THE SINISTER SIGNPOST

Racing cars! Mystery! Adventure! These elements combine to give Frank and Joe Hardy one of the most dangerous and intriguing cases of their careers.

It all starts when their father, Fenton Hardy, is engaged by an experimental race car and motor designer to investigate a series of mysterious accidents. Three of his drivers have crashed because the windshields of their cars were suddenly crazed, thus cutting off forward vision. Frank and Joe uncover one slim clue. Each of the drivers had seen a signpost marked DANGER shortly before his accident. The young detectives investigate, only to discover that the signposts have vanished. What happened to them? And what sinister purpose did they serve?

The attempted theft of a secret experimental motor and the kidnapping of a famous race horse are part of this thrilling case, which proves to be as sinister as the signposts themselves.

The Hardys' escape took the men completely by surprise

Hardy Boys Mystery Stories

THE SINISTER SIGNPOST

BY

FRANKLIN W. DIXON

NEW YORK
GROSSET & DUNLAP
Publishers

Printed in the United States of America

CONTENTS

THE
SINISTER
SIGNPOST

CHAPTER I

Danger on Wheels

"Do you see what I see?" Joe Hardy asked his brother.

"It's a dragster," Frank replied. "They're not supposed to be driven on public roads. At least not in this state."

The Hardys were driving home from Taylorville along Shore Road in their open convertible. It was a sunny summer afternoon. So far, they had encountered almost no traffic. Now Frank was gaining on the slow-moving, bright-orange racing car. In the driver's seat, situated aft of the car's massive rear wheels, sat a helmeted, black-jacketed figure.

"He's sure traveling at low speed," Joe remarked. "I wonder why."

Frank, dark-haired and eighteen, stepped on the gas and attempted to pass the other vehicle. The driver of the dragster increased his own speed

1

and prevented the convertible from going by.

"What's he trying to do? Cause an accident?" Joe said angrily.

Frank was forced to return to his position behind the dragster. As he did, the driver again reduced speed to a snail's pace.

Blond-haired Joe, who was a year younger and more impetuous than Frank, stood up and cupped his hands over his mouth. "Okay!" he shouted at the other driver. "You've had your fun! Now let us by!"

Frank made another attempt to pass. Suddenly the driver of the dragster maneuvered his vehicle in such a way that its left rear wheel slammed up against the right front wheel of the Hardys' car.

"We're out of control!" Joe yelled.

Their car swerved violently as a result of the impact. Frank struggled with the steering wheel and managed to regain control. He quickly came to a stop. The boys watched as the dragster sped down the road out of sight.

"I'd like to get my hands on that clown!" Joe said, fuming.

"So would I," Frank agreed. "But the dragster had no license plates. We'd have a hard time trying to track down the car."

The boys inspected the damage to their convertible. The right front fender was crumpled and the rim of the wheel badly bent.

"We'd better replace the wheel with our spare," Frank suggested.

The Hardys jacked up the car. While they worked, a large, open-panel truck approached on the opposite side of the road. As it flashed by, Joe caught a glimpse of a bright-orange dragster in the rear of the vehicle.

"Look!" he exclaimed. "That must be the same race car that rammed us!"

Frank jumped to his feet and peered in the direction his brother was pointing. By now the speeding truck had vanished around a bend in the road.

"Everything happened so fast," Joe said disappointedly, "I wasn't able to get the license number of the truck."

"Too bad," Frank commented. "It'll be miles away by the time we finish putting on the spare."

When the job was completed, the boys continued their journey home. Mrs. Hardy, a slim, graceful woman, greeted them when they arrived.

"I'm so glad you're back," she announced. "Your father wants to see you right away."

The boys sprinted up the stairs to their father's study on the second floor. Mr. Hardy, a distinguished-looking, middle-aged man, was seated behind his desk.

"Hi, Dad!" Joe greeted him. "Mother said you wanted to see us."

"Hello, boys," he replied. "I just accepted a new case that I'd like to discuss with you two."

Frank and Joe glanced at each other excitedly. Then they took seats near Mr. Hardy's desk. He sat quietly for a moment, studying a myriad of notes he had spread out in front of him.

Fenton Hardy was an extremely meticulous man. Formerly a member of the New York City Police Department, he now worked as a private detective. His exceptional skill in solving baffling crimes had made him famous. In fact, many of his methods were studied and adopted by law-enforcement agencies throughout the world. Frank and Joe had inherited their father's talent, and often assisted him with his cases.

"Yes," Mr. Hardy said finally as he glanced up from his notes. "I believe we're in for a challenging case."

"We?" Joe exclaimed. "Did you say—we?"

Their father smiled. Although in his midforties, he appeared much younger than his years. "That's right," he assured his sons. "I'm going to need your help."

"That's great!" Frank declared. "What kind of case is it?"

Mr. Hardy leaned back in his chair. "Have you ever heard of the Alden Automotive Research and Development Company?"

"Yes," Joe answered quickly. "It's a firm just

a few miles south of Clayton. I believe they experiment with high-speed cars."

"Correct," the detective replied. "The company makes components for regular stock automobiles as well. Also—"

"Isn't Keith Alden the president of the company?" Frank interrupted. "I remember reading about him in the newspapers. He was once a famous racing driver."

"That's right," Mr. Hardy replied.

He went on to tell his sons Alden had designed an experimental turbine motor for his high-speed race cars.

"The power plant is so revolutionary that the government has shown an interest in it. However," the detective continued, "despite his efforts to keep the motor a secret, Mr. Alden suspects that someone has learned about it and is trying to steal the plans."

"Does he have any idea who the person is?" Joe asked.

"None," his father replied. "And here's something else. Two of his cars, in which the motor was installed, met with accidents of a very mysterious nature."

Mr. Hardy stated that Alden wanted to put his motor and car designs to a real test by entering them in road race competitions. "It was during test runs that the vehicles were totally destroyed.

The drivers barely escaped with their lives."

"What happened?" Joe asked.

"The windshields of the cars suddenly crazed," he said, "and cut off the drivers' forward vision. As a result, they went out of control and crashed."

"Windshields crazed?" Joe muttered.

"Yes," Mr. Hardy answered. "They turned almost a milky white."

"But how could that happen?" Frank asked.

"We don't know," his father admitted. "At first, Alden thought the windshields might have been made of a faulty material. But after a laboratory test, that theory proved to be wrong."

"What's Frank's and my assignment?" Joe questioned eagerly.

Mr. Hardy rose from his chair and slowly paced the floor. "I'm going to run a check on all of Alden's employees," he said. "That's just a matter of getting hold of the personnel files at the plant. However, such information seldom reveals the whole story about a man. I'd like to place as many of the workers as possible under close observation, especially the men in the research department."

"And you want Joe and me for an undercover job!" Frank exclaimed.

Their father grinned. "You're way ahead of me," he replied. "But you're right. It's exactly what I have in mind."

"That means we'll have to act as employees

ourselves," Frank said. "The problem is how can we do it without arousing suspicion?"

"I have an idea," his brother answered. "Bayport High introduced a basic automotive engineering course last term. Suppose we say we want to work at the plant to get some practical experience."

"That's it," Frank said. "And the timing is perfect, since our school vacations have just started."

"Sounds good," Mr. Hardy agreed. "You'll have a chance to meet Mr. Alden tomorrow. He's permitting an automobile club to use his private race track for a dragster and a stock-car competition. We're invited to be his guests."

"Great!" Joe exclaimed. "Would it be all right to ask Chet to come along?"

"I don't see why not," his father replied.

Chet Morton was a school chum of the Hardys. He was a plump, good-natured boy, who lived with his family on a farm near Bayport.

Just then Mrs. Hardy announced that supper was ready. The boys and their father were about to leave the study when an object crashed through one of the windows. It landed in a corner of the room.

"Get down!" Frank yelled.

A split second later there was a muffled explosion!

CHAPTER II

Threats

INSTANTLY the room was filled with thick, boiling clouds of smoke.

"What happened?" Joe shouted.

"It must have been a bomb!" Frank cried out.

The Hardys held their breaths and groped their way through the choking smoke. There was no sign of fire. Frank, Joe, and their father soaked handkerchiefs with water, held them over their faces, then began flinging open all the windows on the second floor. Gradually the smoke cleared.

"Eek!" they heard a woman scream. The boys turned to see the tall, angular form of their Aunt Gertrude rushing up the stairs, followed closely by Mrs. Hardy.

"Everything's all right!" Frank announced, in an effort to calm the women.

"Smoke!" Aunt Gertrude cried. "Call the fire

department! Call the police! Do something!"

"No need to get excited," Mr. Hardy said. "There's no fire. Please go back downstairs. We'll explain everything later."

The boys dashed from the house to look for the thrower of the smoke bomb. Not finding him, the young detectives searched in a widening circle. Presently Frank noticed a small glittering object some distance away. He ran to the spot and picked it up.

"Take a look at this!" he called to his brother.

"Why—it's a rifle cartridge case," Joe said as he examined Frank's discovery.

"Let's show it to Dad."

The boys returned to their father's study. Mr. Hardy was examining fragments of the bomb. He held up a metal tube about a foot long. "This is all that's left of what I'm certain was a rifle grenade."

Frank's eyes widened with astonishment. "A rifle grenade?" he echoed.

"Yes," Mr. Hardy replied. "The explosive section is attached to one end of this tube. The other end fits over the muzzle of a rifle. It's then fired from the weapon by means of a blank cartridge shell."

"A shell like this?" Frank said, handing his father the cartridge case he had picked up.

An expression of surprise spread across the older detective's face. "Exactly!" he declared, studying the small object. "Where did you find this?"

"Just a few yards beyond our own grounds," Frank said. "That explains why we saw no footprints on our property."

Mr. Hardy handed his sons a fragment of paper. "This was tied to the shaft of the smoke grenade," he told them.

Frank and Joe were amazed to find that it was a handwritten message which read:

You are being watched. Drop the Alden case, or the next smoke will be lethal!

"Leaping lizards!" Joe exclaimed. "We haven't even started on the case yet, and already we're being threatened!"

"This is something we can't ignore," Mr. Hardy said. "We'll have to be extra cautious. And as for your mother and aunt, I'm going to ask them to take a little trip. We can't risk leaving them alone in the house."

During supper the two women rebuked the boys' father for suggesting that they go away.

"Would a sea captain be the first to leave his sinking ship?" Aunt Gertrude exclaimed. "Not on your life! I, for one, will not budge from this house!"

Mr. Hardy's sister, unmarried, had a peppery temperament. She was always quick to express her opinions openly, and often made dire predictions about the horrible fate awaiting all detectives.

"We know you're concerned for our safety," Mrs. Hardy added in her soft-spoken voice. "But we will not leave here."

"Well—all right," her husband conceded reluctantly. "However, I'm going to call Chief Collig at headquarters and request that a couple of guards be posted near the house day and night."

The next day, Saturday, Mr. Hardy and the boys had an early breakfast. Then, after driving to the Morton farm to pick up Chet, they headed for Alden's private race track near Clayton.

"I can't wait to see the stock-car competitions," Chet said as he peeled a large banana. "In fact, I've been thinking of getting into the sport myself. There's an old car in my father's barn I'm planning to fix up."

"Oh-oh," Joe remarked jokingly. "That's one hobby you had better stay away from."

"Don't worry," Frank added with a laugh. "Chet's car will end up as a diner on wheels, rather than a threat to the racing world."

"Cut the small talk," their friend retorted. "You two masterminds are jealous because I'm the daredevil type. We're a species that eat more because we need tons of energy."

The Hardys and Chet arrived at the track in less than an hour. The area was a beehive of activity. Bright-colored stock cars and dragsters gleamed in the sun as drivers prepared their vehicles for the day's competitions.

"You fellows enjoy yourselves looking at some of these cars," Mr. Hardy said. "I'll locate Mr. Alden and bring him back here."

"Okay, Dad."

The boys began to stroll around the area. Suddenly Joe grabbed his brother's arm and exclaimed, "There's the dragster that rammed us!"

"It sure looks like it," Frank agreed. "Same color. But let's not jump to conclusions. We'll ask the driver some questions first."

The Hardys and Chet walked toward the dragster. A slim, sandy-haired young man was working on the engine of the car.

"Are you the owner of this dragster?" Frank queried.

"Yeah," the young man sneered. "What's it to you?"

"Now hold on!" Joe interjected. "No need to get hot about it. He just asked a simple question."

"Were you driving along Shore Road in Bayport yesterday?" Frank continued.

The drag-strip racer hesitated a moment. "Why don't you guys take a walk?" he shot back finally. "Especially the fat one with you. He looks like he could use some exercise."

"Why don't you take a walk?" the young man snarled

"Who do you think you're talking to?" Chet snapped.

"Just a second," Joe said. He ran his hand around the outer surface of the vehicle's left rear wheel. "The wall of this tire is roughed up. It must have rubbed hard against something."

"Such as our car!" Frank stated.

"Get away from that wheel!" the young man growled.

He gave Joe a shove that sent the boy crashing to the ground. Like a flash Joe was up on his feet. He rushed at his attacker and pinned his opponent's arms behind his back in a jujitsu maneuver.

"Let me go!" the young man cried.

At that moment Mr. Hardy appeared with Keith Alden. He was a tall, slim man with patrician features. His dark hair was slightly gray at the temples.

Mr. Alden looked troubled "What's going on here?" he demanded.

"Are you boys having trouble?" Mr. Hardy asked quickly.

The car manufacturer spoke to Joe in a displeased voice. "Why are you holding onto my son like that?"

"Your—your son?" Frank stammered.

Joe released his grip on the young man.

"Yes," Alden continued. "This is my son Roger."

Mr. Hardy introduced his client to the boys. Except for Roger, everyone was mutually embarrassed.

"These guys," the young man shouted, "are trying to pin some sort of car accident on me!"

Alden eyed Roger suspiciously. "I don't think the Hardy boys would accuse anyone without good reason. If you were involved in an accident, it wouldn't be the first time."

Frank and Joe glanced at each other. It seemed wise not to force the issue. They told Mr. Alden about their encounter with a dragster the previous day, but could not say for certain that the driver of the bright-orange car was Roger.

"Then only my son can clear up this matter," Alden said. He put the question to Roger.

The young man became even more arrogant. "I didn't ram into anybody's car, and I never heard of Shore Road!"

His father was in a quandary. Finally he said, "Until this matter can be investigated further, I forbid you to drive your dragster in the competitions today."

"We'll see about that!" Roger muttered defiantly. He glared at the Hardys, then turned and walked off at a furious pace.

"I don't know what to do about my son," Alden said with remorse. "His mother died several years ago, and I haven't been able to spend much time with him. He's been getting more difficult to live with every day."

"I'm sure he'll straighten out," Mr. Hardy remarked sympathetically.

"I hope so," Alden replied. Suddenly his mood changed. He turned to Frank and Joe. "Now down to business. Your father tells me you two are going to work with him on the case," he said.

"That's right," Frank replied.

"Excellent! I'm sure you have some questions of your own you'll want to ask me. However, I must fly to Washington immediately after the competitions. How about all of us meeting in my office Monday morning?"

The Hardys nodded.

Alden looked at his wrist watch. "It is time for me to get to my post. I'm the official timekeeper for the stock-car runs. Perhaps you would like to join me out on the track."

"Would we!" the boys answered excitedly.

As they started to walk off, Frank bent down and picked up a small packet which had fallen from his brother's pocket during the scuffle. It was Joe's detective kit. Each of the Hardys carried one. Among the items that had spilled out was a magnifying glass and a metal signaling mirror. He handed the kit to Joe.

Suddenly a voice crackled from the loud-speaker of the P.A. system.

"The first trial run will be made by car number twenty-two. The driver is Roger Alden!"

"What!" exploded Alden. "How did he get his hands on a car? I must stop him! Roger doesn't have enough experience for closed-circuit racing!"

CHAPTER III

Prime Suspect

ALDEN rushed toward the starting line with the Hardys close at his heels.

"Stop that car!" he shouted.

But it was too late. Roger roared off.

"Flag that car down!" Alden ordered one of the track officials.

"I'll try to signal him with my mirror when he comes along the straightaway," Joe said.

Frank and Joe ran alongside the track opposite to the direction Roger was headed. They watched him as he skidded dangerously on the far turn.

"Did you see that?" Frank yelled.

"Yes. He took that curve too fast."

The boys hurried down the straightaway. As Roger came around the second far turn, his car spun out of control and crashed through the

18

fence on the sideline. A huge geyser of dust erupted from the spot.

Frank and Joe rushed to the scene of the accident. An ambulance sped by them with its siren screaming. They arrived just as two white-coated men were helping Roger move away from the damaged vehicle.

"Is he hurt?" Joe asked quickly.

"No," one of the men replied. "He's lucky. I think he just had the wind knocked out of him. But we'll take him to the hospital for an examination, anyway."

Shortly Roger's father and Mr. Hardy came running up.

"Are you all right?" Alden asked his son nervously.

"I—I guess so," Roger gasped, still trying to catch his breath. Then he glared at the Hardys and pointed an accusing finger at them. "You guys are the cause of this!" he screamed. "You reflected sunlight into my eyes with that mirror of yours!"

"You're crazy!" Joe retorted.

A rangy young man appeared and gazed at the wrecked car in disbelief. "My car!" he groaned. "It's almost totally demolished!"

"Are you the owner?" Alden queried.

"Yes, I am."

"How is it my son was driving your racer?"

"Roger offered me a hundred bucks if I would let him make the trial run," the young man explained. "Now all I have is a pile of junk."

"Serves you right," Alden snapped, "but I'll pay for the damage."

Roger was helped into the ambulance and taken to the hospital. Although his father was greatly upset over the incident, he did not request that the competitions be discontinued. Instead, Alden told the participants to carry on. At the signal, engines began roaring to life. The Hardys and Chet watched the day's activities and were thrilled by the performance of the skillful drivers.

After dropping Chet off at the Morton farm, the three detectives headed home. When they arrived, Mrs. Hardy announced that supper was ready to be served. As they ate, the boys discussed the day's events.

Aunt Gertrude looked at them scornfully. "Racing of any kind is just dreadful! It should be outlawed!"

"When properly organized," Frank put in, "it's a fine sport."

"I call it utter nonsense!" Aunt Gertrude retorted. She hurried out of the room before her nephews could argue the point.

The next day the boys rose late. After eating a hearty breakfast and attending church services, they settled down to read the voluminous Sunday newspapers. Shortly the telephone rang. Frank scooped up the receiver. The caller was Iola Morton, Chet's sister.

"Chet won't be able to see you later," she sobbed. "He's had an accident!"

Frank and Joe leaped into their convertible and drove to the Morton farm. They arrived to find the entire family standing on the front porch of the house. Chet was seated on the steps, exclaiming that he was all right. His face was blackened with soot.

"I don't need a doctor!" the chubby youth insisted.

"What happened?" Frank asked worriedly.

Mr. Morton, a good-looking, normally jolly man, turned to the Hardys. "Chet was experimenting with a highly volatile fuel on the engine of that old car I keep in the barn. He was pouring some into the carburetor when it suddenly blew up."

"It seems the racing bug has bitten him," said Iola, a slim, pretty girl. She was a witty, light-hearted person and was a school chum of the Hardys. Iola was Joe's favorite date.

"I was afraid something like this would happen," Frank remarked. "However, I didn't expect it so soon."

Mrs. Morton, an attractive, dark-haired woman, hurried to meet Dr. Mills, a Bayport physician, as he drove up to the house. He examined

Chet, then left after saying that fortunately the boy had not been injured.

"You'd better call off your experiments," Joe advised his friend.

"I'll make sure he does," Mr. Morton said. "I'm getting rid of that old car right away."

"But you can't!" Chet protested. "I'm on the threshold of producing the Morton super-duty racing car!"

Frank and Joe helped to convince him that such experiments should be left to the experts. Chet was crestfallen for a moment, then his face suddenly brightened.

"I'll drop the race-car project in favor of another idea," he said. "A rocket-propelled bicycle!" The Hardys shook their heads in despair and returned home.

Monday morning found Mr. Hardy and his sons in Keith Alden's office. The company president was seated comfortably behind his desk, ready to discuss the case with them.

Frank was the first to speak. "Dad says that you suspect someone is trying to steal your experimental motor. Why?"

"My motor," Alden replied, "uses a valve of a very unusual design. In fact, we're not equipped here at the plant to make one. However, I learned of a company on the West Coast that specializes in valve manufacturing. They said they could do the job, so I gave them the green light."

He went on to say that one day Mr. Dillon, president of the valve company, had telephoned him excitedly. A stranger, who refused to identify himself, had appeared with the specifications of a valve exactly like the one to be used in Alden's experimental motor.

Keith Alden rubbed the back of his neck. "Beats me how the fellow got hold of my design."

"What's the name of the company, sir?" Joe asked.

"Exeter Valve. It's a small outfit and, lucky for me, very reputable. Mr. Dillon told the guy he'd like to study the specifications further before agreeing to handle the job. The stranger refused and scooted off."

"Did you get a description of him?" Frank asked.

"Yes," Alden replied. "He was tall, wore black rimmed glasses, and had a beard and mustache that looked phony."

"Obviously a disguise," Mr. Hardy commented.

"I'm certain it was by sheer accident that the stranger went to the same company I was dealing with," Alden declared. "And I'm also sure that his valve sketch was a direct copy of my own design."

"Leaping lizards!" Joe interjected. "Maybe the stranger has the plans to your whole motor!"

"We doubt that," Mr. Hardy said.

Alden grinned. "Your father is referring to the

precautions I have taken to prevent the plans from being stolen."

"What kind of precautions?" Frank asked.

Alden explained that there were only two sets of plans in existence. "One set, the original, is safely hidden. The other is recorded on film slides.

"The work is divided among the technicians here," the man continued. "No one worker knows what the other is doing. Each receives his assignment in the form of a slide, which is placed in a burglarproof projector. He displays it on a small screen and uses it for his job."

"Sounds foolproof," Joe commented.

"That's what I thought," Alden said. "Yet somehow specifications for my motor must be leaking out of the plant."

"So far," Mr. Hardy told his sons, "only half of the slides have ever been seen by anyone other than Mr. Alden. That's why we doubt that the entire design has fallen into the wrong hands."

The boys asked Alden if he had the slightest reason to suspect any of his workers.

"No," he replied. "And just to be sure, I had them all double-checked."

"What about ex-employees?" Joe suggested. "Have you had any trouble in the past?"

Alden rubbed his chin dubiously. "Come to think of it, I did. But that was several months ago."

He stated that Vilno Sigor, an engineer and designer, had worked in his research department. The man had created a number of small, but clever inventions which were used by the company.

"Then one day Vilno came to my office and accused me of picking his brain," Alden said. "I told him that was what I was paying him for, and reminded him of the generous bonuses he received for his ideas. Vilno wanted more. He demanded a partnership in my firm. When I refused, he became furious and left. I haven't seen him since."

"Too bad," Frank muttered. "He might have been our man."

"Now take his twin brother Barto," Alden remarked. "He's still employed in my research department as a sheet-metal worker. An excellent craftsman. His job is to fabricate the bodies of our experimental race cars."

"A twin brother?" Frank exclaimed. "That's a lead. Barto could be in cahoots with Vilno!"

Alden grinned. "You'd be wasting your time investigating him. He's the direct opposite of Vilno in engineering knowledge and in temperament. Even if he got a look at the plans of my motor, he'd never be able to understand them."

Despite Alden's opinion of Barto, the boys were determined to list the sheet-metal worker as a prime suspect.

The young detectives asked about the two experimental cars that had met with accidents after their windshields had been mysteriously crazed. Alden told them that each of the vehicles was powered by a prototype of his motor.

"But whether the accidents were the result of sabotage, I can't say," he added.

Mr. Hardy spoke up. "Right now let's tackle this case one step at a time," he advised his sons. "We have to assume that somewhere in this plant there's a clever crook. He's managing to steal specifications of the experimental motor. Our first job is to find out who he is. And we'll have to find him fast!"

CHAPTER IV

Fingerprint Hunt

"So you want to work in my plant as undercover agents," Alden said, when told about the boys' plan. "I like the idea."

"Thanks," Frank replied. "When do we start?"

"Tomorrow, if that's all right with you fellows," Alden said. He glanced at his wrist watch. "I see it's nearly lunchtime. Let's have some food."

After a delicious meal in the company's cafeteria, Alden conducted the Hardys on a tour of the plant. The boys watched with interest as various machinists turned out parts for the experimental motor. Each of the men worked from a plan projected on a small screen.

The last item on the tour was a visit to the research department. There Alden introduced the boys and their father to Barto Sigor.

"I am pleased to meet you," Barto said in a

quiet voice. He was a short, stocky man with bushy eyebrows and dark, wavy hair. His steel-gray eyes were fixed on the young detectives.

"These two lads will be working here in the plant for a while," Alden told him. "They're taking an automotive engineering course at school and would like to get a little practical experience."

"Ah," Barto responded. "So you want to learn the automobile business. That's good. Do not hesitate to call on me if you have any questions."

"We won't," Joe answered.

Later, while driving home to Bayport, Frank and Joe discussed the case with their father.

Then Joe said, "What's your opinion of Barto, Frank? He seems pleasant enough."

"I agree he's a weak suspect, but—"

"You have something on your mind, son," Mr. Hardy guessed. "What is it?"

"Mr. Alden said that Barto would not understand the motor specifications even if he got a look at the plans," Frank replied. "However, since Vilno and Barto are twins, it's possible that they could have switched identities."

"There's only one flaw in your theory," Mr. Hardy said. "Vilno is not a sheet-metal worker. How could he perform his brother's job at the plant?"

"I didn't think about that," Frank admitted. "Still, I'd like to check it out."

"There's one way of settling the question," the older detective suggested. "Try to get Barto's fingerprints. But do it without his knowledge. We don't want Barto, or anyone else in the plant, to suspect you're working on a case."

The boys retired early that night. The next morning they started for the Alden plant immediately after breakfast. Mr. Hardy, who had been supplied with a microfilm report of all the employees' records, remained at home to check the information against his files on criminals.

The boys spent the morning watching the skilled machinists perform their various tasks. Finally they positioned themselves so they could peer into the research department to observe Barto. The young detectives noticed that he wore a pair of thin rubber gloves constantly. Joe made a casual remark about this to another mechanic.

"Barto always keeps those gloves on," the man said. "He uses certain acids in his work. Also, he says the gloves give him a better grip on his tools."

Eager to discuss the situation, the young detectives retreated to a secluded corner of the plant.

"Those gloves of Barto's make it impossible to get his fingerprints," Joe commented.

"He'll have to take them off sometime," Frank pointed out. "Maybe when he has his lunch."

At noon most of the workers went to the cafeteria. Barto, however, did not leave the shop. Instead, he walked to a clothes rack in one corner of the room and pulled a sandwich, wrapped in wax paper, from the pocket of his jacket. He then sat down on a bench, removed his gloves, and unwrapped the sandwich. The boys watched from a distance.

"We might get a good print from that wax paper," Joe whispered.

"Right," his brother agreed. "Let's see what he does with it."

After Barto finished eating, he crumpled up the wax paper, put his gloves back on, and strolled out of the shop through an exit door. The young detectives rushed to a window and peered outside. There they spotted the suspect walking toward a flaming incinerator. The man tossed the wax paper into it and returned to the shop.

"Well, that's that," Joe muttered disappointedly.

"We can't waste too much time trying to get Barto's prints," Frank said. "Let's follow him when he quits work for the day."

A few minutes before five o'clock the boys hurried to the parking lot to pick up their car. Then they posted themselves outside the main gate. Workers began to spill out of the plant.

"There's Barto!" Joe said.

The boys watched their suspect walk to a street corner and wait. Soon a bus came along and Barto climbed aboard. The boys followed the vehicle. Eventually the trail led them to the center of Clayton. The bus stopped and Barto got off.

"We'll park the car and follow him on foot," Frank declared.

They shadowed their suspect in the best detective fashion. Barto bought a newspaper. Then he stopped at a refreshment stand and ordered a glass of orange juice. When he had finished and walked off, Joe rushed to the stand to seize the glass. But before he could do so, a counterman swept up the tumbler and plunged it into a sink filled with soapy water.

"Out of luck again," Joe grumbled.

Finally Barto led the boys to a small, red-brick apartment house off the main street and entered the building. Frank and Joe waited a few minutes, then dashed into the lobby. They quickly checked the mailboxes and found that Barto lived in apartment 6B.

"Well, there's nothing more we can do today." Frank sighed. "We may as well go home. Maybe we'll come up with an idea before tomorrow."

After supper the young detectives joined their father in his study.

"Sorry to hear you haven't had any luck with your investigation today," Mr. Hardy said. "Neither have I. So far, none of Alden's employees show up in my criminal files."

"Did you check on Barto and his brother?" Frank queried.

"Yes, I have."

Mr. Hardy said that according to their records, the twins had been born in a small Midwest community. When they were still very young, their father had moved the family to Switzerland, where he accepted a job as an engineer. It was there that Vilno attended a university, and Barto had learned the sheet-metal trade.

"The twins returned to the United States several years ago and started a business called Inventions, Incorporated," Mr. Hardy continued. "They didn't do very well and finally closed the shop. After that, it was a matter of job-hopping until they joined the Alden company."

"Hm! Not much to go on there," Frank muttered. "However, I still want to follow through on the fingerprint angle."

"Maybe we could get into Barto's apartment!" Joe suggested.

"We'd need a court order to do that," his brother said. "At present we haven't any reason for justifying such a move."

Frank thought for a moment, then suddenly sat bolt upright in his chair. "Wait a minute! I have an idea!" he exclaimed. "Barto has to grab the doorknob to enter his apartment. I can hide in the hallway and wait until he comes home, then simply lift his prints from the knob."

"Say! That might work!" Joe agreed.

"Go to it, boys. But be careful," Mr. Hardy warned.

The hours dragged by slowly during the boys' second day at the plant. At lunch they reviewed their plan. Frank would leave an hour before quitting time and take the bus to Clayton. Joe would drive their car and shadow Barto as they had done the previous day.

A few minutes before four o'clock Frank hurried from the plant and caught the bus to Clayton. Within half an hour he was climbing the stairs to the sixth floor where Barto's apartment was located. He found 6B, then stepped out through the exit door at the far end of the hallway. The young detective inched the door open so he could watch for his suspect.

"I hope Barto doesn't come home late tonight," he thought.

While Frank waited, an elderly woman in work clothes appeared with a vacuum cleaner and a small trash disposal cart. She unlocked Barto's door and went inside. Shortly she reappeared with a wastebasket and dumped its contents into the cart. Then she went back into the apartment. The whirling sound of a vacuum cleaner could be heard.

"I wonder what was in the wastebasket," Frank mused. "Maybe I'll find a clue."

He dashed to the cart and found several pieces

of crumpled paper. Frank jammed them into his pocket and returned to his hiding place.

Eventually the cleaning woman emerged from the room, locked the door, and disappeared down the hallway with her paraphernalia. Frank ran to the door and wiped it clean so that Barto's prints would be the only ones present.

Half an hour passed. Then, from his hiding place, Frank spotted Barto walking down the hallway. The stocky man unlocked his door, twisted the knob, and went inside. When the door closed behind him, Frank sprang into action.

He dusted the knob with a fine, gray powder. Next, he took a strip of sticky tape from a celluloid container and carefully pressed it on the knob. A split second later he lifted off the tape, placed it back in the container, then rushed down the stairs and out of the building. He saw Joe in their car about a block away.

"Whew!" Frank said, out of breath. "I was afraid Barto was going to open his door any second."

"Mission accomplished?" his brother asked half-jokingly.

Frank held up the celluloid container. "Here are his fingerprints. Let's take them to Chief Collig and have him check them right away."

The boys drove directly to Bayport Police Headquarters. Chief Collig told them that he would send the data to the FBI by teletype and call the Hardys as soon as he received a reply.

Arriving home, the boys had a leisurely supper, then went to their crime lab located above the garage. There they examined the crumpled pieces of paper Frank had found in the disposal cart. All of them proved to be discarded advertising circulars, except one blank page.

"This looks like the backing sheet for a type-written letter," Joe observed as he carefully flattened it out on a table.

"Then there must be word impressions on it," his brother replied. "Let's put it under the ultra-violet light."

The boys treated the blank sheet with a chemical solution and placed it under a special lamp. Gradually, words began to show up clearly. The letter read:

6/2

Dear Eric:

Forgive me for taking so long to write you, but I've been so exhausted from work the last few days that I didn't feel I could write a coherent sentence. How I wish I had the stamina of two hard-working boys who have taken summer jobs at the plant. Any family would be proud to have sons like that.

As I already told you, my brother has left the Alden company. It came as a surprise to me because I did not detect anything in his behavior to lead me to believe he was dissatisfied with his job. I hope he manages to survive his own idiosyncracies. His reasons for leaving were extremely unreasonable, and I hope he eventually sees the error of his ways.

Because of my brother, I feel a bit embarrassed about continuing to work here. I'm sure they're expecting me to leave also. I must admit I have been investigating other possible jobs, but now I realize it would be foolish of me to quit.

Hoping that luck will not continue to evade us, I am

Your friend,
Barto

The Hardys wondered to whom the letter had been sent, and if it might contain a coded message. After close examination, they concluded that the letter was quite ordinary. They kept it on file, nevertheless.

Later Chief Collig telephoned the boys. "I just got a reply on those prints you wanted checked," he announced. "They belong to a Barto Sigor."

The news was shattering. The Hardys no longer had a prime suspect!

CHAPTER V

A Close Call

THE next day and a half at the plant proved disappointing for the boys. Despite their meticulous investigation, they failed to come up with a suspect.

"I'm ready to tackle this case from another angle," Frank said. "We may as well give up our undercover work here at the plant. Nothing more we can do."

"What do you have in mind?" Joe asked.

"Looking into the accidents involving Alden's experimental race cars."

"Do you think there's some connection between the accidents and the stealing of the motor specifications?"

Frank shrugged. "I don't know. Each of the cars was equipped with a prototype model of the motor. Yet why would anyone risk destroying the cars if that's what they were after?"

"Let's have a talk with Alden," Joe suggested.

In a little while the boys were seated in the president's office.

"So you want to investigate the accidents," Alden said. "That's okay with me."

"We'd like to have a talk with the drivers," Frank replied.

"You'll find them in the garage opposite the research department," Alden told them. "They're getting another of my cars ready for a road race competition that's coming up. Their names are Jim Markus and Speed Johnston."

Frank and Joe made their way toward a large, metal-covered building. Inside, a crew of mechanics was busy working on a bright-red experimental race car. Two wiry young men, in their mid-twenties, were watching the proceedings. They turned when the boys called out the names of the drivers.

"I'm Jim Markus," one of them said.

"And my name's Speed Johnston," announced the other, extending his hand in greeting. "What can we do for you?"

Frank and Joe questioned the drivers about their accidents. They told the Hardys that Alden had entered the experimental vehicles in the competitions in order to match their performance against other makes of cars. The explanation of the accidents were the same as Alden had given, except for a couple of interesting facts. First, each of the drivers had experienced a crazing of the windshield immediately after turning a sharp bend in the road. Shortly before it happened, each of them recalled seeing a sign marked DANGER.

"Would you show us on a map where the accidents took place?" Frank asked.

"Sure thing," Johnston replied.

He took out a road map and spread it on the floor. "Mine happened here," he said, jabbing a finger at the spot along a winding red line.

Markus stooped beside his companion. "And my accident took place right here," he added, marking the location with a pencil.

The boys thanked the drivers for their help, then left, taking the map with them.

"The road isn't far from here," Frank commented. "Joe, let's drive there and take a look around."

Half an hour later the Hardys were guiding their convertible along a narrow, winding road. They arrived at the sharply curved segment indicated by Johnston and stopped.

"This is the spot," Frank remarked. "But I don't see a sign marked DANGER."

The boys got out and walked along the shoulder of the road.

"Look!" Joe exclaimed, pointing down at the ground. "There's a little mound of dirt. Someone has filled in a small hole."

"You're right," his brother agreed. "That's where the sign must have been. But why was it taken away?"

Puzzled, the boys returned to their car and drove on to the spot where Markus had said he had his accident. It proved to be another sharply curved segment on the road. The Hardys again examined the shoulder and found a similar mound of dirt.

"Strange," Frank muttered. "I think we're on to something. The only problem is—what?"

It was getting late, so the boys decided to drive home. When they arrived, Mrs. Hardy rushed out of the house to meet them.

"Something has happened to your Aunt Gertrude!" she cried out.

"Where is she?" Frank asked.

"In the living room!"

The boys quickly followed their mother inside. There they found Aunt Gertrude slumped in a chair. Mrs. Hardy had placed a wet towel on her forehead.

"What's wrong, Aunt Gertrude?" Frank asked.

Miss Hardy suddenly came to life. "The telegram I just received!" she moaned. "What a dreadful inheritance! Read it!"

The boys looked down and saw the telegram on the floor beside her chair. Joe picked it up and they read the message. Both tried hard not to laugh.

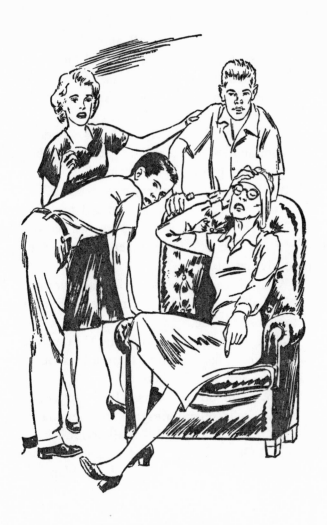

*"What a dreadful inheritance!" Aunt Gertrude
moaned*

"So that's what this is all about," Frank said finally. "You've inherited a stable of race horses."

"A stable of retired race horses, you mean!" she exclaimed. "They're the worst kind. They've already fleeced the public!"

Mrs. Hardy smiled. "I think it's wonderful," she commented. "You might get to like horses. They seem to grow on you in time."

"Laura! How can you say such a thing!" Aunt Gertrude rebuked her. She slumped back in her chair. "And to think that this was wished on me by an old friend I forgot even existed. She apparently has no heirs."

"Where is the stable located?" Joe queried.

"In Baltimore," his aunt replied. "Even that is too close for me."

"What do you plan to do with it?" Frank asked.

"Sell the place!" Aunt Gertrude shot back. "And the quicker the better!"

"Now calm down," Mrs. Hardy urged. "Tomorrow we'll telephone the attorney handling the estate and see what this is all about."

Aunt Gertrude remained silent all through supper. Finally a teasing cry of "Giddap!" from Joe sent her storming out of the room.

The next morning the boys went straight to Alden's office. They told him about the signs the drivers had mentioned and of their own investigation.

"Sounds mysterious," Alden remarked. "But what harm could a sign do?"

"I can't answer that at the moment," Frank admitted. "But I've a hunch it has something to do with the accidents."

Alden eyed the boys with interest. "How do you plan to follow up your hunch?"

"The last time we talked," Frank recalled, "you said that another of your experimental cars was being readied for a road race competition."

"That's right. In fact, the race is scheduled for tomorrow."

"Where is it to take place?" Frank asked.

"On a road not far from the one where the accidents happened. Why?" Alden asked.

"If you'll point out the road for us on a map," Frank explained, "Joe and I will travel the route shortly before the race starts. Maybe we'll spot one of those signs. At least it's worth a try."

Alden pulled a map from his desk drawer and indicated the road to be used for the competition. Then the boys returned home and discussed the plan with their father.

"You might be on to something," Mr. Hardy said. "I'll drive the route with you."

"Thanks, Dad," Frank replied. "But we weren't going to use the car."

"You're not planning to walk all the way?" the detective asked with a look of astonishment. "The race will be over a course of several miles."

"We discussed it on the way home, Dad," Joe put in. "We plan to use our old bicycles. They're still stored in the garage."

Mr. Hardy leaned back in his chair and grinned. "I get it. Bicycles are noiseless. And if there is anything behind this sign theory of yours, you won't scare off whoever's setting them up."

"Exactly," Frank replied.

Before retiring for the night, the boys went to the garage and inspected their bicycles.

"The tires have to be inflated, and a few drops of oil are needed here and there," Joe observed. "Otherwise, they're in good shape."

It took only a few minutes to do the job, then they rode their bicycles once around the block for a quick test run.

"Let's load the bikes in our car," Frank suggested, "so we'll be all set to go first thing in the morning."

Frank and Joe got an early start. Mr. Hardy accompanied them to the starting line. There were about twenty stock cars lined up for the race. Each was painted in a different color scheme. Drivers and mechanics were milling around, waiting for the contest to begin. Alden was there and greeted the Hardys.

"How much time do we have before the race gets under way?" Frank asked him.

"About thirty minutes. My car will be the first one off. Johnston is the driver."

"Then we'd better get going right away," Frank declared.

"Be careful," Mr. Hardy urged.

The young detectives lifted their bicycles from the trunk, then pedaled down the road.

After they had covered most of the route, Joe sighed. "I'd forgotten how slow bicycling can be."

"Keep going," his brother said. "The race will be starting any second now, and it won't take the cars long to travel this far. We should cover as much of the route as we can before they do."

As the boys continued, they noticed that the road was becoming treacherous for racing. It was flanked on one side by a rocky wall, and on the other by a sloping embankment with a drop of nearly a hundred feet.

Eventually Frank and Joe came to a sharp bend in the road. As they rounded it, Frank suddenly locked his brakes. Joe did the same. Just ahead was a large sign marked DANGER!

"Leaping lizards!" Joe declared in a hushed voice.

"That sign is exactly like the ones Johnston and Markus described to us," Frank observed. "Let's take a look at it."

"Maybe we're being watched."

"That's a chance we'll have to take."

The boys laid their bicycles on the embankment and began walking toward the sign. When they reached it, they stopped and gazed at its face.

"What do you make of it?" Joe queried.

"Seems quite ordinary, except for one thing," Frank answered. "It's much thicker than most signs."

At that instant the young detectives heard a faint, whirring noise.

"What's that?" Joe said.

Frank listened. "I'd say it's a generator of some kind," he concluded.

"It's coming from a spot a little farther down the road."

The boys began to inch their way toward the source of the sound. Suddenly the roar of a motor became distinct. Each second it grew louder.

"The first of the race cars is coming!" Joe exclaimed.

The Hardys turned just in time to see Alden's entry tearing around the sharp curve in the road. Suddenly it began to swerve out of control. The vehicle bounced into the air and hurtled directly toward the boys!

CHAPTER VI

Final Warning

THE racing car plunged toward Frank and Joe like some horrible monster eager to crush its prey. In a desperate move the boys leaped down the embankment and went tumbling head over heels to the bottom. They lay stunned. The next thing they knew, Mr. Hardy and Alden were leaning over them.

"Are you all right?" their father asked anxiously.

"I'm—I'm okay," Frank assured him.

"Me too," Joe added, rubbing his head gingerly.

"One of the other drivers saw that there had been an accident and reported it," Alden said. "We got here just as fast as we could."

Frank sprang to his feet. "Your driver Johnston! How is he?"

"Fine, except for a few bruises," Alden replied.

He grinned. "I build very strong cars. My drivers are well-protected."

The boys told the two men what they had seen.

"And you say there was a signpost marked DANGER?" Mr. Hardy asked curiously. "Where?"

Frank pointed toward the top of the embankment. "The one right—" His words trailed off.

"Why—it's gone!" Joe exclaimed.

The boys led the way up the embankment. Then they slowly walked along the shoulder of the road. In a minute they discovered a small hole that had been hastily filled in.

"Here's the place," Frank said. "This is where we saw the sign."

"I'd call it a sinister signpost," Mr. Hardy remarked, rubbing his chin dubiously. "It's here one minute, and gone the next. Obviously someone has carried it off."

Joe casually thrust his hands into the pockets of his jacket. A moment later his face showed surprise and he pulled a piece of paper from one of his pockets. On it was a printed message:

THIS IS A FINAL WARNING!
HANDS OFF THE ALDEN CASE!

"This must have been put in my pocket while we were lying at the bottom of the embankment," Joe said.

"We can be sure of one thing," Frank added.

"Whoever's after Mr. Alden's experimental motor is also responsible for the accidents."

A car roared up and screeched to a halt. Its driver, one of Alden's race car mechanics, leaped out.

"Mr. Alden!" he shouted excitedly. "We just received a call from one of your watchmen at the plant. The research department is on fire!"

"We'll drive you there," Mr. Hardy offered. "There might be a connection with the accident here."

He and his sons hopped into the boys' convertible with Alden. By the time they arrived at the plant, the flames were completely extinguished. Firemen began to rummage through a charred area that once was Alden's research shop.

"This is a terrible blow to my experimental project," he muttered.

The Hardys expressed their regret, then went to talk with the fire chief.

"I can't say what caused the fire," the chief told them. "We'll have to conduct an investigation first."

"Approximately when did it start?" Frank asked.

"We got the alarm about an hour ago."

"I'd appreciate knowing the results of your investigation," Mr. Hardy said as he presented his credentials to the fire chief.

The man recognized the name immediately. "It sure is a pleasure to meet you, sir. And these two boys must be your sons, Frank and Joe. My name's Fred Evans." There was an exchange of handshakes. "You can count on me," the fire chief continued. "I'll let you know if we uncover anything."

The Hardys thanked him, then rejoined Alden who was picking his way through the rubble of his burned shop.

"There's nothing left to salvage," he said dejectedly. "However, I'll set up a temporary research shop in one of the other buildings."

The Hardys expressed their regrets at Alden's loss and returned home. Aunt Gertrude was still greatly upset over her inheritance of a stable filled with retired race horses.

"Fenton!" she exclaimed. "You promised to call the attorney who's handling the estate, and you never did. Please do it right away. I can't rest thinking about that awful place."

Mr. Hardy went to telephone, while the boys had a snack of sandwiches and milk in the kitchen. A few minutes later their father hurried into the room.

"I still have the attorney on the line," Mr. Hardy said. "He'd like us to take a look at the stables. However, I have too much work to clean up here, and I'm sure your aunt won't go. So why don't you two boys hop down to Maryland?"

"Sure thing, Dad," Frank replied.

Mr. Hardy completed his call, then gave Frank and Joe their instructions.

"You can catch an early train to Baltimore in the morning," the detective explained. "The attorney will meet you at the station there. He'll be waiting in front of the information desk. His name is Steve Benson."

Frank and Joe left Bayport aboard the seven-o'clock train. It was nearly noon when they arrived in Baltimore. The boys went directly to the information desk and noticed a tall, even-featured man standing nearby. He appeared to be in his late fifties, and was impeccably dressed.

"Mr. Benson?" Frank queried.

"Yes," the man answered. "And you must be the Hardys. I've heard a lot about you and your father." He extended his hand in greeting. "My car is just outside. The stable isn't far from here."

The boys enjoyed the drive through the lush, green countryside. During the journey, the attorney discussed Aunt Gertrude's situation.

"Your father says that she wants to sell the stable as soon as possible," Benson remarked. "We shouldn't have any trouble doing that. In fact, Norman Fowler, the temporary manager out there, would like to buy the place. Unfortunately he doesn't have the money right now."

Nearly an hour passed before Benson guided

his car through an arched gateway. Spread across the arch, in gold letters, was the name:

SOUTHERN PINES STABLES

"All told, there are about twenty acres here," the attorney announced. "It's not very big, but it's adequate for the purpose."

Ahead, the boys saw a small house and two other wooden structures. All were painted white and appeared to be in excellent condition. The largest of the buildings contained the stalls for the horses. To the left was a large grassy area surrounded by a wooden fence. About a dozen fine-looking horses were lazily grazing there.

Benson brought the car to a stop near the house and got out. The young detectives followed. Standing on the porch was a bulky, deeply tanned man whom the attorney introduced to the boys as Norman Fowler.

"The Hardys have come to take a look around," Benson told him.

"Glad to be of service," Fowler said cordially. "As you probably know, all the horses here have seen the last of their racing days. The owners want to provide a comfortable retirement for them. That's our job."

The manager invited his guests into the house to lunch, then took them on a tour of the stables. As the day drew to a close, Fowler suggested that the boys remain overnight and return to Bayport in the morning.

"All my stable hands are away for the evening at a local affair," he said, "and the bunkhouse is empty. You can sleep there."

Benson announced that he had to leave, but promised to return in the morning to drive the Hardys to the railroad station. After a quick supper prepared by Fowler, Frank and Joe went to the bunkhouse. At ten o'clock they retired for the night. Little more than an hour had passed when the boys were awakened by the muffled sound of men talking.

"That's odd," Frank whispered. "I thought all of Fowler's stable hands were away for the evening."

The boys dressed and crept out of the bunkhouse toward the source of the voices.

"We want fifty percent of the take," they heard one man say.

Joe accidentally stepped on a twig, which snapped with a cracking noise. The boys froze in their tracks and listened. There was only silence.

"Let's move ahead and try to get a glimpse of the men," Frank hissed.

The young detectives cautiously edged their way through the darkness. They saw no one. Then suddenly a voice boomed out from behind them.

"Stay where you are!"

The boys turned to find themselves peering into the muzzle of a rifle.

"Who are you?" Joe demanded.

The armed man directed the beam of a flashlight into the faces of the Hardys.

"Oh, it's you boys," he said. "I thought you were asleep." The man flicked the beam of light onto his own face.

"Mr. Fowler!" Frank exclaimed.

"We heard some men talking out here," Joe explained, "and came to investigate."

"Did you see them?" the manager questioned.

"No," Frank replied. "We never got close enough."

"Well, I heard them too," Fowler said. "But I'm sure they were workers from the farm just across the way. They often use our area as a short cut when they walk back from town." He then said good night and went into the house.

Frank and Joe rose early the next morning. They had just finished breakfast when Benson arrived to take them to the railroad station. The boys thanked Fowler for his hospitality, then hurried off to the train. During the drive, the attorney explained some of the legal points involved in their aunt's intended sale, and handed them some documents that she was to examine.

When they arrived in Bayport, the boys wasted

no time in telling Aunt Gertrude and their parents what they had seen.

"It's too bad you want to sell the stable," Joe said. "The place is beautiful."

"Say no more!" their aunt retorted. "Just give me the documents the lawyer wants me to read, so I can get it over with!"

"Once your aunt makes up her mind," Mr. Hardy commented, "there's no changing it."

The following morning Alden telephoned Mr. Hardy. "Come to the Clayton Police Station right away," he requested. "There's a thief down here who's been stealing information on my experimental motor!"

CHAPTER VII

The Elusive Stranger

MR. HARDY and the boys drove to Clayton immediately. Alden met them at the police station.

"Where is the suspect?" Mr. Hardy asked him.

"Detective Lieutenant Swaze is questioning him in the interrogation room," Alden answered. "He said we were to join him the minute you arrived."

Inside, a thin, untidily dressed man was seated in a chair. Lieutenant Swaze, lanky and middle-aged, was pacing the floor in front of him. Alden introduced the detective to the Hardys.

"This man is charged with burglary," Swaze announced. "He was caught rifling Mr. Alden's office safe by one of the watchmen at the plant."

"When the police searched him," Alden interrupted, "they found several hollow-core impeller blades for my experimental motor in his pocket.

I always keep a supply of them in the safe until an engine is ready for assembly."

Mr. Hardy turned to the suspect. "Whom are you working for?" he demanded.

"I ain't workin' for nobody!" the prisoner shouted. "And I don't know nothin' about any experimental motor!"

"Then why did you take the impeller blades?" Frank asked quickly.

"Them things were made out o' shiny metal," the man replied nervously. "I thought it might be silver and I could get some money for 'em."

The interrogation continued for another two hours. The prisoner stuck to his story. Finally the boys and their father left the room with Alden.

"I'm convinced the suspect is telling the truth," Mr. Hardy concluded. "He's obviously just a small-time crook who would steal anything."

"Then you don't think he's part of a gang trying to get the plans for my motor?" Alden queried.

"At this point, no," the detective said. "But let's see what the police come up with when they check his record."

Alden glanced at his watch and announced that he would have to return to the plant. The Hardys walked to their car and started back to Bayport, disappointed that nothing had come of their trip.

While driving through the center of Clayton, Joe suddenly pointed toward two men standing on a street corner. "Look!" he exclaimed. "There's Barto talking to someone!"

"I wonder why he's not at work," Frank remarked.

"Maybe he has the day off," Joe answered.

The boys noticed that Barto's companion had the collar of his jacket turned up high, and his hat pulled low over his eyes.

"That guy he's with sure looks suspicious," Joe commented.

Frank stopped the car at the next corner. "I'll walk past Barto and try to get a glimpse of the other man's face," he said. "The sidewalk is crowded with pedestrians. Chances are he won't spot me."

Frank made his way toward the two men. When he was within a few feet of them, Barto suddenly gave his companion a hard shove. The man turned and ran down the street. Frank, figuring this was strange, raced off in pursuit.

"Did you see that?" Joe said to his father.

"Yes! Come on! Frank might need our help!"

They leaped out of the car and joined in the chase. Mr. Hardy stopped long enough to fire a question at Barto.

"Who was that man you were talking to?"

Barto appeared surprised. "I—I don't know," he stammered. "He was looking for a handout.

When I refused, he insulted me and I gave him a shove."

Mr. Hardy hurried on and found his sons standing at the entrance of an office building.

"He ran in here," Frank told his father.

"Let's go after him!" Joe urged.

"I'll stay outside," Mr. Hardy said. "In case he gives you the slip, I'll go after him."

The boys ran into the building and discovered that the elevator was out of order. They bounded up the stairs. High above them, the two sleuths heard heavy footsteps.

"He must be heading for the roof!" Joe whispered.

Continuing the chase, the boys soon reached the roof. Their quarry was not in sight, but they heard what sounded like a metal door being slammed shut.

"It came from over there!" Joe said, pointing to the roof of an adjacent building.

The boys leaped across the narrow gap separating the two structures, and found a door leading inside. Pulling it open, Frank and Joe rushed down the stairs to the ground floor. Their father met them as they dashed outside.

"Your man came running out of this building," Mr. Hardy said. "I was too far away to stop him. By the time I realized what had happened, he disappeared in the crowd."

"Too bad," said Frank.

As the Hardys drove home, the detective told his sons what Barto had said.

"Do you believe him?" Frank asked.

"We have no choice but to take his word for it," Mr. Hardy replied. "Yet Barto doesn't strike me as the type that goes shoving people around."

"And why would a man just asking for a hand-out run off like a fugitive?" Joe interjected.

"There's something fishy about this," Frank added.

The Hardys had just finished supper when the telephone rang. Frank answered.

"This is Mr. Alden," the caller said. "I have one more completed race car fitted with my experimental engine. Luckily it was in the garage when the research shop burned down. I plan to give it a test run tomorrow."

"Another competition?" Frank asked.

"No, this will be a private test. I have permission from the highway department to use a straight stretch of road near the plant. I'd like you boys and your father to be present. I don't expect any trouble, but it pays to be safe."

"Wouldn't it be better to use the drag strip at your track?" Frank suggested. "You'd be less likely to find intruders there."

"The strip is too short for my purpose," Alden explained. "Shall we say ten o'clock tomorrow morning?"

"We'll be there," Frank assured him.

The next day the boys and their father drove to the test site. Alden's experimental race car was unpainted, and its highly polished metal surface gleamed in the sun. Mechanics were giving the vehicle a final inspection.

"We'll be ready to start in about twenty minutes," Alden told the boys. "I intend to drive the first couple of runs myself. They will be acceleration tests."

He said that the car was a two-seater designed to carry a mechanic in addition to the driver.

"Since I won't be taking a mechanic with me," Alden said, "how would one of you boys like to go along?"

He suggested that the boys draw straws to decide which one would accompany him. They did, and Frank won.

"That's settled," Alden remarked, then added, "Joe, would you mind helping us with the tests?"

"How?"

"Normally, there's not any traffic using this road," Alden replied. "But we can't be sure. So I'd like to post a man with a walkie-talkie at the far end of the stretch to warn me if anything comes along. I have a radio receiver in the car for that purpose."

"I'm your man," Joe assured him.

He could not help but feel a bit envious of his brother as he watched Frank climb into the sleek car with Alden. Mr. Hardy drove Joe to his post a couple of miles down the road, which at that point was flanked by heavy woods.

As the detective drove off, Joe heard a voice crackle from the speaker of his walkie-talkie. "All clear ahead?"

"All clear!"

Minutes later, Joe could detect the sound of Alden's car approaching. Then he spotted it far down the road. It was a shining speck of silver that grew larger and larger each second.

As Joe watched, he was startled to see a battered automobile emerge from the woods.

"Stop!" Joe cried frantically. "Mr. Alden, stop!"

CHAPTER VIII

Stolen!

THE dilapidated car turned onto the road, picked up speed, and headed directly for Alden's car. Joe raced after it, calling out into the walkie-talkie.

His pleas went unheeded. Joe was horror-stricken at the small gap between the two vehicles. A head-on collision seemed inevitable.

"Frank! Mr. Alden!" Joe screamed. "Watch out!"

Suddenly the mystery car swerved out of control. It went hurtling off the road and tumbled over into a ditch. A split second later the vehicle was a mass of flames.

Alden brought his racer to a screeching halt. He and Frank leaped out and followed Joe toward the disabled vehicle. They managed to get close enough to pull open one of its doors. The three were amazed to find that there was no one inside.

"Get back!" Alden shouted. "The gas tank may explode any second."

His warning came just in time. As Alden and the boys got clear, there was an explosion. A large ball of orange flame rose above the burning car. It quickly transformed into a thick cloud of black smoke.

Minutes later a pickup truck arrived on the scene, carrying a crew of Alden's mechanics. Mr. Hardy was with them. The men scrambled out with fire extinguishers, and directed streams of chemical foam at the burning car. Soon the flames and smoke disappeared.

"You gave us a bad scare," Mr. Hardy said, turning to Frank and Alden. "We saw the smoke and came running. We thought you'd had an accident with the car."

"They almost did," Joe said shakily. He told his father what had happened.

When the car cooled sufficiently to be touched, the Hardys examined it. The heat had turned the vehicle into a charred mass of twisted metal.

Frank, looking underneath, made a startling discovery. To the underside was attached the remains of an elaborate radio-controlled system. Wires ran from it to the throttle and steering mechanism.

"So that's how the car was operated with no driver!" Joe exclaimed. "But why did it go haywire all of a sudden?"

Frank had an answer. "When Joe used the walkie-talkie to warn us, the signal must have interfered with the radio frequency used to guide the car."

Mr. Hardy nodded. "Whoever operated the transmitter would have needed a clear view of the road, and at a point not too far away from this spot."

Frank looked toward a high hill, the top of which loomed above the treetops. "There's a perfect spot," he said, pointing to it.

The boys lost no time in climbing to the summit to investigate. The area was covered with thick brush and grass.

"These bushes would provide good cover for anyone watching the road," Frank stated.

"Look! Over here!" Joe cried out. "Some of the grass has been trampled flat. I'd say it was done recently by two or three men."

Frank examined the spot. "This is where the transmitter was set up," he concluded. "From here you get a perfect view of the road."

A further search revealed no other clues. The boys rejoined their father and Alden. Mr. Hardy stated that he had given the mystery car a thorough going-over, but found nothing that would permit them to trace its owner.

"The vehicle wasn't carrying license plates, and the serial numbers on the engine and chassis had been removed," he continued. "Also, the fact that it was burned to a crisp doesn't help either."

Alden decided to carry on with the tests. When he had finished, the Hardys offered to drive him to his office.

As they started off, Alden rested back in the seat. "After all the excitement we've been having lately, I need a little diversion," he said. "I think I'll spend Saturday giving my race horse a workout."

"Race horse?" Joe queried.

"Yes," Alden answered. "I'm interested in racing of all kinds. I bought the horse several months ago. Great animal! I keep him in a rented stable near the plant."

"Our aunt would tell you off quick if she knew this," Frank remarked laughingly. He then told Alden about Gertrude Hardy's recent inheritance.

"A stable for retired race horses? Sounds like a great idea," Alden said. "I'll keep it in mind. Perhaps someday I'll send my horse down there."

"Not if Aunt Gertrude has anything to say about it," Joe muttered with a grin. "Anyway, she will have sold her stable by that time."

Alden asked the Hardys if they would like to see his horse. The boys' father had to decline because of a business appointment, but Frank and Joe eagerly accepted the invitation.

"And would you mind if we bring our friend Chet?" Frank asked.

"Please do," Alden replied. "Drop by any time. I'll be at the stable most of the day."

Chet was not able to go until the afternoon because of Saturday chores to do. The Hardys picked him up at the Morton farm.

"A real race horse, eh?" Chet said with a grin. He pulled three apples from his pockets and offered one to each of his friends. "What I wouldn't give to own one!"

When they arrived at the stables, Alden was leading a beautiful, haltered thoroughbred around the paddock. His owner spotted the boys and led the animal toward them.

"How do you like him?" he called out. "His name is Topnotch."

"Nice piece of horseflesh," Chet commented, trying to act like a seasoned equestrian.

The horse was completely chestnut in color, except for small white areas above its two front hoofs. The boys watched in admiration as Alden removed the halter and permitted Topnotch to trot freely around the paddock.

As Joe glanced toward a row of stalls nearby, he noticed a sandy-haired young man pitching hay into one of them.

"Mr. Alden, isn't that your son Roger over there?" Joe asked.

"Yes," Alden replied in a determined voice. "I arranged to get him a job here so he could help pay for the race car he damaged. It's about time he developed a sense of responsibility. I'd have given him something to do at the plant, but he can't get along with the other workers."

Chet followed the Hardys to the stall.

"Hello, Roger," Frank said in a friendly voice.

The young man looked surprised. Then his eyes narrowed as he glared at the boys.

"Oh, it's you guys again!" he snapped. "You keep popping up like bad dreams."

"So you're still carrying a chip on your shoulder," Joe retorted.

"You bet I am," Roger shot back angrily. "I've got to work in this lousy place to pay for that stock-race car I had an accident in. You Hardys were the cause of it all!"

Frank kept his temper, but said, "Don't tell us you're sticking to that fairy tale of yours. You know we didn't reflect sunlight into your eyes while you were driving."

"It's my word against yours," Roger snarled. "But what chance do I stand? Because you're the Hardy boys you think you can get away with anything."

Joe's face flushed with anger. However, he managed to exercise self-control. "It's useless trying to talk sense into Roger," he said. "We'd better go."

As they walked away, Chet remarked, "That

fellow is about as friendly as an enraged cobra."

Roger, who overheard the comment, gave Chet a black look. He picked up a large mass of hay with his pitchfork and flung it on top of the chubby youth.

Chet scrambled from underneath the pile. He quickly brushed strands of hay from his eyes, ears, and hair. Then, angry, he grabbed a feed bag nearby and pulled it over Roger's head, down to his elbows. The imprisoned boy stumbled around the stall in a frenzy.

"I'll get you for this!" Roger yelled after his tormentor when he finally pulled the bag free.

The Hardys and their chum strolled back to the paddock. Mr. Alden had been too preoccupied with Topnotch to notice what had happened.

"Let's not say anything to him about Roger," Frank suggested.

The boys spent the balance of the afternoon watching Alden exercise his horse, or taking turns riding the mount themselves.

"He's super," Chet remarked. "Sure beats our farm horses."

At sundown the boys thanked the owner and left.

Frank and Joe spent a relaxing Sunday at home and retired early. The family had been asleep only a short time when the telephone rang. Frank got up and rushed to answer it. His father had already picked up the extension by his bed.

"This is Alden," an excited voice was saying. "Sorry to disturb you. But something terrible has happened and I need your help. I'm at the stable. Topnotch has been stolen!"

CHAPTER IX

Demand for Ransom

FRANK wakened his brother to tell him about Topnotch. The boys and their father dressed quickly, rushed to their car, and headed for the stable.

"This sounds to me like some of Roger's work," Joe suggested.

"Possibly," Frank agreed. "He's pretty mad at his father. Roger could have done it for spite. But stealing a horse is not easy. He'd need help."

"My advice is to wait until we get the facts before coming to any conclusions," Mr. Hardy interjected. "I realize Roger would never win a popularity contest. Yet it's hard to believe he'd be mean enough to do a thing like this."

They arrived at the stable to find Alden still greatly distraught over the theft of his horse.

"The police were here to investigate," he told the Hardys. "They left a few minutes ago."

"What did they come up with?" Joe asked.

"Nothing," Alden replied disappointedly. "The thieves were careful not to leave a shred of evidence behind. Even the foot- and hoofprints leading from Topnotch's stall were swept away."

"But they must have used some kind of a vehicle to carry the horse off," Frank said. "Did the police find any tire tracks in the area?"

Alden nodded and asked the Hardys to follow him. After walking a short distance, he directed the beam of his flashlight toward the ground and pointed to a set of deep, parallel ruts pressed into the soft earth.

"They must have been made by a truck or a horse van," Joe said.

Mr. Hardy stooped down and examined the ruts carefully. "Obviously the thieves covered the wheels with canvas or other heavy material," he concluded. "There aren't any tread marks. Too bad."

"Were there any witnesses to the crime?" Frank queried.

"Only one of the grooms," Alden answered. "But he can't help us. He lives in a room above the stable. When he heard a strange noise in one of the stalls, he came down to investigate and was struck from behind. The police took him to the hospital."

"Has the groom been able to tell when the theft took place?" Mr. Hardy questioned.

"Yes. He regained consciousness. The theft was about five hours ago. The groom had been tied and gagged. It took him over four hours to work himself free after he regained consciousness."

Joe let out a whistle. "Five hours!" he exclaimed. "The truck could be hundreds of miles away by now."

The Hardys did not want to upset Alden any further by asking him about Roger's whereabouts that evening. Instead, they discussed the case from another angle.

"We don't know if this was an inside job or not," Mr. Hardy remarked. "But we can be reasonably sure what the motive is. Ransom!"

"In that case, the thieves will try to contact me," Alden said. "If they do it by telephone, they'll call my office, since I have an unlisted number at home."

"I suggest we go there right away and wait," Frank put in. "The horsenappers may start early to call."

Alden accompanied the Hardys in their car. During the drive, Mr. Hardy outlined a basic plan.

"If you should receive a call demanding ransom," he advised the horse's owner, "stall him off. Tell him you want proof that they actually have Topnotch. That'll give us more time to hunt a lead."

Arriving at the plant, Alden led the way to his office. There he and his companions each selected a comfortable chair and settled down to wait.

"Have you a private line here in addition to your regular company phone?" Mr. Hardy asked the executive.

"Yes, I do," Alden replied, pointing to one of two phones on his desk.

"Good," the elder detective said. "I'll use it to have the call traced if the thieves should contact you."

The night dragged on slowly. The boys were restless and found it difficult to sleep. When morning finally came, Alden arranged to have breakfast served in his office.

It was a little after nine when there was a short buzz on the company phone. Alden scooped it up, listened for a moment, then covered the mouthpiece with his hand.

"It's my secretary in the outer office," he informed the Hardys. "She says a man wants to speak to me. He refuses to identify himself."

"This might be the call we're waiting for!" Joe exclaimed softly.

Mr. Hardy rushed to the private phone. "I'll get to work on having the number traced," he announced quickly. Seconds later, he signaled Alden to proceed.

"Okay, put him on," Alden ordered his secretary.

The boys fixed their eyes on the executive and waited anxiously.

Alden suddenly sat bolt upright in his chair. "You want fifty thousand dollars' ransom to return Topnotch?" he shouted into the phone. "You're out of your mind! I'd want absolute proof before I handed out that kind of money!"

A few seconds later the executive placed the phone down. "He hung up," Alden announced.

Mr. Hardy frowned. "Too bad. There wasn't enough time to trace the call. Obviously we're not dealing with amateurs."

"What did he say when you asked for proof that they had Topnotch?" Frank put in.

"He said he'd think about it and let me know later," Alden replied.

Mr. Hardy stretched out his arms and yawned. "You boys must be as exhausted as we are," he said. "Why don't you go home and get some rest? I'll stay here. You'll hear from me immediately if anything comes up."

His sons readily agreed. But it was not rest that interested them. Their father's suggestion offered an excellent opportunity for them to question Roger without Alden's knowledge.

"Let's go back to the stable and see if he's working today," Frank said as they drove off in their convertible.

When the Hardys arrived, Roger was busy

painting a section of the fence that surrounded the paddock.

"We'd like to ask you a few questions," Frank called out.

Roger quickly glanced at his visitors without interrupting his work. "It's you guys again!" he snapped. "Haven't you got a home? Get lost! I don't have time to answer any of your stupid questions."

"Come off it!" Joe shot back angrily. "You must know your father's horse was stolen last night. That's what we want to ask you about."

There was a momentary pause. Roger nervously fingered his paintbrush and kept his face turned away from the Hardys. "Yes, I heard about it," he muttered defiantly. "But you've come to the wrong guy for information. And even if I did know something about it, I wouldn't tell you."

"Where were you last night?" Frank demanded.

"Why don't you try looking into a crystal ball to find out?" the young man retorted.

"Cut the comedy!" Joe exclaimed. "This is serious. A theft has been committed, and there's no reason why you shouldn't be among the suspects."

"Okay! If you have to know, I was working on my dragster all evening," Roger snapped.

"Where?" Frank questioned.

"At home!"

"Can you prove it?" Joe asked. "I mean, was

"You want fifty thousand dollars' ransom?"
Alden shouted

there anyone with you who can back up your statement?"

"No. I was alone," Roger answered.

"What about your father?" Frank put in. "Didn't he see you?"

"He was visiting friends till late. I was already in bed when he got home."

"For your sake," Joe remarked, "I hope you're telling the truth."

Roger suddenly hurled his paintbrush to the ground. His face was flushed with anger. "I've had enough of you two!" he rasped. "What I do is none of your business!"

"We're making it our business," Joe told him.

Frank wanted to avoid a scene. "Simmer down," he said calmly. "We'll have to take your word for what you told us. But if you should run across any information concerning the theft, I advise you not to keep it to yourself."

The Hardys walked back to the convertible and returned to Bayport. Their mother and aunt were disappointed to see that the boys' father had not come with them.

"I suppose he's chasing after some horrible criminal!" Aunt Gertrude remarked. "Your father won't remember where he lives if he keeps up this sort of thing."

"Now calm down, Gertrude," Mrs. Hardy pleaded in a soft voice.

Joe playfully sniffed the air. "Smells like roast turkey for supper."

"And coconut-custard pie for dessert," announced Mrs. Hardy.

"Let's hope your sons can stay put long enough to eat it," said Aunt Gertrude.

The boys went to bed early that night. They spent the next day puttering around their crime lab and mulling over the case. It was midafternoon when their father telephoned with an urgent message.

"Mr. Alden just received another call from the thieves," said the detective. "He was told that the proof he had asked for would be found in a book entitled *Famous Horses of the World,* at the Clayton Library. Meet us there just as soon as you can."

The boys started out immediately. At the library they found their father and Alden seated at one of the reading tables examining a large book.

Mr. Hardy handed his sons a photograph. "This was tucked in between the pages," he whispered.

The boys' eyes widened with surprise. "It's a picture of Topnotch," Frank said.

"Are you absolutely sure?" Joe asked.

"No doubt about it," Alden replied in a low voice.

"And it's a cul-de-sac when it comes to getting

a line on who placed the photograph in the book," Mr. Hardy said. "I questioned the librarian, but she has been too busy to take note of any strangers."

"May we keep the picture for a while?" Frank queried. "It might provide us with a clue."

"You're welcome to it," Alden replied. He glanced at his watch. "I'd better get back to the plant. The thieves will surely call me again."

Mr. Hardy explained that Alden had had one of his drivers bring them to the library. He turned to the executive. "Why don't you send him back to the plant? You and I can go along with the boys in their car."

"Very well," Alden agreed.

As they drove, Mr. Hardy urged his client to stall for more time. "Tell those crooks that you can't get the ransom money until Friday morning," he said.

"I'll try." Alden sighed. "But I don't want to endanger Topnotch any more than I have to."

Soon the plant came into view. As they drove toward the main gate, Alden's experimental race car suddenly sped out the driveway.

"I didn't give anyone permission to drive that car!" he shouted.

Frank pressed down on the gas pedal and the convertible shot off in pursuit!

CHAPTER X

Suspicious Rendezvous

"THAT racer is too fast for us!" Joe yelled. "We'll never catch it."

"Turn onto that side road just ahead!" Alden ordered. "We might be able to head him off!"

Frank followed instructions. It was a wild, bumpy ride and kept the occupants hanging on to their seats. After a couple of miles, the route led them back to the road along which their quarry was traveling.

"There's the experimental car!" Mr. Hardy called excitedly as he peered out the rear window. "It's about quarter of a mile behind us and coming fast!"

Frank skillfully maneuvered his convertible to prevent the other driver from passing.

"Hang on!" he cried out. "I'm going to start slowing down!"

As the Hardy car came to a stop, the other driver was forced to do the same.

"Good work!" Alden exclaimed, and leaped out of the convertible. The Hardys followed.

"Roger!" Joe exclaimed as a sandy-haired young man slowly emerged from the experimental dragster.

Alden was furious. "What do you think you're doing?" he demanded.

"I—I was just taking your car for a little spin," his son stammered.

"Why aren't you working at the stable?" Alden fumed.

"I took the afternoon off," Roger replied.

Alden glared at his son with a look that would melt ice. "You know my racer is a secret project. How dare you take it for a drive?"

He turned to the Hardys. "I'll meet you back at my office. I'm going to ride to the plant with Roger just to make sure he doesn't get any more wild ideas."

The Hardys reached the office just as Alden finished reprimanding his son.

"Don't send me away to that lumber camp," Roger was pleading.

"I don't see what else I can do with you," his father replied. "I'm fed up with your shenanigans!"

"But I promise to stick with my job at the

stable," Roger replied, "and I won't go near your experimental car again."

Alden rubbed his chin dubiously for a moment. "Well—all right," he finally agreed. "But step out of line once more and off you go."

Roger thanked his father. Then he rushed past the Hardys and out of the office.

At that instant the telephone rang. Alden picked it up. From his expression the Hardys knew it was another call from the thieves.

"Yes, I saw the photograph of Topnotch you placed in the book at the library," Alden informed the stranger. . . . "Will I pay the ransom you demand? I suppose I'll have to. But you must give me until Friday. It'll take me that long to get such a large sum of money."

When the telephone conversation ended, Alden glanced at the Hardys. "They've agreed to wait till noon on Friday. I'm to receive further instructions then."

Frank jumped up. "That gives us two and a half days to find out who stole your horse."

"We'll get to work on it right away," Mr. Hardy said.

"I hope you're successful," Alden commented. "Fifty thousand dollars is a lot of money. But I'll pay it if I have to."

The Hardys hurried home to Bayport. There the elder detective began going through his criminal files. "I'll check to see if I have information on anyone whose specialty is horsenapping," he said.

Meanwhile, his sons hurried off to their crime lab and studied the photograph of Topnotch.

"What are we looking for?" Joe inquired.

"I thought we might find something in the picture that would help us identify the locality," Frank replied.

"Slim chance. Other than the horse, there's nothing but a few bits of shrubbery."

"Wait a minute! That's it! Perhaps a botanist could tell us if the shrubs are indigenous to a particular region."

"Let's call Mr. Scath, curator of the Howard Museum."

Frank rushed to the phone and dialed a number. Soon he had the curator on the line.

"We recently added a botanist to our staff," Scath said. "His name is Mr. Ronald Clause. I'm sure he can be of help to you."

"Would it be possible to see him right away?" Frank asked. "It's urgent."

"Yes," the curator assured him. "We're about to close the museum for the day, but Mr. Clause plans to be here for a couple of hours to work on a new exhibit. I'll tell him you're coming."

The boys hurried to their car and drove to the museum, located in the northwestern section of Bayport. A lanky, scholarly-looking man admitted them.

"I'm Mr. Clause," he announced. "Mr. Scath said you wanted to see me."

The boys introduced themselves, then stated their business. They handed the botanist the photograph of Topnotch.

"Hm! The shrubs are a bit out of focus," Clause muttered, "but I'll see what I can do."

"We realize you're very busy," Frank said. "However, we're racing against time. We'd appreciate it if you could give us an answer as soon as possible."

"I'll get to work on it right away," the botanist answered. "Might take me a day or so. If I come up with something, I'll call you."

The Hardys thanked him and left. As they drove back home, Frank's thoughts returned to Alden's son.

"I'm still not convinced that Roger had nothing to do with the theft of Topnotch," he remarked.

"I'm not either," Joe added. "Say, why don't we shadow him tomorrow? If he is in with the crooks, he might try to contact them."

"We've nothing to lose," Frank agreed. "But it would be safer to have Roger shadowed by someone he doesn't know. That eliminates us and Chet."

"What about Biff Hooper and Tony Prito?" Joe suggested. "They've done a good job of following suspects for us before."

"Good idea. Let's call them when we get home."

Like Chet, Biff Hooper and Tony Prito were classmates of the boys at Bayport High. They always welcomed a chance to work with the Hardys on their cases.

"What's up?" Biff asked eagerly as he and Tony joined the Hardys in their crime lab. "From your telephone call, I'd say it was important."

"It is," Frank assured him. "And we need your help."

Tony Prito, a dark-haired, lively boy, declared, "Count me in!"

Frank and Joe gave their friends a quick rundown on the case, then furnished them with a description of Roger.

"We'd like you to shadow him and give us a report on everything he does," Joe said.

"You'll find Roger at the stable in the morning," Frank added. "Try to be as inconspicuous as possible. We don't want him to suspect he's being watched."

Biff, a tall, blond, athletic-looking youth, beamed with enthusiasm. "You can depend on us!" he exclaimed.

The next day the Hardy boys stayed close to the telephone. It was almost one o'clock in the afternoon when a call came. Frank answered.

The caller was Biff Hooper. "Tony and I followed your suspect to a restaurant in Clayton. He's inside talking to a couple of suspicious-looking characters."

"Are you calling from the restaurant?"

"No. I'm in a public phone booth across the street from it, on the corner of Stanton and Winthrop streets."

"Joe and I will come there right away!" Frank declared. "If Roger leaves in the meantime, stick with him. You can let us know where you are by leaving a message with Mother or Aunt Gertrude. We'll check with them every fifteen minutes."

The boys leaped into their car and headed for Clayton. When they arrived, Biff and Tony were still at their posts across the street from the restaurant.

"Your suspect hasn't left yet," Biff said.

Frank pointed to a building behind him. "Let's hide in that doorway, Joe," he advised. "We don't want Roger to spot us when he comes out."

The Hardys and their companions became impatient as the minutes ticked by. Finally Roger emerged from the restaurant with two rough-looking men. Each of them walked off in a different direction.

Frank turned to Biff. "You and Tony follow Roger," he ordered. "Joe and I will split up and trail those two men he was with."

Each boy hurried off on his assignment. Frank

trailed his quarry for several blocks. Suddenly the man darted into an alley.

"He must know he's being followed," the young detective thought, and cautiously stalked toward the spot. He peered into the alley. There was nothing in it but a pile of discarded wooden crates at the far end.

"That man must be hiding behind them," Frank decided.

As he edged his way forward, the man leaped from back of the crates and flung a small object toward Frank. It hit the ground a few feet from the boy and exploded!

CHAPTER XI

A Prize Catch

A THICK, white cloud of smoke erupted from the spot. Frank felt a burning sensation in his eyes and began to cough uncontrollably.

"It's tear gas," he thought. "I must get out of here!"

Frank stumbled backward away from the smoke. At that instant he saw the blurred figure of a man running past him. The young detective lashed out with his fist and made contact. Then someone grabbed his left arm. Again Frank lashed out with his fist, but his punch was blocked.

"Hold it!" came the voice of his brother. "It's Joe!"

As the effects of the tear gas wore off, Frank saw a man lying unconscious on the ground. Joe pointed at the prone figure. "Looks as if you got your man," he said. "Wish I could say the same."

"You lost the other guy?" Frank asked.

"I had to let him go. He led me around the block and down this street past the alley. Then the smoke attracted my attention and I saw you were in trouble. So I ran to help."

The man regained consciousness. "Who—who are you guys?" he groaned as he struggled to his feet.

"Never mind that," Frank answered. "Suppose you tell us who *you* are?"

"My name's Marty Tempson, if it's any of your business," the man growled.

"Why did you toss that tear-gas bomb at me?"

"I thought you were some guy out for a heist."

"What kind of business did you and your pal have with Roger Alden?" Joe shot at him.

Tempson glared at the boys. "Roger Alden? I don't know no guy by that name," he snarled.

"You're lying," Frank declared. "He's the young man you and your friend were with in the restaurant."

"Never saw him before," Tempson replied. "The restaurant was crowded and he let us share his table."

At that moment a police patrol car arrived on the scene. One of the officers got out and approached the Hardys and Tempson.

"A shop owner across the street reported seeing smoke in this alley," the policeman announced. "What's going on here?"

The boys gave their names and Frank explained what had happened. When Tempson was unable to produce identification, the policeman searched him and discovered a tear-gas bomb in his pocket.

"I'm taking you in!" the officer declared.

Tempson turned pale. "You—you can't arrest me!" he stammered. "I ain't done nothing!"

"That's what you think," the policeman retorted. "There happens to be a law against tossing bombs at people." He glanced at the Hardys. "Will you come to the station and make a statement?"

"Glad to," Frank answered. "We'll pick up our car and meet you there."

Tempson was already being fingerprinted when the boys arrived at Clayton Police Station. The desk sergeant took down their statement, then said that a complete check would be made on the prisoner.

"You boys must be in court when he's brought up for a preliminary hearing," the sergeant added. "That'll be tomorrow morning."

"We'll be here," Frank assured him.

He and Joe left the building and returned to their car.

"What's our next move?" Joe asked.

"Let's find out if Roger went back to the stable," Frank suggested. "If so, I want to question him."

Arriving at their destination, the boys found Roger seated in front of a stall repairing a harness.

He was as belligerent as ever and became enraged when Frank declared that they had seen him in Clayton with two men.

"You lousy snoopers!" Roger yelled. "What right have you to spy on me?"

"Never mind that," Joe put in. "Who were the two men you were with?"

"I don't know," snapped the young man. "I went to the restaurant for lunch. The place was crowded and I let them share my table."

"Very considerate of you," Joe said sarcastically. "What made you so friendly all of a sudden?"

Roger jumped to his feet. "I don't have to take that from you!" he shouted.

In the next instant he swung the harness at Joe. The young detective stepped back, caught the end of the gear, then wrapped it tightly around his opponent's arms.

"Let me go!" Roger demanded.

"Not until you calm down!" Joe shot back.

Frank spoke up. "I don't think you're telling us the truth about not knowing those men."

"I am!" the young man cried out.

"Clayton is about ten miles north of here," Joe said. "Isn't that a long way to go just to have lunch? I've noticed a couple of local restaurants within walking distance."

"I like the food in Clayton," Roger replied mockingly.

"Why did you three walk off in different directions when you left the restaurant?" Frank questioned.

"I went my way, and they went theirs. How am I supposed to know where they were going?"

By now several grooms had collected around the boys. "Hey! Roger's wisecracking must have finally got him in trouble!" one of them yelled to his companion.

"Yeah! And he sure looks funny with that harness wrapped around him," another said, laughing. "I think he should keep it on permanently."

Joe felt a bit embarrassed and released Roger, who glared at the faces around him. Then he stormed off.

The Hardys headed back to Bayport. As they rode along, Joe said, "What do you think about Roger's story?"

"At least it jibes with what Tempson told us," Frank remarked. "But it could have been a pre-arranged alibi between him and the two men."

"If you ask me, there's something fishy about the whole thing."

When the boys got home, they went directly to their father's study.

"Glad to see you're back," Mr. Hardy said. "Detective Tanner of the Clayton police telephoned a few minutes ago. He wants to talk to you two."

"What about?" Joe inquired.

"Marty Tempson. Tanner told me all about

the tear-gas incident," their father replied. "They checked up on him. Seems his name is not Tempson, but Marty Seegan. He's wanted in Michigan for robbery."

"Then it means that Seegan will be extradited," Frank remarked, "and we won't have a chance to talk to him."

"Afraid so," Mr. Hardy commented. "Since the Clayton police are holding Seegan on a lesser charge, the Michigan authorities get first crack at him. I was also asked to tell you," the detective continued, "that the preliminary hearing scheduled in the morning is off."

At that moment the telephone rang. Mr. Hardy answered it. "It's for you, Frank."

"This is Mr. Clause of the Howard Museum," the caller announced. "I have some information concerning the shrubbery you asked me to identify in the photograph."

CHAPTER XII

A Startling Lead

"WHAT did you find out?" Frank asked quickly.

"I've identified the shrubs as Rubus Diparitus," Clause told him. "They're indigenous to Maryland and parts of Virginia."

Frank thanked the botanist for his help. He then informed his brother and Mr. Hardy about Clause's discovery.

"Maryland!" Joe exclaimed. "That's a coincidence. Aunt Gertrude's stable is located there."

"Let's go see Mr. Fowler, the manager, first thing in the morning," Frank suggested. "Maybe he can help us find Topnotch. Is it all right if we have Jack Wayne fly us there, Dad?"

"You have my okay."

Jack Wayne, a tanned, lean-faced man, was the pilot of Mr. Hardy's personal single-engine plane. The boys telephoned him and requested that he be ready for an early departure the next day.

Dawn was just breaking as Jack began his take-off roll at the Bayport field.

"Too bad Dad couldn't come with us," Joe remarked as he watched the ground drop away beneath them.

"Yes," Frank agreed, "but he wants to be within reach of Mr. Alden if something should come up."

It took little more than an hour to reach their destination. Jack landed the plane on a small field located about four miles from Aunt Gertrude's stable. The airport operator, a genial man, lent the Hardys a car which he kept for the convenience of visitors.

"We might be gone for several hours," Frank told the pilot.

"Don't worry about me," Jack said. "I'll stick around here and do some hangar flying with the fellows."

As soon as the boys arrived at Southern Pines Stables, they spotted a short, wiry man standing in front of one of the stalls. His hard features and deep-set eyes gave him a foreboding appearance.

"We'd like to see Mr. Fowler," Joe informed him.

"Whatcha want to see 'im about?" the man asked in a raspy voice.

"It's confidential," Frank said. "We'd appreciate it if you would tell us where we can find him."

The man stared coldly at the boys for a moment.

Then he pointed toward a knoll in the distance. "You'll find 'im on the other side of that hill. He's practice shootin' with his rifle."

The muffled sound of rifle shots could be heard in the distance. Frank thanked the man and the boys started off. As they crossed over the crest of the hill, they spotted Fowler at the bottom of a shallow gully. He was firing at a paper target.

"Well, if it isn't the Hardys!" Fowler called out when he saw them approaching. "What brings you to this neck of the woods? Business?"

"Not exactly," Frank replied. He then told the manager about the theft of Alden's race horse.

"Why are you telling me all this?" Fowler snapped. "I've never heard of Topnotch."

"We're pretty sure that the horse is being kept somewhere here in Maryland or Virginia," Joe explained. "You must come in contact with lots of stable owners. We thought you might have heard rumors that . . ."

"Sorry! Can't help you," the manager interrupted. "Maryland and Virginia cover a lot of territory. That horse could be anywhere." He squeezed off a couple of shots, then turned to the Hardys. "I regret I can't spend more time with you, but I've lots of work to do. I'm sure you understand."

As the boys followed Fowler out of the gully, Frank picked up one of the spent cartridge cases from the manager's rifle. He quickly stuck it into his pocket.

A few minutes later they were back at the stable. The short, wiry man the boys talked to when they first arrived was nowhere in sight.

"Sorry to cut your visit so short," Fowler said, shaking hands with the young detectives. "Come again when I'm not tied up."

The boys walked back to their car.

"Fowler was certainly in a hurry to get rid of us," Joe commented. "He acted mighty suspicious. Why don't we stick around and see what's going on?"

"No. We're flying back to Bayport right away," Frank announced. "If my hunch is right, we'll save a lot of time in our investigation."

"What hunch?"

Frank dipped into his pocket and pulled out the cartridge case he had picked up. "This shell is of the same caliber as the one we found the day the smoke bomb was fired into Dad's study," he said. "But I can't tell whether it was fired from the same rifle until I make a microscopic comparison."

"Leaping lizards!" Joe exclaimed. "If they do check out, it would connect Fowler with the gang that's after Alden's experimental motor!"

"And the same gang might have stolen Topnotch," Frank added.

Soon the boys and their pilot were winging back to Bayport.

Mrs. Hardy greeted her sons when they arrived

home. "I didn't expect you so soon. Your father left on an errand a few minutes ago. Then he's going directly to Mr. Alden's home. He told me he can be reached there in about two hours."

The boys hurried to their crime lab. Frank took the first cartridge case he had found, and placed it with the second in the comparison microscope. He peered into the eyepieces of the apparatus for several minutes.

"What's the verdict?" Joe asked impatiently.

Suddenly Frank leaped to his feet. "My hunch has paid off!" he exclaimed. "Take a look! The markings on the cartridges match exactly!"

"Wait till Dad hears this!"

Frank glanced at his watch. "Let's drive to Alden's home," he suggested. "Dad should be there by the time we arrive."

The boys dashed to their car. An hour went by before they pulled into a driveway leading to a large, white house. It was set back from the road on a spacious, tree-covered lawn.

An elderly servant responded to a single press of the doorbell. "What can I do for you?" he asked.

"We're Mr. Hardy's sons," Joe explained. "We must see our father right away."

"Oh, yes," the servant answered as he pulled the door open all the way. "He arrived with Mr. Alden a few minutes ago. Please come in."

The boys were ushered into Alden's study. Mr. Hardy was surprised to see them.

"Back from Maryland already?" he said. "Have any luck."

"You bet!" Frank replied excitedly.

Their father and Mr. Alden listened with interest as the two boys told them about their startling lead.

The executive sat bolt upright in his chair. "If what you suspect about this man Fowler is true," he said, "then we must do something right away."

"I'm going to call Chief Collig," Mr. Hardy declared. He dialed a number and shortly had the officer on the line.

"Those cartridge cases are strong evidence," the chief remarked when told about Fowler. "I'll contact the Maryland State Police and have him picked up for questioning. You should hear from me within a couple of hours."

Alden arranged to have dinner served while they waited. Nearly three hours passed before the phone rang. Mr. Hardy rushed to pick it up.

"This is Chief Collig," the caller said. "Looks like your suspect flew the coop. The Maryland police went to the stable and found no one around."

"In that case, will you issue an APB on him?" Mr. Hardy asked. "Frank and Joe can give you a detailed description of Fowler."

"I'll send it out immediately," Collig assured him.

Frank got on the phone and furnished the police chief with the necessary information. Then he and his companions mulled over the situation.

"No wonder Fowler was eager to get rid of us," Joe muttered. "He was planning a getaway. But we still don't know if he had anything to do with the theft of Topnotch."

Frank was casually gazing at some photographs mounted on the wall of the study. Suddenly his eyes widened in amazement.

"I—I don't believe it!" he shouted.

CHAPTER XIII

No Trespassing!

"WHAT is it?" Joe asked, surprised at Frank's outburst.

Frank pointed to a photograph showing a small group of men. "Take a look at the face of the man standing next to Mr. Alden in this picture," he urged.

Joe peered at the photograph in astonishment. "Why—it's Fowler!" he exclaimed.

"The picture you're looking at was taken three years ago during a fishing trip I went on with some friends," Alden interjected as he gazed at the boys curiously. "That man's name is not Fowler. It's Norman Dodson. He's a distant cousin of mine."

"I'm sure we're not mistaken," Frank insisted. "He's the suspect we're after!"

"The idea is utterly ridiculous," the executive

countered. "Why would Norman get mixed up with a gang of crooks? He—"

"Think back," Mr. Hardy interrupted. "Did you and Dodson ever have a falling-out in the past?"

There was a momentary pause.

"As a matter of fact we did," Alden said finally. "About a year ago."

"What happened?" Frank asked.

"Norman was once a junior partner in my firm," the executive explained. "However, he became more interested in the raising of race horses than in automobiles. One day he asked to be bought out so he could purchase a stable. Unfortunately, his venture failed and Norman lost all his money."

"The pieces are beginning to fit together," Joe observed.

"Then about a year ago," Alden continued, "he came to my office and demanded more money. He said that I hadn't paid him enough for his share in the firm. I refused, and we had a bitter argument. I haven't seen him since."

"No doubt about it!" Frank declared. "Dodson must have masterminded the theft of Topnotch. And his motive is clear. He's out to get more money from you one way or another."

"I still find it hard to believe." Alden sighed.

The Hardys returned to Bayport. Aunt Gertrude went into a frenzy when she heard about

Topnotch and their suspect. "My stable is not only a haven for retired race horses," she cried, "but for stolen ones as well!"

"Let's call Mr. Steve Benson, attorney for the estate," Frank suggested to his father. "He should be able to give us more information on Dodson."

Frank dialed the number. It took only seconds to reach the lawyer in Maryland. Benson was shocked to hear about the missing stable manager. He stated that Fowler had worked several months for the previous owner before their aunt inherited the business.

"But I only knew him by the name Fowler," Benson added. "He was the most competent of all the workers there. When I was placed in charge of the estate I made him temporary manager."

"Is there anything else you can tell us about him?" Frank asked.

"Only that he was interested in buying the stable when he learned it was for sale," the lawyer said. "However, he was unable to raise the cash. Later he asked if I would help him sell a piece of land that he owned."

"A piece of land?" Frank blurted. "Where?"

"In northern Vermont," Benson replied. "He showed me the exact spot on a road map. It consists of about twenty acres and a cabin. But I wasn't really interested in handling the matter."

Frank quickly obtained a map of Vermont. He

then asked the attorney to describe where Fowler's land was located. Benson stated that it was just west of Highway 15, twelve miles north of the town of Haversville.

After Frank had hung up, he said, "I'll bet Fowler-Dodson has gone to his cabin!"

"It would be a perfect place to hide out with Topnotch," Joe agreed. "But wouldn't he be taking a big chance? After all, he told Mr. Benson where his land was located."

"Dodson might be hoping the attorney forgot about it, or wouldn't think it important enough to mention," Mr. Hardy said.

"How about requesting the police up there to check the area?" Frank spoke up. "It's been more than fourteen hours since we last saw Dodson. He could easily be in Vermont by now."

Mr. Hardy telephoned Chief Collig again. Two hours passed before the Bayport officer called back.

"A couple of officers searched the cabin and some of the surrounding land," he informed the detective. "Afraid you're out of luck. They found nothing."

"Thanks, Chief," Mr. Hardy replied. "By the way, our suspect would have to transport Topnotch in a horse van. Would you send out an alarm to have all such vehicles—spotted within a six- or seven-hundred-mile radius—stopped and inspected? Although I'm sure it's too late for that now."

"I'll do it, anyway," the chief assured him.

"Guess we've run into another blank wall," Joe muttered.

"Not necessarily," Frank commented. He snapped his fingers. "Let's go to Vermont and take a look ourselves. Dodson's pretty clever. He certainly wouldn't keep Topnotch there at the cabin. It's possible he's hiding somewhere nearby."

"I'm with you," his brother said.

"Go to it," Mr. Hardy told them. "I'll have to stay behind and sit it out with Mr. Alden. Remember! Noon tomorrow is the deadline for him to pay the ransom."

The boys alerted Jack Wayne for another flight the next morning. After an early breakfast, they drove to the airport and boarded the plane.

"Flight time should be approximately two and a half hours," the pilot announced. "The nearest field is about twenty miles from where you want to go."

Jack's estimated time to their destination proved to be correct. After landing, the Hardys arranged to rent a car.

"You stick close to the phone here in operations," Frank instructed Jack. "If you don't hear from us in two hours, notify the police."

"Roger," Jack replied. "Good luck!"

Soon Frank and Joe were driving north on

Highway 15. When they were twelve miles north of Haversville, they spotted a crude fence a few yards west of the road. On it was a large sign which read:

PRIVATE PROPERTY
NO TRESPASSING

"This must be Dodson's land," Joe concluded.

Frank turned the car onto a narrow, dirt trail which jutted off the highway. After traveling a short distance he brought it to a stop.

"We'd better continue on foot," he advised.

The Hardys picked their way through an area of dense woods and brush. Soon they came to a small clearing.

"There's the cabin!" Joe declared, pointing to a dilapidated log structure directly ahead.

"Let's watch it from here for a while," Frank said. "There might be someone inside."

Half an hour went by. There was no sign of life, and the only sound was that of the wind rustling through the trees.

"I think it's safe to go in," Joe remarked impatiently.

"Okay. Let's go!"

They skirted the clearing and approached the cabin from the rear. When they reached it, Frank cautiously peered through a window.

"The place is empty except for a couple of pieces of furniture," he told his brother.

The boys walked around to the front of the cabin and climbed two steps to the porch.

"Careful," Frank warned. "These planks are pretty creaky. Step lightly."

The door of the cabin did not have a lock. The boys pushed it open and went inside. A wooden table stood in the middle of the floor with worn-out chairs set at each end. Suspended from the ceiling above the table was an old kerosene lamp.

Joe walked over to a cupboard mounted against the wall. He pulled open the door. "Look at this!" he exclaimed. "A supply of canned food!"

Frank inspected his brother's discovery. "These cans look as if they haven't been here long. No dust on them."

Suddenly the boys heard the voices of men in the distance.

"Someone's coming!" Joe said excitedly. "Sounds as if they're approaching from the woods behind the cabin."

"Let's get out of here!" Frank said.

The boys dashed through the door and across the clearing to the edge of the woods. They took cover in a clump of thick brush. A moment later three men appeared from around the corner of the cabin.

"That tall guy is the one I trailed from the restaurant in Clayton," Joe whispered.

"And we met the short one at the Southern

Pines Stables when we went to see Dodson," Frank hissed.

Neither of the Hardys recognized the third man, who remarked, "Dodson would nail us to a wall if he knew we came to the cabin!"

"I'm hungry," another said. "I can't wait till dark to get some of that canned food!"

The three men hurried into the log structure and slammed the door behind them.

"I'm going back and try to hear what they're saying," Joe announced.

"It's too risky in daylight," his brother warned.

But Joe was already on his way. Frank watched him scoot across the clearing and carefully step up onto the porch of the cabin.

Suddenly there was a loud cracking sound. Frank's pulse quickened. "Some of the planks are giving way underneath Joe!" he thought.

The next instant there was a crash as Joe fell through the porch floor up to his waist. Frank rushed to his aid. As he reached his brother, the three men spilled out of the cabin!

CHAPTER XIV

Daring Escape

THERE was a violent struggle. Frank lashed out at one of the men and sent him hurtling back into the cabin. The remaining two pounced on the dark-haired youth.

"Run for it!" Joe shouted as he frantically tried to free himself from between the planks.

One of Frank's assailants caught him from behind with a headlock. The young detective flipped him high over his shoulder in judo fashion.

"Hold it!" came an order. Frank suddenly found himself staring into the face of Dodson, who patted a rear pocket significantly.

"Er—hi, Boss," one of the men said nervously. "We came to get some canned food and caught a couple of snoopers."

"What did I tell you guys about coming here in daylight?" Dodson yelled. He glared at the

Hardys. "How did you know where to find me?"

"Trade secret," Joe snapped as he finally worked himself free of the planks and rejoined his brother.

"These kids probably told somebody they were coming here!" Dodson said to his cohorts. "We'd better move the horse van to another hiding place."

"But what about the ransom money?" said one of the men. "Kurt will be comin' here after he picks it up."

Dodson looked at his watch. "It's early yet. He'll still be in his room at the hotel in Clayton." He turned to the short, wiry man the boys had met at the Southern Pines Stables. "Beaver! Get to a telephone and call Kurt. Tell him to go ahead as planned, then to drive to the bus terminal in Haversville. We'll meet him there tonight."

"Okay, Boss," Beaver replied as he hurried off.

The boys were ordered to walk ahead of their captors.

"Where are you taking us?" Frank demanded.

"You two went to a lot of trouble to find Top-notch," Dodson snarled. "I'm going to give you a chance to see him."

The Hardys were marched along what appeared to be a very narrow trail through the woods. Actually they saw it was a wide, dirt road, cleverly covered with brush.

Soon the boys were ordered to halt. A huge mound of dried brush loomed in front of them. One of their captors pulled it aside.

"Why—it's a camouflage net," Joe whispered to his brother.

"And it's covering a horse van," Frank answered in a low voice.

"Shut up!" Dodson demanded. "Get inside!"

The boys walked up a ramp which formed the rear door of the van when closed. To the right in the back of the van was a small bedroom for the trainer. Ahead, another door with bars at the top opened into a stall. Inside was Topnotch who began to whinny at the disturbance.

Frank and Joe were roughly pushed into the van. A quick glimpse at the race horse revealed that his distinguishing white marks above the front hoofs had been dyed chestnut to match his coat.

"This animal," Dodson remarked with a laugh, "has been living like a king. After all, he means fifty thousand dollars to me."

"You won't get away with this!" Joe vowed.

"Who's going to stop me?" Dodson retorted. He then barked an order to his pals. "Tie these wise guys up!" His henchmen shoved the boys inside the small room and uncoiled lengths of rope.

"No use resisting," Frank told Joe. He winked. "Just relax." Joe nodded in response.

As they were being tied up, the boys took deep breaths and flexed their muscles hard. The men wound the ropes tightly around the boys' bodies, then they left with Dodson. The rear door was slammed shut.

Instantly the Hardys exhaled and relaxed their muscles. The ropes went slack and the boys had little difficulty freeing themselves.

"Thanks for reminding me to relax," Joe said with a grin. "I had almost forgotten that old trick Dad taught us."

"We're lucky Dodson's men don't know much about tying up prisoners," Frank remarked.

A scraping sound outside told the boys that their captors were removing the camouflage net covering the van.

"They're getting ready to move," Frank said. "We must get out of here fast!"

"Let's make a break for it! It's our only chance."

The boys dashed from the small room, but were dismayed to find the door of the van locked.

"There's no other exit!" Joe said frantically.

"I have an idea!" Frank whispered. "We'll ride Topnotch out of here!"

"What! Through a locked door?"

"We'll force Dodson and his men to open it!"

"How?"

"By raising such a racket that they'll let down the door to investigate."

The boys opened the door to the stall, patted

the horse, who seemed to recognize them, then bridled him. Quickly they led Topnotch to within a few feet of the rear door.

"Hey!" came the voice of one of their captors. "Do you hear Topnotch movin' around?"

"Probably just restless," Dodson replied. "He'll calm down."

Frank leaned close to Joe. "All set?" he whispered.

His brother nodded, and the boys began pounding on the door with their fists.

"What's that?" they heard a man shout. "It's comin' from inside the van."

"Maybe the kids got loose!" Dodson declared. "We'd better check. Quick! Open the door!"

The Hardys leaped onto Topnotch and flattened out on his back. As the ramp was pulled down, they nudged the race horse forward. He sprinted down the ramp, taking the men completely by surprise. Before they could recover, Topnotch had covered a hundred yards.

"They're getting away!" one of the men yelled.

Suddenly Topnotch stumbled and the Hardys were thrown to the ground. They scrambled to their feet just in time to see Dodson take a small object from his pocket and throw it toward them.

"Looks like a tear-gas bomb!" Frank yelled.

Joe darted ahead and caught the object, then tossed it back at their captors. On contact with the ground, the bomb exploded and engulfed Dod-

The men wound the ropes tightly

son and his henchmen in a thick, white cloud of smoke.

As the choking gas began to drift away, the boys, holding their breaths, pounced on them and wrestled the men into the van. They shut and locked the door.

Joe glanced around. "Where's Topnotch?"

"He ran off!" Frank said. "You stay on guard here. I'll go look for him."

After a brief search Frank found the horse behind a clump of trees, entangled in heavy brush. He freed him and led the animal back to the van.

At that moment the Hardys were startled to hear their names called. "Frank! Joe! Where are you?"

"Sounds like Jack Wayne," Joe said. "He must be at the cabin."

Frank sprinted down the brush-covered trail. Reaching the clearing, he saw the pilot and two state troopers standing near the cabin.

"Jack!" Frank shouted as he ran to greet them.

"Am I glad to see you!" Jack said with a sigh of relief. "I jumped the gun a bit. Didn't quite wait out a full two hours. Thought you'd call me long before that. I began to worry and notified the State Police."

"Glad you did." Frank told Jack and the officers what had happened, then led them to the van.

"You're under arrest!" one of the troopers announced as the boys pulled the door of the vehicle down. Dodson and his henchmen staggered out and were handcuffed.

"There was a fourth man with them," Joe put in. "He went to make a call."

"Where's the nearest telephone?" Frank asked the officers.

"There's a public booth about a mile and a half down the highway," one of them replied.

Frank checked his watch. "Let's drive in that direction," he suggested. "Beaver was on foot. He should be on his way back by now."

"We'll use the patrol car," one of the troopers said, and added, "I'll have to radio headquarters for more help."

Leaving Jack and the other officer behind to guard the prisoners, the Hardys and their companion hurried to the highway. Soon they were cruising in the patrol car.

Minutes later, Joe pointed to a wiry figure trekking back along the highway. "There he is! That's Beaver!"

The officer brought the car to an abrupt halt and leaped out, with the boys close at his heels.

"What—what's this?" Beaver shouted as he was placed under arrest. "How did you kids escape?"

"Save your breath," Joe snapped. "You'll soon have enough talking to do."

It was not long before more troopers arrived on

the scene. Two grooms from a nearby stable were summoned to take charge of Topnotch until his owner could claim him.

Dodson and his cohorts were driven to Haversville Police Headquarters. There Frank telephoned Alden's plant.

"Sorry," said the executive's secretary, "but Mr. Alden and Mr. Hardy left a few minutes ago on urgent business. I don't know when they'll return."

"They're probably on their way to pay the ransom money," Frank remarked as he hung up.

"The guy named Kurt is in for a surprise when he arrives at the bus terminal tonight," Joe commented with a grin. "He'll have quite a reception party waiting for him."

"You can say that again," Frank said. He then turned to their pilot. "Jack, fly back to Bayport and keep trying to contact Dad and Mr. Alden. When you do, bring them here."

"Okay."

The Hardys interrogated the prisoners but without success. After an early dinner at a restaurant in town they returned to police headquarters. They were elated to find their father waiting for them.

"Just got here," Mr. Hardy said. "Heard you boys cracked the horsenapping case. Good work."

"Thanks, Dad," Frank answered. "Where's Mr. Alden? Didn't he come with you?"

"He intended to. But just as we were leaving his office, he received word that Roger was involved in an automobile accident," the detective explained. "Jack went back to Bayport and will fly Mr. Alden here in the morning if Roger isn't seriously hurt."

"What about the ransom?" Joe asked.

"Mr. Alden decided to pay it," his father replied. "He received a call precisely at noon today and was instructed to leave the money in a public locker at the Clayton railroad station. I wanted to stick around and try to nab the pickup man, but Mr. Alden wouldn't hear of it. He was afraid of losing Topnotch if anything went wrong."

The boys told him about Kurt.

"This is a great piece of luck!" Mr. Hardy exclaimed.

Frank glanced at his watch. "If Kurt picked up the money and departed from Clayton by one o'clock this afternoon, he should reach Haversville about ten or eleven o'clock tonight."

As the hour neared, the three Hardys posted themselves across the street from the bus terminal. Several plainclothesmen were assigned to accompany them.

The time ticked by slowly. It was almost midnight before a car approached and parked in front of the terminal building. A burly man climbed out.

"That could be our man," Mr. Hardy whispered.

"Trouble is, we don't know what Kurt looks like," Joe muttered.

Frank was struck with an idea. He stepped out of the shadows and nonchalantly walked toward their suspect. "Hi, Kurt!" he said.

The man whirled. "Hi! Er—who are you?" he responded with a startled expression.

"You're under arrest!" the young detective declared.

The man tried to make a break for it, but Frank seized him. Plainclothesmen closed in from all sides.

"What is this?" their captive shouted. "I ain't done nothin'."

"We know who you are!" Frank shot back.

"Where's the ransom money?" Mr. Hardy demanded.

"What money?" Kurt sputtered.

"It's probably in his car," Joe put in. He quickly searched the vehicle and found a package stuffed underneath the front seat.

"That's it," Mr. Hardy observed.

The prisoner was taken to police headquarters. There he was brought face to face with Dodson.

"Gosh, Boss," Kurt began, "I . . ."

"Shut up!" Dodson screamed. "Idiot! You walked straight into a trap!"

"But nobody warned me! How was I supposed to know?"

"As long as you're in the mood for talking," Frank spoke up, "suppose you answer a few questions."

"I told you before," Dodson retorted, "you're not getting anything out of me."

"Is there someone else in this with you?" Mr. Hardy inquired.

A smirk spread across Dodson's face. "Why don't you ask Alden's son?"

CHAPTER XV

Plea for Help

"WHAT do mean by that remark?" Frank demanded.

"You guys think you're so smart," Dodson snapped. "Figure it out for yourselves."

After the prisoners were escorted to their cells, the Hardys went to a local hotel to spend the night. The next morning Mr. Alden and Jack Wayne arrived just as the boys and their father were finishing breakfast.

"You've done a terrific job," Alden said. "And I'm glad to know that Topnotch is all right."

"We've recovered the ransom money too," Joe announced.

"What!" Alden exclaimed. "That's incredible."

After a pause Mr. Hardy inquired, "How's your son?"

"Fine, thank you. It was just a minor car accident, and I was happy to hear it wasn't his fault.

Fortunately Roger escaped injury and reported for work at the stable this morning."

Frank said quietly, "We're sorry that your cousin is one of the thieves."

Alden also expressed some remorse for Dodson. He hinted that he might drop the charges against him.

"But you can't let him go free," Mr. Hardy objected. "We've reason to suspect that your cousin is involved with someone who is trying to steal your experimental motor. He might turn out to be our only link."

Alden finally agreed.

Then the detective said, "We're going to take another crack at questioning Dodson before we fly back to Bayport. You'd better come to headquarters with us. The police will want a statement."

"All right." Alden sighed. "But please don't ask me to be at the interrogation. You understand. Anyway, I want to arrange to take Topnotch home today."

When Dodson was grilled by the Hardys, he continued to be uncooperative.

"You were the one who fired the smoke grenade into our father's study, weren't you?" Frank said.

"I don't know what you're talking about," Dodson insisted.

"No use denying it," Joe interjected. "We have evidence to prove that the grenade was fired from your rifle."

The prisoner nervously gripped the arms of his chair. "You're lying!" he screamed.

"Who's trying to steal Mr. Alden's experimental motor?" Mr. Hardy demanded.

"I don't know anything about a motor!" Dodson shouted. He jumped to his feet. "I want to go back to my cell!"

Shortly he was ushered out of the room. The Hardys then questioned each of the other prisoners in turn. But they too refused to talk. Obviously Dodson had frightened the men into remaining silent.

After lunch Jack Wayne flew the Hardys back to Bayport. When they arrived, Frank suggested that they drive to the stable near Alden's plant and tell Roger about Dodson's remark.

"I'd like to see what his reaction will be," Frank added.

"You boys go ahead. I must get back to another case," Mr. Hardy told them. "I'll take a taxi home."

The boys hurried to the airport parking lot and climbed into their car. Soon they were at the stable confronting Roger with Dodson's insinuation.

"I barely know my father's cousin," the young man yelled. "He's crazy!"

"Then what reason would Dodson have for trying to involve you?" Frank asked.

Roger grew pale. "Don't ask me!" he retorted. "Maybe he's trying to get back at my father through me."

"Then you've nothing to worry about—if you're not involved," Joe said.

"Leave me alone!" The young man nervously fumbled with a bucket he was carrying. "Get out of here! I have work to do!"

"Okay," Frank replied. "But don't forget this. When Dodson and his gang are put on trial, your name is likely to pop up again. If so, the prosecutor will have you subpoenaed."

When the boys returned home, Chet Morton was waiting in the driveway with his bicycle.

"Hi, fellows!" Their friend was bubbling with excitement. "Long time no see!"

"Hello, Chet!" Frank said. "What's with the bicycle? Car break down?"

"No," the plump youth answered. "Remember the rocket cycle I told you I was going to design? Well, this is it!"

Frank and Joe noticed a square canister attached underneath the seat of the bicycle. A long, funnel-shaped nozzle protruded from it.

"Don't tell us it works," Joe said.

"I don't know yet," Chet admitted. "I wanted to wait until you masterminds could be on hand to witness the supreme test."

"Forget it," Frank advised. "That thing looks dangerous."

Chet shrugged off the warning. He leaped onto the seat of the bicycle and flicked a small toggle switch mounted on the handle bar. A crackling sound came from the canister. Then suddenly a long tongue of flame shot out from the nozzle. Chet was carried off with a roar. He maneuvered the bicycle through several wide circles as its speed rapidly increased.

"Cut off the motor!" Joe cried anxiously.

"I—I can't!" their friend stammered.

In the next instant Chet steered on a straight course and vanished down the street in a trail of smoke. The Hardys jumped into their car and took off in pursuit.

"Where did he go?" Joe said anxiously after they had traveled about half a mile.

"Look! Over there!"

Frank pointed to a bicycle, minus its rider, turned over on a spacious lawn. The wheels were still spinning.

"There's no sign of Chet," Joe muttered worriedly.

"I see him!" Frank declared.

He led his brother to a thick hedge a short distance away. Chet's legs were protruding from the top.

"Are you all right?" Joe yelled.

"Yes, I'm okay! Get me out of here!"

The boys pulled their chum free of the hedge. He was badly shaken by his experience, but other than a few scratches he had suffered no injuries.

"Better stick to the old-fashioned way of propelling a bike," Frank urged.

"Guess you're right." Chet sighed. "It wasn't such a good idea, anyway."

The Hardys drove their friend and his rocket bike to the Morton farm. Then they returned home in time to enjoy a delicious dinner. The meal was interrupted by the telephone. Frank answered it.

"This is Roger," the caller announced. He seemed frightened. "I've got to see you right away. But I don't want to come to your home. Meet me at the municipal parking lot in Bayport."

The boys quickly finished eating, then drove off to rendezvous with Alden's son. They found him seated in his car. At Roger's request the boys climbed into the rear seat.

"What's this all about?" Frank demanded.

"You must help me," the young man pleaded.

"Help you?" Joe snapped. "Why should we?"

"I'm in terrible trouble," Roger said shakily. "I *was* in on the theft of Topnotch. But I didn't know the horse was to be held for ransom."

"Then why did you get involved?" Frank asked.

"I wanted revenge for the way my father has been treating me."

"How did you get mixed up with Dodson?" Joe questioned.

Roger stated that he met his father's cousin one night in Clayton. "I realize now that it was not a chance meeting. He must have followed me there after work. Said he'd heard I wasn't on friendly terms with my father. I never thought to ask him how he knew that."

"Hm! Interesting," Frank muttered.

"Dodson then told me that he also had a grudge against my father," Roger continued, "and asked me if I would like to play a joke on him."

"Like stealing Topnotch?" Joe interjected.

"Yes. But Dodson promised that the horse would be returned in a few days. It wasn't until they attacked the groom the night we took Topnotch that I realized the theft was meant to be more than a joke."

"Why did you meet two of Dodson's henchmen in that restaurant in Clayton?" Frank inquired. "By then you knew they were crooks."

"I had to," Roger replied. "Dodson sent them to warn me not to talk; otherwise he'd see that I went to jail with them."

"What made you change your mind?" Joe asked.

"When you told me Dodson had mentioned my name, I thought it over and decided to tell you what I know. I would have before, but I was afraid."

"You made a wise decision," Frank assured him.

"And if you continue to cooperate, we'll do everything in our power to see that you get a break."

"What should I do now?" Roger asked.

"I suggest you tell your father everything you've told us," Frank advised. "You're going to need his help as well as ours."

Roger thanked the Hardys and drove off.

"Roger's completely changed," Joe commented as he and his brother returned to their car.

"He's scared," Frank said. "And it's a good thing. Maybe this will teach him a lesson."

When the boys arrived home, their father greeted them with alarming news.

"Dodson has escaped!" he announced.

CHAPTER XVI

Dilemma

FRANK and Joe were startled by the news.

"I can't believe it!" Joe exclaimed.

"How did he manage to get away?" Frank asked quickly.

"That's the most fantastic part of what I have to tell you," Mr. Hardy replied.

He told his sons that Lieutenant Monroe of the Haversville police had telephoned. The officer had informed him that Dodson escaped while he and his men were being transferred to the county jail in Myles City.

"The prisoners were sent in a patrol car," Mr. Hardy continued. "When they were about halfway to their destination, the windshield suddenly crazed. The driver lost control, skidded off the road, and turned over in a ditch."

"Leaping lizards!" Joe exclaimed. "That's exactly what caused Mr. Alden's race cars to crash!"

"Then what happened?" Frank asked.

"The occupants were badly shaken up," the detective replied. "But one of the officers faintly recalls seeing two masked men run toward the patrol car. They pulled Dodson out and disappeared. That's all he remembers."

"What about the men with him?" Frank inquired.

"They were left behind," Mr. Hardy answered.

"That's strange," Joe muttered. "I wonder why."

"I don't know," their father admitted. "But I suggest we fly to Myles City tomorrow and have another talk with Dodson's pals."

At that moment Aunt Gertrude entered the room and began one of her tirades.

"Horsenappers! Ransom money! It's all too horrible to imagine," she sputtered. "And to think those criminals were connected with that awful stable I inherited."

"It's not really as bad as all that," Mrs. Hardy commented in a soft voice. "Horses are wonderful animals. Think how pleasant it must be for them to have a lovely place in which to retire."

"Fiddlesticks!" Aunt Gertrude retorted. "I'll have no part of it." She glanced at Mr. Hardy. "Are you sure Mr. Benson is doing his best to sell the stable?"

"Yes, he is," the detective assured her. "You'll probably be hearing from him any day now."

"I certainly hope so," his sister said. "The next thing you know, they'll be setting up public ticket booths and holding races in the paddock."

The others smiled, then Frank changed the subject.

Early the next morning Jack Wayne and the Hardys were streaking down the runway on take-off at the Bayport field. Less than three hours later, the boys and their father were at the county jail in Myles City. Lieutenant Monroe was there to greet them.

"We've checked on the prisoners," he said. "They all have police records a mile long."

"We'd like to question them one at a time," Mr. Hardy requested.

"Okay," the lieutenant replied. "We can use the chief guard's office."

Beaver was the only one among the three prisoners willing to talk. "Dodson's left us holding the bag!" he growled. "That rat won't get away with this. Whatcha' want to know?"

"When did you first meet Dodson?" Mr. Hardy asked.

"A couple of months ago in Maryland," Beaver answered. "I was on the lam at the time and came across the stable he was managin'. He was lookin' for workers and offered me a job. I took it 'cause I thought it would be a good place to lay low for a while."

"Was it his idea to steal Topnotch?" Frank questioned.

"Yes," the prisoner admitted. "I got to be on friendly terms with Dodson. Told 'im I had a police record. He said not to worry about it. Later he asked me if I would help his men steal a race horse, and get a couple o' my friends to come in on the deal. Needin' money, I jumped at the chance."

"Do you know if he was involved in any other shady activities?" Joe asked.

"Not that I know of," Beaver replied. "But he was away from the stable two and three days at a stretch sometimes. Maybe he *was* up to somethin' that he never told me about."

"Think hard," Mr. Hardy urged. "Did Dodson ever mention anything about experimental race cars or motors?"

"Not to me he didn't," the prisoner answered.

When the interview was over, the boys and their father discussed the information.

"I believe he was telling the truth," Frank commented.

"So do I," Mr. Hardy agreed. "And it explains why Beaver and the other two prisoners were left behind."

"What do you mean?" Joe queried.

"I'm convinced that Dodson is part of a gang that's trying to steal Mr. Alden's experimental motor. The theft of Topnotch must have been his own private deal. As a result, the gang knew nothing about his horsenapping plans or the men who were helping him."

"Makes sense," Joe remarked. He thought for a moment. "But how did the guys who helped him escape know he was being taken to Myles City?"

Frank turned to Lieutenant Monroe, who was seated nearby. "Did Dodson have any visitors, or make any phone calls from Haversville?" he asked.

"He didn't have any visitors," the officer told him, "but he was permitted to make a call. When I informed him that we were taking him to Myles City, he demanded that he be allowed to contact his lawyer. I dialed the number for him."

"Did you check the number?" Frank asked.

"No," the lieutenant replied. "But I have a record of it back at headquarters. I'll call the desk sergeant and have him check it immediately."

Monroe picked up the phone. Twenty minutes went by before he obtained the information. "It's an unlisted number in Clayton," he said, "registered in the name of Barto Sigor."

"Barto!" Joe exclaimed. "Mr. Alden's chief sheet-metal worker!"

Mr. Hardy jumped to his feet. "There's no time to lose!" he told his sons. "We're flying back to Bayport immediately!"

Shortly Jack Wayne and his passengers were airborne. When they reached their destination, the Hardys drove at once to Alden's plant. They found the executive in his office. He was greatly upset.

"What's wrong?" Frank asked.

"Barto drove off in my experimental car!" Alden declared.

"When?"

"A few minutes ago! I've already notified the police."

"Have you any idea which way he went?" Joe asked.

"No."

"Your car has a bright silver finish and a distinctive shape," Frank commented. "We should be able to spot it from the air."

"Good idea!" Mr. Hardy said. "You boys go aloft. I'll stay here with Mr. Alden in case the police come up with anything."

Frank rushed to the phone and dialed the number of Jack Wayne's office at the Bayport field. Luckily he caught the pilot just as he was about to go home.

"Sorry to ask you to go up again," he said. "You've been doing so much flying the past couple of days you're likely to sprout wings. But this is an emergency!"

"I don't mind," the pilot assured him.

Frank glanced at Alden. "Is it okay if Jack

lands the plane on your private drag strip?" he asked. "It'll save time."

"By all means," the executive said.

Soon the boys and their pilot were cruising high above the plant.

"Where do we start searching?" Joe inquired.

"My guess is that Barto will stick to the back roads," Frank explained. "There are lots of them to the west."

Jack maneuvered the sleek aircraft to a westerly direction. Frank and Joe scanned the terrain below. Thin ribbons of secluded roads cut across the hills and through the heavy forests.

"I'll climb a bit higher so you can take in more area," the pilot said as he advanced the throttle.

More minutes passed. Then suddenly Joe pointed down toward a bright speck moving along one of the narrow roads. "Look!" he cried. "That might be the car!"

"I'll go down on the deck and make a head-on pass," Jack announced.

Descending to almost ground level, the pilot headed toward the oncoming vehicle. The tall trees that flanked the road seemed just inches away from the wing tips.

"It's Mr. Alden's race car all right!" Frank observed. "Barto is pulling it off to the side."

The plane swept by the vehicle at high speed. Then Jack pulled up into a climbing turn and came around for a second pass. As he did this, Frank saw a man run out onto the road. "Must be Barto!" he shouted.

As Jack flew closer, the boys noticed that the man was aiming a long, cylindrical object at them.

"Be careful!" Frank warned the pilot. "It might be a weapon of some kind!"

In the next instant the windows of the plane crazed completely. The occupants were unable to see through the milky whiteness.

"We're flying blind!" Jack cried as he hauled back on the control wheel and soared skyward.

"How can we land?" Frank asked tensely.

CHAPTER XVII

Emergency Landing

THE Hardys sat frozen in their seats. They heard the loud, thudding sound of the treetops whipping against the underside of the wings.

"I veered off course slightly!" Jack cried. "We just managed to clear the trees!"

Seconds later a large, dark shadow flashed over the top of the plane's canopy. This was followed by a severe buffeting that rocked the craft violently.

"What was that?" Joe shouted.

"We almost collided with another plane!" the pilot declared nervously. "I must contact air traffic control. They'll have to handle us just as if we were flying in bad weather!"

Jack switched the radio transceiver to emergency frequency. "Mayday! Mayday! Mayday!" he declared. "Bayport Center! Do you read me?"

There was an immediate reply as the radio's loudspeaker crackled to life. "This is Bayport Center!" came a voice. "Aircraft calling Mayday! Give position, altitude, and identification!"

"This is Skyhawk One-One-Eight-Howe-Boscoe!" the pilot responded. "Now inbound on the two-eight-four-degree radial of Bayport Omni, approximately forty miles from the station! Present altitude, three thousand!" He then explained their predicament.

"Roger, Eight-Howe-Boscoe!" the air traffic operator replied. "Maintain present heading and altitude! Will advise when we have radar contact!"

It was several minutes before the air traffic controller informed Jack that the plane had been identified on the radar screens. He was also told that his craft would be brought down for a landing by means of a Ground Approach. Frank and Joe knew this meant radar operators would detect their aircraft's heading, descent, and distance from a landing runway. Jack Wayne would be literally "talked down."

The boys watched in admiration as he skillfully maneuvered the plane. When finally advised by the controller that he had just crossed the threshold of the runway, Jack chopped the power and settled to the ground.

"Whew!" Joe sighed, mopping his forehead. "I

don't want to go through that again. For a while it was like driving in heavy traffic with your eyes shut."

Jack brought the plane to a stop. "We'll wait here until a tractor arrives to tow us back to the hangar."

After this was done, the Hardys and their pilot examined the windows of the plane curiously.

"I've never seen anything like it," Joe declared.

"It looks as if something had upset the molecular structure of the material in the windows," Jack said.

"Whatever caused the crazing," Frank concluded, "must have had something to do with that gadget Barto was aiming at us."

"Let's search his apartment in Clayton," Joe suggested. "Maybe we'll find a clue."

"Just what I had in mind," Frank said. "I'll call Dad at Mr. Alden's office and ask if he can arrange to get a search warrant."

"I almost forgot," Joe interjected. "Our car is at the plant."

"Use mine," Jack said, tossing a set of keys to the boys. "I'll stay here and see about getting the windows replaced."

The boys hurried off to meet their father at Alden's office.

"The warrant's all set," Mr. Hardy said. "Clayton Police Station is sending a man to meet us at Barto's apartment."

They were greeted by a jolly, sturdily built policeman. "I got a master key from the superintendent," he informed them. "Makes it easier."

The Hardys were not surprised by what they saw when entering the apartment. A chest of drawers had been emptied of its contents and the closets were bare. The general untidiness of the rooms indicated that the tenant had left in a hurry.

"Barto didn't waste any time getting out of here," Joe commented.

"Dodson's call from Haversville obviously scared him away," Frank concluded. "He knew the police might check his number."

"This proves one thing," Mr. Hardy put in. "Barto must be in with the gang that's after Alden's motor. In fact, he might even be the leader."

Frank discovered a single fingerprint on the telephone. He lifted the print with his special tape and placed it in a celluloid container. "Must be Barto's," he remarked. "But I'll ask Chief Collig to check it just to be sure."

Meanwhile, Joe was rummaging through the wastebasket. He pulled out a crumpled, typewritten letter and two sheets of carbon paper. "I've found something," he called to his brother and father. They examined the letter together. It read:

Dear Barto:

I'm sorry to hear that your brother had trouble with his employer and moved on. Perhaps the strain of his labors was too much for him.

I wish you could visit me. I'm still operating my old mansion as a restaurant. One night I had forty customers. They came from miles around. However, I have competition about two miles north of my place. It is called the Claymore. Tonight I intend to go there to see how well they are doing. It is located just off the main highway. I must go now, since it is getting late and I always make a point of retiring by twelve.

Write soon.

Your friend,
Eric

"I wonder who Eric is," Joe mused.

"Too bad we don't have the envelope the letter came in," Mr. Hardy said. "It would tell us where it was mailed."

"What's written looks innocent enough," Frank observed. "Just the same, I want to examine it more carefully, and for luck I'll take these two sheets of carbon paper."

A further search of the rooms revealed nothing more. The Hardys thanked the Clayton policeman who had been assigned to accompany them and returned to Bayport. Frank stopped to give Chief Collig the fingerprint he had lifted from Barto's phone.

"I'll check it right away," the officer said.

"Thanks," Frank responded. "I'll be at home. Please call me there."

The boys and their father arrived home to find Aunt Gertrude in a jovial mood. "I have wonderful news!" she exclaimed. "Mr. Benson telephoned. He's found a buyer. My stable is as good as sold."

"Glad to hear it," Mr. Hardy told her. "That should put your mind at rest."

"Indeed it will," Aunt Gertrude agreed. "But I hope the new owner is an expert in caring for horses. I would dislike the thought of those poor animals being neglected."

"Do I detect a change of heart?" Joe asked with a grin. "How come you're so fond of horses all of a sudden?"

"I always have been," Aunt Gertrude defended herself. "I just don't think they should be raced around a silly track for people's amusement."

Joe said, his eyes twinkling, "Someday I'm going to take you to a race!"

After supper the boys went to their crime lab and examined the letter they had found in Barto's apartment.

"Do you think it contains some kind of a code message?" Joe asked his brother.

"Not any more than the first letter I found in Barto's wastebasket the day I took his fingerprints from the doorknob," Frank replied. "What about the sheets of carbon paper?"

"Haven't had a chance to examine them carefully yet," Joe said. "So far, it looks quite ordinary."

At that moment Chet Morton entered the lab. "Hi, masterminds," he greeted the Hardys. "Got a few minutes to talk?"

"We always have time for you," Frank assured his friend with a smile. "What's on your mind?"

"It's about my rocket cycle," Chet announced.

"Oh, no!" Joe exclaimed. "I thought you gave that up as a bad idea."

"I intended to," Chet replied. "But then I had a brainstorm."

Frank winked at his brother. "This ought to be good," he remarked.

"Okay!" Chet protested. "If you don't want to hear about my invention, just say so."

"I'm sorry," Frank said. "Go ahead."

The chubby youth took a rolled sheet of paper from his hip pocket and spread it out across the table. On it was the rough sketch of a bicycle. "See these tubes underneath the seat?" he began.

"Yes," Joe told him. "How could we forget? They're your rockets."

"Wrong!" Chet declared with a flourish of his hand. "What you see are jet engines. And I won't even have to build them myself. The hobby shop sells these units for model planes and boats. About four of them will produce enough thrust to propel my bike."

"If you insist on going ahead with the project," Frank warned, "just make sure that there are plenty of hedges around for you to fall into."

"Stow the comedy," Chet retorted. "The bike won't run away with me again. Since the jets are operated with liquid fuel, I'll be able to control the power."

"When do you plan to unveil this great invention of yours?" Joe inquired skeptically.

"In a couple of days," Chet announced proudly.

"This calls for a celebration," Frank said. "Aunt Gertrude baked an apple pie today. What say we go to the kitchen and have some?"

"Lead me to it!" their friend exclaimed.

As the boys were being served, Chief Collig telephoned. "I just got the results on the fingerprint you gave me," he said to Frank.

"I assume it's Barto's," Frank commented.

"No," the chief replied. "The print is from his brother Vilno!"

CHAPTER XVIII

Night Chase

"THAT's incredible!" Frank declared.

He and Joe rushed to their father's study to tell him the news.

"Then Vilno was in his brother's apartment," Mr. Hardy concluded. "But why?"

"To help Barto steal the experimental car," Joe suggested.

"If so," Frank argued, "why wasn't Vilno with his brother when we spotted the car from the air?"

"Maybe they decided to go their separate ways after the theft," Mr. Hardy said.

Frank frowned. "I wonder," he muttered, "if Vilno has been posing as his brother all the time."

"Impossible!" Joe said. "Those were Barto's fingerprints you lifted off the doorknob the day you followed him to his apartment. And don't forget, Vilno is not a sheet-metal worker. How could he do his brother's job at the plant?"

"Guess you're right," Frank finally agreed. "But it's an interesting theory."

Mr. Hardy rubbed his chin dubiously. "I'm going to try getting more background on those two," he said. "It may lead up a blind alley. Yet I might discover some useful information."

Their discussion was interrupted by a telephone call from Alden.

"The police have retrieved my experimental car," the executive told Mr. Hardy. "Unfortunately Barto got away."

"What happened?" the detective asked.

Alden explained that a state trooper, who was patrolling the road indicated by the boys, had spotted the car traveling at great speed. He gave chase, but found that his motorcycle was not fast enough to close the gap.

"Then Barto blew a tire and spun out of control," Alden continued. "By the time the officer reached the spot, Barto was gone."

"Was the car damaged?" Mr. Hardy queried.

"A little," Alden answered. "But nothing that can't be repaired in a few hours. In fact, I had considered entering it in a road race that's scheduled near here a couple of days from now. However, I don't think I will."

After hanging up, the detective told his sons what Alden had said.

"I wonder where Barto was taking the car," Joe mused.

"Your guess is as good as mine," Mr. Hardy admitted.

Frank thought for a moment. "I have an idea," he said finally. "Let's ask Mr. Alden to enter his car in the road race. Then the night before the event Joe and I will inspect the route. We might spot one of those signposts."

"It's worth a try," their father agreed.

The following morning Frank telephoned Alden and told him his plan.

"I'll do anything to help clear up the mystery," Alden stated. He agreed to the plan, then described the route of the race.

After Frank put down the phone, Joe said, "I hope you don't plan on our using bicycles like the last time. If you do, I'm going to ask Chet to install a couple of his jet engines on mine."

Frank grinned. "We'll use our car."

"But if there are members of the gang around, they'll hear us coming," Joe objected.

"So far, the signposts have been set precisely beyond a sharp curve in the road. There'll be a full moon. We can cruise along with our lights out, and every time we come to a curve we'll stop and inspect it on foot."

It was clear and cool the night before the event. The boys waited until midnight before starting out for the race site, which was situated a few miles west of Clayton. When they arrived, Frank turned out the headlights and drove slowly along the route described by Alden.

"Maybe we're too early," Joe warned. "If the gang does intend putting up a signpost, we might finish our search before they get here."

"We'll keep patrolling the road till dawn," Frank said. "If they haven't set one up already, they'll have to do it before daylight."

The boys stared into the darkness. As they approached the first sharp bend in the road, Frank stopped the car. He and his brother edged their way around it on foot.

"Nothing there," Joe observed.

The Hardys returned to the car and continued on. They had almost covered the entire route when another sharp bend appeared ahead of them. They climbed out of the vehicle and walked forward.

"Hold it!" Joe ordered in a low voice. "Do you hear something?"

Frank listened, then nodded. "Sounds like several men mumbling to one another," he whispered.

Crouching low, the boys cautiously worked their way around the bend. Then suddenly the Hardys came to a stop. The shadowy images of five men could be seen standing near a pickup truck a short distance down the road. A signpost stood nearby.

"Rotten luck," one of the men growled in a hushed voice. "This generator we brought doesn't work."

"We should've checked it out at the lab," another man added.

"I know those voices," Frank hissed. "It's Dodson and Barto!"

"I wonder if Vilno is with them," Joe whispered.

A couple of men lifted a heavy object onto the back of the truck.

"Slade! You and Tadlow go back and get another generator," Barto ordered. "But be quick about it. Everything has to be set up before it gets light."

Two men leaped into the truck and started off. The driver executed a U-turn and headed in the direction of the Hardys.

Frank pointed to a clump of brush a few feet away. "Take cover!"

The boys managed to conceal themselves just before the truck flashed by.

"They're bound to spot our car!" Joe said anxiously.

A moment later he and Frank were panic-stricken to hear the truck screech to a halt. Soon one of its occupants came running back to rejoin his companions.

"Barto!" the man exclaimed. "There's a car parked beyond the bend. It wasn't there before!"

"Maybe it's the police!" Dodson sputtered.

"I don't think so," Barto argued. "They would've driven up and asked us what we're doing here." He turned to his pals. "Spread out and start searching the area. There must be snoopers around."

The men took out flashlights and began walking down the road toward the Hardys.

"What'll we do?" Joe said.

"Our only chance is to make a break for it," Frank decided. "Head for the car. There'll be only one man to get past."

The boys leaped to their feet and sprinted down the road as fast as they could.

"Look!" Barto yelled as he directed his beam of light toward the fleeing youths. "There go a couple of guys!"

"It's those Hardy kids!" Dodson shouted. "Don't let them get away!"

As Frank and Joe rounded the bend, they saw the driver of the truck standing beside their car. Joe crouched low, shot forward, and buried his right shoulder into the man's midriff. The fellow went crashing to the ground.

Frank leaped behind the steering wheel of the car and started the engine. Joe climbed in beside him just as Barto and his friends bore down on the boys.

"Stop them!" Dodson yelled.

After making a quick U-turn, the boys sped

along the road and away from their pursuers. Joe peered out the rear window. "They're coming after us in the truck!"

Frank gave the convertible more power. "Are they gaining on us?"

"No!" Joe answered. "But we're not losing them either!"

After rounding another sharp bend in the road, Frank noticed a trail ahead which struck off to the right and into a wooded area. "Hang on!" he cried. "I'm going to try something!"

Swerving sharply, Frank turned onto the trail. After they had traveled a short distance, he switched off the engine and lights. A moment later their pursuers raced past and continued down the road.

"Your maneuver worked!" Joe said with a grin.

"We're not out of this yet," Frank warned. "Barto and his men are sure to figure out what happened. We'll get back on the road and drive in the opposite direction."

He restarted the engine and rolled only a few feet when he brought the vehicle to a stop.

"What's wrong?" Joe queried.

"I'm afraid we have a flat!"

The boys climbed out of the car and were dismayed to see that the left front tire had been punctured by a sharp rock.

"What a time to have this happen!" Joe muttered.

The Hardys made a break for it!

At that instant they heard the sound of a vehicle approaching in the distance.

"It must be Barto and the others!" Joe concluded.

"Quick! Let's hide!"

"Where?"

Frank glanced around. "We'll climb a tree. That one over there should be the easiest. Get going! I'll follow you!"

Soon the Hardys were pulling themselves up through the branches, high above the ground. A thick mass of leaves provided excellent cover. There was one small clear spot which permitted them to view the road.

"We made it just in time," Joe said. "There's the pickup truck. Barto and his men are turning in here!"

The boys' pulses quickened as they watched the truck come to a halt immediately behind their car.

"I told you those kids must've turned in here after we didn't see them on the road ahead!" Dodson declared. "Good trick. Lucky I remembered our passing this trail."

"But where are they?" Barto growled. He examined the damaged tire. "I see they have a flat. Why didn't they try to fix it?"

"Probably heard us coming and ran off," Dodson replied. "Just the same, let's take a look around."

Frank and Joe were almost afraid to breathe as they watched their pursuers take out flashlights and search the area. At one point, a beam of light was directed toward the place in which the boys were hiding.

"That was close," Frank thought as the beam was finally turned downward.

"We'd better not waste any more time here!" Barto shouted. "Those snoopers may be on their way to call the police!"

"They've ruined everything," Dodson snarled. "We'll have to forget about using the signpost on Alden's car during the race. Let's pick it up and get out of here."

One of the men walked to the rear of the Hardys' car with a sharp-pointed tool. He proceeded to punch several holes into the fuel tank. Gasoline began to stream from it. "That'll stop 'em from usin' this in case they come back."

Barto and his henchmen climbed into the truck and drove off. The Hardys waited a few minutes before leaving their hiding place.

"Here we are in the middle of nowhere without transportation," Joe said angrily.

"Won't help to complain about it." Frank sighed. "Must be five or six miles to the nearest telephone. Let's start walking."

They began trekking along the road. It had been daylight for more than an hour when they saw a sedan approaching.

"Oh-oh," Joe remarked. "I hope none of Barto's men are in it."

As the car came to a stop, the boys were elated to see Alden behind the wheel and their father seated beside him.

"Am I glad to see you two!" Mr. Hardy called out. "I became worried when I didn't hear from you. I decided to look for you and asked Mr. Alden to come along." He peered at his sons curiously. "Why are you walking? Where's your car?"

The boys climbed into the rear seat of Alden's car and told the men what had happened. Then they drove to the spot where they had seen the signpost.

"This is where it was," Frank announced, pointing to a small hole on the shoulder of the road.

"The gang made certain that they didn't leave any clues behind," Mr. Hardy observed.

"You boys have saved my experimental car from being wrecked," Alden interjected.

"You must be tired," Mr. Hardy said to his sons.

"I insist you come to my home for breakfast and a few hours' sleep," Alden added.

The young detectives readily agreed. They rested until midafternoon, then returned to Alden's office. They had been there only a few minutes when the phone rang. Alden picked up the receiver. He turned pale as he listened to what his caller had to say.

"What's the matter?" Mr. Hardy asked after his client hung up.

"That—that was Barto's brother Vilno!" Alden stammered. "He has Roger! He said unless I give him my experimental motor, he'll harm my son. He's calling again in two hours for my answer."

CHAPTER XIX

Breaking the Code

THE Hardys were shocked by the news.

Alden was almost at the point of collapse. "If Vilno and his gang want my motor that badly, I'll give it to them."

The three detectives were angry. Mr. Hardy exclaimed, "I'd like to get my hands on those scoundrels! They'll stop at nothing!"

"If only we had a lead to where their hideout is," Joe put in.

Frank frowned. "Maybe the lead is right in our files at home."

"What do you mean?" Joe asked.

"Maybe the letters we found in Barto's apartment do contain a code after all," Frank answered.

Mr. Hardy nodded. "Why don't you boys go back to Bayport and work on that angle?" He handed them a set of keys. "Take my car. It's in the plant's parking lot. I'll stay here and be on hand when Vilno calls back."

"Meanwhile," Alden told the boys, "I'll send one of my tow trucks to pick up your car."

Frank and Joe hurried home, took Barto's letters from the file, then went to their crime lab to study them.

After an hour had passed, Joe sighed. "We're no closer to discovering a key than we were the last time we examined the letters."

"Looks hopeless," Frank agreed. "But let's keep at it a bit longer."

Shrugging, Joe turned his attention to the sheets of carbon paper found in Barto's apartment. He scrutinized them carefully and thought they looked a bit different from the usual carbon paper. Suspicious, Joe sandwiched a sheet between two sheets of white paper, picked up a pencil, and began scribbling on the upper one.

Suddenly he sat bolt upright. "This is odd! The carbon doesn't produce a copy except in a few isolated spots."

Frank jumped to his feet. "Joe! You may have discovered the key to the code!"

"I hope so. Fortunately our typewriter has pica type like Barto's machine. I'll type an exact copy of the first of his letters," Joe said. "If our hunch is correct . . ." His words trailed off as he inserted two clean sheets into the typewriter. Then he began tapping out the words.

Dear Eric:

Forgive me for taking so long to write you, but I've been so exhausted from work the last few days that I didn't feel I could write a coherent sentence. How I wish I had the stamina of two hard-working boys who have taken summer jobs at the plant. Any family would be proud to have sons like that.

As I already told you, my brother has left the Alden company . . .

When Joe finished typing the letter, he pulled out the sheets and quickly examined the carbon copy.

"That's it! We've broken the code!" he exclaimed. "Trick carbon paper!"

Joe showed Frank the copy. "Notice that the carbon has transferred only certain words and portions of words onto the copy sheet. First we have the word 'hard.' Next, the 'y' and 's' from the word 'boys.' "

"Spelling out 'Hardys'!" Frank declared.

"And the next word is 'sons,' and so on."

The boys observed that the complete message read:

Hardys, sons of detective, here. I'm sure they're investigating.

Tingling with excitement, Frank handed his

brother the second of Barto's letters and the other
sheet of carbon paper. "Quick! Make a copy of
this!"

Joe repeated the procedure. The carbon copy
revealed the following message:

> moved lab to old mansion forty miles north
> of Clayton on route twelve.

"It must be the location of the gang's hideout!" Frank exclaimed.

He rushed to the telephone and dialed Alden's
private office number. There was no answer.

"It's after office hours," Joe said. "Mr. Alden's
secretary must have left. Why don't you try the
company's main number?"

Following his brother's suggestion, Frank finally got a response from the plant's chief watchman.
"Sorry, I can't help you," the man told Frank.
"Me and my men just came on duty. I haven't
seen Mr. Alden or anyone else."

Next, Frank tried the executive's home. Again
there was no answer.

"I wonder where Dad and Mr. Alden are,"
Frank muttered.

"Maybe they went to meet Vilno."

"Dad would have called us. I don't like this."

"If they're delivering the experimental motor
to Vilno, he and his gang may try to make a getaway after they have it. Let's go to their hideout."

"Okay!" Frank agreed. "But since Mother and

Aunt Gertrude won't get home from the theater till late I'll ask Chet to stand by the phone here. He can tell Dad where we are if he should call."

Twenty minutes later Chet's ancient yellow car rumbled to a stop in front of the Hardy home. The boys noticed that their friend had his jet-propelled bicycle lashed to the rear bumper.

"I'm taking my bike to a secret spot early tomorrow morning," Chet announced. "It's ready for the supreme test."

"Lots of luck," Frank said. "I hope the job we're asking you to do isn't going to interfere with your plans."

"Not at all," the chubby youth replied grandly. "What is it you want me to tell your father if he calls?"

Frank handed him the message they had decoded revealing the location of the gang's hideout.

"I'd rather be going with you," Chet muttered, "instead of having to sit at the telephone."

"We wish you could too," Joe assured him. "But your job is an important one. We'll check with you later."

It was already dusk when the Hardys drove off. Forty miles to the north of Clayton, Joe pointed to a dimly lighted building in the distance. "I think I've spotted the mansion! It's behind those trees over to the right."

Frank brought the car to a stop near the foot of a long wooded driveway. He and his brother continued on foot. The house was situated quite a distance from the main road.

"I don't see anybody or signs of activity," Joe whispered as they neared the building.

"Just the same, be careful. If this *is* Vilno's hideout, he's sure to have one or more guards posted."

The boys crept forward toward the front of the house, keeping in the darkness of the trees. Suddenly Joe grabbed his brother's arm. "Look!" he whispered. "There's a man up ahead, seated on that big rock. He's armed!"

"It's a guard all right, Joe. He's Tadlow, one of the men we saw with Barto and Dodson at the sinister signpost!"

"Then we're at the right place. Let's nab him."

"Okay."

The Hardys stalked their quarry. When they were within arm's reach of the man, he jumped to his feet and whirled around to face them.

Quick as a flash Joe leaped and caught the man squarely on the jaw with a right uppercut. He tumbled to the ground, unconscious. Nearby lay his rifle, which Frank flung into a clump of brush.

The boys dragged the man to a slim tree, put his arms around the trunk, and tied his wrists together with a belt. The placing of a handkerchief gag completed the job.

Moving cautiously, the boys continued toward the mansion. They kept a sharp lookout for other guards, but there were none. When the Hardys reached their goal, they detected a humming sound.

"What do you think that is?" Joe hissed.

"Offhand, I'd say it's some kind of machine," Frank answered. "Seems to be coming from the basement."

The boys started to creep around the outside of the mansion. Soon they discovered a metal air vent in the foundation. Frank peered through it in amazement.

"See anything?" Joe asked in a hushed voice.

"Yes. Looks like a physics or electronics laboratory."

Joe crouched just as three men came into Frank's view. They were Vilno, Barto, and Dodson. The boys pressed their ears against the vent in an effort to hear what the men were saying.

"This is a good setup here," Barto remarked. "Too bad we have to leave it."

"Now that we have the experimental motor," Vilno put in, "there's no reason for us to stick around."

"What about the prisoners?" Dodson inquired. "Alden and his son don't worry me, but that detective Hardy can be dangerous to us."

Frank and Joe gasped. Their father had been captured together with Mr. Alden and Roger!

"Forget it," Vilno told Dodson. "We'll be miles away before anyone finds Hardy."

Frank turned to his brother. "We must rescue them!"

"We can't do it alone! There are probably more members of the gang inside."

Suddenly the tall figure of a man loomed up behind the boys. "Who are you?" he demanded.

Frank and Joe leaped to defend themselves. A wild struggle followed. They crashed against the side of the house several times. Then Frank dealt the man a blow that sent him crumbling to the ground.

Suddenly the young detectives heard another, but louder, humming sound. In the next instant they were horror-stricken to find that they could not move.

"What's happening?" Joe exclaimed.

The boys were frozen in their tracks. Some powerful, invisible force was holding them!

CHAPTER XX

Jet Action

"IT's THE Hardy kids!" Dodson shouted as he, Barto, and two other men arrived on the scene.

"Don't get too close to them," Barto warned his pals, "or you'll get caught in the sonic trap yourselves. Tadlow! Go tell my brother to turn it off."

Within a couple of minutes the boys were released from the mysterious force that had prevented them from moving. The aftereffects, however, caused Frank and Joe to fall to the ground exhausted. Dodson and the others pounced on them and tied the boys' hands behind their backs.

"So! How do you like our little sonic trap?" Barto sneered.

"Sonic trap?" Frank said weakly.

"Yes," Barto replied. "It's another of Vilno's inventions. A device which encloses objects of our choosing within a solid shell of hypersonic vibrations. Your father also had the honor of experiencing its effects."

Frank and Joe were marched into the mansion, then down a flight of stairs leading to the basement. They were awed by what they saw. The area had been converted into a large laboratory, and was filled with various pieces of electronic equipment. In one corner of the room lay several signposts marked DANGER.

"Welcome! Welcome!" Vilno exclaimed with exaggerated politeness. "Looking for your father? Well, you've come to the right place."

"If you've harmed him," Joe began, "or . . ."

"He's perfectly fit," Vilno interrupted, "and is in our storage room with Alden and his son. You shall join them shortly."

For the first time the boys had an opportunity to see Vilno and Barto together. They were identical twins. Other than for a difference in dress, it was difficult to tell who was who.

"Perhaps our guests would like to see some of the things we invented," Barto sneered.

"That *we* invented? You're forgetting it was my genius alone that made our devices possible!" his twin said boastfully.

"How did you manage to craze the windshields of Mr. Alden's race cars?" Frank interjected.

Vilno seemed pleased by the question. He led the Hardys to the signposts. "Inside each of these is a hypersonic generator of my own design. I found that I could disturb the molecular arrangement in some materials with the waves it produces. They are what crazed the windshields of Alden's cars."

"And the windows of our plane!" Joe said angrily.

"Ah yes," Vilno said. A sinister smile spread across his face. He walked to a table and picked up a long, cylindrical object. "Your plane was among the first objects on which I tried the portable version of the hypersonic generator."

"Then it was you, and not Barto, who stole Mr. Alden's experimental car," Frank remarked.

"Precisely," Vilno replied.

At that moment Barto began to roar with laughter. "They still don't know," he told his brother, "that it was you who was working at the plant all the time, posing as me!"

"But how could you carry on the deception?" Joe sputtered. "You're not a sheet-metal worker."

"That's where you're wrong," Vilno shot back. "My brother and I were both trained in sheet-metal work as youths. But I never claimed it as one of my skills. My ambition was to become a scientist."

"Why are we standing around here talking?" Dodson said impatiently. "These snoopers might have told the police they were coming here!"

"Then where are they?" Vilno countered. "You worry too much."

"I don't care what you say!" Dodson retorted. "I . . ."

"Shut up!" Barto broke in. "We should've let you stay in jail for stealing Alden's race horse. Why did you do it? Aren't we paying you enough?"

"And your stupidity didn't end with the horse theft," Vilno added with a touch of irritation. "You made the mistake of telephoning me at my apartment from Haversville Police Headquarters. Idiot! I knew the Hardys were bound to check the number."

Dodson grimaced but said, "You're not so smart. You started a fire in the experimental lab."

Frank broke in. "Vilno, you say you were posing as your brother all the time. Yet it was Barto's fingerprints I found on the doorknob of your apartment the day I followed you home from the plant."

"Quite simple," Vilno answered proudly. "Barto and I were dressed exactly alike and switched places in the lobby. It was he you saw enter the apartment."

"But how did you know you were going to be followed that day?" Joe asked quickly.

"Your taking summer jobs at the plant didn't fool us," Barto put in. "We knew you were probably investigating the Alden case. Vilno guessed that he would be a suspect, and that you would undoubtedly shadow him. So, each day, we wore similar clothes in the event we had to switch places. The plan paid off. You followed the wrong one on the street in Clayton. Vilno pretended a friend was a bum and shoved him away."

"We've told them enough," Vilno growled. "Put them in the storage room with the others."

Dodson and two men marched Frank and Joe out of the laboratory and down a narrow passageway. They came to a stop in front of a heavy metal door. Dodson pulled it open.

"Inside!" he ordered.

The boys entered a small, windowless room made of stone. Before the door was closed, they saw their father, Alden, and Roger.

"Dad!" Joe exclaimed.

"I see you two also had some bad luck," the detective said remorsefully.

The metal door clanged shut and the Hardys and their companions were in total darkness.

"We were surprised to learn that you and Mr. Alden had been captured, Dad," Frank remarked.

"I walked into Vilno's sonic trap," Mr. Hardy explained.

"How did you find the gang's hideout?" Joe asked.

"After you left Mr. Alden's office, I went to Clayton Police Station in Mr. Alden's car to tell them about the situation, and to arrange for help in case we needed it. I planned to return to the plant in time for Vilno's telephone call. When I was driving back, I saw Mr. Alden go by me from the opposite direction in a truck."

"Sorry about that." The executive sighed. "This is how it happened, boys. Vilno called me again shortly after your father left. He told me he'd been watching the plant and saw Mr. Hardy drive off. Vilno was worried he was going to the police and demanded I deliver the experimental motor to him immediately. For Roger's sake, I had no choice."

"What happened then?" Frank asked.

"Vilno ordered me to bring the motor to the Bryant crossroads north of Clayton," Mr. Alden replied. "There, two of his men jumped into the truck with me and told me to drive on. We came here to the mansion."

"I followed the truck," Mr. Hardy interjected. "Too bad I didn't have my own car, or I would have contacted you boys by radio. And unfortunately I couldn't stop to use a telephone."

"You people wouldn't be in this mess if it wasn't for me," Roger muttered.

Frank began to grope around their enclosure, hoping for a way of escape. His father said, "The walls are solid, and you couldn't budge that metal door with a bulldozer."

"The room is completely sealed," Mr. Alden added, "except for an air vent. Thank goodness for that."

"Air vent," Frank repeated, looking for it.

"It's near the ceiling," Mr. Hardy said. "But if you're thinking of an escape route, it's too small for any of us to crawl through."

"Let me try," Joe urged. "I've managed to squeeze through some pretty small spaces before."

Mr. Hardy guided his sons to the rear wall of the room. "The vent should be directly above this spot."

Frank hoisted his brother onto his shoulders. Joe ran one hand along the upper portion of the wall. "I've found it! The vent is covered with a metal grating." There was a momentary pause. "I think I can pull it loose."

Joe tugged the grating hard. Finally it broke free of the wall. "The opening is small, but I'm sure I can manage to get through. Boost me up higher."

Frank grabbed his brother's feet with both hands and shoved him upward. An instant later Joe was gone.

"Be careful, son," Mr. Hardy called.

But Joe was not free yet. He was in an air duct. His arms stretched out in front of him, Joe forced his way through the narrow passageway. Minutes seemed like hours. Finally he was elated to find that the vent led directly outside the mansion.

Another grating, however, barred his way. He grasped the bars with both hands and shoved with all his strength. The grating loosened and dropped outside to the ground.

After climbing out of the vent, Joe scanned his surroundings. Several yards away he saw Vilno and his henchmen preparing to depart in Alden's truck.

Stealthily, the young detective stalked toward the front door of the mansion. Luckily it was unlocked. He raced inside and ran down to the storage room to free his companions.

"Quick! Vilno and his men are getting ready to leave!"

The three Hardys and their friends rushed outside the mansion. They were crestfallen to see that the truck had already pulled away.

"We'll never catch them!" Frank declared.

"Look!" Joe yelled. "What's that glow?"

His companions were startled to see a bright ball of light approaching the truck head-on. Just as a collision seemed imminent, the vehicle veered off the lane. This was followed by a loud crunching sound.

"What's that?" Alden shouted.

They detected a roar as the glow grew closer. Then it suddenly vanished. Seconds later Chet Morton coasted out of the darkness on his jet-propelled bicycle.

"Hi, fellows! Am I glad to see you!"

"Chet! What are you doing here?" Frank exclaimed.

"I began to worry when I didn't hear from you," the chubby youth explained. "So did your mother and aunt. I decided to see what was going on. My car ran out of gas about a mile from here, so I came the rest of the way on my jet bike." His eyes widened. "By the way, I almost ran into a truck! What happened to it?"

The Hardys hurried to the spot where they had seen the vehicle veer off the lane. They found it tightly wedged between two stout trees. Vilno and his pals were desperately trying to open the doors but without success.

Just then a State Police car arrived on the scene. One of the troopers got out. "Did any of you see a wild kid on a bicycle?" he questioned. "We think it turned in here. Looked as if it was on fire."

"I'm the one," Chet admitted sheepishly.

"What were you trying to do?" the officer demanded. "You went by us as if you'd been shot out of a cannon." His attention was attracted by the disabled truck. "What happened here? Accident?"

Mr. Hardy stepped forward. "Let me explain," he said.

After hearing the story, the officer radioed for additional men, then the troopers took Vilno and his henchmen into custody.

"We'd have escaped if it hadn't been for that crazy friend of yours and his bicycle," the gang leader growled.

"That's your hard luck!" Joe told him.

Mr. Hardy said, "We know that specifications of Mr. Alden's motor were leaking out of the plant. How did you manage it?"

Vilno's egotism caused him to forget his predicament for a moment. "Easy! Alden's machinists worked from plans recorded on film slides. I just roamed around the plant and photographed the projected pictures with a spy camera in my wrist watch. Other components I committed to memory and put them down on paper later."

Soon more troopers arrived. The prisoners were herded into patrol cars. The case of *The Sinister Signpost* was over. Frank and Joe always regretted such a moment. They were not restless for long, however, because the mystery of *A Figure in Hiding* soon came their way.

Before departing, one of the officers walked up to Chet. "I should give you a ticket for speeding," he announced, winking at the Hardys.

"I—I wish you wouldn't," Chet stammered. "It won't happen again."

"Well, under the circumstances, I think I can overlook it this time." The trooper sighed, trying not to grin. "Anyway, I wouldn't know how to describe your jet-propelled bike to the judge."

"We warned you about that invention of yours," Joe whispered, nudging his chum. "Lucky for us you didn't listen!"

Your Thyroid Problems Solved

Holistic solutions to improve your thyroid

Dr Sandra Cabot

Margaret Jasinska ND

Your Thyroid Problems Solved
Copyright © 2006 Dr Sandra Cabot & Margaret Jasinska ND

First Published 2006 by WHAS Pty Ltd

WHAS Pty Ltd - Australia
P. O. Box 689, Camden NSW, 2570 Australia
Phone 02 4655 8855

SCB Inc. - United States of America
PO Box 5070 Glendale AZ USA 85312
Phone 623 334 3232

www.whas.com.au
www.liverdoctor.com
www.weightcontroldoctor.com

ISBN: 978 09757436 4 5

1) Thyroid 2) Nutrition 3) Immune system 4) Hormones

Type set by Hero Productions: 0414 539 419

Contents

Introduction

Thyroid disorders are extremely common and unfortunately their incidence is rising. All thyroid conditions are far more common in women than men. By age 50, one in ten women has a thyroid disorder. The symptoms of a mild thyroid imbalance can go unnoticed for many years because they are so general and unspecific. You may have gained a couple of kilos in the previous six months, but put it down to being busy and not as physically active as you once were; or maybe you blame it on menopause. You may feel tired but reason that it must be the extra pressures at work right now. Perhaps you have felt bloated and depressed but just put it down to the weather or that time of the month.

What if the real problem is an under active thyroid gland that has gone undiagnosed? Many people wander around with a thyroid imbalance, yet their doctor may consider them a hypochondriac and not offer any practical help at all. If your doctor does do a blood test for your thyroid gland how will you know if he/she has tested all of the important hormones? And does your doctor understand the importance of testing thyroid antibodies and what they could mean for the potential development of a thyroid disease in the future?

Many people with a thyroid disease are very confused. In Australia and the USA the most common thyroid disorders are Hashimoto's thyroiditis and Graves' disease. Most cases of hypothyroidism are due to the autoimmune disease Hashimoto's thyroiditis; yet the majority of people taking thyroid hormone tablets have no idea their disease is caused by a dysfunctional immune system. Taking thyroid hormone tablets replaces the hormone your body can no longer make, but it does nothing to halt the continued destruction of your thyroid gland by your immune system.

In this book you will learn how to improve the health of your thyroid holistically by working on your immune system, liver and digestive tract with the help of nutritional medicine. You will be treating the cause of your thyroid gland trouble.

Thyroid medication is still essential to take in many cases, but there are several options that you are probably not aware of. If you are one of the thousands of people taking *Oroxine*, (the most common brand of thyroxine, or T4 thyroid hormone) and still feeling tired and overweight there is a reason for this. You will learn which nutrients help thyroxine work in your body; which foods you should be eating more of and those that are best avoided; perhaps you require another medication in addition to thyroxine to obtain the full benefits of thyroid hormones.

Many patients in the early stages of thyroid disease have symptoms that brought them to the doctor, and they may even have an enlarged thyroid gland, but if their blood test results are normal they are sent away. Their doctor cannot offer them any solutions to improve the health of their thyroid and avert a thyroid disease; they can only wait until the disease develops fully, and then offer medication. This book will give you practical help on how to improve the health of your thyroid and also how to read your blood test results, so that you are fully informed.

This book mostly focuses on conditions that cause an under active thyroid gland; also known as hypothyroidism, since this is the most common thyroid problem. However, every major thyroid condition is covered. Thyroid cancer rates are climbing sharply, and it is often younger women who are affected. Several chemicals in everyday use have been linked to the development of thyroid nodules and cancer; you will learn how to protect yourself against these.

No one organ in your body functions independently of the others, and this is very much the case with the thyroid gland. The health of your liver, adrenal glands, immune system and reproductive system all affect the function of your thyroid gland. A truly holistic approach to treating thyroid conditions takes the health of your entire body into account.

Conventional medicine treats thyroid conditions by either supplementing with thyroid hormone if the gland is under active, or destroying or removing the thyroid if it is overactive. However, change of diet, nutritional and herbal medicine can help you greatly if you have a thyroid problem. Correcting your thyroid hormone levels is only one part of the solution and it does nothing to address why the thyroid condition developed in the first place.

> For truly holistic treatment of thyroid disease, your diet, lifestyle and other health conditions must be addressed. Otherwise your thyroid hormone levels may be normal, but you will still feel far from well.

Chapter 1

The thyroid gland: basic anatomy & physiology

The thyroid gland is located in the front of the neck attached to the lower part of the larynx (voice box) and to the upper part of the trachea (windpipe). It is shaped like a butterfly and composed of two lobes that are connected in the middle by a narrow band of tissue called the isthmus. The thyroid cartilage surrounding the gland sticks out in the neck and forms the Adam's apple.

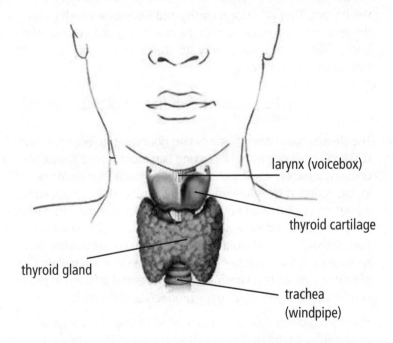

larynx (voicebox)

thyroid cartilage

thyroid gland

trachea
(windpipe)

The word thyroid comes from the Greek word for shield; *thyreos* was an ancient Greek army shield. The thyroid gland is one of the largest endocrine (hormone producing) glands in the body; it weighs approximately 18 grams in women and 25 grams in men. It is densely supplied with blood vessels and appears redder than surrounding tissues.

The thyroid gland contains many follicles, or small spheres. These follicles contain a protein mixture called colloid, where the protein called **thyroglobulin** is found. The thyroid hormones T4 and T3 are made out of thyroglobulin. Parafollicular cells are found between the thyroid follicles; they secrete the hormone **calcitonin** which reduces the concentration of calcium in body fluids and drives it into bones.

Nerves that travel to the voice box (larynx) and control speech, run behind the thyroid. Four tiny glands called the parathyroid glands (parathyroid simply means beside the thyroid) are also located behind the thyroid. They produce **parathyroid hormone** which increases the concentration of calcium in the blood by drawing it out of the bones. Because of these nearby structures, any surgery done to the thyroid gland poses risks.

Function of the thyroid gland

The thyroid gland manufactures two hormones: triiodothyronine (T3) and tetraiodothyronine (T4 and commonly called thyroxine). T3 contains 3 molecules of iodine and T4 contains four molecules of iodine. Iodine is therefore an essential mineral that is required for the manufacture of thyroid hormones, and efficient metabolism in your body. You can read more about the importance of iodine in chapter two. Thyroglobulin (thyroid binding protein) contains numerous tyrosine molecules. Tyrosine is an amino acid that is a building block of protein. We obtain tyrosine in our diet and it is found in protein rich foods like meat, eggs, dairy products and almonds.

The thyroid gland produces much more T4 than T3; they are produced in a ratio of 80% to 20%; however, T3 is known to be five to seven times stronger than T4 in its action[1]. Most T3 in the body is produced out of T4 in other parts of the body besides the thyroid[2]. The thyroid gland only makes small amounts of T3. Small amounts of T1 and T2 are also produced by the thyroid gland; they contain one and two molecules of iodine respectively. T1 and T2 do not have any known hormone activity. Thyroid cells are the main cells in the body that can absorb iodine; they combine it with tyrosine to form thyroid hormones.

Thyroid hormones are responsible for controlling the basic activity of each cell in the body, including metabolism, growth and development. If hormone levels drop below normal, metabolism inside cells slows down and energy levels drop. If thyroid hormone levels become too high, metabolism and all body processes speed up.

Regulation of thyroid hormone secretion

The thyroid gland is controlled by hormones secreted by two different regions in the brain:

- The **anterior pituitary** gland, located at the base of the brain produces thyroid stimulating hormone (TSH), also known as thyrotropin.

- The **hypothalamus**, an area above the pituitary produces thyrotropin releasing hormone (TRH).

The co-ordination between these regions of the brain and the thyroid gland is called the "Hypothalamic – Pituitary – Thyroid Axis". In healthy individuals, this system keeps thyroid hormone levels finely controlled. If blood levels of thyroid hormones become low, the hypothalamus and the pituitary gland detect this and TRH is released from the hypothalamus. This stimulates the anterior pituitary to secrete TSH, which then gives the signal for the thyroid gland to release T3 and T4 thyroid hormones. This returns blood levels of thyroid hormones to normal, which in turn signals back to the pituitary and hypothalamus, suppressing further secretion of TSH and TRH.

The diagram illustrates the coordinated feedback mechanism between the hypothalamus, anterior pituitary and thyroid gland:

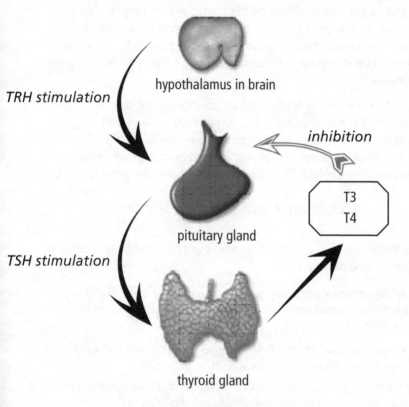

Thyroid hormones in circulation

T3 and T4 hormones are stored in the follicles of the thyroid gland attached to the protein called thyroglobulin. Enzymes called proteinases split the T3 and T4 off the thyroglobulin, and these hormones can then enter the bloodstream. The thyroid gland can store two to three months worth of thyroxine (T4) inside its follicles. Remember that T4 is released in far greater amounts than T3 and it is a pro-hormone; it must be converted to T3 in order to be active.

Most T4 circulates in the bloodstream attached to carrier proteins (such as Thyroid Binding Globulin (TBG), or albumin or transthyretin). The miniscule amount of T4 that is unbound is referred to as free-T4 (fT4).

In order for T4 to become active, it must be converted into T3 by an enzyme called 5'deiodinase (pronounced 5 prime deiodinase); this occurs mainly in the liver and kidneys but can occur in almost any cell of the body. This enzyme depends on selenium for its function, and to a lesser extent zinc and some other minerals. T4 can also be converted into reverse T3 (rT3), or eliminated. Reverse T3 is discussed in detail in chapter seven.

Most (approximately 85%) of the body's T3 is made out of T4, the rest comes directly from the thyroid gland. The majority of the T3 in the body is also bound to proteins, {(either albumin or Thyroxine Binding Pre-Albumin (TBPA)}. Around 8-10% is free-T3 (fT3)[3].

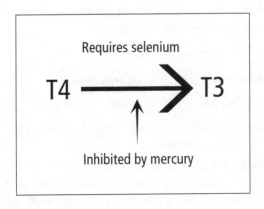

This diagram illustrates the conversion of T4 into its active form T3

Chapter 2

Thyroid Diseases that cause an under active gland

Incidence of thyroid disease

Unfortunately thyroid disorders are quite common. It is estimated that one in 20 people will experience a thyroid disorder in their lifetime; this figure is one in 14 for women. Every type of thyroid disease is more common in women than men, and the incidence of these conditions is rising. Thyroid disorders are very common in the third and fourth decades of life, and after the age of sixty.

The most common thyroid problems are where the gland is under active; not producing enough hormone, or overactive; where it produces excessive amounts of hormone.

Some other common thyroid disorders are:

- goitre, where the gland becomes enlarged;

- thyroid nodules, where lumpy growths develop,

- thyroid cancer, which fortunately can usually be treated effectively if it is caught early.

Thyroid conditions tend to run in families; immediate family members of people with a thyroid disorder are very likely to develop a problem themselves. Thyroid diseases also tend to commonly develop in people who have an autoimmune disease such as type 1 diabetes, lupus or rheumatoid arthritis; or in people who have a relative with one of these conditions.

We will now look at the individual types of thyroid diseases in more detail.

Types of thyroid diseases

Under active thyroid (Hypothyroidism)

> **Worldwide, the most common cause of hypothyroidism is iodine deficiency.**

In developed countries such as Australia and the USA, the most common cause of hypothyroidism is the autoimmune disease Hashimoto's thyroiditis. The body's own immune system attacks and destroys the thyroid cells, producing inflammation and leaving the thyroid unable to manufacture sufficient amounts of thyroid hormone.

After that, the third most common cause of hypothyroidism is iatrogenic, meaning doctor induced. This is usually where a patient has been treated for an overactive thyroid, and because of the treatment, the gland eventually becomes under active.

When the thyroid gland cannot manufacture adequate amounts of thyroid hormones, metabolism and all body processes slow down. The rate of ageing accelerates.

Symptoms of Hypothyroidism

These are all possible symptoms; you will not necessarily experience every one of them.

- Lethargy & fatigue
- Weight gain for no apparent reason
- Decreased appetite
- Increased sensitivity to cold
- Slow heart rate (bradycardia)
- Slow, weak pulse
- Goitre (enlarged thyroid). This will not always be present.
- Depression

- Poor concentration
- Poor memory
- Mental confusion
- Loss of interest in sex
- Dry skin & hair
- Ageing skin
- Scalp hair loss & loss of hair from the eyebrows
- Constipation
- Deeper, hoarse voice
- Muscle weakness, especially of the arms & legs
- Slow reflexes
- Carpel tunnel syndrome (pain at the wrists and numbness of the hands)
- Aches and pains in muscles and bones
- Infertility
- Fluid retention. A severe form of fluid retention associated with hypothyroidism is called myxoedema.
- Puffiness around the eyes.

What Causes Hypothyroidism?

a. Hashimoto's thyroiditis

This is the most common cause of an under active thyroid gland in developed countries. It is named after a Japanese physician called Hakaru Hashimoto, who first described the condition in 1912. Thyroiditis just means inflammation of the thyroid gland tissue. This condition is six times more common in women than men and tends to run in families.

Hashimoto's thyroiditis is an autoimmune disease, meaning that a person's own immune system produces antibodies that attack and destroy their thyroid gland. Why autoimmune diseases develop will be discussed in chapter eight. Hashimoto's thyroiditis can develop very slowly and there may not be any symptoms for many years. Eventually the thyroid loses its ability to produce hormones and hypothyroidism develops. If thyroid antibodies are picked up in a blood test early on in the disease, the progression to irreversible hypothyroidism can be avoided. Hashimoto's thyroiditis causes the symptoms of hypothyroidism described earlier in this chapter.

Sometimes in the early stages of Hashimoto's thyroiditis, the thyroid gland becomes temporarily overactive and churns out excessive levels of thyroid hormones. This can cause symptoms such as anxiety, palpitations, rapid pulse, diarrhoea, weight loss and insomnia. These symptoms usually do not last long because the thyroid gland soon becomes under active and then the symptoms of hypothyroidism develop.

How do we diagnose Hashimoto's Thyroiditis?

A blood test is used to diagnose this condition. A thyroid function test will show an elevated level of TSH and the hormones T4 and T3 are often low. A blood test will also reveal high levels of thyroid autoantibodies. These antibodies are made by the immune system and directed against the thyroid gland. The two main antibodies are:

- Thyroid Peroxidase Antibody (TPO Ab). This is also known as Anti-microsomal antibody.
- Thyroglobulin antibodies (Tg Ab).

Blood tests for thyroid conditions are discussed in detail in chapter six.

How do we treat Hashimoto's Thyroiditis?

Conventional medicine treats this condition with thyroid hormone replacement; the hormone that the damaged thyroid gland can no longer make is taken in tablet form. Usually thyroxine (T4) only is given. Brand names of thyroxine are *Oroxine* and *Eutroxsig*. Sometimes T3 is given to the patient as well.

Hormone treatment is not a cure for Hashimoto's thyroiditis, which is an autoimmune disease; it only replaces the hormone your thyroid can no longer make. It does nothing to halt the production of thyroid antibodies. The immune system will continue to make autoantibodies that destroy the thyroid more and more, and your dose of thyroid replacement may need to be increased over time. With all autoimmune diseases it is essential to do a bowel and liver detox, as well as supplement with the right minerals and antioxidants to heal the immune system. The treatment of autoimmune disease is described in chapter ten.

b. Iodine Deficiency

Deficiency of iodine is the main cause of hypothyroidism in the developing world. Iodine is required in our diet for the synthesis of thyroid hormones. Most of the world's iodine is found in the oceans but a lot is found in the soil too. Usually the older an exposed soil surface, the more likely the iodine in the soil has been leached away by erosion. Throughout the world it is estimated that 740 million people are iodine deficient. The most severely iodine deficient areas of the world include mountainous regions, such as the Himalayas, the Alps and the Andes, as well as flooded river valleys such as the Ganges[4].

Iodine Deficiency in Australia

In Australia the soils are not quite as depleted; Tasmania is the most iodine deficient area because of its mountainous terrain and high rainfall. Other areas known to have iodine deficient soils include the Atherton Tablelands of north Queensland, the Great Dividing Range in NSW, the Adelaide Hills, the eastern region of Victoria and the plains surrounding Canberra.

New Zealand soils are mostly deficient in iodine. Areas like this are usually deficient in more than one mineral, so along with iodine the soils are also low in selenium, magnesium, zinc and other minerals vital for good thyroid function.

Before the 1950s cretinism and goitre were fairly common in Tasmania. At that point children started receiving iodine supplements and some food manufacturers added iodine to salt and bread. Low levels of iodine in the soil means that most foods grown there will be lacking in iodine.

Recent studies done in Tasmania, Melbourne and Sydney have detected mild to moderate iodine deficiency in the Australian population, particularly pregnant women and children. This is probably due to a number of factors. In the past, potassium iodate was added to bread but this was discontinued in 1974 because some people were getting too much iodine and developed iodine-induced hyperthyroidism. Also in the past iodine was used in the dairy industry as a disinfectant in the form of iodophor cleansers. The iodine was used to sterilise milk vats and milking teats and this meant small amounts of iodine found their way into dairy products. But now iodine has been replaced with chlorine-based cleansers. Our environment also contains a number of iodine antagonists; these are substances that compete with iodine for absorption, meaning less iodine reaches the thyroid gland. Iodine antagonists include goitrogens in food, along with fluorine, chlorine and bromine; these are discussed in chapter nine.

Effects of Iodine Deficiency

Without enough iodine, the thyroid gland is unable to manufacture adequate quantities of thyroid hormones. Iodine deficiency can produce a number of conditions, collectively called **Iodine Deficiency Disorders**. People of all ages can be affected but the consequences are most severe in babies.

According to the World Health Organisation, almost 50 million people in the world suffer from some degree of iodine deficiency related brain damage. If a baby does not receive adequate iodine while in its mother's uterus and shortly after birth, it can have severe intellectual impairment and problems with physical development. Thyroid hormone is required for the myelination of the developing central nervous system in the foetus; it is needed for the myelin sheath to form around nerves. Severe iodine deficiency during early development results in a form of mental retardation called **cretinism**. Along with mental retardation, the other symptoms include stunted growth, apathy and impaired movement, speech and hearing. All developed countries, including Australia, New Zealand, Canada and the USA screen infants for hypothyroidism at birth. Congenital hypothyroidism occurs in one in 4000 births.

Iodine deficiency is the most common cause of preventable brain damage in the world. For this reason it is vitally important for pregnant and breast feeding women, as well as young children to receive an adequate amount of dietary iodine. Iodine deficiency in pregnancy can lead to miscarriage and stillbirths.

> It is frightening that recent studies have shown at least 50 percent of pregnant women in Australia have an inadequate intake of iodine[5]. Apart from the obvious and severe form of mental retardation called cretinism, iodine deficiency in pregnancy can have more subtle effects. It increases the risk of attention deficit disorder, learning difficulties, lowered intelligence and hearing loss in children.

In children and adults, enlargement of the thyroid gland is one of the earliest and most obvious signs of iodine deficiency. The thyroid gland enlarges in an attempt to become more efficient when iodine is scarce; the bigger the gland the more iodine it could possibly trap. This is referred to as **goitre** and will be discussed in more detail in chapter four. Goitre can develop whether the thyroid is under active or overactive, but when iodine is deficient the thyroid gland becomes under active and hypothyroidism develops.

People who are iodine deficient are more prone to developing radiation induced thyroid cancer if they are exposed to radiation (in the form of radioactive iodine). If you are iodine deficient, your thyroid gland is also more susceptible to damage by environmental pollutants, pesticides and other toxins. Iodine deficient people are more likely to develop iodine induced hyperthyroidism if their iodine intake increases too dramatically. Iodine deficiency is made worse if a person is also deficient in selenium, vitamin A or iron.

Sources of iodine

We do not need very much iodine to keep our thyroid healthy; a teaspoon over an entire lifetime is all that's needed. But because we can't store iodine in our body for long, we need some in our diet each day. The adult human body contains approximately 17mg of iodine, most of which is found in the thyroid.

According to the World Health Organisation iodine is required in the following quantities:

Group	Amount required per day
Adults	150 µg
Pregnancy and Lactation	200 µg
Children (6-12 years)	120 µg
Infants (0-5 years)	90 µg

µg is the symbol for micrograms.

Because nutrition information panels on foods do not contain iodine, it is very difficult for the average person to work out how much iodine they are ingesting. The iodine content of foods depends on how much iodine was present in the soil on which they were grown or raised. As iodine is plentiful in the oceans, the best dietary source of iodine is seafood. Seaweed (eg. Wakame, nori and kelp) are also very high in iodine. Other foods high in iodine include eggs, meat, dairy products, citrus fruits and cashews.

Iodised salt is a very rich source of iodine. It is produced by spraying salt crystals with an iodine solution while they are travelling along a conveyer belt. This salt contains between 25 and 65 micrograms of iodine per gram. Iodised salt is sold in the supermarket packaged with a green label.

Sea salt is a poor source of iodine; it contains less than two micrograms per gram. Iodised salt is usually not added to salty takeaway foods and snacks, so eating a lot of salty junk food does not provide your body with iodine. The best way to get an adequate intake of iodine is to eat seafood regularly, as well as a variety of animal foods such as meat and eggs. Eating seafood three times a week will provide you with adequate levels of iodine. Fish is also an excellent source of omega 3 essential fatty acids, which provide many health benefits.

> **People who do not eat any fish or seaweed, do not use iodised salt and are vegetarians are most at risk of iodine deficiency.**

It is now possible to buy iodised sea salt; this is regular sea salt that has had iodine added. It is preferable to regular iodised salt because that usually contains the free flow agent 554. This is a form of aluminium called sodium aluminosilicate that prevents the salt from clumping. Aluminium has been linked to the development of Alzheimer's disease, kidney impairment and bone diseases.

Tasmanian bakeries have been running a trial using iodised salt in bread. Results so far have shown a positive improvement in iodine status in children. Currently Food Standards Australia New Zealand is considering compulsory fortification of bread with iodine.

Too much iodine

Iodine is found in many multi vitamin and mineral supplements, usually at a dose of 50 to 150 micrograms. Kelp is a rich source of iodine and some supplements will contain iodine in this natural form. Iodine is also present in the herb bladderwrack, also known as Fucus vesiculosus. Iodine is safe in quantities that do not exceed

1100mcg per day; more can be used under medical supervision. Long term use of high doses of iodine can cause thyroid dysfunction. In normal healthy individuals excessive iodine intake can suppress the production of thyroid hormones. In people who are iodine deficient, a rapid high intake may cause hyperthyroidism. Women who take excessive quantities of iodine while pregnant can have a baby with a goitre and hypothyroidism

Can I take Kelp or Iodine if I have a Thyroid Problem?

People with Graves' disease and other overactive thyroid conditions should avoid high doses of 1000mcg daily or more of iodine because it can trigger a worsening or relapse of the disease.

If your thyroid gland is under active because you have Hashimoto's thyroiditis, taking additional iodine in the form of supplements or kelp will not help your thyroid because this is an autoimmune disease; the problem lies with the immune system and not iodine deficiency. A small percentage of people with a thyroid condition are extremely sensitive to iodine and they react to small quantities. It is usually people with an autoimmune thyroid condition that can react unpredictably to iodine supplements. It is okay to consume iodine as part of a multi vitamin and mineral supplement, but straight kelp supplements should be avoided by these people.

Testing for iodine

Iodine can be tested in the urine; the more iodine you have in your diet, the more will be excreted in your urine. A healthy normal iodine level in the urine is 100 micrograms per litre. The Recommended Daily Intake of iodine for adults is 150mcg per day; if you take in this amount you will be excreting around 100mcg per litre in your urine each day. Having less than 50mcg per litre in your urine indicates you are iodine deficient. However, excretion does vary from day to day, so a one off urine measurement is not 100 percent reliable. It is better to have three tests, each on separate occasions.

Pregnancy causes an increase in the rate of iodine excretion in urine, so it may give a false sense of adequate intake. It is difficult to calculate how much iodine you are consuming each day because it is not listed on nutrition panels on labels. However, if you eat fish three times a week you are assured of getting enough iodine. Other good sources of iodine are iodised salt, meat, poultry and eggs. It is mainly vegetarians who don't eat fish that are at risk of iodine deficiency.

The Chernobyl Accident

On 26th April 1986 the worst nuclear accident in history occurred in the town of Chernobyl, located in the Ukraine district of the former Soviet Union. The Chernobyl nuclear plant experienced an explosion that blew off the reactor's lid. Dangerous levels of radiation were released and more than 30 people died immediately. For ten days after the accident, clouds of radiation were still being released and exposing the residents of Chernobyl to high levels of radiation. Radiation was carried by the wind to Eastern European countries and it contaminated food, especially milk that was exported to several other parts of the world.

The radioactive material released by the Chernobyl reactor contained high levels of radioactive iodine, particularly iodine-131. The thyroid gland cannot tell the difference between regular iodine and radioactive iodine, so it takes up the radioactive iodine readily. People who are deficient in iodine will absorb much greater amounts of radioactive iodine if they are exposed to it.

Radioactive iodine greatly increases the risk of thyroid cancer, especially in children. Children in Belarus, the Ukraine and other parts of Eastern Europe were heavily exposed to radioactive iodine and experienced high rates of thyroid cancer. Currently the rate of thyroid cancer in 15 to 18 year olds in the affected area is three times higher than before the accident happened in 1986. The incidence of thyroid cancer increased ten fold in children living in Ukraine. Iodine deficiency was common amongst these populations, helping to explain the high rates of cancer. People who had an adequate amount of iodine in their diet were not so susceptible to this cancer.

One way of greatly reducing the chance of developing thyroid cancer due to radiation is by taking a high dose of potassium iodide. If potassium iodide is given in a pharmacological (high) dose of 50 to 100mg for adults within 48 hours before or eight hours after exposure to radioactive iodine, it can greatly reduce the thyroid's uptake of radioactive iodine. This means that if the thyroid gland is first flooded with healthy iodine, it will have no room left for radioactive iodine which will just pass through the body.

In Poland the government quickly distributed potassium iodide supplements to the population immediately after the 1986 nuclear reactor accident; this is believed to be the reason why rates of thyroid cancer in children in Poland did not increase significantly compared to other nearby areas[6].

c. Iatrogenic hypothyroidism

Sometimes the thyroid gland becomes under active as a result of the medical treatment of hyperthyroidism. The word iatrogenic means doctor induced. An overactive thyroid is sometimes treated with radioactive iodine that destroys the gland, and sometimes it is surgically removed. Either of these scenarios usually means that the patient would need to take thyroid hormone tablets for the rest of their life. The treatment of hyperthyroidism will be discussed more in chapter three.

d. Secondary Hypothyroidism

The thyroid gland can also become under active as a result of failure of the pituitary gland to produce Thyroid Stimulating Hormone (TSH). This is called secondary hypothyroidism. Secondary hypothyroidism may occur if the pituitary gland is damaged by a tumour or through surgery. It is not a common condition.

If the thyroid gland itself cannot manufacture T4 and T3 this is called primary hypothyroidism.

The Thyroid Gland and Ageing - case history

Miriam was a typical country woman who had had a hard life on the land weathering the hot Australian sun. She had neglected herself and always put her family first. She had come to Sydney to see a relative and decided to pay me a visit at my Camden clinic for a check up. Miriam was 56 years of age but she looked 70, with very puffy and lined skin, and dry brittle thinning hair. She complained of constipation and fatigue but put it down to simply getting older.

Miriam's physical examination revealed slow and delayed muscle reflexes and some muscle weakness and she was also overweight. Miriam's blood tests revealed a very under active thyroid gland with her results showing the following –

MIRIAM'S RESULTS	NORMAL RANGE
Free T 3 = 1.43 pmol/L	2.5 – 6.0
Free T 4 = 5 pmol/L	8.0 – 22.0
TSH = 16 mIU/L	0.30 – 4.0*
THYROID ANTIBODIES	
Anti-thyroglobulin antibodies = negative	(less than 100)
Anti-microsomal antibodies = negative	(less than 100)

* Most laboratories use 4 mIU/L as the upper limit of normal for TSH. However, new research has found that if TSH is above 2 mIU/L, the thyroid gland is probably in the early stages of disease.

Miriam was not a vain woman and did not wear makeup or jewellery but she knew something was not right in the way she looked.

I started Miriam on thyroxine (T4) tablets in a dose of 50mcg daily and over a month I gradually raised her dose to 150mcg daily. She responded well to this dose and after 6 months of treatment she was most pleased with the following improvements –

- Her hair stopped falling out and looked much thicker and less grey in colour.

- She lost 12 kilograms in weight.

- Her muscle strength came back.

- Her memory and mental acuity greatly improved.

- Her bowels were no longer sluggish.

- She was able to work much harder on the farm and achieved much more.

The striking thing to me was that Miriam looked more than 10 years younger and I could see that she was really a most attractive woman, who had just let herself go.

An under active thyroid gland causes the metabolism of every cell in the body to slow down; this results in an accelerated rate of ageing of the body and the brain.

Now that the average life span of a woman has increased so much over the 20th century, fine tuning the hormonal system so that it is working at an optimal level is very important to prevent premature ageing.

Chapter 3

Overactive Thyroid Gland (Hyperthyroidism)

Hyperthyroidism is far less common than hypothyroidism. An overactive thyroid develops in approximately two percent of women and 0.2 percent of men[7].

When the thyroid gland produces too much thyroid hormone, metabolism and all body processes speed up. The most common cause of hyperthyroidism is Graves' disease. This is an autoimmune disease where the body produces an abnormal antibody called thyroid stimulating antibody; it stimulates the thyroid to make too much hormone.

Symptoms of Hyperthyroidism

The following symptoms may develop:

- Rapid pulse & heart palpitations
- Fast heart rate (tachycardia)
- Feeling overly sensitive to heat
- Increased sweating
- Increased appetite
- Weight loss
- Inability to sleep
- Irritability, anxiety, nervousness & even panic attacks
- Diarrhoea or frequent bowel movements
- Hand tremors
- Mood swings
- Goitre – this is not always present
- Raised, thickened skin over the tops of the feet or shins.

- Fatigue
- Shortness of breath
- Weakness
- Thin, moist skin
- Menstrual periods become very light or stop altogether
- Joint pains
- Difficulty concentrating
- Brittle nails
- Eye complaints, especially bulging or gritty eyes
- Muscle weakness, particularly in the shoulders & thighs
- Angina worsens in people with heart disease

Causes of Hyperthyroidism

a. Graves' Disease

This is the most common cause of an overactive thyroid, accounting for 85 percent of all hyperthyroidism. The condition was named after Robert Graves, an Irish doctor who first described it in 1835.

Graves' disease can produce thyrotoxicosis, which literally means toxic high levels of thyroid hormones. Like all thyroid disorders, Graves' disease is far msore common in women; seven times more women than men develop it[8]. It is most common in the third and fourth decades of life. Graves' disease is an autoimmune disease and sometimes develops in people with other autoimmune diseases including type 1 diabetes, vitiligo or Systemic Lupus Erythematosus (SLE).

In this particular autoimmune disease, the immune system produces abnormal antibodies called thyroid stimulating antibody. These antibodies continually stimulate the gland to release thyroid hormone, so eventually far too much thyroid hormone enters the circulation.

Diagnosis of Graves' Disease

A blood test called a thyroid function test will be performed. People with Graves' disease have an abnormally low TSH level, (generally less than 0.30 mIU/L). High levels of the hormones T4 and T3 may also be present. A blood test may also be done to check for the presence of thyroid autoantibodies.

Your doctor may want to perform an ultrasound or radioactive scan of your thyroid gland to see if the entire gland or only sections of it are overactive.

Treatment of Graves' Disease

People with Graves' disease usually require rapid treatment because their symptoms can be so severe, they are incapacitating. There are three treatment options: tablets, surgery or radioactive iodine.

Tablets: there are two categories –

   o Beta-blockers

   o Anti-thyroid drugs

Beta-blockers: These drugs have no effect on reducing the excessive production of thyroid hormones; they merely offer symptom relief. Beta blocker drugs slow down the heart rate. They are commonly used for high blood pressure and angina. Some examples of beta blockers are *Inderal* (propranolol hydrochloride), *Corbeton* (oxprenolol hydrochloride), *Lopresor* (metoprolol tartrate) and *Tenormin* (atenolol).

Beta blockers are effective at easing some of the worst symptoms of hyperthyroidism such as a rapid heart beat, tremors, shakes and sweating. They do this by blocking the effects of excessive thyroid hormones on the heart, skin and muscles. Beta blockers can have side effects, including dizziness, headache, fatigue and vivid dreams. This is not usually a problem because the relief they give from other symptoms is more important and they are not taken for a long period of time.

Anti-thyroid drugs: These work directly on the thyroid gland to reduce the excessive output of thyroid hormones. These drugs usually take a few weeks to produce their effects and need to be taken in high doses initially. Examples of anti-thyroid drugs include *Neomercazol* (carbimazole) and Propylthiouracil. As well as being used for hyperthyroidism, these drugs are used in the preparation of a patient for thyroidectomy (removal of the thyroid gland). In Graves' disease there is a 50 percent chance that a 12 to 18 month course of anti-thyroid drugs will **permanently cure** the condition. Because of this most doctors try the tablets first, and if they do not work or there is a recurrence of the disease, surgery or radioactive iodine treatment are used.

Potential Problems/Side Effects of Anti-thyroid Drugs

Adverse side effects are most likely to occur in the first eight weeks of treatment and may include:

- High doses may cause enlargement of the thyroid gland
- The drug crosses the placenta and enters breast milk, therefore must be used with extreme caution in pregnant and breastfeeding women. There is a risk it may cause hypothyroidism in the foetus or newborn.
- Itchy skin or urticaria (hives)
- Skin pigmentation
- Pins & needles, burning & prickling sensations
- Headache
- Joint pain
- Digestive upsets including nausea, vomiting and stomach discomfort
- Scalp hair loss
- Suppression of the bone marrow
- Mild leukopenia (low white blood cell count)

Excessive iodine intake, either through diet or the use of supplements, reduces the effectiveness of anti-thyroid drugs; therefore a higher dose will be required. On the other hand, iodine deficiency increases the effectiveness of anti-thyroid drugs, so a smaller dose is needed. These drugs can interact with prescription blood thinning medication such as warfarin.

Surgical Treatment of Hyperthyroidism:

Thyroidectomy means removal of the thyroid gland. In 1909 the Nobel Prize in medicine was awarded to Professor Theodore Kocher of Switzerland for making thyroidectomy a safe procedure.

Surgery for Graves' disease is most commonly indicated for patients below 20 years of age in whom a course of anti-thyroid tablets has been ineffective.

Surgery is also needed in patients with goitre, an enlarged thyroid gland, which is so large that it causes blockage of the trachea (windpipe) or oesophagus (food pipe).

Having the thyroid gland removed requires a five day stay in hospital; all but a small portion of the thyroid gland is usually removed. The aim is to leave a small part of the thyroid in place so that it can still produce some thyroid hormone. However, around 80 percent of patients with Graves' disease who have had their thyroid taken out will develop an under active thyroid and will need to take hormone tablets for the rest of their lives.

Side Effects of Thyroidectomy

Straight after the surgery it is common to experience a swelling of the neck, a sore throat and some difficulty swallowing. You may also notice discomfort in the back of the neck from the position it was in during surgery. Sometimes fluid builds up under the spot where the neck was cut and this can be drained with a needle and syringe by a surgeon. If most of the thyroid gland has been removed, the patient can become deficient in calcium for some weeks or months after the surgery. This can be remedied with a calcium supplement and the condition usually corrects itself over time. Calcium levels can become low because of damage or irritation to the parathyroid glands that sit behind the thyroid.

Radioactive Iodine Treatment of an Overactive Thyroid Gland

In the late 1930s doctors learned that the thyroid gland absorbs radioactive iodine in the same way as normal iodine; it can't tell the difference between the two. Shortly after, the use of radioactive iodine to treat hyperthyroidism began. The radioactive iodine damages the thyroid cells so they are no longer able to produce thyroid hormones.

This form of treatment is usually used in patients above 20 years of age because of fears of radiation use in children. The patient is given a capsule or a glass of water that contains radioactive iodine; these have no smell or taste. Once the radioactive iodine gets into your bloodstream it is quickly taken up by your thyroid cells. This type of treatment usually takes several weeks to have its full effect, so anti-thyroid tablets are usually given as well because they work faster and offer symptom relief faster.

Radioactive iodine causes the thyroid gland to shrink and hormone production to fall. Your doctor will try to calculate your requirement for radioactive iodine accurately but sometimes a patient will remain hyperthyroid and will need to take a second dose of radioactive iodine.

A much more common scenario is that several months after treatment the patient will develop hypothyroidism. This is called iatrogenic (doctor induced) hypothyroidism and the patient will need to take thyroid hormone tablets for life. Another problem with radioactive iodine treatment is that it sometimes aggravates the eye problems associated with Graves' disease. These will be described later in this chapter.

Hyperthyroid Case History

Shirley had suffered with an overactive thyroid gland for 2 years and the medication that she took called Neomercazole was only just managing to control the symptoms. She had been diagnosed with Graves' Disease – also known as auto-immune thyroiditis.

Shirley had the classic symptoms of an overactive thyroid gland –

- Weight loss, despite a large appetite – she only weighed 50 kilograms and was 174 centimetres in height
- Tremor of the arms and hands
- Muscle weakness
- Fatigue
- Anxiety
- Headaches
- Diarrhoea
- Palpitations and rapid resting heart rate of 106
- Protuberant large eyes (exophthalmos)

Her doctor had told her that if the Neomercazole did not become more effective, the use of radioactive iodine to irradiate the thyroid gland would be needed. To Shirley this was a last resort; so she decided to try complementary medicine to see if it could calm her thyroid gland down and stop it from pumping out excessive amounts of thyroid hormone.

After taking her medical history, looking at her pathology tests and doing a physical examination, I could see the most important things for her case were –

1. A family history of autoimmune thyroid disease (Graves' disease) – this was also illustrated by the high levels of antibodies against her thyroid gland that her immune system was producing.

2. Her high powered job, which over taxed her emotionally and physically, causing constant stress and lack of sleep.

3. A high intake of caffeine, sugar and cigarettes, which act as stimulants to the thyroid gland. People who smoke cigarettes are more prone to thyroid disease.

4. A diet deficient in antioxidants and minerals.

I recommended the following program for Shirley –

1. A bowel and liver detox, incorporating a gluten and dairy free diet. This was essential since she has an autoimmune disease.

2. A supplement of magnesium to calm her nervous system and reduce her fast heart rate. She would need 400mg of elemental magnesium daily.

3. A supplement of selenium to reduce the amount of antibodies attacking her thyroid gland.

4. Extra vitamin C to calm down her overactive immune system.

5. Fish oil or cold pressed flaxseed oil to reduce inflammation in the thyroid gland.

6. The avoidance of stimulants such as caffeine, cigarettes and excess sugar.

7. A holiday from work – this was easy, as she had plenty of leave owed to her. This would enable her to rest and exercise and get some sunlight and fresh air.

8. She also needed a boost of antioxidants from raw juicing – she did have a juicer, but with her busy schedule she never had time to juice. I always tell busy folks that they can juice a whole weeks' supply of fresh raw juice on the weekend; then freeze it in individual containers for daily use. Once frozen, the juice will retain all its freshness and antioxidant effects for months.

Shirley came back to see me after the 8 week holiday she had taken. She had spent the whole time concentrating on her own health and getting plenty of sleep and exercise. She said that it took her a full 3 weeks to unwind and relax and then she decided to try to quit the cigarettes. She managed to quit with the help of Nicorette patches but did get some withdrawal headaches. Shirley found that once she quit smoking she no longer craved the caffeine, so this made it easier for her.

She had gained 4 kilograms in weight and certainly looked 100 times better, as she had lost that haggard anorexic look. Her pulse rate had come down to 75 and she felt much fitter.

She was still on the Neomercazole medication but was hoping that her specialist would be so pleased with her efforts that she may allow Shirley to start to reduce the dose.

Shirley was very grateful to me – more for the fact that I had insisted she take leave from a highly stressful job for medical reasons. Her new found sense of well being showed her that her health was her greatest asset and not the glass ceiling she was trying to crack at the office.

This case history illustrates the fact that autoimmune thyroid disease can be greatly aggravated, or even triggered, by severe emotional and physical stress and a poor diet and lifestyle.

Thyroid Storm

This is severe hyperthyroidism and is also referred to as a thyrotoxic crisis. It is a possible complication of Graves' disease. Thyroid storm is usually brought on by stress, surgery or a severe infection.

Levels of thyroid hormones become so high that the condition becomes life threatening; this is mainly because of the effects thyroid hormones have on the heart and brain. The condition can occur in people who are not having their hyperthyroidism treated, or when it is treated inadequately.

Patients experiencing thyroid storm may have the following symptoms:

- Chest pain
- Shortness of breath
- Vomiting
- Abdominal pain
- Fever
- Hyperventilation
- Fast heart rate (tachycardia)

- Extreme agitation or irritability
- Disorientation
- Diarrhoea
- Coma

The patient needs to be taken to the emergency department of a hospital immediately; there is no time to wait for blood tests to confirm the diagnosis.

Thyroid Eye Disease

Many people with Graves' disease develop what is known as eye signs (Graves' ophthalmopathy). Early symptoms can include redness, dryness, itching, a gritty feeling, swelling of the eyelids and an inability to wear contact lenses. Symptoms can be especially bad at night, in air conditioned buildings and during windy days. The eyes appear to be slightly bulging because of spasms of the muscles of the lids, giving them a staring appearance. Around half of people with Graves' disease only experience relatively mild symptoms, but another half develop more severe eye disease.

The more severe version of thyroid eye disease is an autoimmune disease of the eye socket and eye muscles in which there is inflammation, swelling and eventual scarring. The immune system attacks and destroys the eyes and surrounding muscles. It occurs most often in people with Graves' disease but can also occur in people with Hashimoto's thyroiditis and thyroid cancer.

There are two phases of thyroid eye disease:

1) Active inflammation and swelling. The eyes are red and inflamed, the lids are swollen and the eyes are "poppy"; this is medically referred to as proptosis. The eyes are usually quite uncomfortable and ache, especially during the night.

2) The muscles that move the eyes start to scar and malfunction. This occurs after the symptoms in phase one start to resolve. The upper eyelid often sits up too high (retracts) and that can produce double vision.

In either phase the eyes can feel irritated, like there is something inside them and the vision can be blurry.

Treatment of Thyroid Eye Disease

The irritation can be relieved by lubricating eye drops. Redness and aching can be relieved by the use of a cold compress over the eyes; this is available from pharmacies. Since symptoms tend to be worse at night, some people find that elevating the head of the bed can give some symptom relief.

During phase one when there is a lot of eye inflammation and swelling, oral steroids like prednisone are often used. This can reduce the swelling and pain. Steroids cannot be used for long periods of time because they have side effects, such as weight gain, indigestion and a worsening of restlessness, which is also a symptom of Graves' disease. Some people require radiotherapy for the swelling.

During phase two when there is scarring, many people need surgery to lower the upper eyelid if it is abnormally raised. Surgery can reduce the "poppyness" of the eyes and also can fix the double vision if the eye muscles are corrected.

Thyroid eye disease is most common in people with an overactive thyroid gland caused by Graves' disease. The Graves' disease is quickly treated by reducing thyroid hormone levels but unfortunately this doesn't help the eye disease very much. For many people, thyroid eye disease becomes a long term problem; the inflammation and swelling pass but around a third of people are left with continual dryness, irritation and sensitivity.

Thyroid eye disease is an autoimmune disease and it must be treated like all autoimmune diseases: a change in diet, supporting the digestion, liver and immune system. See chapter ten for our treatment plan for autoimmune disease.

Graves' dermopathy is a rare skin disease that occurs in some people with Graves' disease. It results from a build up of protein in the skin and makes the skin red and swollen; the texture can resemble an orange peel. The disease usually affects the shins and tops of the feet. The treatment of Graves' dermopathy involves treating the overactive thyroid, cortisone cream and compression with elastic wraps. Sometimes the condition continues even after the thyroid hormones have been normalised. This is because it is an autoimmune disease and the immune system must be treated.

Other Causes of Hyperthyroidism

b. Toxic Multinodular Goitre

This usually occurs in people who have had a longstanding goitre and especially in the elderly and females. A part of the thyroid gland produces thyroid hormones all by itself without regard to TSH (Thyroid Stimulating Hormone) that is produced by the pituitary gland and would normally suppress this. Goitre means enlargement of the thyroid gland, multinodular means that many nodules or growths appear on the thyroid, and toxic refers to abnormally high and dangerous levels of thyroid hormone that are produced. Toxic multinodular goitre produces a less severe version of hyperthyroidism than Graves' disease does, and there is usually no eye disease. The immune system does appear to be involved because around 25 percent of people with the condition have thyroid autoantibodies in their blood. This indicates that it may be an autoimmune disease.

The nodules can vary in size from a few millimetres to several centimetres. Nodules greater than one centimetre in size can usually be felt by a doctor. If a biopsy is performed, the doctor will see that often the nodules have degenerated and a cyst has formed. There can be evidence of previous or current bleeding, there is often a lot of scarring and calcium deposits may be found. Areas of normal thyroid tissue can be found between the nodules and white blood cells often infiltrate the area. If a multinodular goitre has been removed by surgery and carefully examined, approximately four to 17 percent of them contain cancerous cells[9].

Symptoms of Multinodular goitre

- The symptoms of hyperthyroidism are present but usually not as severe as in Graves' disease.
- Enlargement of the thyroid gland, causing a swelling in the neck.
- A tight feeling in the throat
- Difficulty swallowing
- Difficulty breathing
- Coughing
- Hoarseness

Diagnosis of Toxic Multinodular Goitre

- A blood test will show low levels of TSH (Thyroid Stimulating Hormone) and in most cases both T4 and T3 thyroid hormones will be elevated. A quarter of patients will have TSH antibodies in their bloodstream like those found in Graves' disease.

- An ultrasound scan of the neck will reveal an enlarged thyroid and show any nodules present.

- A nuclear thyroid scan may be performed. This is where radioactive iodine is injected into the vein on the inside of the elbow. The iodine travels to the thyroid gland and an image of the thyroid gland is displayed on a computer screen. This accurately displays the nodules in the thyroid gland.

Treatment of Toxic Multinodular Goitre

Most cases are treated with radioactive iodine. Because the thyroid gland is believed to be the only part of the body that takes up radioactive iodine, it destroys the thyroid cells while leaving the rest of the body unharmed. Depending on how much of the thyroid gland is destroyed, it may become under active and then thyroid hormone replacement tablets will need to be taken. If the goitre is very large and interfering with breathing and swallowing it may be surgically removed.

c. Thyroiditis

This is inflammation of the thyroid gland and may cause it to become overactive. There are several possible causes:

• Hashimoto's Thyroiditis.

This is the most common cause of thyroiditis. Hashimoto's thyroiditis normally results in an under active thyroid gland but early on in the disease there may be periods where it is overactive. This is an autoimmune disease and when antibodies attack and destroy the thyroid this creates some inflammation. The inflammation leads to a brief period of excessive thyroid hormone release but eventually the gland becomes under active and hypothyroidism develops.

• De Quervain's Thyroiditis

This is also sometimes called subacute or granulomatous thyroiditis. It was first detected in 1904 and is much less common than Hashimoto's thyroiditis. The thyroid gland swells rapidly, becomes very painful and tender and releases large amounts of thyroid hormone into the bloodstream, causing hyperthyroidism. The thyroid gland then stops taking up any more iodine from the bloodstream and the hyperthyroidism resolves itself within a few weeks.

De Quervain's thyroiditis often produces a fever and sufferers feel so unwell they must lie down in bed. Thyroid autoantibodies are not present in the bloodstream and the condition is not caused by an infectious agent such as a virus or bacterium. A blood test will show a high erythrocyte sedimentation rate (ESR) which is an indicator of inflammation in the body.

The usual treatment is bed rest and aspirin to bring the fever down and reduce the inflammation. Sometimes steroids are used because they are a more powerful way to bring down inflammation. Thyroid hormones are sometimes given if the disease does not resolve itself quickly; this helps the thyroid gland to rest as it does not need to make its own hormones. Most patients recover and their thyroid gland returns to normal in several weeks or months. A small percentage of people develop an under active thyroid after an episode of de Quervain's thyroiditis and they need to take thyroid hormone replacement.

• Post Partum Thyroiditis

This is also called silent thyroiditis and occurs in five to nine percent of women in the six months after giving birth. This type of thyroiditis is usually painless but the gland may be enlarged. Around 80 to 90 percent of women will have thyroid autoantibodies in their bloodstream with this condition, indicating that it is autoimmune based. This disease can follow three possible courses: the thyroid becomes overactive and then returns to normal function; the thyroid becomes under active; or the thyroid is first overactive and then becomes under active. Many women are not aware they are suffering with this condition and put any symptoms they get down to just having given birth.

Post partum thyroiditis usually requires no treatment and 80 percent of women recover completely within three months. Bed rest is the usual treatment; sometimes beta blocker drugs are used to control palpitations if the thyroid is overactive. Thyroid conditions related to pregnancy will be covered in more detail in chapter five.

d. Pituitary Adenoma

This is a benign (non-spreading) tumour of the pituitary gland in the brain. The pituitary gland normally secretes TSH which stimulates the thyroid gland to produce more T4 and T3 thyroid hormones. If a tumour is present on the pituitary it can stimulate it to secrete excessive amounts of TSH, which then leads to excessive production of T4 and T3 thyroid hormones. This causes all the symptoms of hyperthyroidism.

e. Drug Induced Hyperthyroidism

This is most commonly caused by the heart drug amiodarone (Aratac, Cardinorm, Cardarone, Genrx amiodarone). Amiodarone is a type of medication used to treat heart arrhythmias; where the beat or rhythm of the heart is irregular. People who take this medication must have a thyroid blood test done regularly because the drug can cause the thyroid to become overactive.

Chapter 4

Other Thyroid Diseases
Goitre

This is a non specific term that refers to enlargement of the thyroid gland. A goitre can occur when the thyroid gland is overactive (toxic goitre), under active (hypothyroid goitre), or even when thyroid gland function is normal (non-toxic goitre); the word goitre simply means that the thyroid gland is enlarged. A goitre may be diffuse (evenly enlarged) or nodular (asymmetrically enlarged). In the USA the word is spelt goiter.

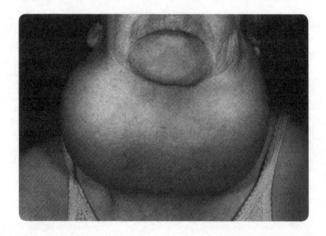

Incidence of goitre

Worldwide, the most common cause of goitre is iodine deficiency. It is estimated that 200 million people in the world have a goitre because they are iodine deficient. In Australia, New Zealand and the USA, the most common cause of goitre is the autoimmune disease Hashimoto's thyroiditis. This produces a hypothyroid goitre.

Goitres are four times more common in women than men. Most of the time a goitre doesn't cause any problems apart from cosmetic disfigurement. How severe it becomes depends on what caused it; large goitres can compress surrounding tissues and cause breathing and swallowing difficulties. In general, the incidence of goitre decreases with advancing age, but thyroid nodules increase with increasing age.

Symptoms of goitre

These symptoms can be present to varying degrees:

- An enlarged thyroid, causing a swelling in front of the neck
- A tight feeling in the throat
- Difficulty swallowing
- Difficulty breathing
- Coughing
- Hoarseness

Causes of goitre

Goitre can be caused by any of the following factors:

- Iodine deficiency and selenium deficiency
- Hashimoto's thyroiditis
- Graves' disease
- Pregnancy can cause slight, uniform enlargement of the thyroid gland, which is normal. See chapter five.
- Postpartum (after childbirth) thyroiditis
- Excess iodine. This usually occurs in people who have pre existing autoimmune thyroid disease, such as Graves' disease.
- Excess doses of the drug lithium. This decreases release of thyroid hormone.
- Goitrogens. These are compounds found in some foods including broccoli and soybeans. They can inhibit thyroid hormone production if eaten in large amounts.
- A pituitary tumour that causes excessive TSH release. This overstimulates the thyroid gland.
- Radiation exposure.

• De Quervain's thyroiditis
• Riedel thyroiditis. This is a very rare form of thyroiditis where the thyroid gland becomes inflamed and merges with surrounding tissues including muscle and the windpipe (trachea).
• Infections of the thyroid gland. This includes bacterial, fungal and parasitic infections.
• Thyroid cancer. This can produce a goitre with a lumpy, uneven texture.

Diagnosis of goitre

The goitre will often be detected first as a swelling in the neck. A blood test will be done to determine if the thyroid gland is overactive or under active; this involves checking levels of the hormones TSH, T4 and T3. A blood test looking for thyroid antibodies should also be done to determine if the goitre is caused by an autoimmune disease such as Graves' disease or Hashimoto's thyroiditis.

Physical examination of the thyroid: The doctor will want to examine your thyroid gland. This is best done when you are sitting upright or standing. Examining your thyroid from sideways usually gives a better view. You may be asked to take a sip of water; your thyroid gland should move when you swallow.

The doctor will feel (palpate) your thyroid when either standing behind you or facing you. Both lobes of the thyroid are checked for size, consistency, nodules (lumps) and tenderness. The doctor should also feel the lymph nodes in your neck (cervical lymph nodes).

Other examinations of the thyroid gland:

An **ultrasound** scan of the thyroid gland will reveal its size and show up any nodules or cysts that the doctor may have missed. Having regular ultrasounds performed will monitor any changes in goitre size, consistency and presence of nodules.

A **CT scan** is sometimes performed. An ultrasound is better at monitoring the size of the thyroid gland but a CT scan can better assess how the enlarged thyroid is affecting surrounding organs. The CT scan is also better at monitoring thyroid cancer.

A nuclear **thyroid scan** may be performed. This is referred to as a radionuclide uptake, or radionuclide scan. During the scan you will have a radioactive isotope injected into the vein on the inside of your elbow. You will then lie back on a table while a camera produces an image of your thyroid on a computer screen. The thyroid scan determines if any nodules present in the thyroid are active (producing hormones). In some cases a biopsy of the thyroid gland is performed.

Treatment of goitre

The treatment of goitre depends on what is causing it, how big it is and what symptoms it is causing.

Treatment can be one of the following options:

- **Observation**. If your goitre is small, your thyroid hormone levels are normal and the goitre isn't causing many symptoms, your doctor is likely to just watch it regularly and see what happens.

- **Medication**. If the thyroid gland is overactive or under active, normalising hormone levels with medication usually reduces the size of the goitre. If the thyroid gland is inflamed, such as in thyroiditis; aspirin or steroid drugs are sometimes given to reduce inflammation.

- **Surgery**. Removing all or part of the thyroid gland is required if the goitre is extremely large and uncomfortable, producing difficulty breathing and swallowing. It is also required if the thyroid has become cancerous. If the goitre contains nodules that are producing excess amounts of thyroid hormone (toxic nodular goitre) part or all of the thyroid gland may be removed.

- **Radioactive Iodine**. This is sometimes used if an overactive thyroid gland is producing the goitre. The radioactive iodine destroys the overactive thyroid cells. This reduces the size of the thyroid but it may also make it under active so that hormone tablets will need to be taken for life.

Thyroid Nodules

Thyroid nodules occur when normal thyroid tissue grows and forms lumps on the thyroid gland. Thyroid nodules are fairly common. A nodule can range in size from a few millimetres to several centimetres.

Thyroid nodules can occur as a single swelling, or be part of a multinodular goitre. The nodules can be solid or fluid filled and in the majority of cases they do not cause any symptoms. Sometimes thyroid nodules can become cancerous; this is more likely with single nodules than with a multinodular goitre. Generally the larger the nodule, the more likely that it may be cancerous.

Types of thyroid nodules

There are four types of single thyroid nodules:

- A fluid filled cyst
- A degenerated benign adenoma (an adenoma is a benign tumour)
- A slowly growing adenoma
- A small percentage are malignant

When there is a single thyroid nodule the rest of the thyroid gland is usually normal. Thyroid hormone production is usually normal. A multinodular goitre is likely to produce too much thyroid hormone and cause the symptoms of hyperthyroidism.

More about thyroid cysts

Thyroid cysts can range in size from less than one centimetre to several centimetres. They can arise very suddenly. A thyroid cyst can be entirely cystic (contains fluid only), or it can be a complex cyst (contains fluid and solid components). Entirely cystic nodules can sometimes enlarge suddenly and this can cause symptoms in the neck such as trouble swallowing, pain, and occasionally it may compress the vocal cords, producing a change in voice. Nodules that contain both fluid and solid components are more likely to contain cancerous cells.

Approximately 15 percent of thyroid cysts resolve themselves and the rest must be aspirated (drawn out) with a fine needle. If you have a thyroid cyst it is very important to avoid eating all dairy products, including milk, cheese, butter, ice-cream, yoghurt and other foods containing milk. Dairy products can promote cyst growth, as can margarine and deep fried food.

Thyroid nodules can also be classified as **hot nodules** (functioning nodules) or **cold nodules** (non-functioning nodules). The distinction is made after the results of a nuclear thyroid scan.

Hot nodules take up a large amount of radioactive iodine compared to surrounding tissues, so they are displayed as hot spots on a nuclear thyroid scan. In more than 95 percent of cases, hot nodules are not cancerous and they usually don't need to be investigated with a needle biopsy unless they are very large, are growing or have an irregular shape. The majority of hot nodules function on their own and cannot be controlled by the pituitary gland like normal thyroid tissue is. Therefore they usually produce excessive amounts of thyroid hormone and eventually produce the symptoms of hyperthyroidism.

When a hot nodule produces excessive amounts of thyroid hormone, the rest of the thyroid gland can shut down production and it shows up as a cold region (non-functioning region) on a nuclear thyroid scan. This is a normal compensatory reaction.

A hot nodule may be found because of its appearance in the neck or because it is giving the patient symptoms of an overactive thyroid gland.

If a hot nodule is small, isn't causing symptoms and thyroid hormone blood tests are normal, it is usually just left alone and observed regularly. But if the nodule is quite large, compresses surrounding tissues or produces symptoms of hyperthyroidism, it will need treatment. This is either surgery or radioactive iodine. If the nodule is producing excessive amounts of thyroid hormone, radioactive iodine will stop this, but it often doesn't reduce the size of the nodule considerably.

Cold nodules do not produce excessive amounts of thyroid hormone. They are also usually not cancerous, but they need to be more closely monitored because they are more likely to become cancerous. With these nodules, thyroid cancer is more likely if there are symptoms such as pain in the neck, difficulty breathing or swallowing, a change in voice and swollen lymph glands in the neck.

Incidence of thyroid nodules

Thyroid nodules are more common in areas of iodine and selenium deficiency and they are more common in women. In autopsy studies up to 50 percent of normally functioning thyroid glands contain nodules[10].

Symptoms of thyroid nodules

Thyroid nodules are usually small and painless, and most do not cause pressure symptoms in the neck. Most people don't even notice they are there; nodules are often discovered by doctors during a check up or investigation for something else. Nodules that are discovered accidentally while looking for something else are given the cute name "incidentaloma". Surprisingly, around 25 percent of these incidentalomas turn out to be cancerous[11]. This is a good reason to feel your neck for lumps regularly. Thyroid nodules are usually firm and smooth; they can be easily felt through the skin if they are larger than one centimetre. Smaller nodules can be seen in an ultrasound.

Cancerous thyroid nodules usually feel very hard, and the lymph glands in the neck may be swollen if the cancer has spread. But it is impossible to distinguish a cancerous from a benign nodule just by how it feels. Hot nodules (functioning nodules) may produce the symptoms of hyperthyroidism if they are producing excessive amounts of thyroid hormone.

Cause of thyroid nodules

Thyroid nodules can occur for a variety of reasons:

- **Heredity**. If a family member such as a parent or sibling has a nodule, it is more likely that you will develop one.

- **Age**. The chance of developing a thyroid nodule increases with age.

- **Gender**. Women are more likely to develop thyroid nodules than men.

- **Some thyroid conditions**. People who have thyroiditis (inflammation of the thyroid gland) are more likely to develop nodules.

- **Previous radiation exposure**. People who received radiation to their head or neck during childhood are much more likely to develop cancerous thyroid nodules as adults. In the United States, in the 1920s until the 1950s, teenagers, children, and sometimes even newborns were treated with radiation on their head and neck for simple conditions like enlarged tonsils, adenoids and acne. Exposure to radiation particles from atomic weapons testing or nuclear power plant accidents also increases the risk of malignant thyroid nodules.

- **Pesticides and other chemicals**. Several chemicals have been linked to the development of thyroid nodules and thyroid cancer. These are covered in chapter nine.

- **Selenium deficiency.**

Diagnosis of thyroid nodules

Sometimes the patient spots the thyroid nodule themselves and sometimes it is detected by a doctor during a routine medical check up. While looking at your neck, a doctor will probably ask you to swallow some water because a nodule on the thyroid will move up and down while you swallow and a lump elsewhere on your neck will not. Once a nodule is detected, it is important to find out if it is cancerous or interfering with thyroid hormone production. This means you will probably have the following tests done:

- **Blood test.** A thyroid function test will check your levels of TSH, T4 and T3 hormones. This will determine if the nodule is functioning (hot) and producing excessive amounts of thyroid hormone. If a blood test is abnormal, the nodule is less likely to be cancerous.

- **Ultrasound scan.** This method uses high frequency sound waves to create an image of your thyroid. An ultrasound can distinguish a cyst from a solid nodule. An ultrasound may also be used to guide your doctor when performing a fine needle aspiration biopsy of the nodule.

- **Fine needle aspiration biopsy.** This is the most sensitive test for distinguishing between a benign and malignant thyroid nodule. A thin needle is inserted into the nodule (much thinner than the needles used to draw blood) and it draws out a sample of cells. Several samples are taken from the nodule, and if you have more than one nodule, samples will be taken from them as well. The procedure takes around 20 minutes. Most thyroid specialists will only perform a biopsy if the thyroid nodule is larger than one centimetre. Rarely a biopsy will not give a definitive answer whether the nodule is cancerous or not; in that case surgery is used to remove the nodule and examine it.

- **Nuclear thyroid scan.** This test involves the injection of a radioactive isotope of iodine into a vein on the inside of your elbow. An image of your thyroid shows up on a computer screen. This is a good way to pick up "hot nodules" because they take up more isotope than surrounding normal tissue. Cold nodules don't take up the isotope hence they look like holes in the image.

A nuclear thyroid scan can't tell the difference between a benign and malignant nodule. The test can get uncomfortable because your neck has to be stretched back during the scan. This test also exposes you to some radiation.

Treatment of thyroid nodules

Treatment may consist of the following:

- **Wait and see**. If the nodule has been confirmed as benign and is not causing any symptoms, nothing will be done and you will be monitored regularly. If the nodule grows or produces symptoms, you will need treatment.

- **Thyroxine (T4) therapy**. Sometimes T4 thyroid hormone tablets are given. The theory is that taking oral thyroxine will suppress the pituitary gland's production of TSH; the hormone that stimulates growth of the thyroid. This treatment is often not effective, and if the nodules do shrink, this can take many months or years.

- **Radioactive iodine**. This is the usual treatment for hot nodules or a multinodular goitre that produce excessive thyroid hormone. The radioactive iodine is taken in capsule or liquid form, travels to the thyroid gland and causes the nodules to shrink. That usually takes two to three months. It's possible for symptoms to worsen for a few days after this treatment because as the thyroid nodules are being destroyed, they release more thyroid hormone into the bloodstream. This would make the hyperthyroidism temporarily worse. Some people develop a tender neck or sore throat after radioactive iodine, and it is possible that too much thyroid tissue will be destroyed, leading to hypothyroidism and the need to take hormone replacement tablets for the rest of your life.

- **Alcohol ablation**. This method is sometimes used for hot (functioning) nodules that are producing too much thyroid hormone. Ethanol is injected into the nodules, which makes them shrink and resolves the symptoms of hyperthyroidism. Sometimes only one injection is needed, but other people will require up to eight; they are usually done in two month intervals. This treatment can cause burning pain at the injection site and headaches, but those side effects should not last more than a few days. The good news is this method does not result in hypothyroidism.

- **Surgery**. If the nodules are cancerous (malignant), they will usually be removed, along with nearly the entire thyroid gland. This is also the best option for large multinodular goitres that constrict blood vessels, the airways or the oesophagus. Sometimes non-cancerous nodules are removed if they are so big that they cause breathing and swallowing problems. If the entire gland is removed, you will need to take thyroid hormone replacement therapy for the rest of your life. Surgically removing the thyroid gland can be risky because there is a chance that the nerves that control the vocal cords may be damaged, causing changes in the voice. The parathyroid glands that sit behind the thyroid can also be damaged. The parathyroid glands control the level of calcium in the bloodstream.

- **Nutritional medicine.** Please refer to chapter ten for our nutritional treatment of thyroid disease.

Thyroid nodules – case history

Kendra came to see me complaining of a moderately swollen thyroid gland, which had been diagnosed as a multi-nodular goitre. Her goitre did not cause her any physical problems but she did not like the appearance, as she was only 32 and was tired of wearing shirts with rolled collars to hide it. She did notice that her goitre swelled at different times of the month, especially before her menstrual period was due, and it became smaller after her period had finished. Her menstrual bleeding was heavy and painful but she did not want to take the contraceptive pill to control this.

Her thyroid scans had revealed a multinodular goitre with several cysts and nodules in the thyroid gland. Her thyroid function tests were normal and she was otherwise well, except for iron deficiency caused by her heavy periods.

Her specialist was seeing her every 12 months at which time he did repeat scans of her thyroid gland and she had had several samples taken of the thyroid nodules with a fine needle, which is known as a fine needle biopsy of the gland. These samples were checked by a pathology laboratory and thankfully none had shown any signs of cancer in the nodules. She had been reassured that the nodules and cysts were only benign and contained a mucus type of substance known as colloid.

Kendra's grandmother had suffered with a huge goitre and had refused surgery. Eventually her grandmother's goitre had bled internally (haemorrhaged) and this had fatally obstructed her airway. Kendra was worried that her goitre would continue to grow and did not like the thought of surgery. She asked me if it was possible to shrink her goitre with the aim of avoiding surgery.

I told Kendra that it was often possible to shrink a goitre and to get the cysts and nodules to gradually dissolve away. I could not promise her that this would result in a total shrinkage of the goitre but it was certainly worth a try. The treatment that I would recommend would also reduce the chances of cancer occurring in her thyroid gland.

Kendra's programme consisted of –

1. A supplement of selenomethionine to provide 100mcg of selenium daily

2. Regular consumption of seafood and the inclusion of seaweed in her diet. Thyroid nodules are more common in iodine deficient people.

3. Regular consumption of raw nuts and seeds, for the minerals and essential fatty acids they contain.

4. Raw juicing with spinach, carrot, red radish and oranges, lemons, limes.

5. The avoidance of mucus producing foods such as margarines, hydrogenated vegetable oils, dairy products, deep fried foods and processed foods.

6. Natural progesterone cream to provide 75mg daily of progesterone; this would lighten her periods and reverse her iron deficiency. Progesterone deficiency can worsen thyroid gland problems and it was most important to restore her progesterone levels.

Kendra was a very good patient and followed my recommendations to the letter. Her tenacity paid off, as six months after her initial visit her goitre was only half its original size, her menstrual bleeding was normal and she felt better in herself. I did instruct her to stay under the regular supervision of her thyroid specialist, as it is important to monitor the progress of a multinodular goitre. Sometimes it is necessary to give a small dose of thyroid hormone tablets to keep the levels of the TSH hormone low; this can also help to shrink the goitre.

Thyroid Cancer

Thyroid cancer is the most common cancer of an endocrine gland, (hormone producing gland). It usually arises out of a lump or nodule in the thyroid gland. The vast majority of thyroid nodules are not cancerous, but a small percentage are. There are a few different types of thyroid cancer; luckily most are easily curable; the most common types are easily removed through surgery. Unfortunately the incidence of thyroid cancer is rising.

Types of thyroid cancer

The main types of thyroid cancer are papillary and follicular; they make up more than 90 percent of cases. Other types of thyroid cancer include anaplastic, medullary (C-cell), thyroid lymphoma and Hurthle cell cancer.

Papillary and follicular cancer can usually be totally removed with surgery and they have an excellent outlook. Medullary cancer is usually more aggressive and harder to treat than papillary or follicular cancer. Anaplastic thyroid cancer grows very quickly and it doesn't closely resemble any thyroid cells. The different types of thyroid cancer will be described in more detail in the section that follows.

Incidence of thyroid cancer

Thyroid cancer affects approximately 15 000 people in the USA each year[12]. In Australia in 1997 there were 860 new cases diagnosed and 71 deaths from thyroid cancer in that year. In Australia it is the sixteenth most common type of cancer. Women are two to three times more likely to get thyroid cancer than men.

Thyroid cancer has a high survival rate; in NSW between 1980 and 1995, 95 percent of people who developed thyroid cancer were still alive five years later. It is the most curable type of cancer in Australia after non-melanoma skin cancer[13].

Symptoms of thyroid cancer

In its early stages, thyroid cancer usually has no signs or symptoms. The gland continues to function as normal and hormone levels on a blood test are usually normal too. As the cancer grows, it can cause the following symptoms:

- A lump in the neck, just below the Adam's apple.
- Hoarseness
- Difficulty breathing
- Difficulty swallowing
- Pain in the neck or throat that may spread to the ears
- Swollen lymph glands in the neck

Cause of thyroid cancer

The genetic material in our cells, called DNA helps them to grow and divide in a normal, healthy way. Generally when it comes to cancer, something happens to alter or damage the DNA. This can cause cells to change and grow in an uncontrolled way, forming a tumour that can eventually spread.

When it comes to thyroid cancer, the only known causes and risk factors are the following:

- **Previous radiation exposure.** Head and neck irradiation in childhood, adolescence and adulthood is the biggest risk factor for thyroid cancer. In the USA between the 1920s and 1950s, X-rays were a common treatment for acne and other skin conditions on the face, fungal diseases of the scalp, tonsillitis, sore throats, coughs, tuberculosis of the neck and even excessive facial hair! These days, people who have radiation treatment for cancer in or near the head or neck are at increased risk of developing thyroid nodules or thyroid cancer later. Radiation exposure from nuclear weapons tests or nuclear power plant accidents is also a risk factor. The thyroid cancer usually doesn't develop until decades after the exposure. Despite this, many people who develop thyroid cancer have not been exposed to radiation.

• **Genetic factors.** Some forms of thyroid cancer run in families. If one of your parents has MEN 2A, MEN 2B or familial medullary cancer, you have a 50 percent chance of having the genetic defect that causes this cancer. If you have this disease and have children, there is a 50 percent chance that they will develop the disease. MEN stands for Multiple Endocrine Neoplasia and refers to many tumours of endocrine glands.

• **Bone marrow transplantation**. Some studies have shown that survivors of bone marrow transplants have a slightly increased risk of thyroid cancer[14].

• **Some inherited diseases**. Having Gardner's syndrome or familial adenomatous polyposis increases the risk of developing papillary thyroid cancer. These are both genetic disorders where large numbers of polyps grow throughout the colon. The polyps always become cancerous if they are not detected and removed. Cowden disease also increases the risk of developing thyroid cancer. This is a condition that produces multiple tumours on the skin, inside the mouth and intestines.

• **Age at pregnancy**. Women whose last pregnancy was when they were 30 or older have more risk of thyroid cancer than women who had all of their children before age 30.

• **Pesticides, insecticides and other chemicals**. Several chemicals are linked to a greater risk of developing thyroid cancer. You can read about them in detail in chapter nine.

• **Race** – Caucasians and Asians have a bigger risk than darker skinned people.

• **Selenium and anti-oxidant deficiency.**

The Types of Thyroid Cancer in Great Detail

Papillary thyroid cancer

This type of cancer is derived from follicular thyroid cells. It is well differentiated, meaning that superficially it looks like normal thyroid tissue. Most of these tumours can still take up iodine from the diet and some can even produce thyroxine (T4).

A papilla is a nipple-like projection. Papillary cancers have many projections, making them look like a fern under the microscope. Papillary thyroid cancer occurs in all age groups and it's the most common type of thyroid cancer, making up around 70 to 80 percent of thyroid cancer cases. Most commonly it occurs in women between 30 and 50 years of age.

Papillary cancer grows slowly. It can eventually spread to other areas of the body via the lymphatic system, in this case the lymph glands in the neck. Around one third of patients who undergo surgery for papillary cancer have got lymph node metastases, (the cancer spread to their lymph glands). This type of thyroid cancer has a very good prognosis whether it has spread to the lymph nodes or not. However, people under the age of 20 who develop this cancer have a higher risk of it spreading to the lungs or bones and of the cancer recurring. The prognosis is also not as good in people over the age of 50.

Follicular thyroid cancer

This type of cancer is also derived from follicular thyroid cells. It makes up around ten percent of thyroid cancer cases and usually occurs in older people than papillary cancer. In general this is a more aggressive form of cancer than papillary. These tumours don't often spread to the lymph nodes but they can enter the arteries and veins inside the thyroid and therefore spread via the bloodstream. From there they can spread to the bones and lungs. Still, this type of cancer usually has a good prognosis too. The outcome is better in people below the age of 50 years.

Medullary thyroid cancer

This type of cancer arises from C cells, which produce the hormone calcitonin. The tumour cells continue to produce calcitonin, as well as a protein that several cancer cells make called carcinoembryonic antigen (CEA). Both of these substances can be picked up in a blood test. Medullary cancer can spread to the lymph nodes or other parts of the body.

There are three types of medullary cancer:

- **Sporadic**. These are the most common medullary tumours. They usually occur between age 40 and 60 and are not inherited.

- **Multiple endocrine neoplasia type II (MEN 2)**. There are two types: MEN 2A and MEN 2B. These tumours tend to occur in younger people and they are passed on from one generation to the next. People with these diseases can also develop tumours in their adrenal glands and parathyroid glands, (the four tiny glands that sit behind the thyroid).

- **Familial**. These tumours are also inherited but people with familial medullary cancer don't usually develop tumours in other organs. This cancer usually affects people in their 50s and 60s.

Anaplastic thyroid cancer

This type of thyroid cancer only makes up around seven percent of cases. It usually occurs in people over the age of 60. It is sometimes called undifferentiated thyroid cancer because the cells making up the tumour look very different to normal thyroid cells. This cancer develops from an existing, undiagnosed papillary or follicular tumour that all of a sudden starts to grow rapidly. Anaplastic cancer is very aggressive; it quickly spreads to lymph nodes and the windpipe (trachea), then on to other organs like the bone and lungs. Treatment such as surgery and radiation are not always successful for this type of tumour. It does not have a good prognosis.

Thyroid lymphoma

This type of thyroid cancer only makes up around four percent of cases. Lymphoma means cancer of the lymph glands, or white blood cells, called lymphocytes. Most people who develop thyroid lymphoma had an inflamed thyroid gland caused by Hashimoto's thyroiditis. Since this is an autoimmune disease, the thyroid gland becomes filled with lymphocytes and the cancer is believed to originate in them. Hashimoto's thyroiditis is very common, but luckily most people with it don't develop thyroid lymphoma.

This type of cancer mostly occurs in middle aged and older people and it has become more frequent in recent years. People with Hashimoto's thyroiditis who develop a goitre, or lump in their neck should be investigated for thyroid lymphoma. The treatment for this cancer is usually a combination of external radiation and chemotherapy.

Diagnosis of thyroid cancer

If a lump has been detected in your thyroid gland, the following tests will be performed:

- **Fine needle aspiration biopsy (FNAB):** This is the most reliable test for distinguishing between a benign and cancerous thyroid nodule. A very thin needle is inserted into the nodule which removes a sample of cells. A few samples are always taken from the nodule which are then analysed under a microscope in a laboratory. A diagnosis of cancer is based on the characteristics of the cells observed.

- **Surgical biopsy.** If a fine needle aspiration biopsy can't give a definitive diagnosis, the entire nodule will be surgically removed and observed under a microscope.

- **Blood tests.** If your doctor suspects medullary cancer, he/she will check for high levels of the hormone calcitonin in the blood. Thyroglobulin will also be measured; it is a thyroid hormone precursor that can be made in large quantities by papillary and follicular thyroid cancer cells.

- **Nuclear thyroid scan.** In the past this was the main way of assessing thyroid nodules. A radioactive isotope is injected into a vein, which then travels to the thyroid gland. An image of the thyroid gland is produced on a computer screen. This test does not distinguish between benign and cancerous nodules.

Treatment of thyroid cancer

1. Surgery

The majority of patients with thyroid cancer will have part or nearly all of their thyroid gland removed. Small pieces of thyroid tissue around the parathyroid glands are left to minimise the chance of damage to these glands. If the parathyroid glands are damaged, it will lead to a severe drop in blood calcium levels. If the cancer has spread to surrounding lymph nodes in the neck, these will be removed also. If most of the thyroid gland has been removed, thyroid hormone replacement tablets will need to be taken for life. As well as supplying needed T4 thyroid hormone, the tablets will suppress TSH release by the pituitary gland. High TSH levels could promote the growth of any remaining thyroid cancer cells in the body. You will need blood tests every couple of months to make sure the dose of thyroid hormone tablets is right for you.

2. Radioactive iodine (Radioiodine)

This therapy is used to destroy any remaining thyroid tissue that was left behind in surgery. It is also referred to as remnant ablation. When used to destroy any residual thyroid tissue, a relatively small amount of radioactive iodine is used and it can be done on an outpatient basis. Radioactive iodine is also used to destroy any thyroid cancer cells that have spread to other parts of the body. Radioactive iodine (iodine-131) is given in capsule or liquid form.

The thyroid gland normally traps and concentrates iodine in the bloodstream and this is stimulated by TSH released by the pituitary gland. Thyroid cancer cells, whether they are in the thyroid gland or spread to other parts of the body also concentrate iodine, but in much smaller amounts. If the level of TSH in the bloodstream is greatly increased, the cancer cells will be stimulated to take up a lot more iodine. Remember that normal and cancerous thyroid cells cannot tell the difference between regular iodine and radioactive iodine.

When the thyroid gland is removed and T4 (thyroxine) hormone is not given, the level of TSH in the bloodstream rises dramatically. This means that when radioactive iodine is given to a patient, any cancerous thyroid cells in their body will take up the iodine readily and be destroyed.

Preparing to receive radioactive iodine is a very unpleasant process. This treatment is usually performed six weeks after thyroid cancer surgery and during this time patients are not allowed to take any T4 (thyroxine) tablets. Patients are usually given T3 (brand name Tertroxin) for four weeks because it has a shorter half life in the body. For the last two weeks before receiving radioactive iodine patients must discontinue all thyroid medication. This greatly increases secretion of TSH by the pituitary gland so that the cancerous thyroid cells will take up as much radioactive iodine as possible. During these six weeks patients are also asked to follow a low iodine diet.

3. Nutritional treatment

Anyone with thyroid cancer is wise to follow our nutritional program outlined in chapter ten. This will reduce the chance of the cancer re-occurring and reduce the risk of new cancers forming.

The low iodine diet

Before undergoing radioactive iodine treatment for thyroid disease, patients are asked to follow a low iodine diet. The aim is to deplete your body of iodine as much as possible, in order to make the radioactive treatment more effective. If your thyroid cells (or cancerous thyroid cells) are deficient in iodine, they will soak up a lot more of the radioactive iodine.

You will be asked to follow this diet for up to two weeks before treatment, and continue it for two days after treatment. Iodine is found in a lot of different foods. The richest sources of iodine are usually iodised salt, fish, processed meats (eg. Deli meats), dairy products, pudding mixes, frozen dinners and food that contains artificial colouring, (iodine is a component of red food dye).

Foods you can eat on a low iodine diet

- Chicken, turkey, beef, veal & pork.
- Potatoes (no skin), rice, pasta, bread (1-2 slices per day maximum).
- All fruit except citrus fruit
- All vegetables except spinach
- Unsalted nuts & unsalted nut butter, except cashews
- Olive oil, vinegar & fresh herbs

Foods that must be avoided on a low iodine diet

- All fish, shellfish and seaweed
- All dairy products – milk, cheese, yoghurt, ice cream and other foods containing milk.
- Bacon, sausages, ham, salami and other processed meats.
- Pickles, sauerkraut
- Canned, frozen and "instant" powdered foods.

When radioactive iodine is used to destroy thyroid cancer cells that have spread throughout the body, a relatively large dose of radiation is given and this requires a one to several days stay in hospital. The patient is admitted to a lead lined room with its own bathroom and cannot leave for several days. Patients are not allowed contact with other people until the radiation levels in their body have fallen to safe levels. They are encouraged to drink large volumes of water so that the radiation leaves their body more quickly.

For the whole week after treatment, patients need to avoid close contact with other people so that they don't contaminate anyone with radiation. This means no hugging, using separate cutlery and sleeping in a separate bed. Ideally patients would keep a distance of two metres from other people. Women are advised not to become pregnant for at least six months after receiving radioactive iodine. Breastfeeding women need to wean their babies before treatment. In men, radioactive iodine can reversibly reduce sperm counts for a couple of years. Some men elect sperm banking if they are planning on having children in the near future.

The most common side effects from radioactive iodine treatment are nausea, vomiting and pain in the salivary glands, which can be relieved by sucking sweets. Because the salivary glands get slightly damaged, patients can be left with a dry mouth temporarily.

External beam radiation

In this case the radiation used comes from a source outside the body. A high energy X-ray machine called a linear accelerator is used to target the cancer cells for a few minutes at a time. Treatment is usually carried out five days a week for a period of six to eight weeks. Patients often feel very tired towards the end of treatment and the skin in the affected area can become red and appear sunburnt. They may also experience hoarseness and difficulty swallowing.

Follow up of thyroid cancer patients

Unfortunately up to 30 percent of thyroid cancers can return, even decades after the initial diagnosis. Therefore it is very important that these patients are monitored long term. The follow up of thyroid cancer patients involves a blood test for thyroglobulin; this is because thyroid cancer cells can produce a lot of this protein, and if high levels are found in the blood it may mean that the cancer has returned. In addition to this, a radioactive iodine scan of the entire body is performed; this way if thyroid cancer cells are present in the body, they will pick up the iodine and can be easily seen. These tests are usually performed every 6-12 months.

In order for these two tests to be as accurate as possible, the patient must have high levels of the pituitary hormone TSH in their bloodstream. The traditional way to achieve this is to ask the patient to stop taking their thyroid hormone medication for six weeks before the tests. This creates all the unpleasant symptoms of hypothyroidism again and is quite traumatic for people.

Thyrogen® is a new medication that eliminates the need for patients to come off their hormone medication for 6 weeks before the tests. This drug is a form of recombinant human TSH and is not currently registered in Australia. Thyrogen® is approved in the USA for use in the follow up of patients with well-differentiated thyroid cancer. This includes papillary and follicular thyroid cancer. Thyrogen is injected into the muscles and it may cause some side effects such as nausea, headaches, vomiting and weakness.

It is vital to not only monitor the cancer, but also to ensure the patient continues to strentghen their immune system.
See chapter ten for more detail.

Chapter 5

Thyroid disease and pregnancy

During pregnancy it is normal for the thyroid gland to enlarge slightly, so it may become more visible. A hormone secreted by the placenta called human chorionic gonadotropin (hCG) stimulates this enlargement because it has weak TSH-like effects. TSH (thyroid stimulating hormone) is the hormone made by the pituitary gland that stimulates the thyroid to make more hormones.

After childbirth the thyroid gland can become inflamed and cause unpleasant symptoms; this is called postpartum thyroiditis.

What is postpartum thyroiditis?

Postpartum thyroiditis (sometimes called silent thyroiditis), is inflammation of the thyroid gland that occurs in five to nine percent of women during the first six months after giving birth. The thyroid gland can become enlarged but this is usually not painful.

Symptoms of postpartum thyroiditis

There are usually two phases to this disease: first hyperthyroidism, then hypothyroidism. In the first phase, while the thyroid gland is inflamed it releases too much hormone into the bloodstream. This phase usually lasts two to four months and it causes the metabolism to speed up. Women commonly experience the symptoms of hyperthyroidism such as: weight loss, a rapid heart rate, anxiety, increased sweating and sensitivity to heat. These symptoms are usually quite mild and many women barely notice them.

In the second phase, the thyroid gland does not produce enough hormones, and this causes the symptoms of hypothyroidism. This phase can last up to a year. Some women develop a goitre (enlarged thyroid gland); other symptoms can include: depression, fatigue, sensitivity to cold, constipation, dry skin and brittle nails, weight gain and hair loss. The condition can be diagnosed by measuring levels of TSH, T3 and T4 thyroid hormones in the blood.

What causes postpartum thyroiditis?

At least 80 to 90 percent of women who develop postpartum thyroiditis have thyroid antibodies in their bloodstream; this means the condition is an autoimmune disease. The body's immune system incorrectly identifies the thyroid gland as a foreign invader and produces antibodies to destroy it. While women are pregnant, their immune system becomes somewhat suppressed so that they don't produce antibodies that would harm the developing foetus. After delivery, the immune system becomes reactivated again and it is during this time that the thyroid gland can become inflamed. Some women have thyroid antibodies in their bloodstream while pregnant and approximately 30 to 50 percent of them will go on to develop postpartum thyroiditis.

Women with the following conditions are most at risk of developing postpartum thyroiditis:

• High levels of anti-thyroid antibodies during the first trimester of pregnancy.

• An immune system disorder or autoimmune disease, such as type 1 diabetes, rheumatoid arthritis, coeliac disease or lupus. Women with type 1 diabetes are three times more likely to develop postpartum thyroiditis than non-diabetic women.

• A personal or family history of thyroid disease, for example Graves' disease or Hashimoto's thyroiditis.

• Goitre (enlarged thyroid gland).

• A history of postpartum thyroiditis. Women who have had this condition with one pregnancy have a 20 percent chance of being affected in subsequent pregnancies.

Treatment of postpartum thyroiditis

In the first phase, when the thyroid gland produces excessive levels of hormones, symptoms are often mild and require no treatment. If tremors and a rapid heart rate are present, beta blocker drugs can be given for a short time to relieve these symptoms. During the second phase, when the thyroid cannot produce adequate hormones, thyroxine (T4) hormone tablets are usually given to restore normal hormone levels. Very little of the prescribed thyroid hormone passes through the placenta to the foetus, or into breast milk. It is also identical to the thyroid hormone made by your own thyroid gland, so it is safe to use while pregnant or breastfeeding. Suffering from untreated hypothyroidism while pregnant or breastfeeding can have dangerous consequences to the intellectual development of a newborn baby.

Most women take prescription thyroxine tablets for approximately six months. After that time, the patient will be told to stop the tablets for four to six weeks and have a blood test for TSH and T4 hormones. This lets us know if the hypothyroidism is permanent, or if the thyroid has recovered and can now produce its own thyroid hormones again. Around 25 to 30 percent of women with postpartum thyroiditis are left with permanent hypothyroidism and they must take prescribed thyroid hormone replacement for life.

Minimising the risks of postpartum thyroiditis

After giving birth, many women experience several months of exhaustion and emotional upheavals. Many women also experience postnatal depression and this can become very debilitating if not recognised and treated. See the book *Hormones - Don't let them ruin your life.* It is very important to have your thyroid function tested regularly by your doctor because postpartum thyroiditis is easily treated and it may be causing you unnecessary suffering.

If you are planning pregnancy, make sure you ask your doctor to do a blood test for antithyroid antibodies and TSH; especially if you:

- Have an autoimmune disease. In particular type 1 diabetes, but also rheumatoid arthritis, lupus, coeliac disease and others.
- Have a goitre.
- Have a thyroid disease.
- Have a strong family history of thyroid disease.
- Have had postpartum thyroiditis before.

Women with antithyroid antibodies in their bloodstream are at increased risk of infertility, miscarriage and postpartum depression[15]. Approximately 90 percent of women who develop postpartum thyroiditis eventually go on to develop Hashimoto's thyroiditis. Clearly, the sooner you find out if you have thyroid antibodies in your bloodstream, the less likely you are to suffer with thyroid disease that is irreversible and requires lifelong medication!

Hypothyroidism in pregnancy

Maintaining adequate thyroid hormone levels during pregnancy is essential for the normal development of the foetus. The mother's thyroid hormone crosses the placenta and is needed in early pregnancy for the neurological development of the foetus. The thyroid gland of the foetus cannot start making its own thyroid hormone until after the first 12 weeks of pregnancy. Even then it still needs the mother's hormones to maintain adequate levels. Babies born without a thyroid gland only have slightly depressed hormone levels, because of hormones from their mother's circulation.

A severe deficiency of thyroid hormones in a foetus or newborn baby can lead to mental retardation and several other disabilities. New research has shown that a mild deficiency will impair the child's intelligence and result in a lower IQ. Therefore, women of childbearing age who are discovered to be hypothyroid should have their hormone levels corrected with medication as soon as possible.

Thyroxine requirements increase during pregnancy

Research published in the *New England Journal of Medicine* has found that 85 percent of pregnant women with an under active thyroid gland need their thyroid hormone medication increased in order to protect their baby. In healthy pregnant women, thyroid hormone levels increase, so that some can be passed to the foetus through the placenta. Women who cannot manufacture their own thyroid hormone must have the dosage of their medication increased.

A study conducted at Brigham and Women's Hospital-Harvard Medical School in Boston, USA recruited 19 hypothyroid women who were planning to become pregnant. The women had their thyroid hormone levels checked before pregnancy and then every two weeks during pregnancy. 17 out of the 20 women needed their thyroid hormone medication increased by an average of 47 percent. This increase in hormone requirement started as early as the fifth week after conception[16].

During the first half of pregnancy, thyroid hormone requirements increase rapidly; after the first 20 weeks requirements stabilise. All women should have a thyroid function test performed by their doctor as soon as they find out they are pregnant, and then every eight weeks. Do not increase your medication on your own; you must be guided by your doctor.

TSH in pregnancy

According to research published in February 2006, the normal blood Thyroid Stimulating Hormone (TSH) levels for each trimester of pregnancy are:

First trimester:	0.24 – 2.99 mIU/L
Second trimester:	0.46 – 2.95 mIU/L
Third trimester:	0.43 – 2.78 mIU/L

Ref. Soldin, Offie, "Thyroid Function Testing in Pregnancy and Thyroid Disease: Trimester Specific Reference Interfals," *Therapuetic Drug Monitor*, Volume 28, No. 1, February 2006.

Pregnant women with above normal TSH levels have a more than three fold increased risk of very premature delivery.

Chapter 6

All about Thyroid Tests

There are many different ways to diagnose a thyroid condition. We will look at the tests your doctor or specialist can carry out, as well as tests you can do yourself at home. The earlier a thyroid problem is picked up, the better the outcome.

Blood tests

The blood test to check thyroid hormone levels is called a thyroid function test. This test checks levels of the following hormones:

• Thyroid Stimulating Hormone (TSH)

• Free Thyroxine (Free T4 or FT4)

• Free Triiodothyronine (Free T3 or FT3)

Free means that the hormones are not bound to carrier proteins in the blood and they are active. In Australia Medicare will only cover the cost of TSH testing in healthy people without known thyroid disease; it will not pay for FT4 or FT3. TSH is produced by the pituitary gland and it regulates T4 and T3 hormone production by the thyroid. If your thyroid gland cannot manufacture enough T4, TSH rises; if it produces too much T4, TSH will fall. If a blood test shows your TSH level to be out of the normal range, only then will Medicare cover the cost of having a FT4 and FT3 blood test. Also, if you are taking thyroid hormone medication, Medicare will cover a TSH, FT4 and FT3 test. Medicare regularly monitors doctors and laboratories to make sure they adhere to this protocol.

This is unfortunate because many cases of thyroid dysfunction and disease are missed by doing a TSH only test. For example, your free T3 (the active thyroid hormone) could be low while your TSH is normal. A solution is to pay for a complete thyroid function test yourself; that way you can have your TSH, free T4 and free T3 levels tested. This costs approximately $55 but varies among laboratories. A thyroid function test is the main way of diagnosing thyroid disease, as well as monitoring doses of thyroid hormone medication in people with a thyroid disease. Knowing your free T3 level is important because it indicates how well your body is converting T4 into its active form T3.

The standard reference ranges for a thyroid function test used by Australian laboratories are:

TSH	**0.30-4.50 mIU/L**
Free Thyroxine (FT4)	**8-22 pmol/L**
Free T3 (FT3)	**2.5-6.0 pmol/L**

The reference ranges for thyroid function tests were based on statistical averages. New research is showing that the TSH reference range may not be accurate; the upper limit of normal TSH is ideally 2 mIU/L. The reason for this is that thyroid disease is extremely common and a large percentage of apparently healthy individuals are in the process of developing a thyroid condition.

Based on new research, the revised reference range for TSH is 0.3-2.0mIU/L.

Research has shown that anyone with a TSH value above 2.0mIU/L is likely to be in the early stages of hypothyroidism!

The standard blood test misses many cases of thyroid disease!

In early 2003 new guidelines for thyroid function tests were issued by the American National Academy of Clinical Biochemistry. The normal reference range for TSH was narrowed from 0.5 to 5 mIU/L to 0.3 to 2.5 mIU/L. Three years later most laboratories are still using an outdated reference range that can miss many people with thyroid disease.

The following statement was issued by the American National Academy of Clinical Biochemistry in their press release, issued January 18th, 2001:

"Even though a TSH level between 3.0 and 5.0 mIU/L is in the normal range, it should be considered suspect since it may signal a case of evolving thyroid under activity."

According to the National Academy of Clinical Biochemistry, more than 95 percent of normal, healthy people have a TSH level below 2.5 mIU/L. Anyone with a higher level is likely to have underlying Hashimoto's disease or another thyroid disease which has not yet progressed to full blown hypothyroidism. This fact is backed up by studying TSH levels in African Americans. This population has a very low incidence of Hashimoto's thyroiditis and has an average TSH level of 1.18 mIU/L[17].

We prefer to use 2.0 mIU/L as the upper limit of TSH because of further studies. A large 20 year study has found that people with a TSH level above 2.0 mIU/L have an increased risk of developing hypothyroidism in the next 20 years, this is especially so for people with thyroid antibodies in their bloodstream, but also applies to people who don't. It is thought that all of these people have low levels of thyroid antibodies in their bloodstream, but current testing methods can't detect low levels[18].

A review published in the British Medical Journal stated that "thyroid stimulating hormone concentrations above 2 mIU/L are associated with an increased risk of hypothyroidism"[19]. The article goes on to say that other research has shown that half of the population fall into this category[20]!

If your TSH level is above 2 mIU/L, don't wait to develop full blown thyroid disease; do something about it now!

If your doctor has performed a thyroid function test on you and told you the result is "normal", ask to see the blood test results yourself. Your doctor is likely using a laboratory that still adheres to outdated reference ranges!

It is vital to find out as soon as possible if you have a thyroid disease, while it is still treatable with diet and nutritional intervention. If detected too late, and there is already thyroid damage, you will need to take thyroid hormone replacement for the rest of your life.

How to Interpret a Thyroid Function Test

The following are possible scenarios:

Low TSH = overactive thyroid gland or pituitary gland in the brain not able to manufacture TSH.

High TSH = under active thyroid gland that is not producing enough T4 and T3 in response to TSH stimulation, or pituitary tumour producing excessive quantity of TSH.

Low FT4 = under active thyroid gland. This can be because the thyroid gland is not able to manufacture hormones, or because the pituitary gland is not stimulating the thyroid to make hormones. If you are currently taking thyroid hormone medication, this result means your dose is not high enough.

High FT4 = overactive thyroid gland. If you are taking thyroid hormone medication this means your dose is too high.

Low FT3 = under active thyroid gland. Your body is not converting T4 into its active form (T3) adequately.

High FT3 = this scenario generally only occurs if you are taking T3 hormone replacement and your dose is too high.

The word *euthyroid* means that thyroid hormone levels are normal.

Thyrotropin Releasing Hormone (TRH) Stimulation Test

This test is not commonly performed; it is mainly used to detect secondary hypothyroidism, or hypothyroidism caused by a defect in the pituitary gland. If the pituitary gland does not produce adequate quantities of TSH, then the thyroid gland will not be stimulated to produce T4 or T3 hormones.

Firstly a baseline TSH blood test is performed. Then the patient is given an injection of TRH (thyrotropin releasing hormone), which is normally produced by the hypothalamus in the brain. This hormone is the stimulus for the pituitary to release TSH. Thirty minutes after this injection another TSH blood test is performed. If the TSH level is very high, this can mean that the thyroid gland is under active and not responding. If the TSH level is low it can mean the thyroid gland is overactive or that the pituitary gland is unable to manufacture TSH.

Reverse T3 test

Reverse T3 is an inactive form of T3 (triiodothyronine). It is produced in large quantities during periods of stress, while following a low calorie diet and in other situations described in chapter seven. High levels of rT3 can suppress the formation and action of regular T3 in the body. This is known as thyroid resistance and can leave you with the symptoms of hypothyroidism despite a normal thyroid function blood test. Thyroid resistance is discussed in chapter seven. The reverse T3 blood test is not covered by Medicare; it costs approximately $45. The normal reference range for rT3 is:

rT3 ....140-500pmol/L

Thyroid Antibody Tests

Thyroid antibodies are tested in order to check for autoimmune thyroid disease like Hashimoto's thyroiditis, Graves' disease and postpartum thyroiditis. This is an important test to have because most thyroid disorders in Australia and the USA are autoimmune.

This test can also pick up a problem in the early stages, before it develops into a hormone deficiency or excess. Your thyroid function test results may be normal, but if you have thyroid antibodies in your bloodstream, your immune system is destroying your thyroid gland and sooner or later your hormone levels will probably be abnormal too.

A thyroid antibody test consists of:

Anti-thyroglobulin Antibody (TgAb)   Cut off titre = 100

Anti-microsomal Antibody Ab (TPOAb)   Cut off titre = 100
(This antibody is also called thyroid peroxidase).

A result above 100 means that your immune system is producing sufficient antibodies to attack and destroy your thyroid gland eventually.

Autoantibodies to thyroid peroxidase and, less commonly, to thyroglobulin are detected in virtually all patients with Hashimoto's thyroiditis. Thyroid peroxidase autoantibodies are usually found in patients with Graves' disease. However, many patients have both types of antibodies in their bloodstream.

Anti-microsomal antibodies are also called thyroid peroxidase antibodies (TPOAb). They are commonly found in Hashimoto's thyroiditis but can also occur in Graves' disease. Approximately 12 to 14 percent of people with normal thyroid hormone levels have thyroid antibodies in their bloodstream. This figure is even higher for people with another autoimmune disease, such as type 1 diabetes, pernicious anaemia or rheumatoid arthritis[21]. This just reinforces the fact that if you have one autoimmune disease you are likely to develop another one. See chapter ten for our recommended treatment of autoimmune disease.

70 to 80 percent of patients with Graves' disease have Anti-microsomal antibodies in their bloodstream, and nearly all patients with Hashimoto's thyroiditis and postpartum thyroiditis do.

Women who test positive for Anti-microsomal antibodies are at increased risk of infertility, miscarriage, IVF failure, foetal death, pre-eclampsia, premature delivery, postpartum thyroiditis and postnatal depression[22]!

This is true even if they have normal thyroid hormone levels. Clearly it is important to have a thyroid antibody blood test.

Approximately 20 percent of patients with follicular or papillary thyroid cancer have raised **anti-thyroglobulin antibodies** in their bloodstream.

TSH Receptor Autoantibodies (TRAb)

There are two types of TSH receptor antibodies that are associated with autoimmune thyroid disease:

1) Thyroid stimulating antibodies (TSAb). These can make the thyroid gland overactive and are found in Graves' disease.

2) Thyroid stimulation-blocking antibodies (TBAb) that block receptor binding of TSH. These make the thyroid gland under active and are sometimes found in Hashimoto's thyroiditis.

These types of antibodies can be found in Graves' disease and Hashimoto's thyroiditis. Usually the higher the antibody levels, the more severe the disease. This is a useful test to determine the cause of hyperthyroidism; if it is due to Graves' disease, antibodies will be present in the blood.

All types of thyroid antibodies can rise significantly after radioactive iodine treatment for thyroid disease.

Who Should Have a Blood Test for Thyroid Disease?

Having a blood test for your thyroid gland is an important part of maintaining your health. According to the American Thyroid Association, everyone should have their thyroid gland function tested at age 35 and every five years thereafter.

If you fall into one of the categories below, you should have a complete thyroid function test (TSH, FT4 & FT3) as well as a thyroid antibody test at least every five years:

- Women over the age of 35 years.
- Anyone with a family history of thyroid disease.
- Anyone who has previously suffered with a thyroid condition, such as postpartum thyroiditis.
- Anyone with an autoimmune disease, such as type 1 diabetes, rheumatoid arthritis, lupus or other.
- People with a family history of autoimmune disease.
- People with coeliac disease (gluten intolerance).
- Anyone who gains weight easily and struggles to lose it.
- If you have lost weight unexpectedly.
- Anyone experiencing fatigue and lethargy.
- People with depression
- Anyone who suffers with infertility.
- People who are taking lithium or amiodarone, as these medications are known to affect the thyroid gland.
- Anyone who has received irradiation to the neck or chest area.
- If you currently take thyroid hormone medication you must have a blood test every six months for TSH, FT4 and FT3.

The best time to have a blood test

If you have just started taking thyroid hormone medication, you should have a blood test for your TSH, free T4 and free T3 four weeks after commencement. Any time that your dose of medication is adjusted, you should have a blood test six weeks later.

Have the blood test done first thing in the morning and do not take your usual morning dose of medication that day. This allows your lowest hormone levels over a 24 hour period to be measured. If you are feeling well on your thyroid medication, you should have a complete thyroid function test every six months.

Calcitonin blood test

Calcitonin is a hormone made by special cells called parafollicular cells (C cells) in the thyroid gland. This test will be ordered if your doctor suspects medullary thyroid cancer. These tumours usually produce abnormally high levels of calcitonin.

Thyroglobulin test

This test is used to monitor patients with thyroid cancer. Thyroglobulin is a protein made in the thyroid gland, and is used to manufacture thyroid hormone and it can be produced in excessive amounts in people with papillary or follicular thyroid cancer.

Thyroid Ultrasound Scan

An ultrasound uses soundwaves to generate an image of the thyroid gland. An ultrasound can determine the following information:

- The size of the thyroid gland.

- Whether nodules are present, their size and how many there are. An ultrasound will often detect nodules that are only a few millimetres in size; too small to be detected by a physical examination.

- Whether the nodules are solid or fluid filled (cystic).

- Areas of calcification in the thyroid gland. This may indicate thyroid cancer.

- Whether lymph nodes in the neck are enlarged.

Remember that some thyroid nodules can contain a combination of solid and fluid components.

An ultrasound* cannot *determine whether a thyroid nodule is benign or cancerous (malignant).

Sometimes a fine needle aspiration biopsy is carried out during an ultrasound. The ultrasound guides the doctor to where to place the needle. If ultrasounds are performed regularly, they can detect changes in the size of the thyroid and any nodules present.

Radionuclide Thyroid Scans (Nuclear scan)

During this scan, a radioactive iodine isotope is injected into a vein on the inside of the elbow. You will be asked to lie on a table while an image of your thyroid is produced on a computer screen. A thyroid scan is useful for detecting inflammation of the thyroid gland (thyroiditis), whether the gland is overactive and the characteristics of any thyroid nodules.

A thyroid scan can detect whether a thyroid nodule is functioning (hot) or not functioning (cold). A functioning nodule readily takes up iodine and uses it to manufacture thyroid hormones; in this same way it will take up radioactive iodine and form a localised hot spot on the image of the thyroid displayed on the computer screen. A non-functioning nodule or fluid filled cyst will not take up iodine and will appear as a "cold" area on the screen. This can be useful in helping to distinguish between benign and cancerous nodules; hot nodules are rarely cancerous. Around five percent of cold nodules are cancerous. This is still not a definitive way to diagnose thyroid cancer.

Fine needle aspiration biopsy (FNAB)

This is also commonly referred to as a thyroid biopsy and is the best way to determine the nature of the cells inside a thyroid nodule. A very fine needle is inserted into the nodule and a local anaesthetic is not usually needed. Your doctor will want to know if you are taking any blood thinning medication that can increase your chance of bleeding during this procedure.

Best results will be obtained if the needle is inserted several times into a few different parts of the nodule; as each nodule can be composed of more than one cell type. Some nodules contain both fluid and solid components. It is possible to experience some neck discomfort for one to three days after this procedure, and some people get mild pain in the thyroid that radiates to the ear.

It is not always possible to distinguish a cancerous from a non cancerous nodule using this method. In this case it may be necessary to have a repeat biopsy performed, or the nodule would be surgically removed and analysed.

Thyroid tests you can do yourself

The Thyroid Neck Check

This is a test advocated by the American Association of Clinical Endocrinologists. You should become familiar with what your thyroid gland looks and feels like; that way you can pick up any changes in its size, or feel lumps at an early stage.

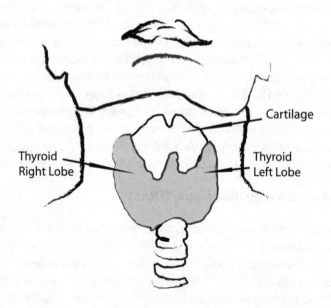

To perform this test you will need a glass of water and a hand held mirror.

1. Hold the mirror out in front of you so you can clearly see the area of your neck just below your Adam's apple and above your collarbone.

2. Tip your head back, while continuing to look at this area.

3. Take a sip of water and swallow.

4. Look at your neck while swallowing. Check for any lumps or bulges while you swallow. Don't focus on your Adam's apple;

your thyroid gland is located further down your neck, closer to your collarbone. Take a few sips of water and repeat this process.

5. If you see or feel any lumps or bulges in this area, see your doctor straight away. A thyroid nodule is likely to move when you swallow, whereas a lump elsewhere on your neck will not.

The Temperature Test

More than 50 years ago, a doctor named Broda Barnes found that the basal (resting) body temperature is a good indicator of thyroid function. An under active thyroid gland can produce a drop in body temperature, whereas an overactive thyroid can increase body temperature. Measuring your body temperature is another tool you can use to diagnose a problem with your thyroid gland. It should be used in conjunction with a blood test, your symptoms, consideration of family history and other diagnostic tests in this chapter.

Instructions for performing the thyroid temperature test

1) It is preferable to use a mercury thermometer. Clean the thermometer with cool, soapy water. Gripping the end opposite the bulb, shake the thermometer down until it reaches 35 degrees Celsius (96 degrees Fahrenheit) or lower. Place the thermometer beside your bed within easy reach, so that you can pick it up while still lying down the next morning.

2) The next morning, as soon as you wake up, place the thermometer in your armpit, so that the bulb is in your armpit. Make sure that there is no clothing between your armpit and the thermometer. Hold the thermometer there for ten minutes and continue lying still.

3) Write down your temperature. You must do this for four consecutive days.

Important tips

Your temperature must be taken as soon as you wake up in the morning; before you have moved out of bed, eaten or had anything to drink. This way you will be recording your lowest temperature of the day. Menstruating women must perform this test starting on the second day of their period; this is because ovulation produces a rise in body temperature and would not give a true reading. Post menopausal women and men can perform this test at any time. Do not do this test when you have an infection, injury or any other condition that can produce a mild fever.

A normal axillary (armpit) body temperature for adults is between 36.5 and 36.7 degrees Celsius; in the Fahrenheit scale this is 97.8 to 98.2 degrees. If your body temperature falls below 36.5 degrees Celsius or below 97.8 degrees Fahrenheit, you should see your doctor for further tests on your thyroid. This method is not always 100 percent accurate and should not be relied on solely; it can be helpful when used in conjunction with other thyroid tests.

Chapter 7

Treatment of Hypothyroidism

The treatment of hyperthyroidism has already been discussed earlier under the various diseases that can cause an overactive thyroid gland. See chapter three.

Here we will focus on the treatment of hypothyroidism with the use of thyroid hormone replacement.

Conventional Medication for the Treatment of Hypothyroidism

The primary treatment for an under active thyroid gland is T4 (thyroxine) hormone tablets. These are sold under the brand names *Oroxine* and *Eutroxsig*. They are both composed of thyroxine sodium and come in a dose of 50, 100 or 200 micrograms. The thyroxine taken in tablet form is identical to the thyroxine that your thyroid gland makes. So it is not like taking a drug; it is simply replacing a hormone that your thyroid gland can no longer make. If you are taking the correct dose of thyroxine, as determined by a blood test, most people do not experience any side effects from this medication.

Thyroxine has a long half life in the body (five to seven days), meaning it stays in your system for a long time. This is good because it keeps your thyroid hormone levels stable and consistent. Your starting dose of thyroxine will vary depending on the results of the blood test that diagnosed you with hypothyroidism. It is important to have a thyroid function test, checking your level of TSH, free T4 and free T3 approximately four weeks after starting thyroxine tablets. A typical dose of thyroxine is 50 to 100 micrograms daily.

It is important to remember that thyroxine (*Oroxine* or *Eutroxsig*), also known as T4, is not the active thyroid hormone. Your body must convert it into T3, which is active and also has a much shorter half life, or duration of action in the body. So if you are taking thyroxine tablets, you must have regular blood tests to check your T3 hormone levels, to be certain that your body is converting the T4 into T3.

Thyroxine tablets are used for the following conditions:

• Hypothyroidism, where the thyroid gland is unable to manufacture enough thyroxine.

• Thyroiditis, where the thyroid gland in inflamed and cannot produce enough thyroxine.

• TSH responsive tumours. Usually thyroid cancer is stimulated by TSH released by the pituitary gland. Taking thyroxine suppresses TSH release, therefore keeping the tumour in check.

Substances that can interfere with the absorption or action of thyroid hormone medication:

• Blood thinning medication (anticoagulants), such as warfarin. These drugs can increase the effect of thyroxine tablets in your body.

• Iron supplements. Make sure you take all supplements containing iron at least three hours away from thyroxine, as iron can interfere with the absorption of thyroxine.

• Calcium supplements. Calcium can also interfere with the absorption of thyroxine, so take calcium supplements at least three hours away from thyroxine.

• Antacids should be taken three hours away from thyroxine, because they can interfere with its absorption.

• Soy. You should wait three hours after taking thyroxine tablets before consuming soy foods or supplements containing soy, because it can inhibit the absorption of thyroid medication.

• Food in general. Therefore do not take your thyroxine tablets with food.

• Lactose. Do not take your tablets with dairy products.

Other medications that may possibly interact with thyroxine include:

- Antidepressants. In particular, tricyclic antidepressants and thyroxine can potentiate each other.

- Antiviral medication, especially that used to treat HIV/AIDS.

- Insulin used to treat diabetes. Insulin may reduce the effect of thyroxine.

- Medication used to treat malaria (eg. Chloroquine and proguanil).

- Beta blockers, used to treat high blood pressure and some heart conditions (eg. Propranolol).

- Corticosteroids (eg. Prednisolone & dexamethasone).

- Medication used for epilepsy (eg. Phenytoin & carbamazepine).

- Digoxin, used to treat heart failure.

- Ciprofloxacin and rifampicin, both antibiotics.

- Bile acid sequestrants, used to lower cholesterol (eg. Cholestyramine). These drugs can bind with thyroxine and prevent its absorption. You must wait five hours before taking thyroxine tablets.

- Amiodarone, used to treat an irregular heart beat.

- Non-steroidal anti inflammatory drugs, such as aspirin.

- Oral contraceptives and hormone replacement therapy containing oestrogen. Women who take oestrogen may need to increase their dose of thyroxine. This is because oestrogen increases the production of a binding protein that binds to thyroxine and makes it inactive. This is especially the case for women without a thyroid. If you have been taking thyroxine for some time and then begin taking oestrogen, make sure you have a blood test for thyroid function six weeks after.

Important points to consider when taking thyroid hormones

• Take the tablets on an empty stomach for maximum absorption. They are best taken first thing in the morning.

• Store unopened bottles of the tablets in the refrigerator.

• After taking the tablet you should wait for one hour before eating anything. Alternatively you may take the tablets three hours after food.

• Fibre can affect the absorption of thyroid hormones. Fibre from foods such as cereals, bread, bran, or powdered fibre supplements can all affect the absorption of the hormones. Fibre is a very healthy addition to your diet so you should continue to consume it; the important point is to eat fibre separately from your medication, keep your diet consistent and try to eat the same amount of fibre each day.

• Watch out for calcium and iron fortified foods, as both of these minerals can interfere with the absorption of thyroid hormones. Calcium and iron can be added to foods like soy milk, orange juice, bread, cow's milk and breakfast cereals.

• If you become pregnant while taking thyroid hormones, speak to your doctor as soon as possible; you may need your dose increased.

• If your dosage of thyroxine is changed, you need to wait approximately six to eight weeks before having a blood test to re check your hormone levels.

• Thyroxine requirements decline with age.

Potential Problems with Thyroxine tablets

Thyroxine, (brand names *Oroxine* and *Eutroxsig*) is the most commonly prescribed thyroid medication, and many people feel well on it and it resolves their symptoms of hypothyroidism. However, thyroxine is only one thyroid hormone and the thyroid gland produces several other hormones such as T3, T2 and T1. In order to be effective, your body must convert the thyroxine (T4) into T3. In some people this conversion is not efficient for a number of possible reasons. These people usually have normal levels of the hormones TSH and T4, but their T3 will be low. Many doctors do not check T3 levels, so they may be convinced you are taking the right dose of medication and there is nothing wrong with your thyroid.

The inability to convert T4 into the active T3 goes by several names, including thyroid resistance, euthyroid sick syndrome and Wilson's syndrome. We will be referring to it as thyroid resistance. People with thyroid resistance usually feel much better when they take T3 in addition to thyroxine. There are several options available including: a combination of T4 and T3; sustained release T3; bio-identical compounded T4 and T3, and porcine desiccated thyroid extract. Along with a change in medication, people with thyroid resistance must take certain nutritional supplements to assist their body with the conversion of T4 to T3.

Thyroid Resistance

To help you understand this condition, we will first briefly review the normal production of hormones by the thyroid gland. The thyroid gland produces two main hormones in response to TSH released by the pituitary gland; they are T4 and T3. The synthesis of these two hormones requires adequate amounts of iodine and the amino acid tyrosine in the diet. Several other minerals are required for these reactions to occur. The thyroid gland secretes much more T4 than T3. Approximately 85 percent of T3 in the body is produced in the liver, kidneys, muscles and other cells out of T4. T3 is a far more potent hormone than T4. The conversion of T4 into T3 is carried out by an enzyme called 5'-deiodinase (pronounced 5 prime deiodinase). This enzyme is dependant on the mineral selenium for its function and it acts to remove one iodine molecule from T4. There are several other vitamins and minerals that are required for the efficient conversion of T4 into T3; these include zinc and vitamins A, D, B2 and B3.

Most T4 to T3 conversion occurs in your liver, so how healthy it is has a great impact on how well this conversion proceeds.

Reverse T3

The thyroid gland also makes very small amounts of a hormone called reverse T3 (rT3). But 95 percent of the rT3 in the body is generated in other tissues such as the liver and kidneys[23]. The enzyme that converts T4 into reverse T3 is called 5-deiodinase (without the prime), and it is not believed to be dependant on selenium.

Reverse T3 is an inactive hormone and under normal conditions 45 to 50 percent of daily T4 produced is converted into rT3. Reverse T3 is able to bind to T3 receptors inside the body's cells and inhibit regular T3 from binding there[24]. Reverse T3 is also able to inhibit the action of the enzyme that converts T4 into T3, called 5'-deiodinase. Having high levels of rT3 and low levels of regular T3 will give you the symptoms of hypothyroidism. This will not be picked up on regular blood tests that do not include all thyroid hormones.

Why is Reverse T3 produced?

In a normal healthy person T4 is converted into both T3 and rT3 continually, and the body eliminates rT3 quickly. But under certain conditions the production of rT3 increases and this reduces the levels of active T3 in the body; slowing metabolism and producing undesirable symptoms. The main stimulants of rT3 production are stress, extreme low calorie diets and starvation, as well as some illnesses (such as liver disease).

Reverse T3 can now be measured in a blood test.

What is thyroid resistance?

Thyroid resistance is the inability of cells and tissues to respond to thyroid hormone. This can cause the symptoms of hypothyroidism despite normal thyroid hormone blood test results. You can be taking the correct dose of thyroid hormone but your body is not responding to it appropriately. There is no definitive, agreed upon cause of thyroid resistance. It is most likely to be due to a combination of:

- Unhealthy cell membranes; consequently T4 and T3 cannot enter your cells properly.
- Nutritional deficiencies, particularly of the minerals required by the thyroid gland.
- Heavy metal toxicity.
- Other toxic chemicals.
- Poor liver function.
- High blood levels of rT3 that are competing with T3 receptors inside your cells.

You can read about how to remedy these problems in chapter ten.

What is Wilson's thyroid syndrome?

Wilson's syndrome is essentially another name for thyroid resistance. The condition was first identified by Denis Wilson, MD in 1990. Officially the symptoms of Wilson's syndrome are low body temperature (below 97.8 degrees Fahrenheit, or 36.5 degrees Celsius) and the symptoms of hypothyroidism.

These symptoms can include weight gain, sensitivity to cold, depression, fatigue, dry skin, scalp hair loss and constipation. People with Wilson's syndrome will typically have normal T4 levels on a blood test, and their TSH can be normal or slightly low. Despite these blood test results, the patient will feel unwell and still complain of the symptoms of hypothyroidism. That is why it is vital to have a blood test for your T3 and rT3 levels.

The enzyme called 5'-deiodinase is required for both the conversion of T4 to T3, as well as the breakdown of rT3. This means that if the enzyme cannot function properly, not enough T3 will be made and rT3 will not be broken down, hence levels will accumulate. This will slow your metabolism and leave you with the symptoms of hypothyroidism.

Factors that impair the conversion of T4 to T3 and promote rT3 production

Under conditions of severe physical or emotional stress, the body slows down to conserve energy. This is a normal mechanism, and when the stress passes, the metabolism should return to normal. But reverse T3 production can continue unabated for several reasons.

These include:

- Ageing
- Burns
- Stress, causing increased blood levels of adrenalin and cortisol.
- Severe injury
- Calorie restriction and fasting
- Cold exposure
- Chemical exposure
- Increased free radical exposure and lack of antioxidants
- Toxic metal exposure, including to cadmium, mercury and lead
- Selenium deficiency
- Chronic high alcohol intake
- Insulin dependant diabetes mellitus
- Liver disease
- Kidney disease
- Haemorrhagic shock
- Severe illness
- Surgery
- Increased levels of cytokines (inflammatory chemicals) in the bloodstream, including interleukin-6 (IL-6), tumour necrosis factor-alpha (TNF-alpha), and interferon-alpha (IFN-alpha). These chemicals are secreted by the immune system in response to stress, infection, obesity and immune dysfunction, including autoimmune disease.

Several drugs have the ability to decrease production of T3 and increase rT3 production; these include:

- Dexamethasone (a corticosteroid)

- Propylthiouracil. This is an anti-thyroid drug used for the treatment of hyperthyroidism.

- Iopanic acid & sodium ipodate (both radiographic contrast agents). Used for some types for X-rays.

- Amiodarone (an anti angina, anti arrhythmic medication)

- Propranolol (a beta blocker)[25]

Alternative Thyroid Hormone Medication

Some people feel that taking thyroxine alone does not alleviate their symptoms of hypothyroidism adequately. This is most likely due to the fact that their bodies are not converting the T4 in these tablets into the active form, T3.

Most doctors prescribe only T4 because they believe the patient will convert it into T3 as needed; however this does not account for the large number of people who have difficulty making this conversion.

There are a number of alternative thyroid medications;
each of them requires a doctor's prescription.
These alternatives include:

- T3 (brand name *Tertroxin*) which can be taken in addition to T4 tablets.

- Sustained release T3 (made by a compounding pharmacy) which can be taken with thyroxine.

- Desiccated porcine thyroid extract can be taken, which is a combination of T4, T3, T2, T1 and probably other thyroid factors.

- Compounded T3/T4 combination capsules can be taken.

T3 (Tertroxin)

Both clinical experience and scientific studies have shown that many people feel better when they take **both** T4 and T3 tablets. If you continue to experience the symptoms of hypothyroidism despite taking thyroxine (T4 tablets), or if a blood test shows you have normal levels of TSH and T4, but low levels of T3, you may need *Tertroxin* tablets.

Tertroxin is a brand name; the drug is called liothyronine sodium. It is really just T3 thyroid hormone which is also known as triiodothyronine. These tablets require a doctor's prescription. According to medical literature *Tertroxin* is used in the following scenarios:

- In patients with thyroid cancer.

- In patients with hypothyroidism who have an intolerance to thyroxine sodium (*Oroxine* or *Eutroxsig*). In this case it would be used on its own.

- In patients with hypothyroidism who are resistant to thyroxine sodium, meaning they are not converting it into T3 adequately.

- In patients who are severely hypothyroid[26].

T3 has a much shorter half life than T4, meaning it does not last as long in the body. For this reason *Tertroxin* tablets must be taken two or three times a day, because they are quickly broken down. The tablets come in one strength only: 20 micrograms, but they can be cut in half or quarters. A typical starting dose is a quarter of a tablet (5 mcg) every four hours, and it may be increased from there. It can be cumbersome having to remember to take *Tertroxin* two or three times a day; to get around this problem you could use sustained release T3 instead.

According to research published in the *New England Journal of Medicine*, when incorporating T3, 50 micrograms of T4 should be replaced with 12.5 micrograms of T3. Do not change the dose on your own; you will need your doctor's guidance.

Fine Tuning the Thyroid Gland – case history

Melanie came to see me in my Brisbane clinic as she was not happy
with the outcome of her thyroid treatment. Melanie was 38 years
of age and had been diagnosed with auto-immune Hashimoto's
thyroiditis at the age of 35; this had caused her thyroid gland to
become under active. She had been treated appropriately with
thyroid hormone replacement in the form of Thyroxine (T4) tablets.

Her doctor was struggling to get her dose of thyroxine balanced,
as she would get side effects from too much thyroxine, which
necessitated a decrease in her dose. After a few weeks on the lower
dose of thyroxine she would become very tired and her blood tests
would show that she needed to increase the dose. Poor Melanie kept
swinging from side effects due to very high doses of thyroxine and
then to the symptoms of hypothyroidism when her dose had to be
reduced.

Her dose of thyroxine was fluctuating from 100 to 300 mcg daily and
yet she still had some symptoms of an under active thyroid gland.
She complained of –

Hair loss

Inability to lose weight

Fatigue

When she took the high dose of thyroxine she developed a racing
heart beat, muscle weakness, insomnia and anxiety – indeed she had
suffered with some panic attacks.

I ordered new blood tests which showed the following –

MELANIE'S RESULTS .... **NORMAL RANGE**

Free T 3 = 1.1 pmol/L ....2.5 – 6.0

Free T 4 = 23 pmol/L ....8.0 – 22.0

TSH = 2.0 mIU/L...0.30 – 4.0*

Thyroid antibodies

Anti-thyroglobulin antibodies = 80 .... (less than 100)

Anti-microsomal antibodies = 1200 .... (less than 100)

* Most laboratories use 4 mIU/L as the upper limit of normal for TSH. However, new research has found that if TSH is above 2 mIU/L, the thyroid gland is probably in the early stages of disease.

Interpretation of Melanie's test results –

The level of her T3 hormone is very low, whilst her T4 level is quite high; the high T4 level is obviously coming from her thyroxine medication.

She has high levels of antibodies attacking her thyroid gland; this means that the Hashimoto's disease is still active and her thyroid gland is inflamed and continually being damaged.

The problem that really shows up well in Melanie's blood tests is that her body is not converting the thyroxine (T4) into T3.

The T3 form of thyroid hormone is much more active than the T4 form. With her T3 levels being so low, it is not surprising that Melanie still suffered with symptoms of thyroid underactivity even whilst taking very high doses of T4. The T4 was not being converted into T3 – it was just building up in her body and making her toxic from its side effects.

I prescribed a treatment program to correct this imbalance which consisted of –

T3 tablets – the brand name is *Tertroxin*; Melanie was told to take one tablet (20 mcg), three times daily. At the same time I reduced her dose of T4 down to 100 mcg daily and told her not to increase this. I also prescribed selenium, as this mineral is essential to thyroid metabolism and the conversion of T4 into T3. Selenium is also essential to reduce the level of the harmful thyroid autoantibodies. Melanie was asked to follow a gluten and dairy free diet, as well as the bowel and liver detox because she has an autoimmune disease. I strongly recommended she follow a gluten free diet for life.

Melanie returned 6 weeks later and was feeling stable and said she did not want to change the doses of her thyroid hormones. I told her to come back in 3 months time with new blood tests to see just how well this dose of T4 and T3 was working.

Three months later her blood tests revealed –

MELANIE'S RESULTS .... NORMAL RANGE

Free T 3 = 5.0 pmol/L ....2.5 – 6.0

Free T 4 = 16 pmol/L ....8.0 – 22.0

TSH = 1.9 mIU/L ....0.30 – 4.0*

Thyroid antibodies

Anti-thyroglobulin antibodies = 40 .... (less than 100)

Anti-microsomal antibodies = 350 .... (less than 100)

* Most laboratories use 4 mIU/L as the upper limit of normal for TSH. However, new research has found that if TSH is above 2 mIU/L, the thyroid gland is probably in the early stages of disease.

This program had worked well, as her blood tests were almost normal. Melanie also felt much better in herself and all her symptoms had improved considerably. This case history illustrates that some patients will need to take two different forms of thyroid hormone replacement to properly balance their thyroid function – namely T4 and T3 tablets.

In a small proportion of my patients, I have found that any synthetic form of thyroid hormone – whether it be T4 or T3, causes unpleasant side effects such as anxiety, palpitations, stress or a lack of well being. In these cases I have found that natural thyroid extract works well and does not cause these side effects. In these cases I am happy to prescribe the natural thyroid extract on a long term basis.

Sustained Release T3

This is also called slow release T3. It is made up by compounding pharmacies and is taken in capsule form. To make the T3 sustained release, it is mixed with a filler (starch) that absorbs fluid inside your stomach and forms a kind of jelly bean. The hormone is slowly released into your body over 12 to 24 hours. This means that most people only need to take sustained release T3 once a day; some people feel better taking it twice a day. Sustained release capsules can be compounded into any strength the patient requires; commonly doses range between 5mcg and 30mcg. These capsules should be stored in the refrigerator to maintain potency. Some people with digestive problems do not absorb sustained release products well. If you have frequent, loose stools, the capsule may pass out of your body incompletely digested.

Desiccated porcine thyroid extract

This type of thyroid medication was first used in 1892. Thyroid glands are taken from specially bred and reared pigs, dried and ground up. The powder is put into capsules and is used to treat hypothyroidism. Desiccated thyroid extract contains both T4 and T3, as well as T1, T2 and other unidentified thyroid proteins naturally present in pig's thyroids and human thyroid glands.

The most common brand of desiccated thyroid is Armour; it is sold in the USA but is also available in many other countries including Australia. This type of thyroid medication is often referred to as "natural thyroid hormone" because it contains both T4 and T3 in the same ratio as they are found in the human body – four parts T4 to every one part T3. Desiccated thyroid is often measured in grains. One grain is equivalent to 65 milligrams. One grain of desiccated thyroid is equivalent to 100mcg of T4 and 25mcg of T3. Many people feel that desiccated thyroid extract is much more effective for hypothyroidism than taking either thyroxine alone, or thyroxine combined with *Tertroxin*.

Opponents of desiccated thyroid extract often state that the dose of hormones can vary from batch to batch and it is not as reliable as synthetically made T4 (*Oroxine, Eutroxsig*) and T3 (*Tertroxin*). This is not the case because analytical tests are performed on the raw material (thyroid powder) and the finished product (capsules or tablets) to measure T4 and T3 activity. In Australia desiccated porcine thyroid extract is available only from compounding pharmacies.

Compounded T4/T3 combination

It is also possible to obtain capsules containing a combination of T4 and T3 in a sustained release form. These capsules are made up by a compounding pharmacy. These hormones are not derived from pigs or any animal source; they are synthesised in the laboratory from the amino acid tyrosine. This is the same protein that our own thyroid gland uses to manufacture hormones. These hormones are bio identical because the finished product is identical to the thyroid hormones made by the body.

T4/T3 combination capsules can be made up into any potency or ratio that the patient requires. For example, T4 and T3 are made by the human body in a ratio of 4 to 1; therefore a common dose present in capsules is 20mcg T4 with 5mcg T3. If a stronger dose is required, this can be increased to 80mcg T4 with 20mcg T3. However, any ratio that the patient needs can be made up. For example, some people with thyroid resistance manufacture high levels of reverse T3 and this inhibits the action of regular T3. People like this need a greater quantity of T3 in their capsules, so the ratio of T4 to T3 may be 3 to 1.

A Comparison of Different Forms of Thyroid Hormone Medication

Thyroxine only – brand names Oroxine and Eutroxsig

Advantages

Least expensive form of hormone replacement.
Eliminates the symptoms of hypothyroidism for most people.

One tablet taken once a day only.

Disadvantages

A significant percentage of patients still experience the symptoms of hypothyroidism while taking thyroxine.

Must be converted into T3 in the body in order to have desired effect.
Only replaces one thyroid hormone.

Thyroxine tablets (brand names Oroxine or Eutroxsig) with Tertroxin (T3) tablets

Advantages

Provides both T4 and the active T3, therefore can help people who can't convert T4 into T3.

Less expensive than compounded hormones if prescribed under an authority.

Disadvantages

T3 is not in a sustained release form, therefore *Tertroxin* tablets need to be taken 2 or 3 times a day.

Tertroxin is very expensive unless prescribed under an authority prescription.
Tertroxin has potential to cause side effects such as palpitations if too much is taken; this is because it is harder to control the dose compared to thyroxine alone.

A Comparison of Different Forms of Thyroid Hormone Medication

Thyroxine tablets and sustained release T3 capsules

Advantages

Provides both T4 and the active T3, therefore can help people who can't convert T4 into T3.

T3 is in a slow release form, so usually one capsule a day is sufficient.

Disadvantages

More expensive than just taking thyroxine only. How well slow release capsules work depends on the health of your digestive tract. People with IBS or frequent stools may need to take T3 more than once a day.

Desiccated porcine thyroid extract –Natural Thyroid Hormone prepared by a compounding pharmacy

Advantages

Provides both T4 and the active T3 in the same ratio made by the human body.

Good for people who have problems converting T4 into T3.

Taken once a day.

Disadvantages

Porcine (pig) origin is not acceptable to some people.

T4 and T3 are present in a fixed ratio of 4:1, therefore more T3 cannot be added if needed. More expensive than taking thyroxine alone because it must be prepared by a compounding chemist.

A Comparison of Different Forms of Thyroid Hormone Medication

Compounded T4/T3 combination capsules – available from compounding pharmacies only

Advantages

Both thyroid hormones are supplied, including the active hormone T3.

Hormones are bio-identical and do not come from a porcine (pig) source.

T4 and T3 can be supplied in any ratio the patient needs – more T3 can be added if needed.

Easier to adjust the dosage of T4 and T3 based on patient's blood test results

Disadvantages

Most expensive form of thyroid hormone medication.

Studies show that patients feel best taking both T4 and T3

A number of studies have been done showing the benefits of taking both T4 and T3 thyroid hormones, rather than T4 alone. Conversely, other studies have shown that there are no additional benefits to taking T3 over T4 alone.

This discrepancy just highlights how individual we all are.

The people who do not feel well taking thyroxine alone probably have a nutritional, genetic, environmental or metabolic factor that prevents them from utilising the thyroxine effectively.

Optimal thyroid hormone replacement

Numerous studies have shown that normal, healthy individuals who do not go on to develop hypothyroidism have a TSH level equal to or less than 2 mIU/L. Therefore, if you are taking thyroid hormone medication, you must have a thyroid function test every six months to check if your dose of medication is correct. Ideally your TSH should be between 0.5 and 2 mIU/L. If it is greater, you may need your medication increased. Do not increase it yourself; you must do this with your doctor's guidance.

Chapter 8

Other Diseases Associated with Thyroid Disease

A number of different health conditions are closely associated with thyroid disease. In some cases, having one of these health problems puts you at risk of developing a thyroid condition. In other cases, if you have a thyroid disease you may be more prone to one of these health problems.

Infertility

Both untreated hypothyroidism and hyperthyroidism can possibly lead to infertility. Having an overactive or under active thyroid can affect your oestrogen levels and your ability to ovulate. Once the thyroid condition is treated with appropriate medication and nutrition, fertility is usually restored to normal.

Effects of hypothyroidism on fertility

Menstruating women with hypothyroidism typically experience heavy periods (menorrhagia), painful periods and more frequent periods; their 28 day cycle can be shortened to 25 days. In some instances hypothyroidism in young girls can trigger early menarche (the beginning of menstruation), before the age of ten.

Women with hypothyroidism have a reduced ability to excrete oestrogen and androstenedione (a male hormone). They are also at increased risk of polycystic ovarian syndrome; a condition that may impair fertility. Recently, studies have shown that some women with polycystic ovarian syndrome have higher levels of antithyroid antibodies in their bloodstream than women without polycystic ovarian syndrome[27]. These antibodies are an indicator of autoimmune thyroid disease. Hashimoto's thyroiditis is the most common cause of hypothyroidism and it is an autoimmune disease.

Sometimes hypothyroidism can increase the levels of a hormone released by the pituitary gland called prolactin. This can cause milk production (galactorrhea) unrelated to pregnancy or childbirth. High prolactin levels can prevent ovulation and this would obviously inhibit fertility. The menstrual period can be irregular or periods may stop altogether. Prolactin can be measured in a blood test.

A failure to ovulate will create a progesterone deficiency. This results in the condition called oestrogen dominance, which means there is too much oestrogen in the body and not enough progesterone to balance it. Oestrogen dominance can create symptoms of PMS, painful heavy periods, reduced fertility and an increased risk of breast and uterine cancer. Oestrogen dominance can further suppress the thyroid, worsening the symptoms of hypothyroidism.

> The majority of women with hypothyroidism need treatment for oestrogen dominance and progesterone deficiency. This is discussed in detail in chapter ten.

In Australia one in six couples suffers with infertility. It is defined as an inability to conceive after 12 months of unprotected intercourse, or being unable to carry a pregnancy to a live birth. If you are experiencing infertility make sure your doctor orders a blood test to check your level of TSH. Ask to see the result; don't just accept the news that you are in the normal range. Some researchers believe that many women will not be able to conceive until their TSH level is between 1 and 2 mIU/L.

If you are suffering from infertility or repeated miscarriages, it is also vital that you have a blood test for thyroid antibodies. This is especially important if your TSH level is above 2 mIU/L. Having thyroid antibodies in your bloodstream means that you are in the early stages of autoimmune thyroid disease; your thyroid is in the process of being destroyed by your immune system. Women with thyroid antibodies in their bloodstream are at increased risk of infertility, miscarriage, postpartum thyroiditis and even postnatal depression. You can reduce or halt the production of thyroid antibodies by following our autoimmune disease treatment protocol in chapter ten.

Women who do fall pregnant while suffering with untreated hypothyroidism are at increased risk of miscarriage and stillbirth. If the pregnancy does go to full term, the child is at increased risk of mental retardation, physical abnormalities and impaired IQ; depending on how severe the thyroid hormone deficiency is.

If you are taking medication for hypothyroidism and become pregnant, speak to your doctor about this as soon as possible because your medication will probably need to be increased.

Effects of hyperthyroidism on fertility

Menstruating women with hyperthyroidism may experience very light menstrual periods, irregular periods, or they may lose their period altogether (called amenorrhoea). They may also fail to ovulate, therefore will not produce progesterone. This can lead to fertility problems. Teenage girls with hyperthyroidism can experience delayed puberty and delayed menarche, past the age of 15. Many cases of hyperthyroidism are due to autoimmune disease, (for example Graves' disease); therefore thyroid antibodies may be present in the bloodstream.

If a woman with untreated hyperthyroidism does become pregnant, she is at greater risk of miscarriage, foetal growth retardation, premature labour, congenital malformations, pre-eclampsia, and even chromosomal errors such as Down's syndrome.

Hyperthyroid women can have two to three times the normal level of oestrogen in their bloodstream during every phase of the menstrual cycle, compared to normal women[28]. Hyperthyroid women often have antithyroid antibodies in their bloodstream and these significantly affect fertility. Hyperthyroid women who smoke cigarettes are more likely to experience menstrual problems than women who don't smoke.

Autoimmune disease

The majority of thyroid conditions in developed countries like Australia, New Zealand and the USA are due to autoimmune thyroid disease: Hashimoto's thyroiditis, Graves' disease and postpartum thyroiditis are the most common. Autoimmune disease is where your immune system fails to distinguish between your own body and foreign tissue, and therefore produces antibodies that attack and destroy your own organs. *Auto* is the Greek word for self. Most autoimmune diseases are more common in women than men. The tendency to develop an autoimmune disease often runs in families, so if a family member of yours has an autoimmune disease you may develop one too. People who have one autoimmune disease are very likely to develop another one; this is especially the case if they fail to address the underlying digestive, liver and immune system dysfunction that caused the disease to develop in the first place. In chapter ten we outline our treatment protocol for autoimmune disease; we have had a great deal of success with this regime in our clinics.

When it comes to thyroid disease, there are some autoimmune diseases that are quite strongly associated with it. If you suffer with one of the autoimmune diseases below, be aware that you are more prone to developing a thyroid condition. This also works the other way around; people with autoimmune thyroid disease are more likely to develop one of the diseases below:

- Coeliac disease
- Type 1 diabetes
- Addison's disease
- Idiopathic Thrombocytopenic purpura (ITP)
- Myasthenia gravis
- Multiple sclerosis
- Pernicious anaemia
- Rheumatoid arthritis
- Sjogren's syndrome

- Systemic Lupus Erythematosus
- Vitiligo

Coeliac Disease

Coeliac disease is also known as gluten intolerance. Gluten is a protein that is found in wheat, rye, oats, barley, spelt, kamut and several other foods. People with coeliac disease cannot digest gluten properly; instead their immune system mounts a reaction as though the gluten were a harmful substance, such as a virus. This causes inflammation and damage to the lining of the intestines, as well as harmful effects in other parts of the body. Most people with coeliac disease will experience digestive problems such as abdominal bloating and pain, diarrhoea and/or constipation, as well as fatigue. However, some people with coeliac disease do not experience any digestive problems at all. This makes it very tricky to diagnose.

The tendency to develop coeliac disease is inherited. Once considered quite a rare condition, research has found that coeliac disease is far more common. Its prevalence in Australia is considered to be somewhere between one in 250 and one in 75 people. Coeliac disease is an autoimmune disease and therefore places sufferers at an increased risk of developing another autoimmune disease. People with coeliac disease often produce antibodies against several organs and tissues. The sooner coeliac disease is diagnosed and treated, the less likely antibodies will destroy other tissues and produce another autoimmune disease.

How would I know if I have coeliac disease?

Coeliac disease can be diagnosed with a blood test. Your doctor should request what is known as "coeliac serology". It is important to realise that this blood test will be a lot more accurate if you are regularly consuming gluten for two months before the test. That means eating at least two pieces of wheat bread or the equivalent in pasta, breakfast cereals, pastry or other foods that are made of wheat flour, as this is the most concentrated source of gluten. Even so, this blood test is falsely negative in three to five percent of people with coeliac disease. The gold standard for diagnosing coeliac disease is an intestinal biopsy, where samples of tissue are taken from the upper part of the small intestine and analysed under a microscope. However, there are milder forms of gluten intolerance that do not show up on any of these tests, but still place an individual at increased risk of autoimmune disease.

You can suspect you may suffer with coeliac disease if you have some of the following symptoms or conditions:

- Irritable Bowel Syndrome (IBS)
- Diarrhoea and/or constipation
- Flatulence, abdominal bloating, abdominal pain
- Anaemia (due to iron and/or folate deficiency)
- Infertility and recurrent miscarriage
- Mouth ulcers
- Easy bruising
- Bone and joint pain
- Muscle spasms
- Osteoporosis
- Skin rashes
- Depression

Gluten intolerance is the most common food intolerance in the world and unfortunately it is very under diagnosed[29]. There are many people who are made sick by eating gluten because they don't know they have this intolerance. There are degrees of severity of gluten intolerance and mild cases sometimes go undetected by the standard blood test and biopsy. Sometimes the best diagnosis is to follow an elimination diet under the supervision of a nutritionist, naturopath or dietician, and see if your symptoms resolve. The longer a gluten intolerant person continues to eat gluten, the more likely they are to develop an autoimmune disease. People with coeliac disease are especially prone to developing Hashimoto's thyroiditis and type 1 diabetes.

Treatment of coeliac disease

The only treatment for coeliac disease is following a gluten free diet for life. This can be tough because gluten is found in so many foods commonly eaten in the Western diet. Gluten is also often hidden in foods, under a different name. The treatment of gluten intolerance, including the gluten free diet will be discussed in detail in chapter ten.

If you have an autoimmune thyroid disease, it is essential that you are tested for coeliac disease. **Research has shown that adhering to a gluten free diet can stop the production of thyroid antibodies in three to six months**[30]!

Other autoimmune diseases associated with thyroid disease

- **Type 1 diabetes:** This is caused by autoimmune destruction of the insulin producing cells (called islet beta cells) in the pancreas. It usually starts in childhood and sufferers must inject insulin for the rest of their life. People with type 1 diabetes commonly produce thyroid autoantibodies and therefore are more prone to developing either an overactive or under active thyroid[31].

- **Addison's disease:** This occurs when the immune system destroys the adrenal glands, which sit on top of the kidneys. It causes a deficiency of the steroid hormone cortisol plus other vital hormones that control fluid and salt balance, blood pressure as well as blood sugar levels. People with Addison's disease are more prone to developing an overactive or under active thyroid gland. The combination of Addison's disease with hypothyroidism is sometimes referred to as Schmidt's Syndrome. If both Addison's disease and hypothyroidism are diagnosed at the same time, it is important that the adrenal gland hormones are replaced first.

- **Idiopathic thrombocytopenic purpura (ITP):** People with this condition produce antibodies that attack and destroy platelets. Consequently they have low levels of platelets in their bloodstream which increases the risk of bleeding. Platelets are necessary for the blood to clot normally. People with ITP have an increased risk of developing autoimmune thyroid disease.

- **Myasthenia gravis:** This is an autoimmune disease that causes weakness in one or more muscle groups in the body. People with myasthenia gravis are at increased risk of both autoimmune hyperthyroidism and hypothyroidism. Both Graves' disease and myasthenia gravis can affect the eyes and impair their normal function and movement.

- **Multiple sclerosis:** In this disorder antibodies are produced against the myelin sheath that covers nerves. Autoimmune thyroid disease is more common in people with multiple sclerosis; particularly in men[32].

- **Pernicious anaemia:** This is usually caused by an autoimmune condition that prevents the absorption of vitamin B12. This vitamin is necessary for the production of red blood cells. People with pernicious anaemia are more likely to develop either Hashimoto's thyroiditis or Graves' disease.

- **Rheumatoid arthritis:** This form of arthritis is caused by antibody destruction of the joint tissue and cartilage. People with rheumatoid arthritis commonly have thyroid antibodies in their bloodstream, and they are more likely to develop autoimmune thyroid disease.

- **Sjogren's syndrome:** In this autoimmune disease, antibodies are produced that destroy the glands that produce tears, saliva and other lubricating secretions. Patients develop dry eyes, a dry mouth, dry vagina, dry skin and a dry nose. Autoimmune thyroid conditions are more common with this disorder.

- **Systemic lupus erythematosus (SLE):** People with this disorder produce antibodies against many different tissues in the body. SLE can affect the skin, joints, heart, kidneys, blood vessels, lungs and the central nervous system. People with SLE are at increased risk of developing Hashimoto's thyroiditis or Graves' disease[33].

- **Vitiligo:** In this disease antibodies destroy the pigment producing cells in the skin (melanocytes), resulting in white patches on areas of the skin. Many people with vitiligo also develop autoimmune thyroid disease.

In all of these conditions it is vitally important to follow our treatment plan for autoimmune disease in chapter ten.

Cardiovascular disease

The heart is very sensitive to changes in thyroid hormone levels. The heart muscle contains receptors for thyroid hormones and they are needed for growth and function of the heart. Either too little or too much thyroid hormone will have a detrimental effect on the health of your heart.

How hypothyroidism affects the heart

An abnormally low level of thyroid hormones in the blood causes metabolism and all bodily functions to slow down. This also causes the heart rate to slow. People with untreated hypothyroidism are at increased risk of heart disease. This is probably because having an under active thyroid gland can cause high levels of the following:

- LDL "bad" cholesterol.
- Triglycerides, (a type of fat that can make the bloodstream thick and sticky).
- Lipoprotein (a). This is a worse form of LDL cholesterol that thickens the walls of the arteries.
- Blood pressure
- Homocysteine. This is a type of protein that has an abrasive effect on the walls of arteries and promotes blood clots.
- C-reactive protein. This is a marker of inflammation in the body. The more inflammation there is in your body, the greater your risk of heart disease.

Hypothyroidism can also result in low levels of HDL "good" cholesterol.

Blood tests are available to measure both homocysteine and C-reactive protein. You can find more information about these substances, how to lower them and how to protect your heart in our book *Cholesterol the Real Truth*.

Research has also shown that people with hypothyroidism have thicker arteries in the neck (carotid arteries) than normal healthy people. This is a risk factor for arteriosclerosis (hardening of the arteries) and subsequent stroke. Replacing the deficient thyroid hormones with medication has been shown to reverse this thickening[34]. Hypothyroidism can weaken the heart muscle in general and it can encourage the accumulation of fluid in the pericardium. This is the bag that surrounds the heart and when fluid builds up there it is called pericardial effusion.

Women with hypothyroidism are 70 percent more likely to have a hardened aorta than women with normal thyroid hormone levels. The aorta is the main artery in the body and takes oxygen rich blood from the heart to the rest of the body. Hypothyroid women have more than twice the risk of having a heart attack. The risk is increased even further in women with Hashimoto's thyroiditis[35].

Research has shown that if you are taking thyroid hormone medication, you should strive to get your TSH level to 2 mIU/L or less in order to lower your cholesterol, triglycerides, homocysteine and C-reactive protein. If your TSH is above 2 mIU/L, you may need your medication dosage increased. Of course there are plenty of other reasons why you may have high blood levels of cholesterol and other substances; an under active thyroid gland is just one of them. Do not attempt to increase the dose of your thyroid medication yourself; this must be done with your doctor's supervision.

How hyperthyroidism affects the heart

Hyperthyroidism usually produces symptoms including a rapid heart rate, faster pulse and palpitations. Some people find that their heart rate goes up much faster when they exercise and it takes longer to get back to normal when they stop. The systolic blood pressure can be elevated in hyperthyroidism; this is the top figure on a blood pressure reading.

In older people, or people who already have heart disease, hyperthyroidism can lead to a dangerous, irregular heart rhythm called atrial fibrillation. This is more likely to happen in men than women. It is not uncommon to first discover an older patient is hyperthyroid because they have complained of palpitations and a racing heart.

Osteoporosis

Osteoporosis is an extremely common condition. It occurs when there is a loss of bone mass and the bones become porous and fragile. It greatly increases the risk of fractures, particularly of the hip, wrists and vertebrae. Our bones are continually being remodelled; bone tissue is broken down and rebuilt on a regular basis. Osteoporosis sets in when more bone is broken down than can be rebuilt.

Hyperthyroidism and osteoporosis

Having higher than normal levels of thyroid hormones in your bloodstream increases the rate of bone breakdown. A recent study has shown that women with sustained, high levels of thyroid hormone are three times more likely to experience a hip fracture and four times more likely to sustain a spinal fracture than women with normal hormone levels. Most of the women in this study were receiving too much thyroid hormone; however some were producing too much hormone of their own. The good news is that if detected early, the bone thinning effects of hyperthyroidism can be reversed. When thyroid hormone levels are brought back down to normal, bone density should be restored to normal[36].

When it comes to osteoporosis risk, the important thing to remember is that thyroid hormones, whether produced in your body or taken in tablet form do not cause osteoporosis. It is only excessive levels of thyroid hormones that create this problem. If you have normal hormone levels and are taking the correct dose of thyroid medication, you are not at increased risk of osteoporosis.

Everyone taking thyroid hormone tablets should have a thyroid function test every six months to check their hormone levels. If your TSH level is less than 0.1 mIU/L, you are either taking too much hormone medication or your thyroid gland is overactive for another reason. You must speak to your doctor about this, as it would increase your risk of osteoporosis[37].

The parathyroid glands

Thyroid disease and especially thyroid surgery can affect the parathyroid glands. The four parathyroid glands are very small and are located behind the thyroid gland; two in the left lobe and two in the right lobe. The function of the parathyroid glands is to keep blood calcium levels within a narrow range. Excessive secretion of parathyroid hormone leads to abnormally high blood calcium levels, and this condition is called **hyperparathyroidism**. If the parathyroid glands do not secrete enough hormone, blood calcium levels fall and the condition is called **hypoparathyroidism**.

The back of the thyroid gland

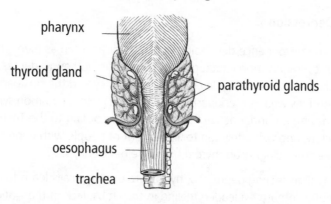

pharynx

thyroid gland

parathyroid glands

oesophagus

trachea

Hyperparathyroidism is often first detected by an abnormally high blood calcium level on a routine blood test. Depending on how severe it is, hyperparathyroidism can lead to the development of osteoporosis, impaired kidney function, kidney stones, stomach upset and ulcers, increased thirst and increased need to urinate. Again depending on the severity, the treatment of hyperparathyroidism usually involves surgically removing one or more of the overactive parathyroid glands.

Hypoparathyroidism occurs when not enough parathyroid hormone is secreted; it results in abnormally low blood calcium levels, called hypocalcaemia. Hypocalcaemia can produce symptoms such as numbness, tingling and muscle cramps or spasms of the vocal cords.

If the thyroid gland needs to be surgically removed, the surgeon will always attempt to preserve and leave behind the parathyroid glands. Sometimes this is not possible if the surgery is difficult to perform or cancer of the thyroid is extensive. In approximately eight percent of patients who have thyroid surgery, the parathyroid glands do not function properly immediately after surgery. This causes blood calcium levels to drop abnormally low and symptoms usually develop between 24 and 48 hours after surgery. Treatment involves taking calcium orally or intravenously, and sometimes vitamin D is given as well. The doses of calcium given are much higher than found in standard nutritional supplements.

Other diseases associated with Thyroid Disease

Depression

Women experience depression about twice as often as men. There are several hormonal factors that predispose women to depression, including menstrual cycle changes, pregnancy and the postpartum period, as well as menopause. Depression is also a common symptom of having an under active thyroid gland. According to the Thyroid Society, approximately ten to 15 percent of people with depression have an undiagnosed thyroid hormone deficiency[38].

As well as feeling depressed, hypothyroidism typically leads to fatigue, lethargy, a leaden feeling in the limbs, lack of motivation and lack of libido. Unfortunately these symptoms often persist for many years before they are traced to an under active thyroid gland. Obviously there are many possible causes of depression, and thyroid disease is only one of them. If you do experience these symptoms it is vital you see your doctor because depression can be effectively treated; there is no need to continue suffering.

If you do have a thyroid disease and suffer with depression, the following points may help you:

- Have a thyroid function test every six months and make sure your TSH level is between 0.50 and 1 mIU/L. According to research, this range may be needed to effectively alleviate depression in some people.

- Try T3 hormone supplementation. Many people find that their depression improves when they take T3 in addition to T4 hormone replacement.

- Have a blood test for thyroid antibodies. Hypothyroidism caused by autoimmune disease may produce a worse case of depression because the production of autoantibodies further weakens and exhausts the body.

- Consider the use of a prescription antidepressant. This should make you feel much better in a relatively short period of time. Then you will have the motivation to start working on improving your diet and lifestyle.

Thyroid hormone treats the winter blues.

Seasonal Affective Disorder (SAD) is a type of depression that is due to a lack of sunlight in the winter months. Researchers have found that taking thyroid hormone improves symptoms of SAD.

12 people living in Antarctica were studied for one year. Researchers found that during the first four months, the individuals' thyroid hormone levels dropped, along with their mood and performance on mental skills tests. Their body temperature also went down.

Over the next seven months half of the subjects took T3 hormone tablets. At the end of the study, those who took T3 had much better moods and did better in mental and exercise tests. It is thought that living in Antarctica causes the muscles to hoard thyroid hormone to keep the body warmer, at the expense of the brain[39]. Other research has found fluctuations in thyroid hormone levels during winter in temperate climates. Perhaps people who experience SAD should have their T3 hormone levels checked during winter.

Fibromyalgia

People with thyroid disease may be at greater risk of developing fibromyalgia. German researchers studying fibromyalgia patients at a university rheumatology clinic found that many sufferers had significantly lower levels of T3 thyroid hormone[40]. Many researchers believe that a high percentage of fibromyalgia sufferers have undiagnosed thyroid disease. Even if your thyroid condition is adequately being treated with hormone replacement, you need to be tested for thyroid antibodies. Antibodies directed against various organs and tissues promote a lot of inflammation, which can cause aches and pains in the body. Patients with autoimmune thyroid disease are more likely to experience fibromyalgia. Our treatment protocol for autoimmune disease is very effective for reducing fibromyalgia. If you do suffer with fibromyalgia, you must also have a blood test for the following hormones: DHEA-S, oestradiol and free testosterone.

Down's Syndrome

This is the most common chromosomal abnormality in humans and affects approximately one in every 800 births. People with Down's syndrome suffer some degree of intellectual impairment and are at increased risk of several diseases. Many people with Down's syndrome develop autoimmune thyroid disease; mostly hypothyroidism. Coeliac disease (gluten intolerance) is also more common in people with Down's syndrome.

Hodgkin's disease/lymphoma

This is a type of cancer of the lymphatic system that is usually treated with radiation and/or chemotherapy. If the neck area receives radiation, the thyroid gland will be exposed to some. People who have received radiation treatment for Hodgkin's lymphoma are at increased risk of thyroid cancer, thyroid nodules, hyperthyroidism and hypothyroidism.

Kidney disease

People with chronic kidney disease are more at risk of developing hypothyroidism[41].

Hepatitis C

Approximately 30 percent of people with the hepatitis C virus have thyroid antibodies in their bloodstream. This is thought to be due to Interferon alpha and Interleukin-2 therapy.

Breast cancer

There does appear to be a relationship between thyroid disease and breast cancer. A study published in the *Journal of Clinical Endocrinology and Metabolism* compared 102 women with breast cancer (before they started any treatment) and 100 healthy women who lived in the same area. All women had a blood test for TSH, T4, free T3 and thyroid antibodies, as well as a thyroid ultrasound. The study found that the overall presence of thyroid disease was 46 percent in breast cancer patients and 14 percent in women without breast cancer. 27.4 percent of women with breast cancer had a non-toxic (non hormone producing) goitre compared to 11 percent of women in the control group. The prevalence of Hashimoto's thyroiditis was 13.7 percent in breast cancer patients compared to two percent in controls. There was not a significant difference in blood levels of the hormones TSH, T4 or freeT3 in both groups, but the presence of thyroid antibodies (specifically thyroid peroxidase) was much higher in the women with breast cancer. This study raises many questions, but it appears there is a significant relationship between breast cancer and thyroid disease, specifically autoimmune thyroid disease[42].

The importance of iodine to breast health

Most iodine in the body is found in the thyroid gland, but some is also found in breasts. There is a documented association between iodine deficiency and Fibrocystic Breast Disease (FBD); also known as lumpy breasts. FBD occurs in around 60 percent of women between the ages of 30 and 50. It is thought to be influenced by hormonal changes of the menstrual cycle and is aggravated by caffeine. Women with FBD may be more at risk of developing breast cancer. Studies have shown that supplementing with iodine does provide symptom relief for women with FBD. Seafood and seaweed are the richest sources of iodine; perhaps the high intake of these foods by Japanese women, rather than soy is one factor that offers them protection against breast cancer.

Chapter 9

Substances that Affect the Thyroid Gland

M any different substances are able to affect the thyroid gland, causing it to become overactive or under active. This section will also cover substances known to cause thyroid nodules or raise the risk of thyroid cancer.

Medications that affect the thyroid gland

A number of different medications can affect the thyroid gland; both prescription and over the counter drugs. Some medications contain iodine, and in some people with thyroid disease this can cause either hyperthyroidism or hypothyroidism. In general, people with thyroid disease should mostly avoid iodine containing medication. Some over the counter cough and cold remedies contain small amounts of iodine, as well as stimulants such as norepinephrine and neosynephrine. These can adversely affect people with hyperthyroidism. Nutritional supplements containing small amounts of kelp or iodine usually do not cause a problem except in people with hyperthyroidism.

Medications that may interfere with thyroid gland function:

- **Lithium:** This is used in some cases of severe depression and manic depression. Lithium is concentrated by the thyroid and it inhibits the thyroid from using iodine. It also inhibits the thyroid from secreting thyroid hormones. TSH levels may rise due to the low T4 and T3 levels that lithium creates. Up to 60 percent of people taking lithium will develop a goitre[43].

- **Amiodarone:** This medication is used to treat irregular heart beats, or arrhythmias. Brand names of amiodarone include *Aratac, Cardinorm* and *Cordarone*. It is also available as an intreavenous injection. Each amiodarone tablet contains a significant amount of iodine. Approximately ten percent of people taking thyroid hormone medication will be affected by amiodarone; it can cause hypothyroidism or hyperthyroidism. Amiodarone is fat soluble, therefore it can be stored in fatty tissues for weeks or months and continue having effects on the thyroid even after it is discontinued. Amiodarone can cause either hypothyroidism or hyperthyroidism. It is a bigger problem if it causes an overactive thyroid gland.

- **Iodine:** This is found in seaweed, especially kelp, and also the herb bladderwrack (also called Fucus vesiculosis). Some vitamin and mineral supplements contain iodine, as well as some cough and cold preparations. In some people with thyroid disease excess iodine can cause either hypothyroidism or hyperthyroidism.

- **Interferon:** Interferons are proteins made in the body that are required for proper immune function. Interferon is also used as a drug in the treatment of hepatitis C, multiple sclerosis and some types of cancer. Some patients with thyroid disease who receive interferon therapy for another disease may have their thyroid gland affected. It is autoimmune thyroid diseases in particular, such as Hashimoto's thyroiditis and Graves' disease that can be affected by interferon. Interferon beta is sometimes used in the treatment of multiple sclerosis; it can cause hypothyroidism or hyperthyroidism in around a third of patients receiving it[44]. Interferon alpha is used in the treatment of hepatitis C and cancer; it may also produce hypothyroidism or hyperthyroidism which usually improves when therapy is discontinued. Anybody receiving interferon therapy should have their thyroid function tested regularly with a blood test.

- **Glucocorticoids (steroids):** Steroids are often used to treat inflammatory diseases and autoimmune diseases such as arthritis, asthma and other lung diseases, collagen vascular diseases, some types of liver inflammation, some skin diseases and granulomatous diseases. Some examples of steroids used include prednisone, dexamethasone, hydrocortisone and methylprednisone. In high doses, glucocorticoids can inhibit the conversion of T4 into the active form T3; they may also reduce the production of TSH by the pituitary gland. Because they suppress the immune system, glucocorticoids can offer some symptom relief to patients with Hashimoto's thyroiditis, Graves' disease and thyroid eye disease. But because of side effects they can only be used for short periods of time.

- **Oral cholecystographic agents:** These drugs are used for visualisation of the gallbladder during diagnostic procedures. They act to inhibit the conversion of T4 into its active form T3, and also the breakdown of reverse T3 into T2. The iodine in these drugs blocks the release of thyroid hormone from the gland.

- **Aspirin:** A study published in the *Journal of Clinical Endocrinology and Metabolism* has shown that aspirin can decrease blood levels of T4, T3 and TSH[45].

Other drugs that may affect the thyroid gland include:

- Sulfonamides: A type of antibiotic.
- Bexarotene: A drug used for some types of skin tumours.
- Ethionamide: A type of antibiotic.
- Some anticonvulsants

Nutritional supplements that affect the thyroid gland

A number of different vitamins, minerals and other nutrients are required for healthy thyroid function. Many of these act as cofactors, allowing enzyme reactions to occur that are needed for thyroid hormone manufacture. In this section we will look at the nutrients that affect the thyroid gland.

- **Iodine:** This mineral is essential for the production of thyroid hormones. T4 (thyroxine) contains four iodine molecules and T3 (triiodothyronine) contains three iodine molecules. Adults need approximately 150 micrograms of iodine each day in order to produce thyroid hormones. Iodine is mainly found in seafood, seaweed and dairy products. Smaller amounts are found in fruit, vegetables and nuts. If you do not use iodised salt or do not eat seafood three times a week you may not be getting enough iodine in your diet. Iodised salt is sold in the supermarket with a green label, but it does contain aluminium to prevent it from clumping. So it is best to get iodine from natural foods or use iodised sea salt.

Goitrogens, found in foods like cabbage and broccoli can inhibit the absorption of iodine from the stomach and upper part of the small intestine. Cooking mostly inactivates goitrogens. You can read more about goitrogens later in this chapter. Pregnant women should take a 100mcg supplement of iodine daily if they do not consume seafood or dairy products; but not women with pre existing thyroid disease. Taking high doses of iodine (more than 1000mcg per day) will not speed up your metabolism and help you lose weight; it can have the opposite effect and inhibit your production of thyroid hormones.

- **Selenium:** This trace element is essential for thyroid hormone production, activation and metabolism. The thyroid gland contains more selenium per gram than any other tissue in the body. Selenium is required by the enzyme that converts T4 into its active form, T3. Selenium deficiency is associated with a greater risk of cancer, including thyroid cancer. Selenium is also essential for healthy immune system function, and can improve the outcome of autoimmune diseases. The majority of thyroid disease in Australia is autoimmune. Many parts of the world, including Australia and New Zealand have selenium deficient soils; therefore crops grown in these soils will be low in selenium also. The best dietary sources of selenium include Brazil nuts, crab, salmon, poultry, pork and walnuts. It is very hard to obtain adequate selenium through diet alone. It is strongly recommended you take selenium in supplement form in a dose of 100mcg daily.

- **Zinc:** Zinc is required for the function of many enzymes in the body, and it is essential for a healthy immune system. Zinc deficiency has been shown to cause low levels of both T3 and T4 in the bloodstream. Zinc is found in oysters, beef, chicken, dairy products, cashews, almonds and chickpeas.

The following nutrients are also essential for the production and metabolism of thyroid hormones:

- **Copper:** This mineral is needed in small amounts for healthy thyroid gland function. Rats that are fed a copper deficient diet develop low body temperature and reduced T3 hormone levels. Getting enough copper in your diet is easy because it is widely found in seafood, grains, nuts (especially Brazil nuts, almonds and hazelnuts), seeds and cocoa. Small amounts of copper are present in most multi vitamin and mineral supplements. Oestrogen promotes copper retention by the body. Copper and zinc compete with each other for absorption, so it is possible to become copper deficient if you have been taking a high dose zinc supplement for some time.

- **Tyrosine:** This is an amino acid (building block of protein) and is needed for the formation of thyroid hormones. In basic terms, thyroxine (T4) is two molecules of tyrosine with four iodine atoms attached. Tyrosine is widely found in protein foods such as meat, fish, dairy products, eggs, nuts and beans. Having good digestion is important for the absorption of tyrosine. If you do suffer with irritable bowel syndrome or another digestive problem, you may need a digestive enzyme supplement to improve the efficiency of your digestive system.

- **Vitamin A:** Thyroid hormone is required for the conversion of beta carotene into vitamin A in the body. Therefore if you have recently been diagnosed with hypothyroidism you may be deficient in vitamin A. The best sources of vitamin A are animal foods such as eggs, fish, butter (preferably organic) and whole milk (not low fat milk). Cod liver oil supplements are very high in vitamin A. Beta carotene is found in plant foods like carrots, pumpkin and sweet potato.

- **Other nutrients required for a healthy thyroid gland include:**
  - **Vitamin D**
  - **Vitamin B2**
  - **Vitamin B3**
  - **Carnitine**, which is a protein

Herbs that have an effect on the thyroid gland

Several herbs can be used to help in the treatment of thyroid conditions. Most of these herbs affect the thyroid because they are high in iodine; Bugleweed can calm down an overactive thyroid gland.

Bladderwrack

This is also known as Fucus vesiculosus and is a type of brown seaweed that is high in iodine. If your thyroid gland in under active because of a lack of iodine, bladderwrack can help to restore normal thyroid function. If you have an autoimmune thyroid disease or your thyroid gland is overactive, you should avoid high doses of bladderwrack.

Kelp

This is a type of seaweed also known as Laminaria. It is light brown to dark green in colour and is similar to Kombu but is thinner and more tender. Kelp is extremely high in iodine, like most seaweed is. Kelp is sold dehydrated, in flake form, powder form and it is present in some nutritional supplements. Like bladderwrack, it is fine to take kelp as a source of iodine, but it should be avoided by people with autoimmune thyroid disease and an overactive thyroid gland. Like most seaweed, kelp is high in a gel like fibre that absorbs toxins in the digestive tract. Therefore kelp can be useful for detoxifying the body of heavy metals and other toxins.

Guggul

This is a resin produced by the stem of the Commiphora mukul tree. This plant is native to India. Guggul is widely used to lower blood cholesterol and triglyceride levels. Some studies have shown that guggul is able to increase secretion of thyroid hormones and promote the conversion of T4 into its active form T3. Therefore guggul has been used to help an under active thyroid gland.

Bugleweed

This herb is also known as Lycopus virginicus and it is used to help mild cases of hyperthyroidism. A close relative of bugleweed is gypsywort, or European bugleweed (Lycopus europaeus) and it has a similar action. These plants are in the mint family. Bugleweed can reduce the ability of TSH to bind to thyroid cells. This herb should not be taken by people with an under active thyroid gland.

Foods that affect the thyroid gland

Foods containing goitrogens

Goitrogens are substances that interfere with thyroid hormone production, and they can even cause enlargement of the thyroid gland (goitre) if consumed in very large quantities. The following foods contain goitrogens:

- Cruciferous vegetables (eg. Cabbage, broccoli, cauliflower, Brussels sprouts)
- Corn
- Sweet potatoes
- Lima beans
- Soy
- Cassava (tapioca)
- Swede (rutabaga)
- Millet
- Peanuts

Cooking mostly inactivates goitrogens in foods, therefore people with an under active thyroid gland should mainly eat the above foods cooked.

Soy

The effect of soy beans on the thyroid gland is a controversial topic. Soy does contain goitrogens but they will not adversely affect the thyroid gland unless you are consuming large quantities of it, or goitrogens in other foods. If you are consuming enough iodine in your diet, studies have shown that soy should not have a detrimental effect on your thyroid. If you take thyroid hormone replacement medication, you should not eat soy or take soy containing supplements until three hours later. This is because soy can interfere with the absorption of thyroid medication.

Gluten

In susceptible people, gluten is capable of stimulating the immune system to produce autoantibodies. These are antibodies that attack and destroy your own tissues and organs. Any organ or tissue can be affected by these antibodies, and quite commonly it is the thyroid gland. Research has shown that a high percentage of people with autoimmune thyroid disease (Graves' disease, Hashimoto's thyroiditis or other thyroiditis) are gluten intolerant. Gluten intolerance is also known as coeliac disease. Coeliac disease typically causes digestive symptoms such as bloating, diarrhoea and abdominal cramps. However, it is now known that a large percentage of people with coeliac disease experience no digestive symptoms at all; the disease affects their body in a more silent and sinister way. If you have a thyroid condition you should be tested for coeliac disease and follow a gluten free diet under the supervision of your healthcare practitioner. See chapter eight for more information about coeliac disease.

Gluten is found primarily in the following foods:

- Wheat
- Rye
- Oats
- Barley
- Triticale
- Spelt
- kamut

Dairy products

In some people, the protein in cow's milk is irritating to the immune system. Casein is the name of a protein found in cow's milk and it can promote excessive mucus production and histamine release. If you have an autoimmune thyroid condition you should be avoiding dairy products. If you have thyroid cysts or nodules you should also be avoiding dairy products because they can aggravate those conditions. Dairy products include cow's milk and all foods containing it, such as cheese, butter, cream, ice-cream and yoghurt.

Chemicals and pesticides that affect the thyroid gland

A number of different chemicals in the environment have a detrimental effect on the thyroid gland.

Fluoride

Fluoride is in a group of chemicals called halogens; other halogens include chlorine, iodine and bromine. Fluoride can cause problems with the thyroid gland because it is chemically very similar to iodine; therefore it is able to displace iodine in the thyroid gland, interfering with thyroid hormone production.

Between the 1930s and 1970s, fluoride was used by European and South American doctors as a drug for the treatment of hyperthyroidism. Fluoride suppressed the production of thyroid hormones, therefore reducing hormone levels back down to normal. The problem is fluoride still does suppress the thyroid. Currently fluoride is added to the drinking water in many developed countries, including Australia and many parts of the USA. Fluoride is added in a concentration of one part per million with the intention of reducing dental caries. Fluoride is also found in many different foods, medications and chemicals, plus it can be absorbed through the skin when we bathe in fluoridated water. The frightening fact is that many people today are consuming fluoride in quantities exceeding those known to suppress the thyroid gland.

Fluoride accumulates in our body; we are never able to excrete all of it. Therefore, the older you are, the more fluoride you will have in your body. Fluoride slows down the production of T3 and T4 hormones in the thyroid gland by interfering with enzymes required for their production. Fluoride also inhibits the secretion of TSH by the pituitary gland; therefore the thyroid is not stimulated to release as much thyroid hormone. Fluoride also competes with TSH for receptor sites on the thyroid gland, therefore less TSH stimulates the thyroid and less T3 and T4 hormones are made.

Why is fluoride added to drinking water?

In some areas the drinking water naturally already contains some fluoride; in other areas it is deliberately added. Fluoride is added to the water supply at a quantity of one part per million with the aim of reducing dental caries. This is a highly debated topic as there are studies to support its benefits and other studies that have shown it offers no benefits at all in preventing tooth decay. A much safer way to prevent dental caries is to practice good dental hygiene and avoid eating sugar.

Excessive ingestion of fluoride can cause problems unrelated to the thyroid. In young children excess fluoride can cause dental fluorosis; this is a mottling of teeth that occurs from defective enamel formation. A very high fluoride intake can also lead to skeletal fluorosis, a condition where excessive fluoride is deposited in the skeleton, weakening the bones. This mainly occurs in developing nations.

Sources of fluoride

It is very easy to get a lot of fluoride into your body because it is found in so many places, such as:

- **Drinking water.** Fluoride is added to the water supply of all Australian capital cities except Brisbane. It was first introduced in 1953 in Beaconsfield, Tasmania. Now almost two thirds of Australians receive fluoridated drinking water. To find out if fluoride is added to your water supply contact the Environmental Protection Agency in your state. If infant formula is made up using fluoridated water it exposes the infant to between 100 and 200 times more fluoride than breast milk.

- **Toothpaste.** Most conventional toothpaste contains fluoride; some herbal toothpastes are fluoride free.

- **Tea.** Tea accumulates more fluoride than any other edible plant; this is mainly through the soil and air.

- **Fluoride pesticides.** Sodium aluminium fluoride is a very common pesticide used on more than 30 different fruits and vegetables.

- **Soft drinks/carbonated beverages.**
- **Some medications.** The selective serotonin reuptake inhibitor (SSRI) antidepressants contain fluoride. Some of these include Prozac, Zoloft and Aropax.

The average person will not be harmed by fluoride unless they consume excessive quantities. If you do have a thyroid condition, or thyroid problems run in your family, it is best to try and avoid fluoride. If your tap water contains fluoride you could purchase bottled spring water; many brands do not contain fluoride. Most water filters do not remove fluoride; you would need a reverse osmosis filter to remove it. Fluoride will do more harm to your thyroid gland if you are iodine deficient. All thyroid toxic substances do more harm in iodine deficient individuals. It is interesting to note that much of Western Europe has abandoned water fluoridation over concerns for public health; around 98 percent of Europe is free of fluoridated water.

Chlorine and bromine

Chlorine and bromine are also halogens, meaning they have a similar structure to iodine and fluoride, and therefore can interfere with thyroid function. Chlorine is widely used in water purification, disinfectants and bleach. It is also used in paper production, paints, plastics and solvents. Animal studies have shown that chlorine suppresses thyroid hormone release. A study conducted in Quebec, Canada found that exposure to chlorine dioxide in drinking water did mildly suppress thyroid function in infants[46].

Bromine is a reddish brown liquid that evaporates easily at room temperature. The gas has a suffocating smell and the name comes from the Greek word *brómos*, meaning stench. Bromine is used to make many products used in industry and agriculture. It is used to make flameproofing agents, water purification compounds, dyes, photographic products and some medications. Bromine is also used in brominated vegetable oil which is used as an emulsifier in many soft drinks.

The main way many people are exposed to bromine is through Brominated Flame Retardants (BFRs). They are used to prevent combustion and inhibit the spread of flames in a number of products including computer monitors and casings; the interior of new cars; televisions; whitegoods; mobile phones; carpet; polyurethane foam in furniture and bedding, and other products. Bromine easily outgases into the environment and it has been found in human blood, liver, fat and breast milk. Brominated Flame Retardants have been shown to disrupt thyroid hormones, mimic oestrogen and promote cancer.

The effects of pesticides on the thyroid gland

Several pesticides have the ability to disrupt normal thyroid gland function. In a September 1998 review article in the journal *Thyroid*, almost 90 separate compounds were identified as having thyroid disrupting properties. Some of these chemicals promote the formation of thyroid nodules or thyroid cancer; some even have the ability to stimulate the production of thyroid antibodies, promoting autoimmune thyroid disease. We will look at different chemicals and their effects on the thyroid gland now:

Chlorpyrifos

This is an organophosphate insecticide that is commonly used in indoor and lawn pest control. It is registered for use in Australia on a wide range of crops. Some brand names of chlorpyrifos include *Dursban, Lorsban, Stipend, Empire* and *Eradex*. Research has shown that exposure to chlorpyrifos can cause immune system disorders in humans. Scientists at the Department of Health, California State University found that people exposed to this pesticide developed autoantibodies against smooth muscle, parietal cells (stomach lining), brush border (small intestine lining), the thyroid gland, myelin and ANA (anti nuclear antibodies)[47].

Amitrole

Amitrole is classed as a triazole herbicide. It works by inhibiting carotenoid synthesis in plants, therefore is used to control weeds. It is used for the control of weeds in orchards, vineyards, eucalyptus and pine plantations, wheat and barley crops and is used to control weeds on roadsides and drains.

Amitrole is known to be an antithyroid agent; it increases the release of TSH by the pituitary gland and therefore has goitrogenic effects (stimulates enlargement of the thyroid). Amitrole is known to cause tumours in the thyroid, pituitary gland and liver in experimental animals. Pesticide workers exposed to amitrole have an increased incidence of tumours[48].

Pyrethrins and Pyrethroids

Pyrethrins are insecticides derived from the extract of chrysanthemum flowers. Pyrethroids are synthetic versions of pyrethrins that are made in a laboratory. Pyrethrins and pyrethroids kill insects because they are nerve poisons. These pesticides are widely used and they are found in indoor fly sprays and bug bombs, human head lice treatments and pet flea sprays.

Research has shown that pyrethroids raise TSH levels and suppress both T4 and T3 thyroid hormones. Chronic exposure can cause the thyroid gland to enlarge, to form cysts and non-cancerous thyroid tumours. Large quantities of pyrethroids have been used in the USA to control the mosquito borne West Nile Virus. Aerial pesticide spraying has been carried out in many areas of the USA, particularly New York and Boston[49, 50].

Grave consequences of heavy pesticide use in Tasmania

In the ten years between 1994 and 2004, the land converted from farms and native forests to monoculture tree plantations in Tasmania increased almost fourfold. Total land covered by tree monocultures is now 207, 000 hectares. Monoculture tree plantations rely heavily on pesticides. Pesticides are dispersed high over tree canopies; from there they drift onto household rooves that collect rainwater for consumption. Creeks and rivers, as well as town water catchments all collect pesticides.

This practice is believed to be a major contributor to the skyrocketing rates of cancer in Tasmania. Between 1980 and 1999 Tasmania experienced:

- A 67 percent increase in non-Hodgkin's lymphoma.

- An 86.4 percent increase in prostate cancer.

- A whopping 273.4 percent increase in thyroid cancer[51].

Other chemicals known to disrupt the thyroid gland

Dioxins and **PCBs (Polychlorinated biphenyls)** are both by-products of PVC (polyvinyl chloride) production, industrial bleaching and incineration. These compounds are persistent organic pollutants, meaning they do not break down readily; they remain in the environment for many years and accumulate in human and animal tissues. PCBs and dioxins are known to cause immune system disorders, reproductive and developmental disorders, as well as cancer. PCBs affect thyroid function by reducing levels of T4 thyroid hormone.

EBDCs are a class of fungicides. They are used on numerous crops including root and leafy vegetables, fruits and cereals. These chemicals inhibit iodine uptake by the thyroid and can cause goitre. The body breaks down EBDCs into ethylenethiourea, which the EPA classes as a thyroid carcinogen. EBDCs lower thyroid hormone levels in rats and inhibit thyroid peroxidase; the enzyme required for the synthesis of T3 and T4[52].

Perchlorate is a chemical that has been detected in drinking water and milk in 35 states in the USA. It is an oxidiser in rocket fuel and is also found in airbags, fireworks and some fertilisers. It is used extensively in the pyrotechnics industry. Perchlorate is known to reduce the ability of the thyroid to absorb iodine from the bloodstream. This is a worry since modern day diets are deficient in iodine already.

Heavy Metals and the Thyroid Gland

Unfortunately most of us live in a highly polluted world. Every day tons of chemicals, including heavy metals are released into the environment. We absorb heavy metals from the food we eat, water we drink, air we breathe, through our skin and in various other ways. The definition of a heavy metal is a chemical element with a specific gravity that is at least five times the specific gravity of water. Specific gravity is a measure of density of a given amount of a substance when it is compared to the same quantity of water. In small amounts, some heavy metals are essential for good health and we refer to them as trace elements; these include zinc, iron, copper and manganese.

A heavy metal becomes toxic when it is not metabolised by the body, but rather builds up in tissues. Heavy metals can create health problems in a variety of ways: they may act as a direct poison on specific organs; they increase oxidative stress in our bodies by acting as free radicals; and they can act as anti-nutrients, blocking the actions of essential minerals in the body.

The following heavy metals have a detrimental effect on the thyroid gland:

Mercury

Mercury is emitted through the earth's crust and volcanic emissions. Large amounts of mercury are used in the mining industry, paper industry and chloralkali plants (chemical manufacturing plants). Mercury that enters the atmosphere travels to all parts of the world by winds and returns to the earth in rainfall. In this way large quantities of mercury accumulate in the oceans and other bodies of water, entering fish and other aquatic life.

How mercury gets into your body

Mercury can enter the body via vapor inhalation, injection, ingestion and absorption through the skin. In the past, mercury was a vital component of many medications, including laxatives, diuretics, antiseptics and antibacterial agents. It was also added to paint as a fungicide until 1990. These days the biggest source of mercury is environmental pollution because agricultural products and fossil fuels both contain it. People commonly get exposed to mercury in one of three ways:

- **Occupational exposure**. Mercury is used in battery, thermometer and barometer manufacturing. It is used in fungicides and was used in paint before 1990 to prevent mildew. Dentists regularly use mercury in amalgam fillings and it is still used in some antiseptic agents in medicine. Mercury is currently used as a preservative in most vaccines, called thiomersal.

- **Fish consumption**. Mercury accumulates in fish mainly from coal-fired power plants that release mercury containing emissions into the air, and these emissions eventually end up in the oceans. Mercury gets concentrated in fish and moves up the food chain. Larger fish have more mercury in their bodies which they obtain through eating lots of smaller fish. According to the US Environmental Protection Agency, one in six pregnant women has blood levels of mercury high enough to cause foetal damage.

- **Mercury amalgam fillings.** These have been used in dentistry for almost 160 years. They are composed of 50% mercury, 34-38% silver, 12-14% tin, 1-2% copper and 0-1% zinc. In Australia today, around 75% of all single tooth fillings are made of this material. The theory has always been that mercury is bound up with the other metals and therefore does not leach out of the fillings. However, research has shown that mercury is released from the fillings every time we chew, swallow and even breathe. As the mercury is released, it interacts with body chemicals and bacteria to form methylmercury, the most toxic form of the metal.

Symptoms of mercury toxicity

Mercury in the body is highly fat soluble and becomes distributed throughout the body. It especially accumulates in the brain, kidneys, liver, hair and skin. Mercury is able to cross the blood brain barrier and placenta and can enter red blood cells.

The symptoms of mercury toxicity can be mild and varied so they often go undiagnosed. They can mimic several other diseases; that's why it's important to consider whether you have been exposed to mercury in one of the three ways listed above. Possible symptoms of mercury toxicity include:

- Tremors
- Gingivitis (inflammation of the gums)
- Insomnia
- Memory loss
- Emotional instability
- Depression
- Blushing
- Uncontrolled perspiration
- Anorexia (loss of appetite)
- Headache
- Excessive salivation
- Ataxia (loss of coordination)

Acrodynia is the name of the disease caused by chronic mercury toxicity. The word literally means pain in the extremities, such as the hands and feet. Acrodynia is also known as Pink Disease and symptoms include pink discolouration of the hands and feet, irritability, photophobia (sensitivity to light), and polyneuritis (painful, inflamed nerves).

How mercury affects the thyroid gland

Mercury can promote hypothyroidism because it reduces the thyroid gland's production of T4 and it also inhibits the conversion of T4 into the active form T3. Mercury is a selenium antagonist and selenium is required by the enzyme that converts T4 into T3[53]. Mercury also disturbs the immune system and promotes the production of autoantibodies that are involved in autoimmune thyroid disease.

Pregnant women with high mercury levels may be placing their unborn baby at risk. It is well known that mercury is toxic to the foetus and can cause spontaneous abortion, developmental delays or retardation. However, mercury can also deprive the foetus of thyroid hormones. Mercury can inhibit T3 hormone production in the mother and foetus, placing the foetus at risk of developmental delays due to thyroid hormone deficiency.

Cadmium

Cadmium is a by-product of the mining and smelting of zinc and lead. It is used in nickel-cadmium batteries, paint pigments and PVC plastics. Cadmium is found in many insecticides, fungicides and fertilizers; in fact the most widely used fertilizer in Australia, Superphosphate is high in cadmium. Cadmium is also present in cigarettes, motor oil and exhaust. Between 15 and 50 percent of the cadmium in your body gets there through inhalation. Symptoms of chronic cadmium toxicity include hair loss, anaemia, migraines, arthritis, learning disorders, osteoporosis, loss of taste and smell and poor appetite. Animal studies have shown that alcohol consumption can increase the absorption and accumulation of cadmium in the body[54].

How cadmium affects the thyroid gland

Cadmium blocks the action of selenium and zinc and can deplete levels of these minerals in your body. Both selenium and zinc are required for the conversion of T4 to T3 thyroid hormone; therefore cadmium can produce an under active thyroid gland[55].

Lead

There are several ways you can be exposed to lead. The main sources of lead are leaded gasoline, lead-based paint, lead batteries, rubber products, glass and lead contaminated water. Lead has been removed from most paint and leaded fuel has mostly been discontinued. Older homes will still contain lead based paint; the lead can be ingested as flakes or inhaled in dust.

In Australia, Broken Hill is the city with the highest levels of lead poisoning, followed by Mt. Isa, Lake Macquarie and Port Pirie. This is due to mining and smelting activity in these towns. In 2005, 25 percent of children in Broken Hill were found to have blood lead levels higher than the national safety standard of 10 micrograms per deciliter of blood. Some children recorded between 60 and 70 mcg/dL, and the occasional child had 100mcg/dL of lead in their blood. These extreme levels are being attributed to 130 years of mining in the city centre and outskirts; much of which was done in open cut mines. The high levels of dust in the town contain a lot of lead which gets into people's homes and is inhaled. Since then the city has changed to underground mining and residents have implemented measures to keep the dust levels at bay. Fluoride in drinking water increases the absorption of lead present in water.

Lead poisoning is associated with many negative health effects such as brain dysfunction in children, neurobehavioral changes in adults (including a reduction in IQ and cognitive abilities, and personality changes), high blood pressure and chronic kidney disease. High blood lead levels have been shown to suppress the conversion of T4 into the active thyroid hormone T3. Research done on people occupationally exposed to lead has proven this[56].

The effects of radiation on the thyroid gland

The thyroid gland is sensitive to all types of radiation: ionising radiation such as through X-rays; fission products used to produce nuclear energy; as well as radioactive iodine (I-131). The thyroid gland takes up large quantities of iodine from the bloodstream and it cannot distinguish between regular iodine and radioactive iodine. So most people exposed to radioactive iodine will accumulate large amounts of it in their thyroid.

Radiation exposure can cause a variety of thyroid diseases: an under active thyroid, thyroid nodules and thyroid cancer.

How much radiation is required to affect the thyroid?

Apart from some genetic diseases, radiation exposure is currently the only officially accepted cause of thyroid cancer. It is not known what the minimum dose required to cause thyroid disease is. Radioactive iodine is used both medicinally (to treat hyperthyroidism and thyroid cancer), as well as diagnostically (in thyroid scans). People receiving radioactive iodine as treatment for thyroid cancer typically receive between 50 and 150 gray.

People who receive radioactive iodine as part of a nuclear thyroid scan typically receive only 0.5 to 1.5 gray.

Some people exposed to radiation from the Chernobyl accident, as well as Hiroshima and Nagasaki bomb survivors were exposed to much more radiation. Some of the children exposed to radiation from the Chernobyl accident received 50 grays of radiation. The higher the dose of radiation, the more likely thyroid cancer is to develop.

Who is most susceptible to radiation induced thyroid disease?

Children are far more susceptible to radiation induced thyroid disease than adults. The younger a person is during exposure, the greater the risk of problems developing. People who are iodine deficient are far more likely to develop radiation induced disease. If you have an adequate amount of iodine in your thyroid gland because you eat iodine rich foods, your thyroid gland will be "full" and will not take up as much radioactive iodine if you are exposed to it. It is well known that taking a potassium iodide supplement immediately before or after exposure to radioactive iodine (such as through a nuclear accident) will greatly reduce the risk of developing thyroid cancer. Unfortunately many of the areas surrounding the Chernobyl nuclear power plant were iodine deficient.

Risk of thyroid cancer in Hiroshima and Nagasaki atomic bomb survivors

Long term follow up of Hiroshima and Nagasaki atomic bomb survivors has found that the risk of thyroid cancer remains high long after exposure. Research published in the *Journal of the American Medical Association* studied over 4000 survivors 55 to 58 years after the bombing. The average age of study participants was 70 and 67 percent of them were women. People who received high levels of radiation were compared with those who received less. Investigators checked for incidence of thyroid cancer, benign thyroid nodules and cysts, as well as autoimmune thyroid disease.

The study found that:

- 32 percent of men and 51 percent of women had a thyroid disease.

- 2.2 percent of people had thyroid cancer. The incidence was higher in those who received more radiation.

- Benign thyroid nodules were more common in people who received a high amount of radiation.

- There was no increased incidence of autoimmune thyroid disease.

- In this group, radiation exposure was believed to account for 37 percent of thyroid cancers, 31 percent of benign thyroid nodules and 25 percent of thyroid cysts[57].

Effects of radioactive iodine on other types of cancer

Some studies have shown that patients exposed to radioactive iodine for the treatment of hyperthyroidism or thyroid cancer are at increased risk of other cancers. According to the National Cancer Institute's Surveillance, Epidemiology, and End Results (SEER) database, women between the ages of 30 and 34 who were treated with radioactive iodine for thyroid cancer are at high risk of developing breast cancer. The breast cancer may develop between five and 20 years later[58]. This is probably because some iodine is stored in the breasts and regular iodine can be a remedy for breast cysts, (thought to increase the risk of breast cancer). Therefore radioactive iodine can accumulate in breast tissue also. Other studies have shown that there is an increased risk of cancer of the small intestine following radioactive treatment for hyperthyroidism[59].

How smoking cigarettes affects the thyroid gland

Many people believe that cigarette smoking only affects the lungs and throat. This is not true; cigarettes contain toxins that affect each part of the body. Smoking significantly increases the risk of developing thyroid problems. A study published in the *Archives of Internal Medicine* recruited 132 pairs of twins. It found that smoking cigarettes caused a three to five fold increase in the risk of all types of thyroid disease. This was especially so for autoimmune diseases (eg. Graves' disease and Hashimoto's thyroiditis)[60].

Smokers are more likely to develop an enlarged thyroid gland, and are twice as likely to develop Graves' hyperthyroidism. It is also known that smokers are more likely to develop thyroid eye disease in association with Graves' disease; they are also far less responsive to treatment for eye disease than non-smokers[61].

Why does smoking affect the thyroid gland?

Cigarettes contain thousands of different chemicals, many of them having as yet unknown effects on the body. Cigarettes contain a significant amount of the heavy metal cadmium. Cadmium can cause an under active thyroid gland by inhibiting the conversion of T4 into its active form T3. Cigarettes also contain cyanide, which is converted into thiocyanate. This compound acts as an anti-thyroid agent by blocking iodine uptake and the manufacture of thyroid hormones.

There are obviously also compounds in cigarettes that irritate the immune system and stimulate the production of autoantibodies which lead to the development of autoimmune disease.

The effects of oestrogen and adrenal hormones on the thyroid gland

A number of different hormones can affect the function of the thyroid gland, in particular the sex hormones and hormones secreted by the adrenal gland.

Oestrogen dominance and the thyroid gland

All thyroid conditions are much more common in women, and it has long been thought that female hormones are responsible for this.

> The main function of thyroid hormones is to convert the calories in food into useable energy for the body.

Oestrogen functions to store energy as fat, therefore these two hormones have opposing actions. Oestrogen has many other functions, including breast growth and thickening the lining of the uterus. Progesterone has opposing actions to oestrogen and acts as a check or balancer on oestrogen. It prevents oestrogen from having an excessive or dominant effect on the body.

Oestrogen dominance is an extremely common condition in women. This is where not enough progesterone is produced in the body to counteract the effects of oestrogen. It is very prevalent now for several reasons: women are having fewer children and having them at a later age, (large amounts of progesterone are produced during pregnancy); stress and nutritional deficiencies can impair progesterone production; and many chemicals in today's world act as xeno-estrogens, (they are not oestrogen but fool the body into thinking they are). Symptoms of oestrogen dominance can include PMS, swollen breasts, bloating, mood swings, sugar cravings, heavy, painful periods, endometriosis, menstrual migraines, loss of libido, short menstrual cycles and fibroids. Oestrogen dominance is often at its worst during the peri-menopausal years, because this is when progesterone levels markedly decline. Quite often thyroid problems first surface around the same time.

It is known that high levels of oestrogen block the effect of thyroid hormones and can result in hypothyroidism. This is thought to be mainly because oestrogen stimulates greater production of thyroid binding globulin; a protein that binds with thyroxine in the bloodstream and makes it inactive. Therefore, oestrogen excess causes lower amounts of free thyroxine in the bloodstream. Thyroid binding globulin levels usually increase during pregnancy and oestrogen administration (such as in the oral contraceptive pill and hormone replacement therapy), and during the acute phase of infectious hepatitis. This will result in lower levels of free T4.

Oestrogen excess also stimulates the body to retain copper. Copper and zinc antagonise each other, so high oestrogen levels can result in zinc deficiency. Zinc is important in thyroid gland function and is needed for the conversion of T4 into T3. Therefore high copper levels can interfere with the production and utilisation of thyroid hormones.

Women who have hypothyroidism and are taking thyroid hormone usually need to have their dose increased when they begin taking oestrogen, such as in hormone replacement therapy (HRT) or the oral contraceptive pill. If you have an under active thyroid gland and have recently commenced taking oestrogen therapy, it is essential to have a blood test for your TSH as well as free T4 and free T3 six weeks after starting oestrogen.

Correcting oestrogen dominance is an essential component in the treatment of thyroid disease. There are several things you can do for yourself, or use progesterone creams that require a doctor's prescription. For more information see chapter ten.

The adrenal glands and the thyroid

An adrenal hormone imbalance can often be associated with a thyroid gland disorder. There are two adrenal glands which are pyramid shaped and roughly the size of a Brazil nut. The adrenal glands sit on top of each kidney. Each adrenal gland is composed of two segments: the medulla, which is the inner part of the gland, and the cortex, which is the outer part.

The adrenal medulla secretes adrenalin and noradrenalin; both of these hormones are primarily released in response to stress. The adrenal cortex consists of three different regions, each of which produces a different group of hormones; these include aldosterone, cortisol and sex hormones (including DHEA and pregnenolone).

Adrenal exhaustion

This is a condition that usually occurs after prolonged intense stress, both emotional and physical. It may also be brought on by nutritional deficiencies, excessive exercise, sleep deprivation and overwork.

Symptoms of adrenal exhaustion can include the following:

- Fatigue and exhaustion
- Unrefreshing sleep, or waking up fatigued
- Feeling most energetic in the evening
- Hypoglycaemia
- Feeling faint
- Low blood pressure, especially when standing up quickly
- Cravings for sweet or salty foods
- Loss of libido
- Feeling rundown and catching infections frequently
- Tired and achy muscles
- Fibromyalgia
- Depression
- Feeling stressed and easily overwhelmed
- Difficulty concentrating, foggy brain
- Sensitivity to cold

Many of the symptoms of adrenal exhaustion are the same as hypothyroidism. This is important to remember because some patients who do not feel better after taking thyroid hormone replacement may in fact have adrenal exhaustion. If you have an under active thyroid gland and still experience some of these symptoms, it is important to have your adrenal hormones tested.

Chapter 10

The Nutritional Treatment of Thyroid Disease

This chapter describes in detail our treatment protocol for patients with thyroid conditions. It is a six point program. It is most beneficial for autoimmune thyroid conditions such as Hashimoto's thyroiditis and Graves' disease, but will reduce your risk of all thyroid diseases, including thyroid cancer.

1. Treat Autoimmune Disease

The word "auto" means self in Greek. An autoimmune disease is where the immune system mistakenly attacks your own body, targeting your own cells, tissues and organs. Autoimmune diseases are extremely common, and many people do not even realise that their condition is an autoimmune disease. They are more common in women than men and especially common during a woman's childbearing years. Many people have autoantibodies in their bloodstream but have not yet developed full blown autoimmune disease.

Who is more likely to develop an autoimmune disease?

The genes you have inherited from your parents contribute to your susceptibility for developing an autoimmune disease. Some autoimmune diseases run in families, where several family members have the same condition. In other cases, several family members have an autoimmune disease but it is not the same one; for instance one person may have lupus, another may have rheumatoid arthritis and another may have type 1 diabetes. Having an autoimmune disease in your family is no guarantee that you will develop one yourself. Something is needed to trigger off the disease; potential triggers include stress, a viral infection, food allergies or intolerances, nutritional deficiencies or pregnancy.

Autoimmune disease is the most common cause of thyroid gland disorders in the Western world. Hashimoto's thyroiditis, Graves' disease, postpartum thyroiditis, and possibly other forms of thyroiditis are all autoimmune diseases.

> Many people who take thyroid medication don't even realise they have an autoimmune disease.

They focus on their thyroid gland and don't realise that improving their immune system can help the symptoms of hypothyroidism such as fatigue, fluid retention and weight excess.

Our program for autoimmune disease involves the following two points:

a) A bowel detox

b) A liver detox

a) The Bowel Detox

The purpose of the bowel detox is to treat leaky gut syndrome; this will be discussed in more detail in the section that follows. Leaky gut syndrome is thought to be the origin and aggravating factor of most autoimmune conditions.

Your digestive tract is the foundation of your health. This makes sense because it is where you obtain the nutrients from the food you eat and excrete toxins that would be harmful to your body if left to remain. The health of your liver and immune system is directly affected by the health of your digestive tract. Many people worry about the chemicals and toxins they are exposed to in the outside world; but the fact is that a far greater quantity of toxins can be generated inside your own body if you have poor digestion. Toxins can build up inside your digestive tract and leach out into the rest of your body. Toxins in the gut also create a great deal of inflammation in the body, and it is inflammation that produces most of the damage in autoimmune disease.

Most people with an autoimmune disease have at least one food allergy or intolerance which is contributing to the disease.

What causes food sensitivities?

In a well functioning digestive system, food is broken down into its smaller molecular components and then passes through the gut wall into the bloodstream or lymphatic system, then to the liver. However, food can sometimes make its way through the gut wall in a larger, partially digested state. Once in the bloodstream, the immune system views these food molecules as foreign particles and mounts an immune reaction against them. Antibodies and inflammatory chemicals are then released.

Sometimes an immediate, acute allergic reaction can occur, such as in people allergic to peanuts or strawberries. Other times the reaction is much more subtle and delayed, so that it becomes very hard to identify the foods at fault. The delayed reactions can be responsible for symptoms such as chronic fatigue syndrome, irritable bowel syndrome, excess mucus and chronic skin problems. If the immune system is hyper stimulated like this long term, the likelihood of producing antibodies that attack and destroy your own body is increased in genetically susceptible individuals.

What is leaky gut syndrome?

Leaky gut syndrome is thought to be a major contributing factor in the development of autoimmune disease.

The lining of the small intestine is designed to allow nutrients we have digested to be absorbed into the bloodstream or lymphatic system. Many kinds of beneficial bacteria and yeasts live there, helping us to digest and absorb nutrients. A leaky gut occurs when the mucous lining of the gut has become more porous than it should be. This allows undigested food molecules, bacteria, fungi, metals and toxic substances to gain entry into the bloodstream. These toxins travel straight to the liver, inflaming it, and then spill out into the bloodstream where they irritate the immune system. It can cause the immune system to spill out antibodies and inflammatory chemicals. People with leaky gut syndrome always have an imbalance between good and bad bacteria in their digestive tract. This will encourage the overgrowth of Candida, which can lead to fungal infections elsewhere in the body, producing thrush, jock itch or athlete's foot.

What causes leaky gut syndrome?

Each of the following factors can cause leaky gut syndrome:

- Food allergies and intolerances

- Stress

- Overuse of medications such as antibiotics, steroids and non-steroidal anti inflammatory drugs such as aspirin, ibuprofen and naproxen.

- Poor diet high in sugar, refined carbohydrates and processed foods (eg. White bread, sweets, soft drinks).

- High alcohol consumption.

- Food poisoning and gastrointestinal infections, which deplete good gut bacteria.

- Nutritional deficiencies.

The role of gluten and dairy products

Gluten is the protein found in wheat, rye, oats, barley, spelt, kamut and other foods. People who are gluten intolerant do not digest this protein adequately; it is able to slip through the intestinal lining and stimulate an immune response. Gluten intolerance, also known as coeliac disease is a very common and under diagnosed condition. Research has shown that a high percentage of people with autoimmune thyroid disease have undiagnosed gluten intolerance (coeliac disease). Adhering to a strict gluten free diet can halt the production of thyroid autoantibodies.

Dairy products, including milk, cheese, yoghurt, ice-cream and all other foods containing casein (milk protein) also create immune system problems for many people. Milk protein is difficult to digest and can encourage the production of mucus and histamine by immune cells.

Bowel detox for autoimmune disease instructions

The bowel detox will run for approximately eight weeks. During this time you must follow a gluten free diet and also a dairy free diet. You will also need to avoid any food you feel unwell after eating and suspect you may have an allergy or intolerance to. Below you will find a description of the gluten free diet and dairy free diet.

GLUTEN FREE DIET

Approximately 1 in 133 people are gluten intolerant. Half of these people do not experience gastro-intestinal symptoms. Gluten intolerance can compromise your immune system, making you more likely to develop allergies and autoimmune diseases.

All foods containing gluten need to be eliminated. These include wheat, rye, triticale, oats, barley, spelt, kamut and the many foods that contain these grains. Non-gluten grains you can eat include rice, corn, buckwheat, quinoa and amaranth. When baking, you can use flour made from the non-gluten grains mentioned above, as well as flour made from arrowroot, tapioca, soy beans and peas. There are many gluten free baking mixes available from health food stores and supermarkets.

Bread, Pastry and Cereals

GLUTEN FREE FOODS

• Gluten free bread, biscuits and baking mixes.
• Plain rice and corn cakes, buckwheat crispbread.

• Puffed rice and corn, gluten free muesli and cereals.
• Gluten free pasta, vermicelli made from rice or mung beans. Sago, tapioca.

• Flour: Corn/maize flour (check labels – only 100% corn flour is allowed). Potato flour, rice flour, polenta.

GLUTEN CONTAINING

• Ordinary bread, bread rolls, soy & linseed bread, rye bread, scones, muffins, waffles, bagels.

• All other breakfast cereals including rice bubbles and corn flakes (they contain malt extract which is derived from barley). All porridge and bran.

• Ordinary pasta, egg pasta, soy pasta and noodles.
• Custard powder, semolina, cous cous, burghal. Most corn flour is 70% wheat.

• Baking powder unless it's gluten free (eg. Wards). Holy bread, pretzels, most chips/crisps.

Milk and Milk Products

Dairy products must be avoided for the duration of the detox and should not be consumed by people with autoimmune disease. This list is simply to make you aware of which dairy products contain gluten, and which are gluten free.

GLUTEN FREE FOODS

• All milk – evaporated, condensed, powdered. Most yoghurts – plain and flavoured.

• All cheese.

• Milk puddings made without added flour or custard powder.

• Some ice-cream.

GLUTEN CONTAINING

• Custard made with custard powder, rice pudding made with "wheaten corn flour".

• Flavoured milk drinks, esp. malted milk eg. Milo, Ovaltine.

• White sauce, cheese sauce thickened with flour.

• Ice-cream containing cake or biscuit crumbs or sauces or maltodextrin.

• Ice-cream cones/wafers.

Fats

GLUTEN FREE FOODS

• All except wheat germ oil.

GLUTEN CONTAINING

• Wheat germ oil.

Soups

GLUTEN FREE FOODS

• Clear soups and those thickened with rice, split peas, arrowroot or gluten free corn flour.

GLUTEN CONTAINING

• Soups thickened with wheat flour, barley (in "soup mix"), noodles or pasta.

Beverages

GLUTEN FREE FOODS

• Tea, coffee, dandelion beverage, cocoa, milk, cordial, soft drinks.

• All distilled alcohol & alcohol made from grapes – eg. Wine, port.

GLUTEN CONTAINING

• Malted milk drinks, eg. Milo, Ovaltine, Aktavite.

• Most coffee substitutes, soy milk containing malt or maltodextrin (derived from wheat).

• Beer, ale, lager.

Condiments

GLUTEN FREE FOODS

• Sauces – most tomato sauce, most vinegar (except malt), honey, jam, nut butters, tahini, plain potato crisps, gelatine, jelly, agar, psyllium, slippery elm, meringue made with corn flour, gluten free baking power and custard powder, tamari, rice malt, carob.

• Wheat derived glucose syrup (in confectionary) is gluten free.

GLUTEN CONTAINING

• Malt vinegar, soy sauce, oyster sauce, fish sauce, some baking powder, mixed seasonings.

• Vegemite and other brands of malt extract, mayonnaise containing flour or thickener.

• Lollies containing wheat starch.

• Foods containing modified food starch.

Vegetables/Salads

GLUTEN FREE FOODS

- All fresh, frozen, canned.

GLUTEN CONTAINING

- Vegetables prepared with cheese sauce thickened with wheat flour. Vegetables with breadcrumbs or gravy.

- Tabouli, Caesar salad or salad dressed with malt vinegar.

Fruits

GLUTEN FREE FOODS

- All fresh, frozen, canned and dried fruit.

- All fruit juices.

GLUTEN CONTAINING

- Fruit pies, pastries, crumbles.

- Fruit cakes, biscuits.

Meat/Meat Alternatives

GLUTEN FREE FOODS

• Fresh meat, fish, poultry, (for gravy use arrowroot or gluten free corn flour).

• Eggs

• Dried peas, beans, lentils.

• Gluten free canned baked beans.

• Casseroles or stews made without added pasta or flour.

GLUTEN CONTAINING

• Small goods such as salami, ham, cabanossi and sausages – gluten free versions of these are available.

• Casseroles, stews thickened with flour, pasta.

• Meat or fish coated with breadcrumbs or battered.

• Vegetarian meat alternatives.

• Fish fingers, chicken nuggets, pies, pastries, hot chips (contain dextrin), hamburgers, pizza, Chiko or spring rolls, sausage rolls, stuffing.

• Packet "soup mix".

DAIRY FREE DIET

Foods that must be avoided

- Cow's milk – full cream, low fat, skim milk, evaporated and condensed milk, powdered milk and buttermilk.

- Cheese of all kinds, cheese spreads, cheese flavoured chips and snacks, cheese based sauces.

- Yoghurt, cream, ice-cream, mousse, custard, dairy desserts, cheesecake.

- Milk chocolate and white chocolate. Some brands of dark chocolate are dairy free.

- Butter and margarine, (some contain small amounts of milk protein).

- Casein, milk solids.

You can eat whey and foods that contain whey, such as whey protein powder. Avoid dairy products made from goat or sheep milk for the duration of the detox.

Substitutes for cow's milk

Soy milk, rice milk, almond milk or coconut milk.

You could also drink tea and coffee black. You can use cow's milk alternatives on breakfast cereals, or eat something else for breakfast such as eggs or gluten free toast.

Foods high in calcium

The following foods are all good sources of calcium:

- Canned sardines and salmon – it is the bones that contain calcium, so you must eat them.

- Calcium fortified soy milk. Check to see if the milk contains added calcium.

- Almonds, sesame seeds, tahini, sunflower seeds and Brazil nuts.

- Green vegetables such as broccoli and Asian leafy vegetables such as bok choy.

- Figs
- Baked beans
- Seaweed

Gluten and dairy products must be strictly avoided for the duration of the detox. After that time you may need to keep avoiding these foods, particularly gluten. A growing body of research is showing that all people with an autoimmune disease should avoid consuming gluten long term. The production of thyroid antibodies can be halted by following a gluten free diet. This bowel detox will clear your digestive tract of toxins, kill the Candida, yeast and other bad bacteria you may have present, as well as heal leaky gut syndrome. Approximately 70 percent of the immune cells in your body are located in your digestive tract; therefore cleaning up your digestive tract will greatly improve your immune system. It is important to avoid alcohol for the duration of the bowel detox.

Sample menu for a gluten free and dairy free diet

Breakfast:

Rice porridge (made with rice flakes) sprinkled with nuts and chopped fresh fruit, with a cow's milk alternative.

Gluten free muesli with cow's milk alternative.

Eggs & vegetables – eg. Omelette, scrambled, poached eggs, etc.

Gluten free toast with egg, baked beans, sardines, almond butter, etc.

Fruit salad sprinkled with LSA (ground linseed, almond, sunflower mix)

Lunch:

Canned tuna or salmon with salad

Salad with left over cold meat or chicken

Rice or corn cakes spread with hummus, avocado or sliced boiled eggs with salad.

Left over meat and vegetable stew or curry served with rice.

Dinner:

Stir fry with chicken or red meat served with rice or rice vermicelli noodles.

Baked fish or roast meat with salad or cooked vegetables.

Spaghetti bolognaise or lasagne made using gluten free pasta.

Lamb & vegetable stew with rice, potatoes or salad.

Snacks:

Raw nuts, seeds & dried fruit mix.

Fresh fruit.

Vegetable sticks with salsa, hummus, baba ganoush or guacamole.

Gluten free crackers with above spreads.

Whey protein powder smoothie made with fresh fruit

Important supplements to be taken during the bowel detox

These supplements must be taken in the following order:

- **A laxative.** This must be taken first, as it will clear your bowel of accumulated toxins. The best laxative is called Picoprep, which you can pick up from a pharmacy. Dissolve one sachet in water and drink it in the morning. Most people only need to use one sachet, but if you regularly suffer with constipation you will need to use a second sachet. Follow the directions inside the packet. You do not need to fast or follow a liquid only diet; continue eating three meals and snacks but make sure you follow a gluten and dairy free diet.

- **Detox 123 herbs.** The next day take a supplement containing a combination of the herbs wormwood, thyme and barberry in tablet form. All of these herbs have antibiotic effects in the body, particularly in the digestive tract. They are able to destroy Candida and other gut parasites. Take one tablet three times a day with meals. Take this supplement for 1 month.

- **Slippery elm.** When you have finished the course of detox herbs, begin a slippery elm supplement. This herb is healing and soothing to the digestive tract; reducing inflammation and helping to heal a leaky gut. Slippery elm contains fibre that provides food for good bacteria in the digestive tract. It is available in capsule form and should be taken in a dose of two capsules three times a day before meals. Take this for 2 weeks.

- **Glutamine powder.** This is to be used at the same time as the slippery elm capsules and also for 2 weeks. Glutamine is the main source of fuel for cells lining the intestinal tract; helping to repair and regenerate them. It reduces intestinal permeability and the ability of pathogenic bacteria to adhere to the intestinal wall. Glutamine is available in powder form and it is best to take four grams per day, split into two doses before meals.

- **A probiotic.** When you have finished the course of slippery elm and glutamine, take a supplement containing acidophilus and other beneficial bacteria. Good bacteria are essential for repairing leaky gut syndrome and improving the health of the immune cells that live in the digestive tract. Take this supplement for a minimum of 2 weeks. It is beneficial to take probiotics long term.

Depending on your individual case, you may need to repeat this bowel detox. Please feel free to phone our Health Advisory team on (02) 4655 8855 so that we can help tailor make this program for you.

b) The liver detox

Once you have completed the treatment for leaky gut syndrome it is important to do a liver detox. Repairing a leaky gut will greatly reduce the amount of toxins that enter the liver from the digestive tract. Your liver is where the majority of T4 thyroid hormone is converted into its active form T3. If you have a fatty liver or a sluggish liver, this conversion will not be effective. If you are taking thyroid medication but still not feeling better, it is vital that you do something to improve the health of your liver.

Detoxification in your liver occurs in two steps: In **phase one**, liver enzymes transform toxins into an intermediate state, whereby they are temporarily more harmful. **Phase two** reactions act to convert the toxins into a water soluble form, so that they may be excreted more readily. A common problem in today's world is that many substances we are regularly exposed to stimulate phase one liver detoxification reactions, and phase two reactions lag behind. This means that you will be left with a whole lot of harmful free radicals that cause inflammation and damage to your liver and other tissues.

The following factors can all speed up phase one liver detoxification. This can be a problem because phase 2 cannot keep up leading to an overload of intermediate toxins.

- Alcohol
- Dioxin
- Exhaust fumes
- Stress
- Cigarettes
- Acetate
- Paint fumes
- Sulfonamides (a type of antibiotic)
- Carbon tetrachloride
- Organophosphate pesticides
- Steroid hormones
- Obesity
- Nicotine
- Chronic inflammation
- Caffeine
- Selective serotonin reuptake inhibitors

To enhance your liver's detoxification ability you should try to minimise exposure to these substances as much as possible. It is important for phase one and two reactions to proceed in a balanced, co-ordinated way. Phase two reactions require several vitamins, minerals, amino acids and antioxidants in order to operate efficiently.

Essential principles for liver detoxification

- **Follow a liver friendly diet.** The type of food you eat each day has the greatest impact on your liver and overall health. Make sure you eat at least five serves of vegetables each day.

You should also eat two serves of fruit each day but not more than that if you are overweight or a diabetic. Vegetables and salads are more important to eat because they are higher in minerals and lower in sugar than fruit. Some vegetables must be consumed raw. You also need to eat adequate protein each day; your liver needs the amino acids in protein to carry out phase two detoxification reactions. Good sources of protein include fish, as well as free range or organic eggs, chicken and red meat. Dairy products provide some protein but they should be avoided for the duration of this detox. If you are a vegetarian you can obtain enough protein if you combine three of the following at the same meal: grain, nut, seed or legume. Eating some fat is also important for your liver; you can find healthy fats in foods like fish, avocados, raw nuts and seeds, olive oil, flaxseed oil and organic virgin coconut oil.

- **Increase the amount of raw food in your diet.** It is important to eat a raw vegetable salad each day; many people only do this in summer. Your liver desperately needs the antioxidants found in raw foods. Raw foods are high in enzymes, which will improve your digestion. A great way to add raw foods into your diet is to make raw vegetable juices. They will flood your body with antioxidants in an easy to absorb form. Any combination of vegetables will be good; avoid too much fruit because it is high in sugar. Here is a recipe for a liver detox juice; you can find more recipes in the book *Raw Juices Can Save Your Life.*

Liver detox juice

½ lemon, peeled
A large handful of dandelion leaves*
1 carrot
1 small beetroot
¼ red onion
1 broccoli floweret
Pass all through a juicer and drink immediately.

* Dandelion is extremely cleansing to the liver. You can purchase medicinal dandelion, (called Taraxacum officinale) from nurseries

and plant it in your garden. If you cannot obtain dandelion, you can use chicory leaves, endive leaves or any dark green leafy vegetable. Chicory and endive are available from most supermarkets and green grocers, although you may not have heard of them.

- **Eat foods that are high in natural organic sulphur.** Sulphur is required by your liver to carry out phase two detoxification reactions. Sulphur containing amino acids such as taurine and cysteine are needed for the production of bile. Bile is a major exit route for toxins in your body, so it is important not to have a sluggish bile flow. Sulphur foods promote better bile flow. Good sources of sulphur include eggs, cruciferous vegetables (eg. Cabbage, cauliflower, broccoli, Brussels sprouts), and vegetables in the onion family (eg. Onion, garlic, leek, spring onion). You can also obtain natural sulphur in powder form to hasten the detoxification in your liver. This natural sulphur is called MSM and is well tolerated by people who have allergies to sulphur based drugs.

- **Be careful about the fats you eat.** Some fats are essential for good health and others are harmful. All of the cell membranes in your body are primarily made of fat. Fat performs many important functions in your body and helps to keep your immune system strong. If you have a fatty liver it means there is inflammation in your liver and your liver cells have been injured. You need the right fats in your diet to heal and repair your liver cells. In most cases people did not develop a fatty liver because they ate too much fat; they ate too much sugar and high carbohydrate foods like bread, pasta and potatoes which their liver converted into fat. However, some fats can promote a fatty liver and they include most vegetable oils excluding extra virgin olive oil, cold pressed flaxseed oil and virgin coconut oil. The fats found in margarine and processed foods like donuts, hot chips, crisps and biscuits are usually harmful. Healthy types of fat are also found in avocados, oily fish (eg, sardines, salmon, mackerel) and raw nuts and seeds.

- **Go easy on the carbohydrates.** It is important to avoid sugar and all foods with added sugar. High carbohydrate foods like bread, pasta, rice, cereals and potatoes are rapidly digested into sugar in your body. If you are overweight you need to avoid or severely restrict your intake of these foods. If carbohydrates are eaten in excess, they will be converted into fat in your liver and will contribute to the formation of a fatty liver as well as obesity. If you are overweight there is an effective weight loss eating plan in the book *Can't Lose Weight? You Could Have Syndrome X*.

- **Lose weight from around your abdomen.** This follows on from the point above. If you carry excess weight around your tummy it is dangerous because it is too close to your liver. Free fatty acids are released from fat cells around your abdomen and they travel directly to your liver causing inflammation and the accumulation of fat inside your liver. This is a sure way to develop fatty liver disease. Excess fat on the thighs and buttocks is not as dangerous to your health as fat around your abdomen, because fat here gets inside your vital organs and impairs their function.

- **Include liver cleansing foods and herbs in your diet.** Some foods and herbs have particularly beneficial effects on your liver function. They work in a variety of ways to improve the detox abilities of your liver and act as powerful antioxidants, to mop up the free radicals produced during detoxification. Some of these substances include:

St Mary's thistle: This herb is also known as Milk thistle and it contains the powerful liver protector silymarin. This compound can protect the liver cells from toxic damage, enhance repair of liver cells and it is a strong antioxidant. Silymarin increases levels of glutathione in the body; this is the body's most powerful antioxidant. Clinical trails have shown that the most effective dose of silymarin is 420mg per day.

Green tea: Green tea comes from the same plant as ordinary black tea but it is higher in antioxidants because the leaves have not been processed in the same way. It contains a group of antioxidants known as catechins, of which the most powerful is epigallocatechin gallate (EGCG). Catechins are thought to be a 200 times more powerful antioxidant than vitamin C. Along with reducing the risk of cancer and heart disease, green tea improves the efficiency of phase two liver detoxification reactions.

Turmeric: This is a plant in the ginger family. Turmeric has a bright yellow colour, is a component of curry powder but has a very mild flavour. The active component of turmeric is curcumin; it is a powerful antioxidant, raises levels of glutathione in the body and may offer protection against cancer.

Sesame seeds: Sesame seeds contain sesamin, a compound that protects the liver cells from damage. It is a powerful antioxidant and reduces the breakdown of vitamin E in the body, thereby increasing levels in the body. Sesamin particularly protects the liver cells from the effects of alcohol.

Watercress: This herb is in the same family as cabbage and broccoli. It contains the compound pheny-lethyl-isothiocyanate (PEITC). It promotes the excretion of cancer causing substances and may particularly protect against lung and colon cancer. Watercress enhances phase two liver detoxification pathways. Try to include some watercress in your salads and vegetable juices.

Limonene: This is a compound found in the rind of citrus fruits, particularly lemons. It is responsible for much of the smell of lemons. Limonene is a powerful antioxidant and is capable of blocking the harmful effects of many different free radicals. You can include some citrus rind in your raw vegetable juices and salads, but only if it is organic.

Other nutrients required for a liver detox

Glycine: This is an amino acid needed for bile production and phase two liver detoxification. When cells of the liver engulf foreign substances they can suffer some damage; glycine helps to minimise this damage.

Taurine and Cysteine: These are both sulphur containing amino acids needed for bile production and phase two liver detoxification. Taurine reduces the tendency to develop a fatty liver and it helps to protect the liver against the damaging effects of alcohol. Cysteine is a precursor of glutathione, the body's most powerful antioxidant. Cysteine helps to protect the liver from damage caused by alcohol and rancid fats, (found in most fried takeaway food).

Methyl donors: These are a group of vitamins that participate in chemical reactions by donating a part of their chemical structure. Methyl donors include folic acid, biotin, inositol and others. Methylation occurs in the liver and is particularly important in detoxifying fat soluble chemicals and heavy metals.

The most important nutrients for the liver can be found combined together in the one liver tonic. Please phone our Health Advisory line on (02) 4655 8855, where a naturopath can help you find a liver tonic that's right for you. Or go to our website www.liverdoctor.com for more information on how to keep your liver healthy.

All people with autoimmune disease also require a mineral supplement and an omega 3 oil supplement, such as fish oil or flaxseed oil. Selenium is the most important mineral to supplement; it has numerous immune system benefits and research has shown it can dramatically reduce the body's production of thyroid antibodies. Minerals and beneficial fats are covered in detail in the section that follows.

Hidden Thyroid Disease – case history

Dianne was a very interesting patient of mine and illustrates that thyroid dysfunction can be hidden and thus hard to diagnose – unless one knows what to look for!

Dianne was a 55 year old post menopausal woman who complained of the following –

Fatigue

Puffy fluid retention around her legs and eyes

Unwanted weight gain

Deterioration in her vision

Her local doctor had correctly ordered blood tests to check her thyroid gland function and these tests revealed an essentially "normal" function of her gland. I asked Dianne to measure her basal body temperature in the mornings and keep a record of this on a chart.

Let's take a look at Dianne's blood test results –

DIANNE'S RESULTS .... NORMAL RANGE

Free T 3 = 2.46 pmol/L ....2.5 – 6.0

Free T 4 = 11 pmol/L ....8.0 – 22.0

TSH   = 3.97 mIU/L...0.30 – 4.0*

Thyroid antibodies

Anti-thyroglobulin antibodies = negative .... (less than 100)

Anti-microsomal antibodies = 1600................ (less than 100)

* Most laboratories use 4 mIU/L as the upper limit of normal for TSH. However, new research has found that if TSH is above 2 mIU/L, the thyroid gland is probably in the early stages of disease.

Interpretation of Dianne's test results –

Her levels of T3 hormone are slightly low, which could be responsible for her symptoms of an under active thyroid gland. Her levels of T4 hormone are at the lower limit (bottom) of the normal range and thus are not optimal. Her TSH hormone level is within the "normal" range, however since new research has shown that people with a TSH level above 2 likely have underlying thyroid disease, this is not ideal.

Note that the level (titre) of her antibodies was abnormally high with a value of 1600, when it should have been less than 100. This is proof that she is in the early stages of a thyroid disease which has not yet greatly affected her hormone levels.

This high level of antibodies was attacking and destroying her thyroid gland and was the cause of her sluggish thyroid gland function. This also proved that Dianne had the auto-immune disease known as Hashimoto's thyroiditis and that unless this was treated, her symptoms and her thyroid gland function would only get worse. Dianne's body temperature chart proved normal with all her readings over a whole month showing temperatures greater than 36.5 degrees centigrade.

Dianne was not happy to just sit and wait until her thyroid gland became more under active, especially because she was not feeling well with her symptoms of an under active thyroid. However, because her levels of the TSH hormone were considered "normal", according to the laboratory reference, her doctor did not think it necessary to give her any treatment.

I suggested to Dianne that we could first try to reduce the levels of the destructive antibodies that were destroying her thyroid gland and also supply her gland with extra nutrients to help it manufacture higher levels of T4 and T3 hormone itself.

To achieve this I prescribed –

Selenium 100 mcg daily

Zinc 10 mg daily

The inclusion of culinary seaweeds in her cooking. Nori can be used to make sushi rolls, added to soups or sprinkled over salads.

An increase in the amount of oily fish, beans, nuts, seeds and tahini paste in her diet.

A bowel and liver detox along with the exclusion of gluten and cow's milk from her diet.

Raw juices daily – carrot, beetroot, oranges, lemons, limes, cucumber and capsicum.

Dianne tried this program for 4 months and found that she felt a lot better and her vision returned back to normal. She lost 8 kilograms of weight and her bowel actions became more regular with less abdominal bloating.

Her antibody level came down to 400 (remember it was 1600), and I was pleased with this result after only 4 months.

Dianne was still troubled by some fatigue and puffiness of her eyes and legs and wanted to try natural thyroid hormone. I was not adverse to this; however I always think it best to start with low doses. I prescribed desiccated porcine thyroid extract in a dose of 32.5 mg twice daily; this would provide her with a daily total dose of 65mg. Desiccated thyroid extract must be made up by a compounding pharmacist and generally speaking, 65 mg of natural thyroid extract is equal to 1 grain, which is equal to 100mcg of thyroxine.

Dianne continued with my nutritional program and the desiccated porcine thyroid for 6 months with an excellent outcome – her antibody levels were now only 150, her level of T3 hormone was normal and all her symptoms had resolved completely. During this time she remained on a gluten and dairy free diet. She now had the energy to exercise, which enabled her to continue with weight loss to reach her goal weight.

Dianne's case history indicates that if a patient has the symptoms of thyroid disease, one must do a full range of tests for thyroid function, including thyroid antibody levels and a basal body temperature chart. We must start to treat the thyroid gland dysfunction, even if it is subtle, in order to avoid progression of the disease and to alleviate the patient's symptoms. Dianne's condition was treated as an autoimmune disease by improving her immune system, digestion and liver function.

An expectant approach, where no treatment is offered is not good enough, because even subtle degrees of thyroid dysfunction can have a huge impact on the quality of life.

2. Supplement with the right minerals

Your thyroid gland has a high requirement for a variety of minerals. If you are deficient in one or more of these minerals, you will have difficulty producing enough thyroid hormones. Minerals are required by the enzymes that manufacture and activate thyroid hormones, and minerals are important because they compete with toxic heavy metals in the body. We are all inevitably exposed to high amounts of heavy metals and these will accumulate and be more toxic if you are deficient in the following minerals. Sometimes when the thyroid gland is only slightly under active, it can be restored to normal function by supplementing with the right minerals.

The following minerals are essential for healthy thyroid gland function:

• Selenium

Selenium is a trace element that is essential for the body in small amounts. It was named after the moon goddess Selene, by the Swedish chemist Jons Jakob Berzellius in 1817. Selenium's importance for animal health was first discovered in 1957, but its importance in human health was not discovered until 1973[62]. Selenium is not just important for thyroid function; it is essential for a healthy immune system, helping to fight viral infections and reduce the risk of cancer; it improves fertility and reduces the risk of arthritis and heart disease.

Regarding the thyroid gland, selenium is a component of the enzyme that helps convert T4 into the active form T3. This enzyme is called 5'deiodinase and the majority of this conversion occurs in the liver, kidneys and other tissues; only a small amount of it occurs in the thyroid gland. If you are deficient in selenium you will not be able to manufacture enough T3 hormone, and this can result in hypothyroidism. Research published in the **New England Journal of Medicine** stated that "selenium deficiency can result in thyroid injury and decreased extrathyroidal triiodothyronine production"; meaning reduced T3 production in tissues other than the thyroid gland[63].

Because selenium is vital for healthy immune system function, it is very helpful for autoimmune disease and inflammatory states; therefore it is very important for people with Graves' disease, Hashimoto's thyroiditis and all types of thyroiditis. Research has found that a deficiency of selenium can contribute to the development of autoimmune thyroid disease. Research reported at the 83rd Annual Meeting of the Endocrine Society in Denver, Colorado in 2001 found that supplementing with selenium may slow down the progression of autoimmune thyroid disease. It is especially effective in the early stages of thyroiditis. Researchers looked at 72 women with an average age of 42. All of the women had autoimmune thyroiditis and they all had thyroid antibody (TPO and Tg) levels higher than 350 U/mL. Half of the women received a selenium supplement (200mcg per day) for three months. At the end of the trial period nine women taking the selenium supplement had antibody levels that returned to normal. Two women in the placebo group also had their antibody levels return to normal[64]. Selenium is a very strong antioxidant and reduces inflammation in the body, and therefore can protect your thyroid gland from autoimmune destruction.

Selenium is essential in the treatment of all autoimmune disease. An ideal dose of selenium is 100 to 200mcg per day. Selenium works best when combined with the other antioxidants: vitamin E, zinc and vitamin C. You can find all of these nutrients combined together in the one tablet.

Unfortunately, many parts of the world have selenium deficient soils. This means that most crops grown there will be low in selenium also. Australia, New Zealand and some parts of Europe are known to have selenium deficient soils; North and South America have a higher content of selenium in the soil. If you live in Australia, it will be almost impossible to obtain an adequate amount of selenium from diet alone.

The following foods are all good sources of selenium:

- Brazil nuts
- Crab
- Salmon
- Brown rice
- Chicken
- Pork
- Beef
- Walnuts

Selenium enriched bread is also now available. The wheat used in the bread is grown in selenium enriched soil. Selenium deficiency exacerbates the effects of iodine deficiency.

• Iodine

Iodine is absolutely essential for the production of thyroid hormones. If you do not get enough iodine in your diet, your thyroid may not be able to produce sufficient levels of hormones. Long term iodine deficiency can cause the thyroid gland to enlarge and form a goitre. Iodine deficiency during pregnancy or infanthood can lead to reduced IQ or mental retardation. Adults require 150 micrograms of iodine each day. You can easily obtain this amount if you consume seafood three times a week. Iodine is also found in high amounts in seaweed such as kelp, kombu and nori. Dairy products, red meat, eggs and fruit contain smaller amounts of iodine. Vegetarians who do not eat fish are at greatest risk of iodine deficiency. If you do not regularly consume iodine rich foods, you may need to use iodised salt. This is available from supermarkets. It is best to use iodised sea salt because this does not contain aluminium (food additive code 554) to prevent the salt clumping.

Ensuring you get enough iodine in your diet is the best way to protect your thyroid against substances that are toxic to it. For instance, people who are iodine deficient are more susceptible to radiation induced thyroid cancer as well as the toxic effects of fluoride, bromine, chlorine and the various pesticides and insecticides that affect the thyroid. Goitrogens in foods like raw cabbage, soy, peanuts and other foods can inhibit your thyroid gland from absorbing iodine. If you eat a lot of goitrogen rich foods it is even more important that you get enough iodine in your diet.

Other nutrients essential for a healthy thyroid gland include zinc and vitamins D, A and B complex. A powerful multivitamin and mineral formula can supply your body with all of these nutrients. Please phone our Health Advisory team on (02) 4655 8855 and speak to a naturopath if you would like advice about multivitamins.

• Tyrosine

Tyrosine is not a mineral; it is an amino acid (building block of protein) and is essential for the production of thyroid hormones. Tyrosine is not classed as an essential amino acid because our body can make it out of another amino acid called phenylalanine. Its name derives from the Greek word for cheese: *tyros,* because it was first identified in cheese.

Tyrosine is required in large amounts to manufacture the thyroid hormones T4 and T3. In addition to its role in thyroid health, tyrosine is also required for the synthesis of the pigment melanin and the hormones adrenalin, noradrenalin and dopamine. A deficiency of tyrosine can lead to low levels of thyroid hormones as well as depression and mood disorders. Tyrosine is also a mild antioxidant. Deficiency of tyrosine is rare because it is found in a wide variety of foods and our body can manufacture it. Tyrosine is found in dairy products, red meat, eggs, almonds, avocados and bananas. If you have poor digestion you may not absorb the tyrosine you consume in food. Common symptoms of poor digestion include bloating, flatulence, irritable bowel syndrome and heartburn. The digestive enzyme called protease is required for efficient protein digestion; it is available in supplement form to be taken with meals.

Please call our Health Advisory line on (02) 4655 8855 and speak to a naturopath if you have questions about digestive enzymes.

3. Eat the Right Fats

Fat is an essential component of a healthy diet, but it is vital that you know which fats to eat and which to avoid. Fat performs many important functions in your body; some of these include insulation, enhanced absorption of some vitamins, healthy immune function and hormone production. Fat is also a major component of the cell membranes that surround every cell in your body.

Healthy cell membranes

Healthy cell membranes are very important if you want healthy thyroid function. This is because T3 and T4 need to enter cells in order to have their effects. With most hormones in the body, the receptor for the hormone is found on cell surfaces. However, both T4 and T3 have to enter cells. This means they have to pass through your cell membranes. Once T4 is converted into T3, it interacts with the mitochondria inside cells or with the DNA.

If you have unhealthy cell membranes this is just one more thing that can go wrong with trying to balance your thyroid hormones. You may have normal levels of thyroid hormones but still feel unwell because the hormones cannot fulfil their actions. If the hormone cannot get into your cells it cannot have its action.

Cell membranes can be disrupted by the following factors:

- Consuming trans fatty acids, found in partially hydrogenated vegetable oil.
- Consuming oxidised or rancid omega 6 fats, found in foods fried in polyunsaturated vegetable oil.
- Very low fat diets.
- Fat soluble toxins such as plastic and PCBs (Polychlorinated Biphenyls).
- A lack of antioxidants in the diet, enabling free radical damage to the fats in cell membranes.

The biggest determinant of the health of your cell membranes is the type of fat you eat each day.

The wrong fats

Today most people in the world eat predominantly the wrong types of fat, or fat that has been processed and damaged. Both omega 3 fats and omega 6 fats are essential for wellbeing; the problem is that people now eat far too much omega 6 fat; much more than humans ever have before in history. Our ancestors evolved over millions of years to consume omega 3 fats and omega 6 fats in a ratio of 1:1 or 1:4; now with modern diets the ratio is between 1:20 and 1:50. An excess of omega 6 fats promotes inflammatory diseases such as asthma and arthritis; research has shown that in excess these fats can also promote cancer. Excess inflammation is a major feature of all autoimmune diseases, including autoimmune thyroid disease.

Deficiency of omega 3 fats can promote cardiovascular disease, depression, reduced IQ and impaired visual ability. Modern diets are lacking omega 3 fats because many people do not eat fish regularly; the most reliable source of these fats. Fish that has been fried or smoked has lost much of the beneficial omega 3 fats it once contained. Also much of the fish we do eat has been farmed; this type of fish has not been fed its natural diet, consequently its flesh is far lower in omega 3 fats. Also meat, chicken and eggs are higher in omega 6 fats than they used to be because the animals are predominantly fed grains rather than pasture.

Fats to avoid

You should avoid the following fats:

- Margarine
- Trans fatty acids. Sometimes these are listed on the nutrition panel on a label. Trans fatty acids are also usually found in partially hydrogenated vegetable oil.
- Vegetable oil found in processed foods like crackers, biscuits, pastries and cake.
- Fried foods, especially takeaway foods.
- Processed meat like salami and other smallgoods. The fat in these foods is usually oxidised.

Fats to include in your diet for a healthy thyroid

All the fat you eat should be in a natural state, meaning not processed, heated or refined. Avocados, nuts, seeds and fish are all great, natural sources of fat. If you use vegetable oil it should be cold pressed or virgin. The following are all healthy sources of fat to include in your diet:

- Oily fish such as sardines, salmon, mackerel, herring and anchovies. Canned fish is okay. Make sure that the fish you eat is wild, not farmed.
- Raw nuts and seeds. These should not be roasted or salted. Examples include walnuts, pecans, almonds, macadamia nuts, Brazil nuts, hazelnuts, pine nuts and cashews.
- Virgin organic coconut oil. This is a very versatile fat that can be used for cooking, as a salad dressing or a spread in place of margarine. It has many benefits for the thyroid gland. NiuLife extra virgin coconut oil is 100% organic and fair trade.
- Cold pressed Extra virgin olive oil.
- Cold pressed flaxseed oil.
- Dairy products, free range or organic meat, poultry and eggs. These foods contain some saturated fat and cholesterol; both

of which our body requires in small amounts for healthy cell membranes. Dairy products should not be consumed while on a detox.

4. Correct Oestrogen Dominance

Oestrogen dominance is an extremely common condition among women and it may be contributing to your case of hypothyroidism. Oestrogen is essential for female characteristics and reproduction, but when it is not balanced with progesterone it can create problems. High levels of oestrogen reduce the amount of free T4 in circulation because they increase blood levels of the protein that binds to T4, making it inactive. Therefore oestrogen dominance can suppress your thyroid function.

Progesterone deficiency can occur for a number of reasons. In order to produce progesterone you must ovulate; many women do not ovulate regularly or at all. Ovulation can be inhibited by stress, poor diet and high insulin levels. Elevated insulin is a feature of Syndrome X and this occurs in women who have polycystic ovarian syndrome. Oestrogen dominance is a common cause of PMS, infertility, uterine fibroids and endometriosis. Women with too much oestrogen typically feel bloated, tired, and irritable and they crave sugar. Correcting a hormone imbalance and promoting increased progesterone is essential not just for a healthy thyroid, but for a healthy reproductive system.

The following methods will all help to correct oestrogen dominance:

a. Improve your diet: Your daily diet has an enormous impact on your hormone balance and it is the first thing to think about when trying to correct the problem. The following points are important:

- Drink at least eight glasses of pure water each day. Ideally the water should be filtered to remove environmental pollutants.
- Eat a raw vegetable salad each day. You can also eat cooked vegetables and fruit, but the raw salad is most important for the antioxidants it provides. Including an oil dressing such as olive, flaxseed or coconut oil will increase the absorption of antioxidants from the vegetables.

- Eat enough protein each day. Protein should be consumed at each meal because this stabilises your blood sugar levels; keeping energy levels high and reducing hunger and cravings. Good sources of protein include fish, organic or free range eggs, chicken and red meat. Dairy products, legumes, nuts, seeds and grains provide smaller amounts of protein.

- Include beneficial fats in your diet. Fat is the building block of hormones, so you must consume enough of it. Good fats are found in oily fish, raw nuts and seeds, avocados, extra virgin olive oil, cold pressed flaxseed oil and organic virgin coconut oil. One theory as to why polycystic ovarian syndrome is so common is the prevalence of low fat, high carbohydrate diets.

- Limit sugar and high carbohydrate foods like bread, pasta, rice, potatoes and breakfast cereals. Avoid all foods with added sugar and limit foods that are made of flour. This will greatly help to rebalance hormones in women with polycystic ovarian syndrome. Avoiding these foods can increase your chance of ovulating. If you suffer with polycystic ovarian syndrome see the book *Hormones: Don't Let Them Ruin Your Life* for more information.

- Include foods that contain phyto estrogens in your diet. Phyto estrogens are also called plant oestrogens and they help to balance and modify the oestrogen in your body. They are predominantly found in legumes, seeds, nuts and grains. More than 300 foods have been found to contain phyto estrogens. If you have an under active thyroid it is best to not consume too much soy; you are better off getting phyto estrogens from a range of other foods.

There are three main classes of phyto estrogens: isoflavones, coumestrans and lignans. Isoflavones are found in soybeans, chickpeas, green peas, nuts, lentils, spinach and other vegetables and fruits. Coumestrans are found in liquorice, peas, spinach, cabbage, soybeans and green beans.

Flaxseeds (linseeds) are the richest dietary source of lignan precursors. When flaxseeds are consumed, bacteria in the intestinal tract convert the lignan precursors into two types of lignans: enterolactone and enterodiol. There is evidence that these lignans may alter oestrogen metabolism in a way that makes it less harmful and less likely to promote breast and uterine cancer. However, these lignans will only be formed if you have plenty of good bacteria in your gut. Studies have shown that people who recently took antibiotics did not form these lignans in their gut. Also, to be effective the flaxseeds must be ground; you will not get these benefits from whole linseeds, such as found in linseed bread. Flaxseed oil does not contain lignans, it is only the ground flaxseed meal that does.

b. Improve your liver and bowel function: After oestrogen has had its effects in your body, it is taken to your liver to get broken down. The oestrogen enters your bile, this is secreted into your intestines and some oestrogen is excreted when you have a bowel movement, while some is reabsorbed back into your bloodstream. If you have a sluggish liver and are constipated you will reabsorb most of the oestrogen and end up with high blood oestrogen levels. If you have an overgrowth of bad bacteria in your digestive tract they can turn the oestrogen into a more harmful state, which is then reabsorbed back into your body.

Follow the gut and liver detox guidelines in this chapter. Make sure you have between one and three bowel movements every day. The best way to ensure this is to drink eight glasses of water each day, exercise and eat plenty of fibre. Fibre can be found in vegetables, fruit, legumes, nuts, seeds and grains. Increased bowel movements mean increased oestrogen excretion.

c. Avoid environmental oestrogens: Many chemicals in the environment have an oestrogen like effect in our body; they are not oestrogen but they can mimic oestrogen. These substances are usually referred to as xeno-estrogens; *xeno* means foreign. These substances increase the oestrogen load in the body and they are very difficult to detoxify through the liver. They are believed to greatly increase the risk of hormone dependant cancer such as breast, uterine and prostate cancer.

By-products of the pesticide and plastic industry are the biggest source of xeno-estrogens. Some xeno-estrogens include organochlorins, bisphenol A, dioxin, DDT, PCBs as well as insecticides, herbicides, fungicides and many industrial chemicals.

How to minimise exposure to environmental oestrogens

- Minimise your exposure to pesticides, insecticides and fungicides as much as possible. Purchase organic food if it is fresh and affordable. Coffee is a heavily sprayed crop, so choose organic; purchase organic olive oil, since most chemicals are fat soluble and accumulate in the oil.
- Drink filtered water.
- Do not microwave food in plastic containers, and especially avoid covering food with plastic wrap in the microwave. Heating plastic will cause some of the plastic molecules to enter your food. This way your body can accumulate large amounts of bisphenol A and phthalates.
- Use laundry and dish washing chemicals that are fragrance free and biodegradable.
- Avoid moisturisers and cosmetics with toxic chemicals, especially parabens. Organic virgin coconut oil makes an excellent face and body moisturiser.
- Avoid nail polish and nail polish remover.
- Do not use chlorine based household cleaners.
- Do not use dry cleaning. Your clothes will retain perchloroethylene residues. If you must have something dry cleaned, air it outside for a day so that fewer chemicals enter your home.
- Do not eat farmed fish. This can contain high levels of dioxins, PCBs and bromine containing flame retardants. Before you purchase fish ask where it came from.
- Use unbleached paper products. This includes tissues, toilet paper, tampons, coffee filters and tea bags. Bleached products contain dioxin residues that can enter your body.
- Do not drink hot liquids out of Styrofoam cups. Bisphenol A will enter your drink and it is a major hormone disruptor.

d. Use natural progesterone cream: A mild case of oestrogen dominance can be helped with the diet and lifestyle suggestions above; however moderate to severe cases will require the use of a natural progesterone cream. This will rebalance the hormones well, give symptom relief and help your thyroid hormones to function properly. This cream requires a doctor's prescription and is also referred to as bio-identical progesterone cream.

Natural progesterone is made in a laboratory from a plant hormone called diosgenin, which is extracted from yams and soybeans. Slight physical changes are made to the diosgenin so that it becomes identical to the progesterone normally made by the body.

Natural progesterone in a cream is made up by a compounding pharmacy and typical doses are between 25 and 100mg daily. Progesterone cream is usually applied to the skin during the last two weeks of the menstrual cycle, but this can vary and your doctor may modify this in your case. The progesterone in this cream is different to the synthetic progesterone (progestins) found in some contraceptives and hormone replacement therapy.

If you need help finding a doctor who can prescribe bio-identical progesterone cream contact our Health Advisory team on (02) 4655 8855 or visit the website www.whas.com.au.

5. Do a Heavy Metal Detox:

Heavy metal toxicity is a common problem in today's world and it is a big contributor to impaired thyroid function. Mercury is the worst metal for the thyroid gland because it inhibits the conversion of T4 into its active form T3. This section of the book will focus on mercury detoxification, but these suggestions will work well for all heavy metals, including lead and cadmium, which can also suppress thyroid function.

How to test your mercury levels

At this stage there is no definitive test to determine if a person is suffering from prolonged exposure to low levels of mercury. The symptoms of mercury toxicity can be extremely varied and are present in a great number of different health conditions. This is why it is important to be aware of the sources of mercury in the environment, and try to avoid exposure to it as much as possible.

When mercury enters the body it is quickly distributed to most tissues. Hair contains a lot of sulphur and mercury forms bonds with this. Hair analysis is commonly used to test for mercury toxicity, but it is not always accurate and tends to have a high rate of false positives. A mercury concentration above five parts per million should indicate mercury toxicity. Lead levels should be checked at the same time because mercury and lead act synergistically and are more toxic than either one is on its own. If selenium levels in hair are low, supplementing with this mineral will help to detoxify mercury.

A urine challenge test can be done to measure mercury levels. A chelating drug is given to the patient, which binds with heavy metals and increases their excretion. Penicillamine is a chelating drug that is used orally and DMPS is used intravenously. A urine sample is taken before the patient is given the drug and another one while the drug is in their body. People that have mercury amalgam fillings in their teeth commonly show a ten fold increase in urinary mercury levels. Blood tests can also be done to measure mercury; levels should not exceed 50mcg/dL.

How to detoxify your body of mercury

To detoxify your body of heavy metals you need to follow the steps below:

- Make sure you eat enough protein. Protein is required by your liver to carry out detoxification reactions. Good sources of protein are fish and free range or organic eggs, poultry and red meat. Dairy products also provide some protein but should not be consumed in excess because they can cause immune system problems. If you are a vegetarian you must consume three of the following at the same meal: legume, nut, seed or grain. If you experience abdominal bloating, gas and irritable bowel syndrome, you may not be digesting protein adequately. A digestive enzyme supplement taken with meals would help you enormously. For more information on how to improve your digestion please call our Health Advisory line on (02) 4655 8855.

- Ensure you have good levels of friendly bacteria in your digestive tract. Detoxification starts in the intestines and many of the detox enzymes present in your liver are also present in your gut. If you suffer with Candida overgrowth, irritable bowel syndrome, bloating and flatulence, your digestive tract needs help. Start off by taking herbal tablets that combine the three herbs wormwood, thyme and barberry. These herbs promote better digestion and kill off Candida and bad bacteria in your gut. After this you will need to take a probiotic, or good bacteria supplement such as acidophilus.

• Ensure you have regular bowel movements. Most of the heavy metals in your body are eliminated through the stool. You need to have between one and three bowel movements each day. If you are constipated, make sure you drink at least eight glasses of water each day and get some exercise each day. If you have stubborn constipation you may need a fibre supplement containing rice and soy bran, pectin, ginger, peppermint and powdered vegetables. This is a gentle, non habit forming laxative that will give your bowels a thorough cleanse.

• Be careful which fish you eat. Some species of fish accumulate much more mercury and toxins than others. Generally, the larger the fish and the higher up in the food chain it is, the more toxins it has accumulated. Food Standards Australia New Zealand recommends that pregnant women, women planning pregnancy and young children limit their consumption of the most contaminated fish species. Shark (flake), broadbill, swordfish and marlin should be limited to not more than one serving a fortnight, with no other fish to be eaten during that fortnight. Orange roughy (sea perch) and catfish should be limited to not more than one serving per week, with no other fish to be eaten during that week. A serve is equal to 150 grams for adults and 75 grams for children. If you have a thyroid problem it would be very wise for you to totally avoid these fish species.

The safest fish to eat are:

• Sardines
• Herrings
• Wild salmon (not farmed)
• Anchovies
• Summer flounder
• Canned tuna (fish used for canning are smaller, short lived varieties)

- Take a selenium and vitamin E supplement. Research has shown that these nutrients can reduce the toxicity of mercury in the body. Neither of these nutrients works as well when used on their own; selenium and vitamin E should be taken together, ideally in a dose of 100mcg of selenium and 200IU of vitamin E per day. Please phone our friendly Health Advisory team if you need help finding a suitable supplement on (02) 4655 8855.

- Sulphur helps your body to get rid of mercury. Good sources of sulphur include eggs, garlic, onion, leek and spring onions. The supplement MSM provides a high dose of organic sulphur. It is available in a powder form combined with vitamin C. An ideal dose is half a teaspoon twice daily and this can greatly help with mercury detoxification.

- The herb coriander is known to help detoxify the body of mercury. Try to include the fresh herb in your diet regularly; it is delicious in salads, raw juices and Indian curries.

- Chlorella is a singled celled algae plant that lives in fresh water. It has the ability to bind with mercury and other heavy metals and transport them out of the body in bowel movements. It is available in supplement form.

6. Address your Stress

Severe or prolonged stress can bring on or worsen nearly any illness. Many studies have shown a connection between stress and autoimmune disease. There is a well known relationship between the onset of Graves' disease and major stress. Stress also negatively impacts on the prognosis of the disease. It is thought that stress can bring on Hashimoto's thyroiditis as well; however this disease often develops more slowly and can go on undiagnosed for longer than Graves' disease. The main cause of thyroid disease in Australia and the USA is autoimmune disease. You are born with the tendency to develop an autoimmune disease, and stress, viral infections or nutritional deficiencies are some of the factors that can trigger the disease.

Stress can also slow down your metabolism by suppressing thyroid hormone production. The stress hormones cortisol and adrenalin are known to increase the production of reverse T3 (an inactive thyroid hormone), thereby suppressing the conversion of T4 into the active hormone T3. This can give you the symptoms of an under active thyroid gland and will not be picked up on a regular blood test if your doctor only measures your TSH level.

How to effectively manage stress

Different methods work for different people, so you need to find what activities or thought patterns work best for you.

Here are some tips:

- Take a look at the thoughts that regularly go through your head. When it comes to stress, it is often not the event itself, but rather the way we think about it that causes us greatest stress.

- Look after your body physically as best as you can. Get enough sleep, eat a nutritious diet and get regular exercise. Avoid eating sugar, artificial sweeteners and processed foods full of chemicals. Avoid stimulants like nicotine and caffeine. Don't rely on alcohol to manage your moods. Poor health is a big stress on your body physically.

- Exercise deserves a special mention. Try to exercise aerobically (meaning something that makes you huff and puff) for at least 30 minutes most days of the week. Exercise causes your brain to release endorphins and no problem feels quite as bad after a hard workout.

- Spend some time nurturing the significant relationships in your life. Keep the channels of communication open and try to say what is on your mind. When life gets you down it is your friends and family that can pick you back up again.

- Make the time to do things that are important to you. Life is short and there are so many great things to experience. Don't get bogged down in work and responsibilities; allow yourself the time to do what makes you happy.

- Remember to breathe slowly and deeply. How you breathe affects your blood pressure.

Chapter 11

Thyroid hormone trouble shooting

In this section we summarise the common problems experienced by those with thyroid disease and give you simple solutions. All of the information in this section can be found elsewhere in this book in more detail.

Thyroid Hormones Normal but Still Suffering Symptoms

A significant percentage of people with hypothyroidism have normal thyroid hormone levels on a blood test yet they still suffer with the symptoms of hypothyroidism. If you are still feeling tired, can't lose weight and find it hard to concentrate and think clearly, your thyroid gland may not be adequately treated. If you are taking thyroid hormone medication but still feeling unwell, here is a checklist to help you discover why:

- Make sure your TSH level on a blood test is between 0.50 and 2 mIU/L. To control the symptoms of hypothyroidism most people require their TSH to be at or below 2 mIU/L.

- When you have a blood test make sure that all three thyroid hormones are tested: TSH, free T4 and free T3. Many doctors fail to include a test for free T3 and it is the most important test because T3 is the active hormone.

- Take your basal body temperature for four consecutive days. If your temperature is below 36.5° C or 97.8° F, your thyroid medication may not be acting effectively in your body.

- Make sure you are not ingesting substances that interfere with the absorption or action of thyroid hormone medication. Food, calcium supplements, iron and lactose can all impair thyroid hormone absorption. Thyroid hormone is best taken first thing in the morning on an empty stomach.

• Ensure you have healthy cell membranes. T3 thyroid hormone must enter your cells in order to have its actions. The best way to have healthy cell membranes is to eat healthy fats and avoid harmful fats.

• Supplement with the nutrients that are required for the conversion of T4 into its active form T3. If you take thyroxine (brand names *Oroxine* or *Eutroxsig*) only, your body will need to convert this to T3 in order to have its effect. The most important mineral is selenium.

• Improve the health of your liver. The liver is the main site of T4 to T3 conversion. If your liver is sluggish, you have a fatty liver or other liver disease; this process will not be efficient.

• Do a detox. A bowel and liver detox combined with a gluten and dairy free diet will help your immune system and can halt the production of thyroid autoantibodies. This is essential if you have an autoimmune disease. A heavy metal detox will reduce the heavy metals that inhibit the action of thyroid hormones in your body.

• Try compounded T4 and T3 thyroid hormones as an alternative to thyroxine on its own, or try thyroxine and T3 (brand name *Tertroxin*).

• Perhaps you are suffering from depression. This can cause symptoms such as fatigue, lethargy, weight gain and poor concentration. Depression can mimic the symptoms of an under active thyroid gland. High stress levels promote the production of reverse T3, inhibiting the action of T3.

• If you can't lose weight it could be because you are suffering from a metabolic disorder such as Syndrome X. This results in high blood insulin levels, which suppress the fat burning hormones in your body. An effective weight loss eating plan is in the book *Can't Lose Weight? You Could Have Syndrome X*.

• Have a healthy lifestyle. Get enough exercise, sleep and fun because chronic exhaustion and poor health can cause symptoms of hypothyroidism such as lethargy, depression, a foggy head and weight gain.

• Consume raw vegetable juices regularly. Very few people get enough antioxidants in their diet. Raw juices are a great source of these.

Thyroid Dos and Don'ts

This section gives you a summary of the beneficial foods and potentially harmful foods to the thyroid gland.

Beneficial foods for the thyroid gland

- Brazil nuts and other nuts and seeds including almonds, walnuts, hazelnuts, cashews, sunflower seeds, pepitas and pine nuts. Brazil nuts are high in selenium and all nuts and seeds are high in minerals and beneficial fatty acids.

- Fish. The healthiest fish to eat include sardines, wild salmon, herrings and anchovies. Farmed fish should be avoided. Fish is a great source of omega 3 fatty acids that help to keep your cell membranes healthy and reduce inflammation in your body. Seafood is the best food source of iodine. If you do not eat any seafood you should be using iodised sea salt. Iodine is the best protection for your thyroid gland against thyroid toxic chemicals and radiation.

- Seaweed such as kombu, wakame and nori is extremely high in iodine and other minerals. Seaweed also binds with heavy metals and takes them out of your body. Large quantities of seaweed should be avoided by people with an overactive thyroid gland.

- Protein rich foods such as eggs and red meat are good sources of the amino acid tyrosine, needed for the formation of thyroid hormones. It is preferable to eat organic or free range versions of these foods. Avocados, almonds and bananas are other good sources of tyrosine.

Potentially problematic foods for the thyroid gland

- RAW cabbage, broccoli, cauliflower & Brussels sprouts can worsen an under active thyroid gland because they contain goitrogens, which can suppress thyroid function. Cooking mostly destroys goitrogens. These foods are ok in small to moderate amounts for people with an under active thyroid gland. Eating these foods raw will not harm you if you have an overactive thyroid.

- Other foods high in goitrogens include peanuts, corn, soy, millet, sweet potato and Lima beans. These foods are usually eaten cooked, so should not pose a problem unless you eat a great deal of them.

- Dairy products such as cow's milk, cheese, ice cream, butter and yoghurt should be avoided by people with thyroid nodules or cysts because they can make them worse. Dairy products can also irritate the immune system and worsen autoimmune thyroid disease. It is okay to eat small amounts of organic or biodynamic plain yoghurt, or cheese made from goat or sheep milk.

- Gluten, which is present in wheat, rye, oats, barley, spelt, kamut and many other foods, will worsen autoimmune thyroid disease. If your thyroid problem is caused by an autoimmune disease, you are best off avoiding gluten. This can stop the production of thyroid antibodies that attack your thyroid gland.

Thyroid solutions

In this section we will look at some common symptoms of thyroid disorders and give you a checklist for what you can do about them. Many of the symptoms of thyroid disease are common to other disorders, so it is important to rule out another condition.

• How to lose weight if you have a thyroid condition

Weight gain is one of the most common symptoms of an under active thyroid gland. Even after your thyroid hormones have been normalised, it is common for some stubborn kilos to hang around. To effectively lose weight you need to address the following factors:

- Reduce the amount of carbohydrate you eat and increase your protein intake. There is a very effective low carbohydrate eating plan in the book *Can't Lose Weight? You Could Have Syndrome X.* Syndrome X is a metabolic imbalance marked by high blood insulin levels. Insulin promotes fat storage and it stimulates hunger and cravings. To effectively lose weight you need to avoid or drastically reduce sugar and high carbohydrate foods like bread, pasta, rice, cereals, potatoes and foods made of flour. Your diet should be based on vegetables and salads, fruit, seafood, chicken, eggs, red meat, legumes, nuts and seeds.

- Eat healthy fats. Fat is an essential component of your diet because it helps you to feel full for longer. A great way to stop craving sugar is to eat more fat. Some fats have the ability to boost your metabolism and promote fat burning; they include omega 3 fats and organic, virgin coconut oil. Include fish in your diet at least three times a week, or take a fish oil supplement. Coconut oil can be used in cooking, as a salad dressing or taken off the spoon. We recommend the Niu Life coconut oil; if you would like some advice on incorporating coconut oil into your diet please phone our friendly Health Advisory team on (02) 4655 8855.

- Drink approximately two litres of pure water each day. This will speed your metabolism, flush toxins from your body and suppress hunger and cravings.

- Address the emotional factors that may be causing you to overeat. Stress, depression, loneliness, anger, grief and other emotions trigger many people to overeat or crave unhealthy foods.

- Exercise is essential, not only for weight loss but for overall health. Exercise increases the amount of muscle you have in your body; people with more muscle have a higher metabolic rate. As you age, more and more muscle is lost and fat is gained. Exercise helps to counteract some of this.

- Improve the health of your liver. Your liver is the main fat burning organ in your body, therefore controls your metabolic rate. If you have a fatty liver, your liver is storing fat rather than burning it. If you carry excess weight around your waist and abdomen, your liver needs help. Follow our liver detox in chapter ten. You may also need a liver tonic.

• Dealing with hair loss

Your hair is a good indicator of your overall health. Hair cells are one of the fastest growing cells in your body, and if your body is stressed or unbalanced, hair loss may result. Scalp hair loss is common in people with an under active thyroid gland, but it can also be caused by a number of other factors such as:

- High blood levels of male hormones (androgens) in women. This is a common feature of polycystic ovarian syndrome but may also occur during menopause. Blood tests called a Free Androgen Index (FAI) and Free Testosterone can detect your level of free male hormones.

- Postpartum hair loss is not uncommon and usually resolves itself within six months. If you are breastfeeding make sure your diet is as nutritious as possible, because many nutrients are lost in breast milk.

- Some autoimmune diseases can cause hair loss. See your doctor and follow our bowel and liver detox for autoimmune disease in chapter ten.

- Stress and nutritional deficiencies can lead to scalp hair loss. Deficiency of iron and B vitamins is most commonly at fault. Very low calorie diets can also produce scalp hair loss.

- Some medications can produce hair loss as an unfortunate side effect. These include drugs for blood pressure and heart conditions, gout, arthritis and some antidepressants.

• Overcoming fatigue

Fatigue is an incredibly common complaint in today's world. There is usually more than one factor responsible for it though. Here are some tips for getting your energy back:

- Make sure you get enough sleep and rest. Sleep restores and repairs your entire body and it is very important for the health of your adrenal glands, (which secrete stress hormones). The most important hours for restoring your adrenal glands are between 10pm and 3am; hopefully you are fast asleep during that period. If the quality of your sleep is poor, see the book *Tired of Not Sleeping*; it covers 68 possible causes of insomnia.

- You could be suffering with adrenal exhaustion. A blood test can be done to measure your levels of the hormones DHEA-S and cortisol. If they are low, a supplement of magnesium, vitamin C and B vitamins can help to restore your adrenal glands. If the hormone deficiency is more serious, you may need a hormone cream containing DHEA and/or pregnenolone. If you would like more information about adrenal exhaustion please contact our Health Advisory team on (02) 4655 8855.

• You may be suffering with depression. Long term stress inevitably leads to some degree of depression and a common consequence is fatigue. Overcoming depression involves making changes to your diet, lifestyle and thought patterns. Magnesium and the herb St John's Wort can help. St John's Wort cannot be taken with antidepressant medication and it interacts with several other medications; consult your doctor. Sometimes overcoming depression necessitates the use of prescription antidepressant medication.

• A weak immune system could make you feel tired and rundown. Fighting a chronic viral infection is very exhausting for the body. Many people unknowingly have hidden chronic infections in their body. These infections may be hidden in the sinuses, gums, respiratory tract, pelvic cavity or other parts of the body. Selenium is an essential mineral for a strong and healthy immune system. It helps to reduce the ability of viruses to replicate. A good daily dose of selenium is 100 to 200 micrograms. Selenium works best when it is combined with vitamin E, vitamin C and zinc.

• Fixing fluid retention

Fluid retention is a common problem and may be present in the feet, ankles, fingers, abdomen and face. In people with an under active thyroid gland fluid retention can be severe. If you are taking the right dose of thyroid hormones but still experiencing bloating and puffiness, the following factors may be at fault:

• Poor circulation can be the cause of fluid retention, especially if you notice it after sitting or standing in one spot for a long time. The best way to get your circulation moving is to exercise regularly. Dry skin brushing before having a shower can also help. Strong and healthy blood vessels are essential for good circulation; you can achieve this by increasing your intake of vitamin C and the bioflavonoid rutin.

• Fluid retention may be a symptom of premenstrual syndrome. The fluid retention occurs ten to 14 days before a menstrual period and disappears during the period. Fluid retention like this usually occurs in women with oestrogen dominance. You can read about reversing oestrogen dominance in chapter ten.

- A food allergy or intolerance can be behind fluid retention. Commonly this will be to dairy products, yeast, wheat or gluten. Eating something you are intolerant to places a great deal of stress on your immune system and the chemicals released as a consequence promote excess fluid.

• Coping with depression

Depression is approximately twice as common in women as men, and it is a typical symptom of hypothyroidism. Depression can interfere with your ability to work, sleep, eat a healthy diet and enjoy life in general. Some of the symptoms of depression include persistently feeling sad, hopeless, anxious and pessimistic. You may experience an empty feeling, lose self confidence and either lose your appetite, or want to eat a lot more. If you are experiencing persistent depression despite having normal thyroid hormones, the following tips may help you:

- Learn effective stress coping techniques. Long term stress inevitably leads to depression.

- Exercise aerobically for at least 30 minutes most days of the week. Intense exercise that makes you huff and puff releases endorphins in your brain that have an antidepressant and anti-anxiety effect.

- Get enough omega 3 essential fatty acids in your diet. A great deal of research has shown that omega 3 fats can help to prevent depression. The best source of these fats is fish, such as sardines, wild salmon, mackerel, tuna and anchovies. If you are currently experiencing depression, you should take a fish oil supplement to top up your omega 3 levels quickly.

- Try to get outside into the sunshine several times a week. This depends on the weather of course, but make a conscious effort to go outside for a few minutes during a sunny day. Sunshine has a mood elevating effect and too many people spend all day indoors and arrive home from work when the sun has already set.

- Magnesium and the herb St John's Wort (Hypericum) may help you. Magnesium is often described as "the great relaxer" because it helps your body to cope with stress better. It is excellent for

191

anxiety, muscle tension and can promote better quality sleep. St John's Wort is an effective herb for mild to moderate depression. However, it cannot be taken with prescription antidepressant medication and interacts with several other medications. Consult your doctor or naturopath if you wish to take it.

• Sometimes a prescription antidepressant medication is necessary. This will lift the depression so that you can put into place the lifestyle changes that can improve your life. These medications are not addictive.

• Help with anxiety and palpitations

Anxiety and heart palpitations are typical symptoms of an overactive thyroid gland. However, anxiety is very common in modern society. A recent study has shown that anxiety is more prevalent in people with both a mildly overactive and a mildly under active thyroid gland[65].

Palpitations are a common feature of hyperthyroidism as well as thyroiditis. These symptoms can also occur if your dose of thyroid hormone medication is too high. Once your thyroid hormone levels are normal, you should not be experiencing any anxiety or palpitations. If you continue to experience these symptoms, it could be because you are deficient in magnesium, calcium or vitamin D.

In summary

Thyroid disease is a hidden epidemic; the incidence of thyroid disorders is growing and thousands of Australians remain undiagnosed. By the age of 50 one in every 10 women has a thyroid problem. These statistics are unacceptable and should not be occurring in this day and age.

Thankfully they will change for the better because this ground breaking book takes away the ignorance and dispels the myths surrounding thyroid problems. This book also inspires as well as educates those with thyroid problems so that they can finally reclaim control of their health.

You have learnt that -

• Most people with a thyroid disease have a problem with their immune system and true healing of thyroid problems involves much more than simple thyroid hormone replacement.

- The regular screening tests for thyroid function will miss a lot of hidden and insidious thyroid problems – this leaves people inadequately treated for years.
- Thyroid hormone controls the conversion of food energy into physical energy – this is called the metabolic rate; if this is not occurring efficiently many people will find it impossible to control their weight.
- An under active thyroid gland will speed up the rate of ageing and this is important to know for our ageing population.
- An under active thyroid gland will cause a much higher rate of heart disease and strokes.
- Deficiency of the minerals iodine and selenium is common in Australia and leads to an increased risk of thyroid disorders and thyroid cancer.
- Conventional treatment with thyroid hormone replacement will be inadequate in many sufferers of under active thyroid and yet people continue to suffer with poor health because they are not offered correctly balanced hormone therapy.
- There are tests of thyroid function you must have that your doctor probably won't order.

This book has enabled you to be your own thyroid doctor! Well almost!

You now probably know more about thyroid problems than the average GP and even quite a few hormone specialists. Indeed you will probably be advising and guiding your own doctor!

But if the outcome of better communication - even though it may ruffle a few feathers, is better patient care, then it's got to be good!

Of course you need to remain under the care of your own doctor; however we are here to help you, both via this book and via our Health Advisory Service. Feel free to send us your questions via –

Phone (02) 4655 8855
Email – contact@whas.com.au
Postal mail – P. O. Box 689 Camden 2570 NSW
www.whas.com.au and www.liverdoctor.com and
www.weightcontroldoctor.com

Thyroid cancer is exploding

A recent NSW report by the Cancer Institute is very worrying and researchers are scratching their heads as to why the incidence of thyroid cancer cases in NSW women has skyrocketed by 84%. The Thyroid Cancer in NSW report found that more than half of the women affected by thyroid cancer were under the age of 50. The incidence of thyroid cancer in men has also increased by 40%. The incidence of most other types of cancer has remained stable so there are obviously specific factors related to the health of the thyroid gland that must urgently be identified and remedied.

Experts are targeting deficiency of the mineral iodine and increasing exposure to radiation as some of the causal factors.

Why has the incidence of thyroid diseases, including thyroid cancer, increased so dramatically?

We believe there are several factors-

- Deficiencies of the minerals iodine and selenium
- Exposure to radiation from medical procedures, mobile phones and computers etc
- Working in certain industries – the manufacture of prefabricated wooden buildings, electric installations, working with fertilisers, oilseed and grain, working with toxic chemicals such as dry cleaning fluids, solvents, pesticides, glues, paints and plastics etc

There is only one piece of good news in all this – the survival rate of patients with thyroid cancer is over 90%.

Our recommendations for keeping your thyroid gland healthy include:

- Ensure that you have a healthy diet, rich in nutrients required for healthy thyroid gland function. These include iodine, selenium and vitamin D.
- Consume adequate high quality protein. The thyroid gland requires the amino acid tyrosine in order to manufacture thyroid hormones. Tyrosine is found in protein rich foods such as red meat, fish, poultry, but also almonds, avocados, bananas and

pumpkin seeds.

- If you have an under active thyroid gland, avoid consuming large quantities of goitrogens. These are substances that can suppress the thyroid gland if consumed in large quantities. Foods rich in goitrogens include raw cabbage, broccoli, cauliflower and Brussels sprouts; soy, millet, peanuts and corn. Cooking these foods inactivates the majority of goitrogens.

- In Australia the majority of thyroid conditions are caused by an autoimmune disease; meaning the immune system is responsible for causing the thyroid to become either under active or over active. Research has shown that gluten intolerance can be a triggering factor in autoimmune thyroid disease. Gluten is a protein found in wheat, rye, oats and barley. Many thyroid patients benefit from following a gluten free diet.

- Ensure you have a healthy liver. The liver is the main site of conversion of T4 into its active form T3. A sluggish or fatty liver may impair the efficiency of this process.

- Ensure your diet contains adequate levels of beneficial fatty acids, as found in oily fish (salmon, sardines, anchovies, mackerel), raw nuts and seeds, cold pressed olive oil and organic coconut oil. These fats can reduce inflammation in autoimmune thyroid disease, and improve the health of cell membranes, allowing thyroid hormones to function more efficiently.

- Minimise your exposure to the heavy metals mercury, cadmium and lead, as they can interfere with the manufacture of thyroid hormones.

- Minimise your exposure to pesticides and insecticides, as some have been linked with the formation of thyroid nodules and autoimmune thyroid disease.

Essential nutrients for a healthy thyroid gland

Iodine

Iodine is a trace mineral and forms part of the structure of thyroid hormones; therefore consuming adequate iodine is vitally important for normal thyroid hormone production.

Iodine deficiency can be one cause of an under active thyroid gland (hypothyroidism). Long term iodine deficiency can cause the thyroid gland to enlarge and form a swelling called a goitre. Obtaining adequate iodine during pregnancy is vitally important for the healthy intellectual development of the infant. Iodine deficiency in infanthood can lead to reduced IQ.

Iodine deficiency is an increasingly common problem in Australia. The majority of the world's iodine is found in the oceans; however small amounts are also found in the soil. Unfortunately many parts of Australia, especially inland areas, have soils very deficient in iodine. Studies done in the last five years have identified iodine deficiency as a common problem among adults, children and pregnant women. Your iodine level can be checked with a simple urine test.

Seafood that comes from the ocean (rather than that which is farmed) is a good source of iodine. Seaweeds (such as kelp, arame, wakame, nori and kombu) are an excellent source of iodine; unfortunately they are not commonly eaten by most Australians.

Recommended supplemental dosage is: 160mcg daily

Selenium

A healthy thyroid gland contains more selenium per gram than any other tissue in the body. Selenium is required for the activation and metabolism of thyroid hormone.

Selenium is required by the enzyme that converts T4 thyroid hormone into its active form, T3. If you are deficient in selenium you will not be able to manufacture sufficient T3 and you may experience the symptoms of an under active thyroid gland, such as fatigue, easy weight gain, dry skin, dry hair, constipation, rapid ageing, depression and scalp hair loss.

A selenium deficiency can contribute to the development of autoimmune thyroid disease and thyroid cancer.

Selenium is deficient in Australian soils and obtaining adequate selenium from diet alone is very difficult because very few foods are a rich source of selenium. Brazil nuts, crab and salmon provide some selenium, however using a selenium supplement will ensure you receive optimal levels of this vital mineral.

Recommended supplemental dosage is: 100mcg daily

Vitamin D

Vitamin D is a hormone-like substance that is produced in the skin during exposure to sunlight.

Vitamin D helps to regulate cellular replication in a very important way. Specifically vitamin D helps cells to differentiate (become specialised), and inhibits cells from proliferating, or growing in an out of control way. It is thought that these are the reasons why vitamin D deficiency increases the risk of various types of cancer.

Vitamin D deficiency increases the risk of autoimmune disease. Surprisingly vitamin D deficiency is a common problem in the sunny country Australia. A study conducted in 2001 detected mild or moderate vitamin D deficiency in more than one in three women during summer, and one in two in winter. Inadequate levels of vitamin D may increase the risk of autoimmune thyroid disease and cancer. Prolonged sun exposure can be hazardous and inconvenient, and vitamin D is found in very few foods; therefore supplementing with vitamin D may be the best option.

Recommended supplemental dosage is: Vitamin D 3 1000 I. U. daily

- Vitamin D, selenium and iodine are needed for healthy thyroid gland cells and healthy thyroid gland tissue- these things can thus reduce the risk of the thyroid tissue becoming cancerous.

Thyroid Health Capsules contain iodine 160mcg plus selenium 100mcg plus Vitamin D 1000IU

Glossary

Anti-microsomal antibodies (TPOAb): Also known as thyroid peroxidase antibodies A type of antibody produced by the immune system that destroys the thyroid gland and is found in autoimmune thyroid disease.

Anti-thyroglobulin antibodies (TgAb): A type of antibody produced by the immune system that destroys the thyroid gland and is found in autoimmune thyroid disease.

Antithyroid antibodies: A general term for antibodies made by the immune system that attack and destroy the thyroid gland. Also referred to as autoantibodies. Found in autoimmune thyroid diseases such as Hashimoto's thyroiditis, Graves' disease and postpartum thyroiditis.

Armour Thyroid: An American brand name of desiccated porcine thyroid extract, containing T4 and T3 hormones, as well as T2 and T1. Available in Australia from compounding pharmacies.

Autoantibodies: Antibodies made by the immune system that attack and destroy the body's own tissues.

Basal body temperature: The temperature of the body at rest, first thing in the morning before any activity.

Bladderwrack: A herb high in iodine. **Also known as Fucus vesiculosis**

Calcitonin: A hormone produced by C cells of the thyroid gland, (also known as parafollicular cells). Calcitonin reduces the amount of calcium in the bloodstream. Medullary thyroid cancer cells usually produce high levels of this hormone.

Cold nodule: A lump on the thyroid gland that does not produce hormones and does not take up radioactive iodine on a thyroid scan.

Compounded thyroid hormone: Bio-identical thyroid hormones, T4 and T3 that are made up by a compounding pharmacy.

Cretinism: Mental retardation and stunted body growth in infants as a result of iodine deficiency while in the mother's uterus and shortly after birth.

Desiccated thyroid extract: Porcine thyroid hormones. Includes the hormones T4, T3, as well as T2 and T1.

Euthyroid: Means normal levels of thyroid hormones.

Exophthalmos: An abnormal protrusion of the eyeballs from the socket, which can occur in Graves' disease.

Follicular thyroid cancer: The second most common type of thyroid cancer, derived from follicular thyroid cells.

Goitre: An enlargement of the thyroid gland. Spelt Goiter in the USA.

Goitrogen: A substance found in some foods that inhibits the thyroid gland from utilising iodine, and can cause enlargement of the thyroid. Found in foods such as raw cabbage and soy.

Graves' disease: An autoimmune disease that is the most common cause of an overactive thyroid gland.

Graves' ophthalmopathy: Also known as thyroid eye disease. An autoimmune disease that causes inflammation in the eyes and affects some patients with Graves' disease.

Hashimoto's thyroiditis: An autoimmune disease that is the most common cause of an under active thyroid gland.

Hot nodule: An active thyroid lump that produces thyroid hormones. It usually causes hyperthyroidism.

Hyperthyroidism: An overactive thyroid gland that produces excessively high levels of thyroid hormones.

Hypothyroidism: An under active thyroid gland that cannot produce sufficient levels of thyroid hormones.

Myxoedema: Fluid retention associated with severe hypothyroidism, including puffiness of the eyes and cheeks.

Nodule: A lump or growth that can occur on the thyroid gland.

Papillary thyroid cancer: The most common type of thyroid cancer, arising from follicular thyroid cells.

Parathyroid glands: Four small glands located behind the thyroid that secrete parathyroid hormone. This hormone increases the amount of calcium in the bloodstream.

Postpartum thyroiditis: Inflammation of the thyroid gland that occurs shortly after giving birth.

Radioactive iodine: A radioactive form of iodine that can be used to both treat and diagnose thyroid disease.

Reverse T3 (rT3): An inactive form of T3 that is produced in the body. High levels are produced during stress, low calorie diets and nutritional deficiencies.

T3 (triiodothyronine): The active form of the thyroid hormone T4. Mostly produced out of T4 in the liver, kidneys and other tissues.

T4 (thyroxine): The main hormone produced by the thyroid gland. Much of the T4 in the body is converted to its active form T3.

Thyrogen: The name of a drug given to thyroid cancer patients before a diagnostic scan. It is a form of the hormone TSH and allows patients to keep taking their thyroid hormone medication, therefore avoiding the symptoms of hypothyroidism.

Thyroglobulin: A protein made in the thyroid gland from which T4 and T3 are synthesized. It is produced in excessive quantities by some types of thyroid cancer.

Thyroid peroxidase antibodies: See anti-microsomal antibodies.

Thyroid stimulating hormone (TSH): Also known as thyrotropin. A hormone made by the pituitary gland in the brain that stimulates the thyroid gland to manufacture hormones. A TSH blood test is considered the most important test to diagnose an overactive or under active thyroid gland.

Thyroid storm: A sudden, life threatening increase in the level of thyroid hormones. Typically occurs in people with hyperthyroidism, (such as Graves' disease), and can be brought on by stress, infection or surgery.

Thyroidectomy: The surgical removal of all or part of the thyroid gland.

Thyroiditis: Inflammation of the thyroid gland.

Thyrotoxicosis: Excessive quantities of thyroid hormones in the bloodstream. Can occur as a result of hyperthyroidism, (eg. Graves' disease), or taking too much thyroid hormone medication.

Thyrotropin: See thyroid stimulating hormone.

Thyrotropin releasing hormone (TRH): A hormone made by the hypothalamus in the brain, which stimulates the pituitary gland to release TSH.

Thyroxine: See T4.

Toxic goitre: An enlarged thyroid gland that is producing excessive quantities of thyroid hormones.

Triiodothyronine: See T3.

Tyrosine: An amino acid (building block of protein) from which thyroid hormones are manufactured.

Wilson's thyroid syndrome: A condition whereby the symptoms of hypothyroidism exist despite normal thyroid hormone levels. Also referred to as thyroid resistance. Wilson's disease is an inherited disorder where the body stores excessive quantities of copper.

Helpful Websites

If you would like to research your thyroid condition further, you will find the following websites very helpful:

- Mary Shomon's Thyroid Guide
  http://thyroid.about.com/ and http://www.thyroid-info.com/

- New York Thyroid Center
  http://cpmcnet.columbia.edu/dept/thyroid/index.html

- Thyroid Manager
  http://www.thyroidmanager.org/
  This website offers very technical information about thyroid disease.

- Thyroid Australia Ltd.
  http://www.thyroid.org.au/
  A support organisation for people with thyroid disease and their family/ friends.

- The Thyroid Foundation of America
  http://www.tsh.org/index.html

- Thyroid Foundation of Canada
  http://www.thyroid.ca/index.html

- Australian Centre for Control of Iodine Deficiency Disorders
  http://www.icpmr.gov.au/accidd/nins/idd.htm

- British Thyroid Foundation
  http://www.btf-thyroid.org/

- Thyroid UK
  http://www.thyroiduk.org/

- Thyroid Cancer Survivors' Association
  http://www.thyca.org/index.htm

References

1. Kohrle J. Thyroid hormone deiodinases – a selenoenzyme family acting as gate keepers to thyroid hormone action. Acta Med Austriaca 1996;23:17-30.

2. Visser TJ. Pathways of thyroid hormone metabolism. Acta Med Austriaca 1996;23:10-16.

3. Robbins J. Factors altering thyroid hormone metabolism. Environ Health Perspect 1981;38:65-70.

4. Hetzel BS, Clugston GA. Iodine. In: Shils M, Olson JA, Shike M, Ross AC, eds. Nutrition in Health and Disease. Vol 9th. Baltimore: Williams & Wilkins; 1999:253-264.

5. www.mydr.com.au

6. Nauman J, Wolff J. Iodide prophylaxis in Poland after the Chernobyl reactor accident: benefits and risks. Am J Med. 1993;94(5):524-532.

7. Thyroid Australia Ltd. www.thyroid.org.au

8. Dr Peter Baratosy MS BS PhD FACNEM It Could Still Be Your Thyroid. Dr Peter Baratosy 2005.

9. Sugenoya A, Masuda H, Komatzu M, Jokojama S, Shimizu T, Fujimori M, Kobajashi S, Iida F. Adenomatous goitre: therapeutic strategy, postoperative outcome, and study of epidermal growth factor receptor. Brit J Surg 79:404,1992.

10. MJA Practice Essentials. Thyroid nodules and thyroid cancer. Emily J Mackenzie and Robin H Mortimer. Vol 180 1 March 2004.

11. Kang. HW. Et al. Prevalence, clinical and ultrasonographic characteristics of thyroid incidentalomas. Thyroid 2004 Jan;14(1):29-33

12. Thyroid Foundation of Canada.

13. Thyroid Australia Ltd

14. Ann Intern Med 1999:131:738-44.

15. Thyroid Australia Ltd.

16. Alexander, Erik K. M.D., et. al. Timing and Magnitude of Increases in Levothyroxine Requirements during Pregnancy in Women with Hypothyroidism, *New England Journal of Medicine*, Volume 351:241-249 July 15, 2004 Number 3.

17. Wartofsky L, Dickey RA. The evidence for a narrower thyrotropin reference range is compelling. J Clin Endocrinol Metab. 2005 Sep;90(9):5483-8.

18. Vanderpump MPJ, Tunbridge WMG, French JM, Appleton D, Bates D, Rodgers H et al. The incidence of thyroid disorders in the community; a twenty year follow up of the Whickham survey. Clin Endocrinol 1995; 43:55-68.

19. Weetman AP. Hypothyroidism: screening and subclinical disease. BMJ 1997;314:1175-8.

20. Tunbridge WMG, Evered DC, Hall R, Appleton D, Brewis M, Clark F et al. The spectrum of thyroid disease in a community: the Whickham survey. Clin Endocrinol 1977;7:481-93.

21. Hollowell JG, Staehling NW, Hannon WH, Flanders WD, Gunter EW, Spencer CA, and Braverman LE. 2002. Serum thyrotropin, thyroxine, and thyroid antibodies in the United States population (1988 to 1994): NHANES III. 2002;J Clin Endocrinol Metab 87:489-99.

22. Assay of thyroid hormones and related substances. Last revised by Carole Spenser, Ph D February 6, 2004. www.thyroidmanager.org

23.Chopra IJ. An assessment of daily production and significance of thyroidal secretion of 3,3',5'triiodithyronine (reverse T3) in man. J Clin Invest 1976:58:32-40.

24. Robbins J. Factors altering thyroid hormone metabolism. Environ Health Perspect 1981;38:65-70.

25. Greg Kelly. Peripheral Metabolism of Thyroid Hormones: A Review. Altern Med Rev 2000;5(4):306-333.

26. Schedule of Pharmaceutical Benefits, 1 February 2004.

27. Janssen OE, Mehlmauer N, Hahn, S, Offner AH, Gartner R. High prevalence of autoimmune thyroiditis in patients with polycystic ovary syndrome. Eur J Endocrinol 2004;150:363-9.

28. Akande EO, Hockaday TDR. Plasma oestrogen and luteinizing hormone concentrations in thyrotoxic menstrual disturbance. Proc R Soc Med 1972; 65:789-790.

29. Accomando S, Cataldo F. The global village of celiac disease. Dig Liver Dis. 2004 Jul;36(7):492-8.

30. *Digestive Diseases and Sciences*, February 2000;45:403-406

31. Umpierrez GE, et al. Thyroid dysfunction in patients with type 1 diabetes: a longitudinal study. Diabetes Care 2003 Apr;26(4):1181-5.

32. Niederwieser G, et al. Prevalence of autoimmune thyroiditis and non-immune thyroid disease in multiple sclerosis. J Neurol 2003 Jun; 250(6):672-5.

33. Pyne D, et al. Autoimmune thyroid disease in systemic lupus erythematosus. Ann Rheum Dis 2002 Jan;61(1):70-2.

34. Monzani F, et al. Effect of levothyroxine replacement on lipid profile and intima-media thickness in subclinical hypothyroidism: a double-blind, placebo-controlled study. J Clin Endocrinol Metab 2004;89:2099-106.

35. Annuals of Internal Medicine February 15, 2000;132:270-278.

36. Karga H, et al. Bone mineral density in hyperthyroidism. Clin Endocrinol (Oxf) 2004;61:466-72.

37. Annuals of Internal Medicine April 3, 2001;134:561-568.

38. The Thyroid Society. Can depression be caused by thyroid disease? www.the-thyroid-society.org

39. The Journal of Clinical Endocrinology and Metabolism, January 2001;86:110-116

40. Riedel W, Layka H, Neeck G. Secretory pattern of GH, TSH, thyroid hormones, ACTH, cortisol, FSH, and LH in patients with fibromyalgia syndrome following systemic injection of the relevant hypothalamic-releasing hormones. Rheumatol 1998;57 Suppl 2:81-7.

41. Lo JC, et al. Increased prevalence of subclinical and clinical hypothyroidism in persons with chronic kidney disease. Kidney Int 2005 Mar;67(3):1047-52.

42. Giani, P Fierabracci, et al. Relationship between breast cancer and thyroid disease: relevance of autoimmune thyroid disorders in breast malignancy. Journal of Clinical Endocrinology & Metabolism, Vol 81, 990-994, 1996.

43. Lazarus JH The effects of lithium therapy on thyroid and thyrotropin-releasing hormone Thyroid 1998 Oct;8(10):909-13.

44. Effect of 1 year treatment with interferon-beta1b on thyroid function and autoimmunity in patients with multiple sclerosis. Eur J Endocrinol 1999 Oct;141(4):325-31.

45. The Journal of Clinical Endocrinology & Metabolism. Variable effects of non-steroidal anti inflammatory agents on thyroid test results. M.H. Samuels, K. Pillote, D. Asher and J.C. Nelson, Vol. 88, No. 12, 5710-5716, December 2003.

46. Quebec National Institute of Public Health.

47. Jack D. Thrasher Ph. D., Roberta Madison, Alan Broughton. Department of Health Science, California State University.

48. Centers for Disease Control National Institute for Occupational Safety and Health USA. www.cdc.gov/niosh/pel188/61-82.html

49. National Pesticide Telecommunications Network.

50. EXTOXNET The Extension Toxicology Network

51. World Rainforest Movement. www.wrm.org.uy/bulletin/97/Australia.html

52. Environmental Health Perspectives Volume 105, Number 10, October 1997.

53. K awada J; Nishida M; Yoshimura Y; Mitani K Effects of organic and inorganic mercurials on thyroidal functions. J Pharmacobiodyn, 3(3):149-59 1980 Mar.

54. Sharma G; Sandhir R; Nath R; Gill K Effect of ethanol on cadmium uptake and metabolism of zinc and copper in rats exposed to cadmium. J Nutr, 121(1):87-91 1991 Jan

55. *Environ Res* 1987 Apr;42(2):400-5.

56.Liang QR, et al. Effects of lead on thyroid function of occupationally exposed workers. Zhonghua Lao Dong Wei Sheng Zhi Ye Bing Za Zhi. 2003 Apr;21(2):111-3.

57. Imaizumi M, et al. Radiation Dose-Response Relationships for Thyroid Nodules and Autoimmune Thyroid Diseases in Hiroshima and Nagasaki Atomic Bomb Survivors 55-58 Years After Radiation Exposure. JAMA 2006;295:1011-1022.

58. Annual meeting of the American Academy of Otolaryngology – Head and Neck Surgery Foundation Washington, D.C. October 2000.

59. Lancet June 19, 1999 353:2111-5.

60. Archives of Internal Medicine 2000;160:661-666.

61. Annuals of Internal Medicine, 1998;129:632-635.

62. Rotruck J.T., et al. Science 179:588-90 (1973)

63. NEJM Volume 339:1156-1158 October 15, 1998 Number 16

64. Thyroid Newsroom Supplementing With Selenium May Help Thyroiditis Mary Shomon About Thyroid

65. Mustafa Sait Gonen, et al. Assessment of anxiety in subclinical thyroid disorders. Endocr J Vol. 51:311-315, 2004. NEJM Volume 339:1156-1158 October 15, 1998 number 16

Pasco JA, Henry MJ, Nicholson GC, et al. Vitamin D status of women in the Geelong Osteoporosis Study: association with diet and casual exposure to sunlight. Med J Aust 2001; 175: 401-405.

Index